WHAT
HAPPENED
THAT NIGHT

Also by Nicci French

Frieda Klein Novels
Blue Monday
Tuesday's Gone
Waiting for Wednesday
Thursday's Child
Friday on My Mind
Saturday Requiem
Sunday Morning Coming Down
Day of the Dead

Other Novels
The Memory Game
The Safe House
Killing Me Softly
Beneath the Skin
The Red Room
Land of the Living
Secret Smile
Catch Me When I Fall
Losing You
Until It's Over
What to Do When Someone Dies
Complicit
The Lying Room
House of Correction
The Unheard
The Favour
Has Anyone Seen Charlotte Salter?
The Last Days of Kira Mullan

NICCI FRENCH

WHAT HAPPENED THAT NIGHT

SIMON &
SCHUSTER

London · New York · Amsterdam/Antwerp · Sydney/Melbourne · Toronto · New Delhi

First published in Great Britain by Simon & Schuster UK Ltd, 2026

Copyright © Nicci French, 2026

The right of Nicci French to be identified as author of this work has been asserted
in accordance with the Copyright, Designs and Patents Act, 1988.

1 3 5 7 9 10 8 6 4 2

Simon & Schuster UK Ltd, 1st Floor
222 Gray's Inn Road, London WC1X 8HB

For more than 100 years, Simon & Schuster has championed authors and the
stories they create. By respecting the copyright of an author's intellectual property,
you enable Simon & Schuster and the author to continue publishing exceptional
books for years to come. We thank you for supporting the author's copyright
by purchasing an authorised edition of this book.

Simon & Schuster Australia, Sydney
Simon & Schuster India, New Delhi

www.simonandschuster.co.uk
www.simonandschuster.com.au
www.simonandschuster.co.in

The authorised representative in the EEA is Simon & Schuster Netherlands BV,
Herculesplein 96, 3584 AA Utrecht, Netherlands. info@simonandschuster.nl

Simon & Schuster strongly believes in freedom of expression and stands against
censorship in all its forms. For more information, visit BooksBelong.com

A CIP catalogue record for this book is available from the British Library

Hardback ISBN: 978-1-3985-2418-7
Trade Paperback ISBN: 978-1-3985-2419-4
eBook ISBN: 978-1-3985-2420-0
Audio ISBN: 978-1-3985-2421-7

This book is a work of fiction. Names, characters, places and incidents are either
a product of the author's imagination or are used fictitiously. Any resemblance
to actual people living or dead, events or locales is entirely coincidental.

Typeset in Sabon by M Rules
Printed and Bound in the UK using 100% Renewable Electricity at CPI Group (UK) Ltd

MIX
Paper | Supporting
responsible forestry
FSC
www.fsc.org   FSC® C013604

To Kate and John, friends for all seasons

PART ONE

PART ONE

He woke long before the bell, as he had done every morning, and for several minutes lay quite still, his eyes closed. On some days, it had been so cold that his bones ached, and on others a fetid heat had pressed down on him, trapping him, but today it was mild. A milky light came through the barred window set high in the wall. Out there in the late spring, birds were singing. Out there, the sea rolled onto the shingle and mud, under a huge sky.

Tyler Green swung his legs onto the floor and stood up: a big man in a small room. He took two steps to the small basin and splashed water onto his face. He lowered himself to the stone floor and, as always, did twenty-five press-ups, twenty-five lunges. There had been thousands of mornings just like this one: not thinking, not looking back or looking forward, day by day leaving his youth behind, his vigour, his possibility, but focusing only on the moment, the pump of his heart.

He took care to make no noise. His bare feet landed softly, his breath was measured. He was alone now, but for most of his sentence he had shared a cell. There had been another body in the bunk above him or below him, someone else's sounds and smells and night terrors and morning glumness; someone else using the toilet behind the curtain, and brushing their teeth in the basin, and eating slop off the tin plate, and swearing and weeping when they thought they couldn't be heard. The last had been Mo with the wild laugh and glass eye, who had hanged himself three months before he was released.

This cell was like a holding pen, this prison on the east coast a stepping stone to freedom. Tyler had been transferred from the high security prison in the Midlands to a Category D open prison just weeks ago. He had worked in the garden, the wind cold against his face where the scar still ached, and had had a couple of temporary releases to get him ready for the real world – that was what his probation officer called it, though it hadn't felt like the real world, more like one of the dreams he used to have. For the first time in almost three decades, he had seen the sea. He had stood for several minutes, gazing out at the grey heave of it, container ships blocky on the horizon, gulls circling and dipping, and he had briefly let himself remember being a child on a beach, a teenager on a beach, skimming stones over the frothy hem of water and watching them bounce, one, two, three, four, into the lip of a wave. But memories can be dangerous; he had pushed them deep inside himself, where he could not feel them hurt.

He was fifty-one years old, and he had been in prison for twenty-eight years and ten months. Today, he would leave.

The morning alarm sounded. Sounds came from other cells. Footsteps in the corridor outside. The window in Tyler's door slid open and he saw a round pink face topped by a sandy bristle of hair. The face grinned.

'Last breakfast for you.'

As if he was about to die.

Tyler didn't eat the breakfast, although he drank some milky tea. He stripped off his sweatpants and T-shirt and rolled them into a ball. He wouldn't wear them again. He pulled on some jeans which were slightly too big for him and a dark blue T-shirt. He tugged on his trainers. Then he used the toilet, washed, brushed his teeth. He confronted himself in the speckled mirror, his hooded eyes, the scar running from ear to jaw, no smile. His hair had turned white long ago.

He dropped his toothbrush and toothpaste into the canvas bag under the small table. He had come in with nothing and was leaving with little more: basic toiletries, a few clothes which however often they were washed would always smell of prison, his reading glasses, a few books, including the anthology of poetry his friend Will had awkwardly handed to him the last time he visited. That was years ago now. The trickle of visitors Tyler had once received had dried up.

The door was unlocked with a rattle of keys. The prison officer entered with a colleague.

'We've got to search you.'

This seemed mad, even in this world of madness. Who smuggled contraband *out* of prison. But Tyler knew better than to answer back. Nothing good would come of it. Clothes lifted, hard fingers pressing and poking at him. He could smell coffee and cigarettes on their breath.

'Bend over.'

He did. He concentrated on the marks on the floor.

'You're okay.'

Tyler stepped into the corridor. A few other inmates were already out of their cells, towels over their shoulders for the shower. One of them raised his hand.

'Off then?'

'Looks like it.'

'Good luck, mate.'

He followed the prison officer down the corridor, through

a double door, another longer corridor, to the Booking Reception.

'Tyler Green,' he said to the man at the desk.

'You're going today?'

'That's what the form says.'

The man grunted, took a long swig from a bottle of Coke.

'There are three of you leaving. And just me. I don't know what they expect.'

Tyler didn't say anything. The man scowled at the computer in front of him.

'There's quite a bit of paperwork, you know.'

Tyler inclined his head.

'You'll have to bear with us a bit. The computer's playing up. Take a seat.'

Tyler sat, folded his hands in his lap, waited. The man tapped, cursed, stabbed at the keyboard.

'Fuck this,' he said, standing up with an ugly scrape of the chair, and disappearing through the door behind him. About ten minutes later, another man came through the door, holding a cardboard cup in his hands.

'It's this new system,' he said, tapping at the keyboard experimentally. 'Just when we get used to something, they change it.'

Tyler went to the long window. He watched the sea beyond the coarse grass and reeds wrinkle and glint in the morning light. The sun moved behind a cloud and the silver waves darkened. The hands on the clock jerked forward.

'Good to go,' said the man at last. 'Just printing this lot out.'

Tyler didn't turn. The printer whirred.

'Here. You have to read all of this through, then sign it.'

Tyler took the pages held out to him and sat back in his chair to read them, though he had been over the conditions with his probation officer already. He knew he must not behave in a way which undermined the purpose of the licence period; not commit any offence; keep in touch with his supervising officer and receive visits from the officer in accordance with instructions; reside permanently at an address approved by the supervising officer and obtain prior permission for any stay of one or more nights at a different address; not undertake work unless approved by the supervising officer; not travel outside the United Kingdom, the Channel Islands or the Isle of Man except with the prior permission of his supervising officer; tell his supervising officer if he used a different name to the one on his licence. And more, so much more.

He knew his licence period was for the rest of his life.

When he had finished, he picked up the pen he had been given. At first it wouldn't write. He had to dab at the tip with his tongue.

'You understand it all?'

'Yes.'

'You need to see your probation officer today,' said the man. 'Or you're straight back in.'

'Yes.'

'Here's your B79. You'll need it when you apply for benefits. You've been told about universal credit?'

'I have.'

'And you've got somewhere to stay?'

'Yes.'

'Just your money then. And a travel pass.'

He unlocked a drawer and took out a wad of notes, licking his finger and thumb and counting aloud.

'Twenty, forty, sixty, seventy, eighty. And two. Plus twenty, thirty, forty pence. Don't spend it all at once.'

Tyler put the money into his pocket.

'My watch,' he said.

'What?'

'They said at the last place that they'd make sure my watch came here for when I left.'

'After thirty-odd years?'

'Yes.'

The man stared at him, scratched behind his ear, shrugged and disappeared through the door once more.

Tyler stayed where he was, waiting. He heard footsteps returning.

'You're in luck.' The man slid a brown envelope towards Tyler, who took it and pushed it into his pocket.

'Is that it?' he asked.

'Don't forget your pass. It'll get you to wherever you're going.' He pushed it across, then scratched at his drinker's nose. 'Anyone meeting you?'

'No.'

'People find it hard,' the man said. 'Even though it's what they've been holding on for. Have you got a plan? Like, for out there.'

Tyler looked at him for a few seconds as if considering, then nodded.

'Yes,' he said slowly. 'There's something I've got to do.'

The man at the desk hesitated, then laughed.

'As long as it's legal,' he said. 'Good luck then. You're free to go.'

Free to go. Free.

Tyler picked up his canvas bag. He paused for a few moments, then pushed open the door.

His probation officer had told him he would probably feel anxious, but he didn't. He didn't feel much of anything. Not excited, not happy, not scared. His body felt clumsy as he walked down the gravel track. His eyes were sore in the shining day. At the junction with the main road, he stopped. Plastic bags and shreds of litter were caught in the hedge. Cars in primary colours raced past. They were going so fast it made him feel slightly dizzy. There was a plane above him, leaving a white trail.

He took the envelope out of his pocket and tore it open, removing his watch. It had a large round face with Roman numerals on it, and a leather strap. Its battery had run down decades ago, but Tyler put it on his wrist. It felt cool and solid.

Across the road was a small cafe and he made his way over to it, pushing open the door and walking up to the counter.

'What can I get you?'

'A coffee, please.'

He touched the money in his pocket for reassurance.

'What kind?'

'What?'

'Americano, cappuccino, macchiato, flat white . . . '

'Just ordinary coffee.'

She looked at him with something like contempt. She knew where he had come from.

'Filter?'

'Yes.'

'Milk? Oat milk?'

'Milk,' he said. 'Please.'

'Anything else?'

'No.'

'That's three pounds twenty then.'

He tried to keep his face expressionless.

'Three pounds and twenty pence,' she repeated.

Sitting at a table by the window, his fingers felt huge as he lifted the cup. The coffee burned his lips. It was so bitter and so good.

Sitting on the coach from Ipswich to London, his canvas bag on his lap as if he was cradling a toddler, he gazed out of the window at the impossible greenness of the May landscape. Then at the light industrial units and scattered houses and landfill sites. At last the city reared up at him in its startling density and height. Tyler flinched. The apartments, towers and cranes seemed to be leaning towards him, toppling in slow motion between floating white clouds, like a night terror he had lurched awake from in his narrow cell.

It felt as if he was watching a film of himself: the middle-aged man convicted of murdering his friend Leo Bauer twenty-nine years ago, coming home at last, with something to do.

I

Beatrice Macmillan, King's Counsel, watched as the woman gathered up the flowers, wrapped them in brown paper, and then tied them with raffia. It was cool and fragrant in the shop, while outside the day was still fierce, heat rising from the pavement and beating off the walls. For a moment, she wished she could stay in this unhurried green world, among the peonies and mimosa and silvery stems of eucalyptus.

She looked at her watch. In half an hour, they would start arriving. She felt a flash of anxiety, her chest tightening and a strange taste in her mouth, metallic, like iron or blood. For a moment, she was light-headed with the strangeness of what lay ahead. Seven people, once her most intimate friends, would arrive at her house. They hadn't so much drifted apart as been violently wrenched out of each other's orbit, to spin off into different lives. For years, she had felt their absence like a physical fact: something missing, like a cracked tooth the tongue searches for, a limb that the brain refuses to acknowledge is missing. Tingling, hurting. She occasionally still saw Will and Ali, but that was almost worse than separation. They kissed each other on the cheek when they met, told each other how well they were looking, smiled without meeting the other's eyes, talked with fake animation about things that didn't matter. Their wary politeness wasn't much more than a reminder of what had been lost. Their old selves were like hazy figures in the far distance.

Beatrice touched the vivid blue bells on a delphinium and steadied herself, forcing her thoughts to the practicalities of the evening. The food would be delivered soon. The table was already set. There was white wine and sparkling water in the fridge, gin in the freezer. Did everyone still drink? Did they eat fish? Would she recognise them all? Will and Ali hadn't changed much, just hardened into caricatures of themselves, but what about the others, the ones she'd lost touch with entirely? What about Tyler?

She picked up the bouquets, cradling them like a baby. The past had lain undisturbed for decades. Now they were disturbing it with a reunion. What's more, they were disturbing it in her house. Will had said it was the obvious spot. In London, and the only place large enough. It somehow made her responsible. It would be different if her husband Sebastian was here, being placid and diplomatic, but he was away. Nottingham, wasn't it? Another speech at another conference. It was probably for the best that he wasn't there.

She wanted to see Tyler again, had wanted it ever since she heard he was to be released. But she had imagined it as an encounter between just the two of them, on neutral ground, maybe walking somewhere together and not having to look at each other while she tentatively, softly, asked him questions about what really happened on that terrible weekend. He hadn't wanted that. He wanted them all, everyone who had been there. She thought they wouldn't come, but they were coming. All of them except Rudi.

She was a lawyer, a King's Counsel. Dealing with sudden crises was what she did, putting a story and a structure around an ugly mess. This felt different. No one knew the rules, and she couldn't wear a wig and robes and hide behind the machinery of the law. Besides, she didn't really feel like a fifty-year-old barrister who was married to a cabinet minister and lived in a large house in Tufnell Park, and whose life was smoothly successful, oiled by money and connections and a daily help. She felt like young, shy, eager Beatrice Macmillan, unsure of herself and of her place in the group, wanting so badly to belong.

Beatrice stepped out of the shop, the fragrance of the flowers in her nostrils, the sun on her face like a warm hand. She felt unanchored. She was fifty. She was twenty-one. She was walking on legs that were suddenly unsteady towards her grand house, and she was lying on the grass with her friends, by a small, brackish lake in a cotton dress, tanned legs bare, sluggish with heat and looking up through half-closed eyes at the green leaves above.

'Who fancies a swim?'

That had been Leo. He was already pulling off his T-shirt. His body was strong, muscled. He had dark hair on his shoulders and his chest, a line of hair running down his stomach like an arrow. He pulled off his jeans, then his boxers. White buttocks, broad shoulders. He walked towards the water, calling over his shoulder for them to join him.

Beatrice propped herself on an elbow to look at him, and then at the rest of the group who were scattered on the grass. A few feet away lay Tyler and Ali, their limbs entangled. Tyler wore cut-off jeans and a white T-shirt, Ali a strappy yellow dress that had ridden up to her thighs. Her dark head was on Tyler's stomach; his hand was on her sharp-boned hip. Ali's eyes were closed, but his were open and he was watching her, an expression on his face that mingled tenderness with desire. Tyler was the only one in the group who would return to university in the autumn: he was a medical student and had two more years to go. The rest of them were celebrating being free. That's how Marco put it. Free as birds, he said.

Marco was sitting bare-chested and cross-legged near the lake, strumming the same chord over and over on his second-best guitar. Beatrice heard twangs of sound, occasionally an experimental word or phrase. His voice was gravelly, but pleasant and somehow arresting. He was concentrating intently, trying something out. One day, she thought, he would be famous: everyone would be impressed that she knew the singer-songwriter Marco Burney. But he wouldn't let it go to his head. He'd always be part of their group, playful, ironic and joyful. Their troubadour.

The light was bouncing off the lake in refracted spears. Beatrice put a hand up to shield her eyes. Leo was in the water, heading out to the middle of the lake. And there was Will, standing in the shallows, skimming stones. He had rolled up his jeans and his shirt sleeves, but even from here looked hot. He was a plump young man, self-conscious about his body even while he made self-deprecating jokes about it. Last night, after they'd unpacked the car, he had made a meal for them all, and got boisterously drunk. He had danced on the table and broken a serving dish that belonged to Leo's aunt, whose house they were borrowing for the weekend.

Will stooped low, took aim. A flat stone skittered across the surface.

'Six!' he cried. 'Who can beat that? Rudi. Come on, mate. Stir yourself.'

Beside her, Rudi Scott groaned and half sat. She smiled at him and he smiled back. His little finger grazed the edge of her hand, and a pulse of electricity ran through her.

'Bea,' he said, very quietly. 'You know what I would like to be doing right now?'

'Shh. Someone will hear.'

She and Rudi were a secret, because she had a boyfriend back home. She'd been with Sebastian since she was sixteen, and they planned to move in together now that she had done her finals. She told herself that was what she wanted; she mustn't derail a future she had worked so hard for. Soon, Rudi would just be a shiver of memory, something delicious, erotic, against the grain of her careful life and her sensible plans. If her friends knew, they might let it slip. She could even imagine Leo doing so on purpose, pretending it had been a mistake, an act of mischief or casual malice.

Through slitted eyes, she looked at the group as they lay scattered on the coarse grass. Perhaps they already did know, she thought. Perhaps the reason it had to be a secret was because there was a part of her that was ashamed. She didn't want to acknowledge to herself that she was betraying Sebastian, who trusted her, and who liked to think of her as shy and innocent, his childhood sweetheart.

Rudi's hand brushed against hers. The sun poured down. She closed her eyes.

'Come on, Rudi!' Will called.

Rudi stood up. He was wearing a singlet and drawstring trousers. He was paler than Tyler and Leo, with an aquiline, clever face; long, thin hands and feet. Beatrice thought he looked a bit like a monk in a medieval painting, bookish but somehow carnal. Desire turned her body soft and boneless. There was a stag beetle on her calf; the red varnish on her toenails was beginning to chip.

Leo was in the middle of the lake, calling for them to join him. From behind her, with a crunching of twigs and a squeal of delight, came naked Ellen Hooper, her long hair streaming behind her like a banner, her curvy body milky-pale. She ran past Beatrice, past Ali and Tyler, and with a whoop threw herself into the water where she lay on her back, her white breasts bobbing, her arms and legs spread out, a starfish adrift.

Clara and Jay came through the trees and into the sunlight. They were holding hands. Clara wore shorts and a baggy, short-sleeved shirt. She had a graze on her knee, new freckles on her face. Her short fair hair was a muss of curls. Beatrice thought she looked like a child – but the expression on her face as she turned to Jay wasn't childish at all. It was grave, almost sad. As Beatrice watched, she lifted his hand and kissed his knuckles and he stopped. He had a thin, nervy face and tense shoulders. Tyler always said Jay was too clever for his own good, too defenceless: he lacked the extra layer of skin that most of us need to cope with the world.

Tyler stood. He held out his hand for Ali, who came to her feet in one fluid movement. He took off his clothes, folding them carefully, as if he was in a bedroom. Ali slid out of her yellow dress; underneath she was wearing a two-piece. Her legs were slender, her stomach flat and her breasts shallow; her black hair was short and spiky and her almost-black eyes were like sloes. They were a beautiful couple, thought Beatrice, as they went towards the water. Everyone's beautiful, she thought dreamily. She took off her own dress, trying not to feel shy, then piled her hair high on her head. The floor of the lake was soft mud that her feet sunk into; the water was cool and silky. She told herself she would always remember this.

Later, back on the grass, damp clothes clinging to their bodies, skin streaked with mud, the midsummer sun still high in the flawless sky, Marco lit a spliff. They passed it between them. Soon they would go back to the house, drink beer and wine and vodka and the strange cocktails that Ellen insisted on concocting. They'd play increasingly raucous games, burn sausages on the barbecue, take drugs, dance, stay up till the early hours, or not sleep at all. Because why sleep? Tomorrow they would leave. Nothing would ever be the same again.

'We'll always be friends, won't we?' she said impulsively. 'No matter what?'

She sounded like a small girl, but no one laughed, not even Leo. Ellen put an arm around her shoulders and kissed her cheek.

'Yes,' said Marco, and picked gently at the strings.

'Of course we will.' Tyler smiled across at her. 'How could we not?'

A car horn blared. Beatrice stumbled on the pavement, clutching at her flowers. She felt as if the bright sun was inside her own head, blinding her.

Leo. Rudi. Will. Ali. Marco. Clara. Jay. Ellen. Tyler. The past was a broken dream.

She stood up straighter, walked at a brisker pace. Who was she now? Who had that young woman become? Beatrice Macmillan, KC.

She would wear her green trousers, she thought, and a white silk shirt. One gold necklace. Not much make-up. Casual but classy. Unspoilt by her luck. That's who she would be this evening. That's who Tyler would see when he stepped into her house, and she would smile at him, and hold out both her hands with their manicured nails, and say: 'I am so glad to see you. After all these years.'

2

Ali Marais looked in the hall mirror, moving her face this way and that. Carefully, with the tip of the nail of her right little finger, she smoothed the line of her lipstick. She stepped back. It had been difficult to decide what to wear. Crimson dress just below the knees, small gold chain, little gold studs in her ears. It seemed just about all right.

She aimed a smile at herself, saw the wrinkles around her eyes, the little stitches above her mouth, the short dark hair with threads of grey. Behind the face, she saw her younger face, as it had been then: bright and keen with youth. Twenty-nine years. Who would she see? Who would he see? Would they still know each other? Her heart fluttered, a trapped bird in her chest.

She looked round at her husband and frowned.

'Aren't you getting ready?' It sounded more like a statement than a question.

Will Garvey was a different shape from his wife: bulky where she was slender, blurry where she was clear and precise. He looked down at himself. He was dressed in jeans, a checked shirt, a dusty blue jacket and trainers.

'It's a group of old friends meeting up,' he said. 'There's no dress code.'

'We look like we're going to different events,' she said.

He lifted up the bag for life he was carrying.

'I've brought some asparagus from the allotment. I'll take it along for dinner.'

'I'm sure that Beatrice has already planned the meal.'

'You can always add a bit of asparagus. I saved these specially. Did you know that summer solstice is officially the last day of asparagus season?'

'I did not.'

'Shall I put Benjy in his room?'

'I'm taking him.'

'What do you mean?'

'He gets sad when he's left at home alone.'

'Sad? He's a dog. You're complaining about me bringing a bunch of asparagus and you're bringing an animal that is extremely likely to bite someone.'

'Benjy doesn't bite.'

'If you say so.'

'What's that supposed to mean?'

'I was just thinking of all the times when Benjy has actually, you know, bitten people.'

Ali bent down to the small, ageing terrier at her feet and stroked the top of his head.

'Benjy's just like anyone, aren't you, darling? Sometimes people frighten you, and you might a give a little yap of protest.' Her tone became sharper as she addressed her husband. 'Benjy's a part of our family. They'll be happy to meet him.'

Her husband rubbed his cheek. He looked slightly bewildered, she thought, or maybe he'd already had a glass of something.

'Are you nervous?' he asked.

Ali shrugged. Her face was inscrutable; it hurt to breathe and it hurt to swallow, but he couldn't see that.

Will looked at her as if he didn't know her, though they had been married for nearly a quarter of a century.

'How can you not be nervous?'

She turned and faced him properly.

'I didn't want to do this. I think it's a horrible idea. I don't know why you would agree to it, and I don't know why he wants it.' She couldn't bring herself to speak his name out loud. 'I don't know why the rest of them have gone along with it. I'm going because you begged me to go, begged and pleaded, and in the end I said yes. I plan to get through the evening, be polite, and leave as soon as we decently can.'

'Can't it be more than that?'

'More?'

'A way of, I don't know . . . '

He rubbed a hand over his broad, creased face. There was still dirt under his fingernails. He had tried many times to talk to Ali about Tyler, but in the first months after the murder, she had seemed too crushed and vulnerable, like a wounded bird who just needed cradling in careful hands. Then, bit by bit, time had seemed to close over the gaping event, like a thin skin gradually hardening, thickening, becoming increasingly impenetrable. They had been married for twenty-three years, but it remained a walled-off area.

'Ali, darling.' He was pleading, but not knowing what it was he wanted to say, or ask.

'The past is past, Will,' Ali said. 'It's over. What do you want from this? Some kind of healing?'

She said the word as if it was a nasty joke.

'This is Tyler we're talking about. Tyler, who killed our mate under our nose, but who's still my friend. In some way he's my friend,' he added doubtfully. 'Some elemental way.'

And who was your boyfriend, he didn't say; who was head

over heels in love with you; who you've never seen since that day, and who we never talk about.

'Is he?'

'Yes. Or at least, I am his. I made that promise. I need to keep faith.'

Ali looked at him. Her eyes were dark. He felt he could stare into them, and it was like staring into a tunnel that he couldn't reach the end of. He reached out and touched her hand, withdrew it.

'There's something else.'

'What do you mean?'

Will cleared his throat.

'He doesn't know.'

'Doesn't know what?'

'That we're together. Married. I never told him.'

Ali briefly closed her eyes. She told herself that it was nothing, compared to everything else that had happened.

'It doesn't matter,' she said.

But it did matter. She felt a memory dislodge itself. Not of that last terrible weekend, of her last sight of Tyler as he lowered himself into the police car, the look he gave her. No, not that – and she put a hand to her throat. But the time Tyler took her to meet his mother, who'd come for the day to visit him. Ali had been anxious, but Tyler had been blithe.

'What if she doesn't like me?' she asked.

'Why on earth wouldn't she like you?'

'Because she's your mother, and you're her only son. She'll think I'm not good enough.'

Really, it was Ali who felt she wasn't good enough. Tyler had an uncomplicated ease about him, a self-assurance that wasn't arrogance, but which came from always being popular, smart, successful, loved. She didn't understand why he was so captivated by her. One day, she thought, he would see her as she was, all her sharp, dark corners.

'I'm not as nice as you are,' she said.

Tyler was pulling on his jacket, but now he came and stood behind her, wrapped his arms around her, pulled her in close. His breath was warm on her hair.

'Ali,' he said. 'It'd be great if you and Mum got on, and I'm sure you will, but I don't care. It's not her you're going to marry.'

Ali stood quite still in his arms. The words hung in the air; had he meant to speak them? She felt Tyler's mouth smile against the crown of her head.

'What?' he said. 'What's the matter?'

'Nothing,' she said confusedly. 'Nothing. I just – Tyler.'

'Not yet,' he said. 'But we will get married, one day. When I'm qualified. Won't we?'

'Are you proposing? Now, when we're already going to be late for lunch with your mother?'

'I'm just saying that we're going to be together.' He turned her to face him, kept his hands on her shoulders. 'Aren't we?'

'I'm twenty-one.'

'So? I'm twenty-two.'

'You're scaring me.'

'How could me saying that I want to be with you scare you?'

'Because you're so certain.'

'Why is that scary?'

'What if you stop loving me? What will happen to me then?'

'I'm not going to stop loving you.'

'How do you know?'

'I know,' he said. He kissed her on her neck, at the hollow beneath her ear, on her closed eyes, on her mouth. 'I just know.'

She pushed her hands into his thick hair, pulled him closer. His hand cupped her buttocks.

'Don't you know as well?'

'Your mother,' she murmured into his mouth, and he groaned, then stood back with a laugh.

They went to a bistro near the university's medical department. Izzy Green was waiting, sitting very upright with a menu in her hand and a glass of white wine already in front of her. She was tall, like Tyler, with a strong, decisive face and a straightforward, almost bossy manner. They ate quiche and salad, followed by a chocolate mousse shared between the three of them. Mother and son joked with each other, easy and affectionate. Under the table, Tyler put his hand on Ali's thigh. Izzy Green asked her about her studies, her interests, watching her carefully as she replied, weighing her up.

'You're not what I expected,' she said to Ali at the end of lunch, holding her hand for a few seconds longer than was necessary.

'What did you expect?'

'I don't know. Someone softer, more charming.'

'Mum!'

'No, I mean it in a good way. You're not trying to please me. I like that.'

'You're not what I expected either,' said Ali, suddenly bold.

'And what did you expect?'

'Someone more motherly.'

Izzy laughed.

'She's all right,' she said to Tyler.

'Oh, she is.'

They both looked at her, and she sat in the glow of their approval.

Standing in the hall with Will, her tight crimson dress like armour and her make-up a disguise, Ali remembered that moment. Tyler's mother smiling at her, Tyler's hand warm and heavy on her thigh, her young body supple and soft; the sense that although she might not be good enough for such luck, and although she could never love Tyler with the open-hearted passion he felt for her, she was going to have a golden life: safe, protected, beloved.

She sprayed perfume under her ears, onto the inside of her wrists, slid on a bangle, took it off again. That terrible week-end stirred in her mind, ominous, trying to push up into her consciousness. Leo's murder. The smell of burnt meat and alcohol and tobacco and blood, screams inside the house and inside her skull.

'I meant to tell him about us,' Will was saying, his words coming from far away. 'But somehow I couldn't. So I kept put-ting it off, and then it was too late.'

Ali stared at herself in the mirror, put the bangle back on, ran her fingers over the fine lines beside her eyes. She looked at Will's pleasant, distressed face, and took pity on them both.

'It's all right,' she said. 'We'll get through it together.'

3

'Aren't we going to be late?'

'This won't take long.'

Marco was finishing a spliff, inhaling deeply, holding it in his lungs, letting the smoke out slowly. His thin, weathered face wore a look of deep concentration. His shaved head gleamed, and his single earring winked. His tie-dyed shirt was slightly grubby.

'It stinks in here now,' said Kristin. She yanked the window open.

'I need it.'

'How do I look?'

Marco held the joint away from him, its ash lengthening, and examined her. They had met three years ago, moved in together a year and a half later, though he couldn't really remember why now. She was much younger than he was, and on a different scale to him: tall and curvy, with a thick blonde mane of hair and an unnervingly loud voice that ricocheted round their small flat. Even her whisper carried. She was wearing a lacy cream dress that was sheer when she stood in the light, and platform shoes that made her several inches taller than Marco.

'Fine, I guess. It doesn't matter. No one will be looking at you.'

'Charming!'

'You know what I mean.'

'It's going to be so weird.' Kristin licked her lips. Her eyes gleamed. 'So fucking strange. I've never met a murderer. That I know of, anyway.'

Marco took another long drag. His chest burned. The air was beginning to soften and waver around him. Time slowed. The blood in his veins slowed. Better, he thought. Kinder.

'You have told them?'

'Told them what?'

'That I'm coming with you?'

'It'll be fine.'

'Because I don't want to intrude.'

'You were the one who insisted.'

'I thought you might want my support,' she said. 'I mean, it's a huge thing, isn't it?'

She made an extravagant gesture with both arms. Marco took a final drag. Ash crumbled onto the carpet.

'Are you dreading seeing him?'

'Totally.'

'Then why are you doing it?'

'I've got to. I owe it to Leo. The friend I lost.'

As he said the words, he wondered to himself: what exactly *did* he owe to Leo? And then he answered his own question: everything, in a way.

When Marco had first arrived at university, it didn't just feel like leaving home. It felt like leaving Earth and moving to another planet. He was the first person in his family to go to university. When he was sixteen, a teacher had casually asked him what subject he was thinking of doing at university, and he had been startled. He'd known about universities. He'd known about people going to them. But, like pensions and death, he had never really thought about it applying to him. It was too strange, too far off in the future.

In the first days on campus he had wandered around alone while it seemed like everybody else was already at home there. He was the only person from his school who had come to this university. Other people seemed to have arrived as part of a group. At the freshers' fair, he was bemused by all the clubs. Who were all these people who had come to university ready to go hiking or play chess or put on plays or do comedy or go rowing? How did they know? Had they already done it at school? What if you had never rowed or played chess? Was it too late to start?

He remembered the exact moment when it all changed.

'Don't,' said a voice behind him.

He looked round. Standing behind him was a young man with an amused expression dressed in a checked shirt over a white T-shirt.

'What?'

The man gestured at the stall in front of them. It was the folk music society. An anxious-looking girl in a flowery dress was handing out leaflets.

'Just don't,' he said. 'Don't go there.'

'Why? I like folk music.'

'Let's go for a drink,' said the boy. 'You can always come back afterwards. Folk music will still be here.'

Marco hesitated. Why was this stranger asking him for a drink? It was a question he went on asking himself the next day, the next month and even years later. What had Leo seen in him?

'All right,' he said and they went to the bar in the union and Marco ordered what Leo ordered and Marco talked to Leo in a way he'd never talked to anyone before.

There must have been other meetings, but what Marco remembered, looking back after all these years, was the first time that Leo came to Marco's room. He brought some weed and they smoked together. Leo noticed Marco's acoustic guitar, leaning against the wall.

'Are you in a band?'

'I just play a bit for myself.'

'What kind of music do you like?'

'Old stuff. Nick Drake, Richard Thompson.'

Leo looked blank.

'You've never heard of them,' Marco said. He got up. 'I'll put some Nick Drake on.'

'No,' said Leo. 'I don't want to hear them. I want to hear you.'

'No. As I said, I just play a bit for myself.'

'Then just play for yourself.'

Marco had never played in front of anyone but the weed had loosened something in his brain and he picked up the guitar and played a song he'd been messing around with. He looked down at his fingers, partly so he wouldn't be aware of Leo looking at him.

'That's it,' he said, when he was finished.

'Who wrote it?'

'Nobody wrote it. It's just a thing I put together.'

Marco felt that he had shown part of himself. Maybe more than he should. But Leo didn't say much. They just carried on smoking for the rest of the afternoon.

A few days later, Leo appeared in Marco's room again. He said that there was going to be a show in the union.

'It's an open mike night,' he said. 'Bits of comedy, bits of music. You just have to put your name down.'

'Not in a million years,' said Marco. 'I've never played in public. I couldn't do anything like that.'

'I thought you'd say that,' said Leo. 'That's why I did it for you.'

Marco would never forget that moment or the expression on Leo's face. Was he being helped or set up? The whole idea was insane and impossible. At first Marco was furious, but Leo just smiled. And a few days later, Marco sat in the student union watching a comedian performing to stony silence. When the young man shambled shamefacedly away, the host looked down at his paper, read a name and Marco realised that it was his.

As he made his way through the crowd, clutching his guitar, he felt as if it was all happening to someone else in a dream. His hands were clammy and his mouth was dry. He thought he wouldn't be able to play at all. But when he started, he looked down at his fingers and something strange happened. He felt at home. The room had fallen silent. When he began to sing, he knew that his voice felt frail, but it was his voice, and he heard it as if for the first time.

When he finished and gave a shy nod, there was a roar of applause. He stepped off the little platform that served as a stage and saw Leo sitting to one side clapping and smiling at him. Next to him was a girl, a dreamy vision of curves and smiles.

'This is Ellen Hooper,' said Leo. 'I've told her all about you.'

Marco was about to put his hand out for her to shake, but she stepped forward and hugged him in a cloud of perfume. He felt her breasts against his chest.

'That was amazing,' she said. 'I wanted to cry.'

She looked at him with a directness that made him almost faint. Nobody had ever seemed so interested in him before.

Ellen, he thought to himself. Ellen. It wasn't just Tyler he was nervous about meeting again. He was anxious about the others as well: not seeing them, but them seeing him, seeing what his life had become, and how the years had led him down a dwindling path to this poky flat, to singing covers in pubs on a Friday night and giving guitar lessons to middle-aged men who were going through their own mid-life crises. At least Tyler couldn't make him feel bad about himself.

'Come on,' he said, standing up, lurching slightly, reaching for his leather jacket. 'Let's do it.'

4

The train from Derby was crowded, so that Jay Murphy had to stand in the corridor. A few feet away, a little girl sitting on her mother's lap was wearing a garland of flowers in her hair and a frothy tutu over her leggings. She saw him looking at her and stared back until he smiled, and then she turned away, burying her face in her mother's shoulder.

Midsummer's Day. He should be walking in the hills. He should be sitting with a book. He shouldn't be here. But Clara had called him up and cajoled and insisted. She was the only one he had stayed in touch with and that had been her doing, not his. Seeing her was a special kind of pain. But she had refused to give up on him, so he owed her, he supposed, although it was a complicated kind of debt. She was the strongest, steadiest person he had ever known. He had loved her with gratitude and wonder, and terror she would abandon him, and she had wrecked his life by leaving him at the time he needed her most. For a long time, he had believed it was impossible to survive without her, had made two botched attempts to end his life in the aftermath of her decision to end their relationship, but it had been years since they had last met.

Clara, he thought. Clara Keane. A stranger now, with a life he knew nothing about. He remembered the way she had led him from the house after Tyler had been taken away. Her hand had been firm and warm, her face pale and stricken.

Jay often thought about the past and about that terrible weekend. But it was like trying to make out the shape of something that had happened in a wild fever dream; he could barely see the faces through the whirling, jammed-up chaos of it. He could barely see himself either – that young man was a virtual stranger, from a world that had disappeared. Jay had stripped his life of everything that had made it unbearable. He'd found peace in his reclusive, pared-back existence. Yet here he was on a train that was taking him back to the people and the memories he had fled.

The train rumbled; there was a hiss of brakes. The people in the carriage swayed slightly. Jay swallowed hard and clenched his fists as dread churned in him. He closed his eyes, heard himself give a groan, opened them again to see the little girl staring at him. She looked scared. He tried to smile, but that only made it worse. He closed his eyes once more.

'I'm all right,' he said to himself, or was it out loud?

He put his hand over his eyes, tried to calm the raggedness of his breath, summoned pictures of the moors rolling away under his feet, the hills folding into the bright distance. But it wasn't working. Other images broke through. Leo smiling at him, radiant with curiosity, urging hm on – as if Jay was an experiment he was conducting.

Jay saw another face, snarling and ecstatic. It was the face of the other Jay, the one who he mustn't think about, mustn't acknowledge. He saw the other Jay hurl something, a window shattering; heard a whoop of wild laughter. Objects swiped off shelves with one mad gesture. Things falling, breaking. A feeling in him that was so strong it was impossible to name: something like fury, like exultation, like release, and like despair.

'Go away,' he said. 'Go away.'

The train rocked. He opened his eyes. The little girl was still gazing at him, and so were other people in the carriage. He rubbed his face, pulled his water bottle out of his bag and took several gulps. The images were receding. He was himself again: meek, kind, damaged Jay, his face a map of past suffering.

'Sorry,' he muttered to no one. 'I must have been having a dream.'

5

Clara Keane was also on a train, coming from South London to Tufnell Park. North London was like another city to her; she kept checking on her phone app for directions. She wore loose cotton trousers and an oversized black shirt, and carried a small bunch of flowers which were beginning to wilt in the heat.

She thought of them all converging on Beatrice's house from different parts of the city and the country, and pressed the back of her hand to her mouth. It had a violent unreality. When she had first read Beatrice's email – a rather formal invitation to meet up for a reunion that might seem surprising and even distasteful – she had sat for several minutes staring at her screen, pondering what her response should be.

Clara had always kept her emotions under control. She meditated, did yoga, took long walks when she was unsettled or distressed. She waited before she spoke her feelings, taking time to gather her thoughts and to let sudden impulses settle down and be absorbed. She was patient; everything she did was rational and considered. The invitation disturbed her more than she cared to admit, stirring up old, unwelcome feelings. She had waited for two days, and then contacted Jay. She had persuaded Jay, at first reluctant, that they should go together.

Sam, her partner, had asked why on earth they were all going along with this reunion, and Clara had shrugged.

'I can't speak for the others, just me.'

'Okay, why are you going then?'

Clara hesitated a long while before replying.

'It's not really for me. I want Jay to go.'

'*Jay*? Why on earth?'

'I think it might help him.'

'Help him in what way?'

'It might be a way of facing up to what happened. I think he's somehow still in hiding.'

'God, Clara, don't you think that's for him to decide, not you?'

'I'm just going with him.'

Sam frowned at her.

'You're not responsible for him, you know.'

'I know I'm not.'

'That's not how it sounds. It's been nearly thirty years. Another life.'

'Another life,' said Clara softly. 'Yes.'

'You were children, for goodness' sake.'

'I didn't feel like a child.'

'You want to rescue him. That's a dangerous impulse.'

'I don't.'

'You can't. You never could.'

'I don't want to talk about it anymore.'

On the train, Clara let herself remember her last sight of Tyler Green – not on the front of newspapers or on news bulletins, but as she had actually seen him when he was taken away, his tall frame bowed, his handsome face turned from them until his last anguished gaze back at them all. She had assumed that none of them would ever see him again, and it felt now as if someone long dead was heaving up the gravestone, shouldering his way back into a life that had tried to forget him.

Her thoughts slid back to Jay, not as he had been over the weekend of Leo's death when he was jittery and paranoid before the murder, frantic after it, but a short time later, when she had moved to London and was sharing a house with four strangers. She had left her old life behind, but was still living in the awful aftermath of Leo's death. At her request, Jay had come down by train to meet her. She was waiting for him at the ticket barrier, and she saw him before he saw her. For a brief moment she looked at him with the eyes of a stranger. He was very thin. His bones seemed to jut through his clothes, and his eyes were red-rimmed in his mobile, restless face. He was wearing a heavy coat, even though the weather was warm, and walked quickly, but with a curious disarticulated gait. As he came nearer, she saw a sheen of sweat on his forehead, a rash on his jaw. He looked unwell, she thought, with a lurch of tenderness that was a world away from desire. He also looked odd, something askew about him.

His eyes found her and his face brightened. He smiled. She smiled back, feeling slightly sick. He came through the ticket barrier after pushing his hand into all his many pockets for the ticket, which he eventually found. He put his arms around her, pulled her into the itch of his coat. He smelt medicinal. There was a bruise under one eye, and Clara wondered if he'd been in a fight. She kissed his cheek, suggested they have coffee. His rucksack, when he put it down on the floor of the cafe they went to, was bulging with hardback books. He wanted to pay for the drinks, but couldn't find his wallet, pulled out the books, a clatter of pens, a meagre toilet bag, a pair of faded boxers and a rolled-up ball of red socks. There was a squashed packet of Brie he had bought as a present for Clara, who loved cheese.

'Sorry,' he kept saying. 'It'll be somewhere.'

'I need to tell you something,' Clara said when they were eventually sitting in a dark corner, each with a coffee in front of them.

'I don't want to talk about Leo and Tyler. I can't.'

'This isn't about Leo and Tyler.'

He looked at her, and then away. He knew what she was going to say. He put his hands out as if to avert the words.

'Let me speak first,' he said. 'It's been a bad time. Leo, Tyler, the nightmare of everything. And coming after what happened to me at uni.' He swallowed; she saw his Adam's apple bob, sharp in his thin neck. 'What I did, I mean. I know I haven't been coping, and that's been tough for you, and not fair. But, that's all going to change. I'm going to get better, and I'm going to be better. Better for you, I mean. A better boyfriend.'

'Jay.'

'I'm going to stop taking drugs. I promise. I'm going to take myself in hand. You'll see. It'll be like it used to be.'

She had rehearsed what she would say. She just had to say it.

'It's no good, Jay,' she said. 'We can't go on.'

He leaned forward, seized one of her hands in both of his.

'You can't do this now. Not after what we've been through. I know I've been useless. I mean, why would anyone want to be with me? I get that. But I love you, Clara. I'm going to get work; I'm already looking. I'm going to turn myself round. You'll see. Everything's going to be different. Give me a chance to prove myself.'

'I gave you a chance. More than one.'

He was gabbling now, mouth forming strange shapes around the words.

'I swear to God I'm going to change. But I can't do it without you. You can't walk away when I need you the most.'

'Why?' Clara asked, and a violent flare of irritation made her cruel. She felt like an assassin. 'What about me? I'm not your mother, you know. I can't be with you just because you'll go to pieces without me. That's not how it works. I can't do it anymore.'

And she couldn't, she knew that, although when she saw his brimming eyes, all she wanted to do was take him in her arms and comfort him for the hurt that she was causing.

'But I love you,' he said again. 'I love you, Clara. And you love me. Don't you?'

'Not like that,' she said, and made herself look into his eyes. 'Not anymore.'

He stared at her. His pupils were enormous. A single tear trickled down his cheek, which he made no attempt to brush away. His chin quivered as though he would sob in earnest.

'You don't love me?' he whispered, a small boy at her mercy.

'Not like that,' she repeated.

'Oh,' he said, like a sigh escaping him. 'I get it.'

'I'll always care about you and be your friend,' she said, re-membering the words she had practised, which sounded empty and fraudulent. 'I'm very sorry for this pain.'

He rubbed his eyes.

'What's going to happen to me?'

'Jay,' she said tiredly, 'I can't be responsible for that anymore.'

And yet, she thought, sitting on the train on her way to Beatrice's, holding her little bunch of wilting flowers, her part-ner had been right. Clara had always felt somehow responsible for Jay, and tied to his emotional state. Twice, he had tried to take his own life. The first attempt had been a few days after she had ended their relationship, and her guilt was complicated rather than lessened by the anger she felt towards him for seeking to so brutally punish her. The second time was several months later. He had phoned her, weeping, telling her he loved her and was sorry, so sorry for everything, that he wished her happiness and that everything was his fault. His voice had been slurred, and in a panic she had called the emergency services. When she visited him in hospital, after his stomach had been pumped, Jay had been calm, sweet, defeated. She had kissed his hands and stroked his hair, and he had smiled up at her as if he was her child.

She sent him a cheery message: *fancy a drink before we face everyone?* Then added an emoji of two glasses tilted together in a toast, and a smiling face.

6

Rudi Scott stared at the screen of his computer. Over the years, he had experimented with different ways of writing. He had tried notebooks. Loose sheets of paper. Index cards. A laptop, which could be used anywhere. Recently he had decided that writing was a craft, and just as if he was a carpenter, he needed his own workshop. He had converted a room in the back of the house, looking out on the lawn.

The room had been repainted in an undistracting shade of grey and he had bought undistracting framed reproductions for the wall: abstract paintings by Rothko and Kandinsky. He had a computer so powerful he could have edited a Hollywood movie on it. The room was like a shrine to creativity.

He had read somewhere that Graham Greene had written 350 words a day before breakfast. That wasn't so much, just two or three paragraphs. If you wrote that every day, you'd have a full-size novel in less than a year. Even if you wrote 250 words a day. Good words. You'd still get a novel.

But what if you wrote no words a day? Or what if you wrote minus words? That is, you wrote almost a hundred words on one day, then reread them the following day and not only deleted them, but deleted what you had written the day before that? You could do that for all eternity and end up with less than when you had started.

People talked about 'that difficult second novel'. After a

handful of short stories published in magazines and anthologies, Rudi was still on his first novel, and that was difficult enough. There were so many distractions. So many things in the world, so many books, so many films, so many coffees to drink, so much happening outside the window.

Now there was Tyler Green. Back in his life and back in his head. It was by far the biggest thing that had ever happened to him. For years he had thought that he should write about it, and he had tried, but he had failed. The murder of Leo Bauer and the arrest and conviction of Tyler Green was like a bleeding oozing chunk of reality that had been dumped in front of him, and he had found himself incapable of turning it into words, shaping it into a story. He had tried it as a novel, he had tried it as a memoir, and then he had tried to forget about it and write about something different. He had written about many different things. The remnants of them were in different files somewhere on his computer, but none of them had amounted to anything.

When he received the message from Beatrice he had immediately thought: no, absolutely not, no way. He'd never liked the idea of school reunions. If you'd stayed in touch with people from the past, then why did you need a reunion? If you had lost touch with them, then you'd lost touch for a reason. But he could imagine what they would be like. People boasting about what they'd achieved, still trying to show they were cool after all these years.

But going to Beatrice's house, meeting Tyler, that was on a whole other level. He was interested in seeing Beatrice, of course. He was curious about what had happened to the girl he had known, now that she was all grown up and a big lawyer married to a famous man. The thought of her gave him an ache in his chest. But he knew it was a curiosity that should be resisted.

He was curious about Tyler as well. What did he want with them? Why would he do this? But there were so many reasons he shouldn't go. He had never even considered staying in touch with Tyler, let alone actually visiting him in prison. For twenty-nine years, Rudi had thought of him as dead and buried. He had tried to forget him. So why would he go and see him now? Only bad things would come of it.

He had talked to his wife, Celia, about it and she had agreed.

'I think you're absolutely right,' she said.

'You said that very quickly. Why? I mean, I'm glad you agree, but why?'

Her face took on a stern expression that he had come to recognise and slightly to dread.

'You've never told me much about your past,' she said, 'and I haven't asked you about it. But from the little you've said, I can tell that there was something very wrong about that group you got mixed up with. I know that we all go a little astray when we're young . . . ' She paused and gave Rudi a meaningful look.

He didn't reply. He was sure that Celia had not gone astray at all at any time, except, perhaps, when she had married him.

'I think you did a good thing when you left all that behind,' she continued. 'I truly hope that Tyler Green has repented for his terrible crime. But I don't know what he's doing, wanting to see you after all this time. I wonder whether he's trying to suck you all into some terrible scheme.'

'On the other hand,' he said in what was almost a mumble, 'it might be a way of making sense of it all.'

'What does that mean? Making sense of it all?' She said the phrase as if she was holding it with tongs. 'He's a convicted murderer.'

'He's part of my life. I can't deny that.'

'He's a part of your life that you managed to escape. I think you might be better off working on your novel than mixing yourself up in all of that.'

Rudi wished he hadn't mentioned it at all, and in the days that followed he had said nothing. But now, looking at his blank screen, he was thinking not of his novel, but of his old friends, old lovers. Were they all now making their way across the country towards Beatrice's house in North London? He felt like he was sitting in an old haunted house, hearing creaking sounds in the attic. They were probably nothing but he had to look, just to be sure.

He got up. He had decided.

'You don't need to go.'

'I know that.'

'I mean you really don't need to go. I thought we'd decided.'

Rudi Scott kissed his wife on the cheek, breathing in her musky scent, the same perfume she had worn when he had first met her on a skiing holiday with friends, all those years ago. That was before he knew she was rich. But of course she was rich. Only those born into wealth have such poise, such assurance about their place in the world.

He took off his grey linen jacket and folded it neatly on the passenger seat before climbing into his car. He rolled up his shirt sleeves.

'I don't think you should. It feels all wrong.'

'I won't stay long. Everyone else has said yes.'

'That's no reason.'

Rudi looked at her solemnly.

'I'm a writer,' he said, with a self-deprecating smile so she could take it as a joke if she wanted to. 'This is rich material, a tap root into my past. I'll just drop in, get the lie of the land, drive home. I'll be back before midnight.'

'It's a long drive, especially on a Friday evening.'

'It'll be fine. Don't wait up.'

'Be careful. Don't drink.'

'Of course not. You don't need to tell me that.'

But when he was out of Burford and before reaching the flyover, Rudi pulled over and took a hip flask out of the glove compartment. He removed his wire-rimmed glasses and tilted the mirror to check up on himself. He pushed his silver hair back, crinkled his face into the smile he gave for the camera. Not too bad for fifty-one. He took a gulp of whisky and then another, before putting his glasses back on and pulling out onto the road, swerving to avoid a cyclist.

7

'Georgia!' Ellen Sweeney called down from the spare room.
'Come and tell me if I look the part.'

Her friend mounted the stairs and pushed open the door.
Ellen was standing at the foot of the bed, in front of a long
mirror. She turned and held her arms out.

'Well?' she said.

She had travelled up that day from Bristol, arriving at
Georgia's front door in a dress that was a bit like a colourful
festival tent. Now she was wearing a pale blue, calf-length skirt
with an elasticated waist, and a short-sleeved checked shirt.

'Well,' Georgia replied cautiously. 'It depends on what part
you were wanting to play.'

She thought, but didn't say, that Ellen looked as if she had
stepped out of the 1950s, and was about to play rounders with
her children. She had five of them – her football team, she
always called them – though only the three youngest still lived
at home.

'Good question.' Ellen sat on the bed, and started to vigorously brush her thick grey hair.

'And why do you need to play a part anyway?'

Ellen nodded approvingly at her.

'Another good question. We play parts all the time, even if
we don't admit it. Don't you agree?'

'I don't know about that,' said Georgia. The Ellen she had

met twenty-five years ago, when they were both single, had been blonde, extravagant, bursting with life and excitement. She wore bright, tight-fitting dresses and red lipstick. She had announced firmly that they should be friends, and so they were. They'd gone on slow, panting runs together, Ellen laughing and gasping all the way; to tennis classes; they had joined an amateur dramatic society. Then Ellen had met Michael, had started wearing long-sleeved, high-necked clothes and flat shoes, and had soon disappeared to Bristol and motherhood.

'So what part are you playing this evening?'

'Unthreatening,' Ellen said firmly.

'Unthreatening?'

'With nothing to prove. Someone people can talk to, confide in.'

She stood up and went to the mirror, where she started to tie her hair into a single, bulky plait.

'Do you want them to confide in you?'

'Only if they want to.'

'And will you confide in them?'

'Me?' Ellen turned her head. 'I shouldn't think so.'

No, thought Georgia, looking at her friend's open, smiling face with a mixture of affection and exasperation. Of course you won't. She couldn't remember a single time over the twenty-five years they had known each other that Ellen had confided in her. She seemed emotionally open, wept in films, expressed her appetites and desires, was full of strong opinions, and appeared to wear her heart on her sleeve. But she never talked about sadness, doubt, insecurity. Sometimes she would be quieter than usual, but if Georgia asked her if she was all right, she would always beam and say that goodness, yes, she was just fine, just thinking.

'It sounds appalling to me. Like some kind of crazy group therapy.'

'Nothing wrong with group therapy,' said Ellen cheerfully, who for fifteen years had worked as a couples' counsellor. 'In my humble experience.' She snapped a rubber band on the end of the crooked plait, leaned forward into the mirror to examine herself. 'You sound a bit dubious.'

'It's just that you seem . . . ' Georgia hesitated.

'Seem what?'

'Like this was just any old reunion.'

'It is a reunion.'

'Ellen, come on! This man killed your friend.'

'Leo was his friend too.'

'Which makes it even worse. It must have been utterly traumatic for you all. I can't imagine it.'

'I believe in atonement,' said Ellen, suddenly solemn.

'I don't even know what that means.'

'And in redemption.'

'That sounds almost religious.'

'Tyler did a terrible thing. He took a life, and was given a life sentence in return. Now he's served his time. His slate is wiped clean. We should forgive him.'

'Has he asked for forgiveness?'

'He hasn't had a chance. Perhaps it's what this evening is all about.'

'If you're so forgiving, how come you never visited him in prison?'

'I don't know,' said Ellen vaguely. 'At first, it was utterly shocking, like a violent blow, and I think I kept my distance a bit. I was very young, remember. And then, well, my children came along and it rather took over. You know how it is.'

Georgia didn't: she had never had children. Every time she visited Ellen in Bristol, she was struck by how competent her friend was, in spite of her breezy manner, her apparent tolerance for chaos. Her house was always neat; she laid down rules for her family which they largely obeyed; she cooked large meals, worked, and seemed to take everything in her stride.

'I'm not sure what Michael would have felt about me traipsing off to see a murderer in the middle of all the mayhem. He's quite stern about things like that.'

'What was he like?'

'Tyler?' For a moment, Ellen's face became grave with memory, a disconcerting glimpse of someone else beneath the jolly surface. 'Oh, Tyler was a dreamboat. Who knows what he'll be like now.'

'Did you write to him?'

'Now you're making me feel bad.' Ellen laughed to show she was joking. 'But you need to understand, we didn't keep in contact with each other either. I tried to at first, but it didn't work; it felt awkward and constrained, as if we were being polite to each other. It was as if our group only worked as a group. Like some kind of organism. Maybe the others did better.'

'Will you talk about it all to Tyler?'

'It's always good to name what everyone's thinking. Shine a light.'

'That sounds ominous.'

'Not at all,' said Ellen reprovingly. 'It's healthy. Now I should go. I'm not sure what time I'll be back. Don't wait up; I have a key, and I'll try not to wake you.'

They went downstairs together. Ellen took her cotton jacket from the hook in the hall, fidgeted with the waistband of her skirt, patted her badly plaited hair, then hesitated by the front door.

'I wonder how everyone's turned out,' she said. 'We were so young. We were like children playing at being adults. And now, well, look!'

She pointed at herself: a stocky, middle-aged woman in matronly clothes, with a weathered face and a bulky grey plait. Georgia realised her friend was nervous after all.

'I hope it goes well.'

'I'll tell you all about it in the morning.' She opened the door and stepped out into the blue evening. 'Thanks for everything,' she said over her shoulder. 'Wish me luck.'

8

Tyler Green had spent the whole day walking. He had gone north up the canal to Islington, then found the Green Link and walked to the Hackney Marshes and along the River Lee. London was so changed from the city he remembered as a young man – larger, louder, poorer, richer, more crowded, more oppressive – but the river was the same. Only the flocks of screeching parakeets were new. Today there had been families picnicking, and pubs with their doors thrown wide open, advertising iced coffee, Aperol spritzes, lunch, but Tyler hadn't stopped or even slowed his pace. He looped back again, on side roads, following his instinct, until at last he was back in familiar territory.

His bedsit just north of King's Cross was drab and anonymous, and he tried to spend as little of his time in it as possible. He wouldn't stay there much longer; he didn't even know if he would remain in London. He could live anywhere, as long as he checked in with his probation officer and kept to the conditions of his licence. His mother had left money to him in her will, and although it wasn't a vast amount, it gave him safety, and it gave him time. Time to think, and time to let his thoughts sink into his mind. On most days, he walked like this – fast, but without a goal or purpose, feeling the wind on his face, the sun and rain, hearing voices around him. Sometimes, when he had tired himself out, he would sit on a bench in a park or a green square for hours. Was this freedom?

Now he slid the pay-as-you go mobile that he had bought a few weeks ago into the pocket of his jeans. It only had a handful of numbers on it, including his probation officer's. He looked at his watch, then stepped out of the room into the corridor. He double-locked the door and slid the key into his back pocket. On the threshold of the building, he stopped for a moment and tipped his head slightly, letting the warmth and light flow into him. He had spent so long in darkness or under flickering yellow lights, ten thousand days and nights. The tick of the clock, the shrill of the alarm every morning, the turn of the key in the lock, the partition in the cell door sliding open and someone staring in at him whenever they felt like, the visits not made, the letters not received, the memories locked away in the basement of the self, and only in dreams did he hear them banging at the door.

There were little children playing in the fountains in Granary Square, jumping in and out of the jets of water. People spilled out of restaurants and bars or sat on the roofs of the boats that lined the canal. Cyclists weaved their way through the crowds and the pigeons.

Tyler was still unused to the ceaseless movement on the streets, the way young men on electric scooters or teenagers on skateboards swerved past him, barely slowing, the way people talked loudly as they passed, gesticulating and grinning. At first, he had thought they were troubled, like poor Mo from prison had been troubled, voices jabbering and sneering in his head; then he understood they were on their phones. Everyone seemed to be on their phones, even the ones in groups were talking to someone somewhere else entirely.

He walked at an even pace, unencumbered and in no hurry. He had waited for nearly thirty years.

9

Beatrice took a long, calming breath. She opened the door.

'Beatrice,' said Will, his face creased in a smile.

She had put on dark lipstick, which made her face look paler than usual. The freckles she used to have as a young woman had all but gone, except for a few faded marks on her cheekbones. Her tawny hair had faded as well. She looked well cared for, Will thought, and elegant, which the old Beatrice had never been, but a bit rubbed away by the years.

She smiled back, put a hand on his arm.

'Will. It's good to see you.'

'Are we the first?'

'Someone has to be, and I'm glad it's you.' Then her expression altered.

'It's Benjy,' said Ali briskly, stepping forward. 'Benjy, Beatrice. Beatrice, Benjy. I hope it's all right bringing him. He's very housetrained.'

'I've got a cat. Is he all right with cats?'

'He gets a bit nervous around them. We might want to try and keep them apart.'

Benjy started barking, and there was the rattling sound of a cat flap from the other side of the house.

'He's just saying hello,' said Ali.

'Speaking of hello,' said Will, stepping inside and putting an arm around Beatrice. He held her for a moment and then stood back. 'You look great, Bea.'

'You two don't look so bad either,' said Beatrice.

But Will was jowly and unkempt and had put on too much weight, she thought, while Ali had lost too much. She had always been slender, with her triangular face and big dark eyes; now she was thin, all angles and bones. Beatrice could feel her smile stiffen, a mild headache starting up. How do we do this, she wondered. It was a mistake; she should never have agreed to it.

Will had a bag in his free hand and he held it up.

'I've brought some asparagus from the allotment. It was in the ground two hours ago. Interesting fact: midsummer is officially the end of the asparagus season. After this evening, we have to wait until next spring.'

'Beatrice probably has the food all prepared,' said Ali.

'It'll be lovely.'

'You don't have to worry,' said Will. 'I'll cook it.'

Beatrice led them through into the living room. Will looked round at the mass of flowers in tall vases, the pictures, the huge mirror over the fire with his own face in it, the giant cream-coloured sofa, the rug, everything immaculate, co-ordinated. Double doors stood ajar, showing a smaller, book-lined room with a piano and another fireplace.

'This is amazing.'

'Haven't you been here?' said Beatrice.

She knew they hadn't. Since Leo's death they had met, less and less frequently as the years went by, on neutral ground. Early evening drinks, always with something else they had to get to afterwards; or brief, polite encounters in crowded rooms. They all knew they belonged to different worlds now, with little in common except for a past they wanted to forget.

'It's extremely beautiful,' said Ali.

'I just want it to be comfortable. Somewhere we can flop down in the evening with a drink.'

Ali walked across to the large French windows, which opened out onto a terrace, then shallow stairs leading to the garden, the grass lush green in the middle of this heatwave, the water sprinklers arcing over well-tended beds, stiff alliums in a row, a mass of roses, the wooden bench under the apple tree. She felt a stab of envy.

'Is Sebastian here?'

'He's away on business. But he probably wouldn't be here anyway. He's often in the House until late.'

Will laughed.

'You say it so casually.'

'It's just another office,' said Beatrice. She took the bag of asparagus from him. 'Thank you for this.'

'I can roast it,' he said. 'Or steam it, whichever you prefer.'

'Or save it for tomorrow,' added Ali. 'If you've already planned your menu.'

'It's not really a menu,' said Beatrice. 'I've had food delivered. It's very simple, lots of salads and things. It'll be good to have asparagus with it.'

'Oh, God, listen to us,' said Will. 'We're talking to each other like strangers, people who've just been introduced and have nothing in common. We all know what this is about. It's wonderful of you to host this, Beatrice. Really wonderful. But I've got to admit I'm feeling a bit nervous about it all. And just, well, amazed that it's really happening.'

Beatrice nodded.

'To be honest, I'm wondering why I ever agreed to it. It would be one thing to meet him again – but to meet him like this, with all of us gathered.'

Except there was no *us* anymore, she thought, and felt bemused all over again at how quickly and easily their group had dissolved.

'It's my fault,' said Will. 'I asked you.'

'No. You passed on a message. Tyler asked me, and I didn't need to say yes.'

'There. We've said his name at least.'

'Why does he want to see us all?' Ali asked. She was still standing by the window, looking out at the beautiful early evening, the light just beginning to thicken, but she had been listening to their conversation. 'I know why I'm here. I'm here because it meant a lot to Will that I should come. I know why Will is here – he has a romantic attachment to the idea of friendship and loyalty.' Will flinched slightly. 'But what does Tyler want?'

Will shrugged.

'I've no idea.'

'Didn't you ask?'

'Of course I did. He just said it was important, and he would say more when he saw us. Maybe he needs to acknowledge the past. Catharsis.'

Ali watched Beatrice's cat stalk past on the gravel path outside. Benjy stiffened and gave a small growl.

'How many times did you visit him in prison?' Beatrice asked.

They were all still standing; Beatrice was holding the bunch of asparagus. Her throat felt tight. She could feel the dampness under her arms and hoped it wouldn't show through her white silk shirt. She felt as if she was on stage, just before the curtain rises, mouth dry and limbs tense, trying to remember lines that no longer made sense.

'Not enough. I've lapsed a bit lately. I haven't seen him for a few years.'

'More than a few years,' said Ali.

'Yes, more than a few.'

'Nearer ten.'

'Okay,' Will said wearily. 'Nearer ten. I feel bad about it. It depressed me, if you want to know. It started to feel so pointless. He didn't want to see me. That was clear enough. He'd just sit there watching me and giving monosyllabic answers. I'd gabble away about stupid things. He started to look so different, thin and hard, a nasty scar on his face. He frightened me a bit, if I'm honest, and there was no way I could get through to him. He was entirely closed off. I kept having to remind myself that this was Tyler, my old friend.'

'You did better than me. I never visited him at all,' said Beatrice. 'And I didn't hear about the release when it happened. The parole board don't make a fuss about releases like his. It's all done very quietly and discreetly, unless it gets into the papers.'

'What do the family think about it?'

'Leo's? They'll have been told, and I'm sure Conrad Bauer doesn't like it one little bit. After all, he was one of the reasons Tyler served so many years. I mean, no one stays in prison that long. But Bauer doesn't have a say in the release.'

The case was already notorious before Leo Bauer's father became involved. The tabloids had gone wild over what was for them the perfect story: sex, drugs and murder on the moors. Conrad Bauer added the element of celebrity. He had been an actor in a long-running soap. After his son was murdered, he had appeared on countless TV shows, and done multiple interviews in the papers, insisting that life should mean life. He had formed an activist group on behalf of victims and their families. And he struck it lucky with the judge on the case: Judge Roger Kendall had strong views about modern society, about drugs and permissiveness.

Beatrice looked down at the asparagus. 'Let me go and put this in the kitchen.'

She left the room, and they could hear her going down the stairs that led to the lower ground floor. Neither of them spoke. There was a knock at the door, and then the doorbell chimed. Benjy started barking frantically.

'Shall I get it?' Will asked, not moving.

Ali raised her eyebrows at him and went into the hall. She closed her eyes briefly, put a hand on her throat where she could feel her wild pulse. Then she pulled open the door.

10

Relief flooded through Ali as she saw it wasn't Tyler. She took Marco's nicotine-stained hand in hers and held it for a moment, trying not to show that she was taken aback by his appearance. He'd always been slightly grungy. Now he looked coarsened and frayed. But his eyes were the same, and when he smiled at her, she could see the old Marco, ironic and yet vulnerable.

Marco noticed Ali's reaction. He saw himself through her eyes, and felt the last of his self-confidence shrivel and die. His smile broadened and tightened, until he felt it was clamped onto his face.

'Welcome,' said Beatrice, joining them. 'How good it is to see you, Marco.'

She was being the hostess, cordial and gracious and a thousand miles away.

'I don't believe this,' said Marco, looking from one to the other. 'It's like a dream.'

His voice felt rusty. He wanted to weep, to flee.

'Hello?' Beatrice turned to Kristin, who stepped forward with a beam.

'I'm Kristin,' she said. 'Thank you so much for having me.'

'Kristin?' Beatrice's forehead corrugated into a puzzled frown.

Kristin turned to Marco.

'You didn't tell her I was coming?'

'I'm sure I mentioned it.'

'No,' said Beatrice. 'You didn't.'

'Sorry about that. I just thought Kristin might be interested in an evening with the old folks. You don't mind, do you?'

'Don't you worry,' said Kristin. 'I know all about it, so I'm fully prepared. Marco told me everything when we first met. You guys, your friendship, the murder. He said it had made him who he was.'

'Really?' Ali's voice was tart.

'Yes. So of course, I wanted to come. But if it's a private reunion, I can leave.'

As she spoke, she stepped firmly into the house, looking around her with a greedy interest.

Beatrice shook her head resignedly. They filed into the living room. Will walked across to Marco, arms out, and the two men hugged. They stepped back and looked at each other.

'Hey, man,' said Will, 'you're looking great. I'd say you're unchanged but . . . ' He tapped the top of his head.

'Yeah, there's a cruel moment where you've got to face reality and ask for a number one. You on the other hand look exactly the same, but more so.'

Will grinned.

'You mean I'm fatter.'

'You're more yourself.'

'I like a man of appetites,' said Kristin enthusiastically.

She was the only one of them who seemed at her ease.

Beatrice left the room and returned holding a wine bottle in each hand.

'When everyone's here, we'll have a proper drink, but in the meantime, I've got some red and some white.'

She poured the wine into glasses and handed them round, except to Kristin, who just asked for water.

'I like to keep a clear head,' she explained.

'Why?' Ali asked, and at first Kristin thought she meant it as a joke, but Ali didn't seem to be joking.

She was, decided Kristin, a neurotic woman. She had an instinct for things like that. She took to Will, though. He was like an amiable bear.

'So how did you meet?' Beatrice asked her.

'He was teaching my brother guitar. He took me along to see Marco play in a pub.'

'It's a venue,' said Marco.

'It's a room in the back of a pub,' said Kristin.

'Is your brother a musician?'

'He's a lawyer,' said Kristin. 'The guitar's just a hobby.' She looked around. 'Nice place.'

'Thank you.'

'Is everyone going to be here?' asked Marco.

'Almost everyone,' said Beatrice. 'People are making a real effort. Ellen's coming from Bristol. Jay's coming from wherever he's living now.'

'What about Rudi? I googled him. He's out in the Cotswolds in a mansion, isn't he?'

'Yes,' said Beatrice. 'We lost touch, but it seems he married well, like in a Jane Austen novel. I assume he's not going to make it. He didn't reply.'

'You and Rudi had a thing, didn't you? Back in the day.'

Beatrice flushed.

'I don't know why you say that.'

It made no sense that she still felt the need to conceal her brief affair with Rudi. It had been secret then because of Sebastian, and perhaps secrecy had sharpened the desire. Now she understood that everyone had probably known or suspected all along, and she felt embarrassed for her artless twenty-one-year-old self.

'Are you blushing?' said Marco with a small chuckle.

'Are you stoned?' Ali squinted at him over her glass.

'He wanted to take the edge off his nerves,' Kristin said.

'We're all anxious,' said Will soothingly.

'What about you then?' Marco said. 'Are you married?'

'Yes.'

'Who's the lucky woman?'

'Me,' said Ali.

Marco swivelled towards her.

'What?'

'I'm the lucky woman.'

'I had no idea.'

'Why would you?'

Marco grinned across at Will.

'You certainly played the long game,' he said.

An expression of distaste crossed Ali's face.

There was another knock, then the sound of cheerful shrieking. Beatrice walked back into the room with Ellen, who hugged everyone for longer than necessary, then introduced herself to Kristin.

'You don't know what you've let yourself in for,' she said.

'I'm excited. I've heard so much about you all.'

'That's not true,' said Marco. 'I never talk about you. You're all water under the bridge.'

His pupils were dilated, and his words were slurred. He had finished his wine already, but then, so had Will.

'When we were last all together,' Ellen said to Kristin, 'we were younger than you are now. Probably quite a lot younger.' She gestured around her. 'And now look at us. We have grey hair and wrinkles. We probably seem old and respectable to you. Young people don't realise that old people were once young.' She looked round the group, her face glowing with memory. 'We grew up together, didn't we, my dears? And then we left ourselves behind. And now we've come back – and well, I want to say that I think this is amazing. Amazing,' she repeated with added intensity. 'Do you know what I think?' She didn't wait for a reply. 'I think we're all very brave. I think in spite of everything, our hearts are still open.'

'Speak for yourself,' said Marco. 'I'm here because I'm angry. And when he arrives, I want to tell him that.'

'Maybe this evening's not the right time for that,' Beatrice said nervously.

But Ellen nodded approvingly.

'It's good to acknowledge anger.'

'I'm acknowledging it all right.'

'And you?' Ellen turned to Ali. 'Why are you here?'

'I don't want to disappoint you, Ellen,' said Ali, 'but I'm only here because it meant so much to Will.'

'To Will?'

'My husband.'

Ellen's face went slack with surprise.

'I didn't know, but how lovely. It still takes courage. For you above all.'

There was a constrained silence, then the doorbell rang again and Beatrice left the room.

'Is it him, or not?' said Kristin, her eyes gleaming. 'Exciting, isn't it? And I'm just an outsider.'

11

It wasn't Tyler, but Jay and Clara. Soon they were in the room being greeted and hugged. Clara was holding a small bunch of anemones which she handed to Beatrice, noticing at the same time the vases full of flowers and taking in the garden bright with blooms.

'Lovely,' said Beatrice, looking around for somewhere to lay them.

'Yeah, well,' said Clara, 'I didn't want to arrive empty-handed. Isn't he here yet?'

'You and Jay aren't a couple again, are you?' asked Marco. Somehow his wine glass was full again. 'Because Ali and Will are. I mean, not again, because they never were before. That I know of. I think I was often in the dark. But are you?'

Jay ducked his head and mumbled something. Clara laughed.

'We really have lost touch with each other, haven't we?' she said.

'The way you arrived together brought back memories. You were such a sweet pair. Always holding hands.'

'I told you I shouldn't have come,' said Jay in an undertone to Clara.

'It's okay.' Clara put her hand on Jay's arm. 'Marco, Jay and I arrived together not because we're a couple, but because we agreed that we both needed to meet for a pre-party drink to give us the courage to face you all. There are other reasons we're not a couple. One is that that was all a long time ago when we were scarcely more than children, and we now live about two hundred miles apart. Another, which is probably a bit more important, is that one of the discoveries I made in my twenties is that I'm gay.'

There was a very brief pause followed by a flurry of affirmations and congratulations. Clara held her hands up to stop them.

'It's nothing to make a big deal of. I'm not asking for a medal.'

'I'm not going to give you a medal,' said Beatrice, 'but I am going to give you a drink.' She clapped her hands. 'How many of us are there?' She counted heads. 'Eight of us.' She looked at Kristin. 'But you don't drink, right?'

'Not alcohol.'

'Sensible. We should all follow your example. But not tonight. I've prepared something that might remind you of the old days. It's already in the freezer.'

She left the room and there was a sound from the floor below of glasses clinking. She returned carrying a tray with cocktail glasses, a lemon and a knife and a jug of clear liquid. The liquid was so cold that steam was coming off it. She picked up the lemon and the knife and cut a series of fat slices of peel and placed one in each glass. Then she carefully poured the drink into the glasses, one by one.

'Six parts gin to one part vermouth,' she said. 'Remember?'

Ali picked up a glass and held it up to the light so that it sparkled.

'I don't normally drink spirits, but maybe tonight doesn't count.'

'I remember the last night we had them,' said Jay, taking a

glass. He hadn't smiled once since arriving. 'It's not a happy memory.'

'Are you all right, my love?' Ellen asked him, motherly and concerned.

She wrapped an arm around his shoulder and pulled him towards her. He looked small and defenceless, standing against the comforting bulk of her.

'I hope that's the point of this evening,' said Beatrice. 'Instead of running away from what happened, we can turn towards it, face it.'

'That's exactly my idea,' said Ellen energetically, still holding on to Jay.

Ali wrinkled her nose.

'Not mine.'

Kristin leaned close to Ellen.

'I don't know why everyone drifted apart. You must have been so close.'

Ellen gave a conspiratorial smile.

'Later in the evening you'll probably hear a bit more about how close we were.'

'Why don't you tell me now?'

Ellen took a gulp of her dry martini.

'I,' she began in mock solemnity, 'am the mother of five children ... '

'Five?' said Kristin.

'Yes, five. Ranging in age from twenty-two to thirteen. I have five children and I am a couple's therapist.' She took another sip. 'I'm a respectable woman and a pillar of the community. Consequently, it's going to take at least another of these drinks and then some wine before I can tell you all about our shared past. I will tell you that he' – she jerked her chin in Will's direction – 'lost his virginity to me.'

'Oh!'

'He pretended it wasn't his first time, but I could tell. As for your Marco – well. You should have known him back when he had hair.'

'You mean, you had sex with him as well?'

Kristin didn't seem displeased. She cast an affectionate look at Marco, who seemed to sense they were talking about him and glanced over nervously.

'Didn't he tell you?' Ellen gave a chuckle. 'Well, I suppose it was so long ago. Why would he? It was a time when we were all exploring. Exploring ourselves and other people. That's what you should be doing when you're twenty. I had fun. I was free. I wasn't hurting anyone.'

'What does your husband feel about your past?'

'Michael?' Ellen chuckled. 'He doesn't know anything about it. He probably thinks I was a virgin when I married him. He was, poor man. He'd be very disapproving. He thinks I'm quite staid, old-fashioned like him. It's quite sweet. Actually—'

There was a ring at the doorbell. Ellen stopped abruptly, and everyone fell silent and looked round.

'Is it him?' said Ali. 'It must be him.'

She looked thinner than ever, as if she'd tightened every muscle. Her eyes were dark. Tyler Green had been her boyfriend. He had been in love with her like nobody had ever been since, like nobody ever would be again. She hadn't seen him for twenty-nine years. She never talked about him, not even to Will when he returned from his sporadic prison visits looking harrowed; but not a day went by that she didn't think of him or miss the person he had allowed her to believe she could be.

Beatrice straightened her shoulders and smiled at them all encouragingly.

'Let's see,' she said.

12

The group stood suspended in silence. Ellen cleared her throat, as if about to speak. Marco passed a hand over his naked scalp. Ali put her fingers to the gold chain around her neck. Kristin pulled at the skirt of her lacy dress and shifted on her platform heels. Benjy had retreated to the empty fireplace, where he glared out at them, emitting menacing growls.

'I'm so glad to see you,' they heard Beatrice say. 'After all these years.'

'Well, it's not her husband,' said Marco.

The front door shut and there were footsteps coming down the hall.

Tyler Green stood before them.

Someone took a raspy breath. Will. He put his hand to his eyes as if to shade them, then took a step towards his old friend.

In Ali's memory, Tyler was tall, strong, dark-haired, smooth-skinned. He had smiled readily, used his hands eloquently, been vital and alert and responsive, as if life pulsed through him. The man she saw now was thin. He had silver-white hair, cut very short. His face, with its high cheekbones, was unnaturally pale and lined. There was a deep scar running from his left ear to his jaw. Only his eyes, walnut-brown flecked with almost-gold, remained the same. She stood absolutely still as they briefly settled on her, no sign of recognition, then passed to the next person.

For a few seconds that felt like minutes, the group endured Tyler's wordless examination. Each of them in their turn felt themselves judged and then dismissed. Ali stood absolutely rigid, as if she had been turned to stone. Marco felt his anger grow inside him until there was room for nothing else. Even Ellen couldn't find her smile.

Will was the first to speak.

'Tyler, mate,' he said, and crossed the room.

He put his arms lightly around Tyler's frame, patted him awkwardly on the back a few times, then let go and stepped back.

Kristin gave Marco a firm push in the small of his back, and he stumbled over, his resolve to hold firm to his righteous anger disintegrating.

'This must be very strange for you,' he said. 'It is for me.'

He tapped Tyler on the shoulder. It felt hard, unyielding.

Tyler looked at him. It was as if he had forgotten how to smile.

Jay made a sound that could have been a greeting or a whimper. There was an expression on his face that Clara recognised. It had been there when she ended their relationship not long after that terrible weekend: as if it was something he had always known was going to happen, had been waiting for; perhaps there was even relief that the expected blow had fallen.

She was not going to be cowed by this man who had done such harm to them all, to Jay above all, and who now stood among them as if they were the ones who were guilty of something. She raised her hand with the glass of martini in it.

'Hello, Tyler,' she said.

She would not lie and say she was glad to see him. He nodded at her. She didn't even know if he recognised her, so she said her name.

'I knew that,' he replied. 'I know who you all are.'

The voice was the same at least, but it seemed to Clara that he spoke more slowly than he used to, separating the words as if considering them in turn.

'You don't know me,' said Kristin, her voice like a trumpet blast in the hushed room. 'I'm Kristin, and I'm Marco's partner. For my sins.'

'What sins?'

She gave a laugh.

'It was just an expression. But you knew that, right? Anyway, Marco's told me all about you.'

'No, I haven't. Only . . . you know.'

'The murder,' Tyler said.

'Would you like a dry martini?' Beatrice held out a glass.

'Just water.'

'Sparkling?'

'Just from the tap.'

Beatrice had met a few men who had been in prison. Even a few years inside did something to a man. It was like the aftershock of a traumatic accident. You could see it in their eyes, in their gestures: something frail, something wounded. They were marked by what they had gone through. Sometimes they could be aggressive, and sometimes they could be submissive, but both were a response to that world of locked doors and drugs and violence and madness. That was after a short sentence. They used to say that after ten or fifteen years, people didn't really want to be released at all. Prison had become their entire world.

Tyler Green was different. It wasn't that he was unmarked, but she had the feeling of utter containment. He didn't smile, but he didn't look hostile either. She felt a shiver of dread run through her, a sense of danger.

'You can watch while we get plastered,' said Ellen, stepping forward. 'Hi there.'

She started to hold out her arms and then dropped them. Her smile had become slightly confused.

'Hello, Tyler.' Ali didn't move from where she stood. She was aware of everyone's eyes on her. Her voice was scratchy. 'I don't know what to say.'

'Then maybe don't say anything.'

His mottled brown eyes were on her once more. Will put a proprietorial hand on her shoulder, put an arm around her, claiming her in front of Tyler. Tyler watched them both, his eyes moving from their faces to their hands, their matching gold wedding bands. A tiny smile twitched at his lips. Ali felt glassy and brittle; if she was dropped, she would shatter into a hundred pieces. Hell, she thought. This is hell.

Beatrice handed Tyler his water, then tapped on the edge of her glass with a spoon.

'At this point, it seems fitting,' she began, and then shook her head vigorously. 'Sorry, sorry. Everyone, I want us to raise our glasses to Tyler, so long absent. Does anyone need a top up?'

'Me,' said Marco.

'And me,' Ellen said. 'I'm starting to feel beautifully woozy.'

Beatrice refilled their glasses, and then Will's and her own. Her hair had come loose, and a coil of greying chestnut hair stuck to her hot cheek.

'To Tyler,' she said.

'To Tyler,' said Will and Ellen and Kristin. Marco muttered something, while Ali put her fingers to her mouth, letting a small sound escape her. Clara linked her arm through Jay's and whispered something into his ear.

Tyler looked round the room, a tiny smile on his lips, then turned away from them to stare out to the garden, where shadows lengthened on the lawn. Warm air blew through the French windows, carrying the fragrance of roses.

He seems so calm, Beatrice thought, the only one among us who isn't nervous. She herself was agitated, feeling responsible for an evening which was already jangled and ominous. She glanced down at her watch. It was too early to eat yet and the nine of them felt locked together in a constrained group, attempts to break the awkwardness falling flat. She felt a flare of resentment towards Will for putting her in this position, but it was her fault. She could have refused.

She looked at Tyler and a feeling she couldn't identify rose in her, hot and stifling, making her want to scream. She couldn't talk to Tyler like this, it was impossible. He was unreachable. She had never visited him or written to him. She had gradually stopped thinking about him. What was it like? How did you survive? How is it being out again? What will you do? What are your plans? Anything would sound cheap, trivial. Her tone would be too bright, her smile self-conscious. Everything sham, hollowed out.

What do you remember? What do you have to forget?

'Let's all go into the garden,' she said loudly. 'It's a beautiful evening, and after all, it's the longest day of the year and we should make the most of it.'

She practically shooed them through the French windows, and onto the decking that led to the steps. She saw how unsteady Marco was on his feet, and how Will had laid his hand on the small of Ali's back, guiding her. She could make out Ali's spine through her tight crimson dress, the knobbly vertebrae.

'It's like something out of a magazine,' said Kristin, and half tripped on the top step, holding out a hand to steady herself and laughing exuberantly.

'I haven't even had anything to drink,' she said.

Beatrice looked down at her garden. She suddenly felt ashamed of its manicured elegance. She felt ashamed of her own successful, comfortable, well-tended life, and then furious at the shame. Hadn't she worked for it, earned and deserved it?

She drained her second martini and watched the group in the garden, and didn't join them.

13

There were roses climbing up the apple tree and up the spindles of a narrow spiral staircase that led to the first floor. Sweet peas were trained onto a wigwam of bamboos. Somewhere there was a water feature. They could hear the tinkling sound of a fountain. On the patio outside the sliding glass doors to the lower ground floor was a long iron table, an oversized barbecue and several terracotta pots full of herbs.

People moved about on the smooth green lawn. Ali sat on the bench, took a new pack of cigarettes from her small bag and tore off the cellophane wrapping. She struck a match but the flame fired then died.

'Here,' said Marco, joining her. 'Let me.'

He sat beside her and took the matches, striking one and shielding the flame with a hand while she leaned forward and sucked at it. He could smell her perfume, spicy like cloves.

'I'm trying to cut down to a couple a day,' she said. 'But I don't think this evening counts.'

'It definitely doesn't count.'

'Do you want one?'

'I don't usually nowadays, but sure, why not?' He lit his own cigarette and leaned back, letting smoke fill his lungs. 'Are you all right?'

'Yes, thank you,' she said woodenly, because she wasn't

going to let her defences crumble for an instant, and certainly not in front of Marco. 'Are you?'

He didn't answer but took a long drag, blew smoke out luxuriously.

'Do you have any idea why Tyler wants us here?'

She shook her head.

'Will thinks it's to do with catharsis.'

'Catharsis. That means feeling better, doesn't it? He killed someone, so why should he get to feel better about it? More to the point, why should we help him feel better about it?'

'That sounds rather harsh,' Ali said.

'Heaven forbid I should be harsh about someone who stabbed my friend to death.' He looked round at Ali.

'Can I ask you something?'

'Of course,' she said warily.

'Why did you and Will marry?'

'I'm sorry?'

'Don't take that the wrong way. I'm pleased for you and all that. I'm sure you're very happy together. Will's great, of course he is. Everyone loves Will. But our group was blown apart by what happened. Nobody kept in touch in any real way – except Clara and Jay a bit, I guess. It was like we couldn't bear to see each other. But you and Will went and got married.'

'We did.'

She looked at the glowing tip of her cigarette and didn't meet his eye.

'Is that all you've got to say?'

'It's private.'

'Did you ever go and see him?'

'No.'

'Why?'

She frowned at him.

'You didn't go either.'

'It's hardly the same. You were together. God, you were so together it was sometimes hard to be in the same room as you.' Ali stared at the cigarette between her fingers, its growing column of ash. 'Weren't you tempted?'

She glanced up at him quickly, then down again.

'It was all or nothing. I couldn't.'

Marco dropped his butt and ground it out with his heel.

'Did it take you ages to get over it?'

'Over it?'

'*It*,' he said roughly. '*It*. The murder. The man you were with turning out to be a murderer.'

She dropped her own butt, put the toe of her shoe on it.

'I don't want to talk about it.'

Marco felt a rush of irritation.

'Why are you here then, Ali, if you don't want to talk about it? What's this fucking reunion for, if not to talk? I mean, really, why did you come? You're moving around as if you're an automaton. Are you literally going to ignore Tyler, pretend he's not here? I *do* want to talk about it, as it happens. Very much. I want to go over to Tyler and look him in the eye and tell him what I think. Give it to him straight.'

'Go on then.' Marco shifted uneasily on the bench, and Ali smiled ironically. 'Now's your chance. There he is. Talk to him. Tell him. Have your say.'

'He's talking to Will.'

'Will won't mind.'

'I'm biding my time.'

Will was stooping down to examine the redcurrant and blackcurrant bushes when Tyler approached. He stood up hastily, wiped his hands down his trousers.

'This garden,' he said. 'It's quite something.'

Tyler looked around him as if noticing for the first time quite how gorgeous it was.

'I like the dog roses,' he said. 'They remind me of my childhood.'

Will was searching for a way to speak to Tyler, but Tyler pre-empted him.

'I want to ask you something,' he said.

'Ask away,' said Will.

'Why did you come and visit me in prison?'

This wasn't what Will had expected.

'You're my friend.'

'That's all?'

'Isn't that enough? I mean, I thought that whatever had happened, whatever you'd done, you were still my friend. I wanted to stand by you, be there for you.' He gave a wobbly laugh. 'I can tell you now that I found those visits pretty difficult. You just sat there, and I talked and talked, like an idiot. You were so weirdly calm.'

Tyler stared into Will's face.

'I should have told you about Ali.' Will spoke in a rush. 'Every time I saw you, I was going to. But when it came to it, I couldn't. I felt awful about it.'

'Not so awful.'

'What do you mean?'

'Not so awful it prevented you from marrying her.'

'You were in prison. What should she have done? What should I have done?' Will was imploring.

'None of that matters now,' said Tyler.

'I'm sorry I stopped coming.'

'I was glad you stopped.'

Will let out a sigh that was almost a laugh.

'I guess it was pretty nightmarish for both of us.'

Tyler left a pause before speaking.

'Will, did you ever think that I might not have done it?'

'That's not the point. The point is that whatever you'd done, you were still my friend. Are,' he corrected himself. 'Are my friend.'

'Or did you *know* I hadn't done it?'

Will blinked at him.

'Sorry?' he said eventually.

Tyler didn't respond, simply waited.

'Tyler, what are you saying? You were convicted. The jury only took four hours. The judge said it was a clear case of justice being done.'

'I know what the judge said. I was there.'

'And now you've served your time.'

'And you're my friend. And you're there for me.'

'Don't say it like that.'

'I don't need friends.'

'Everyone needs friends,' said Will lamely.

'Do you think that's what I'm here for? Friendship?'

'I don't know. Why are you here?'

'You'll find out later.'

'You can't tell me?'

Tyler considered for what felt like a long time.

'It's something to do with saying goodbye.'

14

Beatrice was on the point of going down the steps to join her guests in the garden, when she heard the bell ring. She put down her empty glass and went to the front door. When she opened it, not knowing who to expect, she was momentarily confused. A middle-aged man stood in front of her. He was dressed in grey linen trousers, a matching jacket over his arm, a white cotton shirt rolled up to the elbows, classy green loafers. He had round, wire-rimmed spectacles, silver hair, and he was smiling at her. And then she realised.

'It's you.'

'It's me,' Rudi said, stepping over the threshold. 'And it's you.'

He dropped his jacket and held out his arms, and she stepped into their circle. Standing in the empty hall, smelling his scent, feeling the warmth of him, Beatrice closed her eyes. She laid her head against Rudi's chest and for that brief moment, the years rolled back, and she wasn't a middle-aged wife and mother, she was young and eager Beatrice Macmillan feeling desire rise through her body.

She opened her eyes and stepped back, half laughing and mildly embarrassed.

'I didn't expect you.'

'I wasn't going to come, and I should have replied to tell you that. But there must have been something inside me that always knew I would, because suddenly, this evening, I was sitting in my study and I realised that of course I had to. Why did I ever imagine I could stay away? Is it all right to turn up like this, at the last minute?'

'I'll just lay another place at the table.'

'You look wonderful. I can't believe this is happening.'

'I know.'

'Since I got your message, it's all I've been able to think of.'

'And yet you didn't reply.'

'It's complicated,' he said, and was serious. 'It wasn't just about seeing Tyler, which is weird enough, or meeting up with people I deliberately didn't make the effort to stay in touch with. It was about seeing you. You were the only one I wanted to meet again.'

'I haven't drunk enough for this conversation,' said Beatrice, turning and making her way towards the living room.

After Leo had been killed, Beatrice had gone back to her family in Dorset. Sebastian was in London by then, working in the City, but he came down most weekends to see her. He seemed strangely incurious about the trauma she had gone through, as if it was just a blip in her life, something mildly distasteful. He was a solid, dependable man who seemed much older than he was, with a clear sense of where he was going. It was a relief for Beatrice to be with someone who felt safe and steady. The memory of the past months' febrile intensity made her nauseous.

Rudi had phoned her house several times, but she had told her parents she didn't want to speak to him. Three months later, she went to London to do her legal practice course, then her two-year traineeship. She moved in with Sebastian, put all her energies into her work, and she gradually became inured to the memories of the past. Over the years, she had thought of

Rudi, of course, and wondered what had become of him. Every so often, she let herself imagine meeting him again: at a party, at the theatre, walking down the street and suddenly seeing him coming towards her. But she never tried to contact him. Why would she? That vulnerable young woman was gone, and the past was like a dream that slips away, leaving only wisps of itself drifting through the mind.

Beatrice stepped into the living room, and Rudi followed her.

'Where are the others?' he asked.

'In the garden. Shall we join them?'

'Wait,' he said, touching her arm. 'I'm not ready. Is everyone here?'

'Yes.'

'Tyler too?'

'Yes.'

'What's he like?'

Beatrice suddenly found it hard to speak.

'Scary, I think,' she said. 'I don't know. I haven't spoken to him properly. You'll see what I mean.'

'Is this the first time you've seen him since, you know?'

'Will was the only one who visited him. He's married to Ali, by the way, just to warn you. I know, odd, isn't it? I don't know why I didn't see him. I mean, there were lots of reasons, but I think . . . ' She stopped. 'I haven't offered you a drink,' she said. 'We're drinking dry martinis.'

'Ah, those martinis. I'd love one. What were you going to say?'

'Say?'

'You were going to say something about why you didn't visit him.'

'I shouldn't. Forget I spoke.'

'Tell me what you were going to say, Bea.'

'The honest truth is,' said Beatrice, 'I've never been absolutely certain that Tyler did it. I know he was found guilty, but I was never one hundred per cent certain. And so – I realise that this makes me a coward – maybe the reason I didn't visit him or write or anything was because that was such a terrifying thought and I couldn't bring myself to confront it.'

'Terrifying?'

'Yes. He was locked away in prison, so I needed to believe that was the right thing, he deserved to be there, otherwise . . . well.' Rudi was about to respond, but she held up a hand. 'Of course, I realise I'll never know for sure. But maybe that's why I agreed to host this: because it's possible that a terrible wrong was done to him and I just turned away. Almost . . . ' She wrinkled her nose in self-disgust. 'Almost for my own convenience. Anything else would have been such a ghastly mess. Simpler to find an answer and consider the matter closed. Done with.'

'*We* turned away.'

'Did you have doubts too then?'

'Me? No. I guess I just assumed—'

'That justice was done?'

'Something like that.'

'Anyway,' said Beatrice. 'He's out now.'

'And in your house.'

She put her arm through his.

'In my house. Or my garden. Come and meet everyone. The old gang.'

'God, I've missed you,' he said.

15

In the garden, Ellen had joined Tyler and Will.

'I've been waiting for the chance to speak,' she said, 'but I didn't want to crowd you. This must be overwhelming. I'm feeling very emotional myself.'

Tyler brought his glass of water slowly to his mouth and took a sip.

'I'm coping,' he said.

'You were saying something to Will about goodbyes.'

'Yes.'

She waited, but he didn't say anything else. Will murmured something about getting another drink, but stayed where he was.

'As you might have heard, I work as a psychotherapist.' She was speaking with the brightness of someone trying to make conversation. 'Does that surprise you?'

'Not so much.'

'It surprises me sometimes,' Ellen said. 'But there you go. And one of the things I have thought a lot about is the importance of acknowledging acts and feelings, no matter how ugly or distressing they might be. No matter that they challenge our sense of who we are or want to be. Acknowledging them, naming them, accepting them. Only then can we be in control of them, rather than the other way round.'

She waited, but Tyler didn't speak.

'I think you're very courageous to bring us all together like this,' she continued. 'It must have been extremely hard. But in my view, everyone can atone.'

'Atone,' said Tyler.

She nodded vigorously.

'Yes, atone. You have spent all those years in prison, which must have been a terrifying experience. Now you deserve to be forgiven.'

'You've got it wrong,' Tyler said softly. 'I'm not asking to be forgiven.'

'You don't look as if you're having a good time,' Kristin was saying to Jay.

'It's quite hard.'

'I can imagine.' She nodded her head several times. 'I can imagine. You're Jay, aren't you?'

'Yes.'

Kristin studied his bony face, his large liquid eyes in their hollow sockets. There was something compelling about him. He clearly wasn't one for small talk.

'Marco said you were the genius of the group.'

'No,' said Jay. 'I was never a genius.'

Jay had entered the friendship group later than everyone else, when he started dating Clara, and he had largely left it before the fatal weekend. The rest of them had found him touching, intriguing, but also slightly unnerving. He had studied philosophy, and they had all assumed he was headed for a stellar degree and a career in academia. Sometimes they called him Prof, and teased him because of his intensity, his studiousness, his habit of sitting for hours stooped over a book, the way he would readily spend Saturday nights in the library. He was naturally quiet, but sometimes, especially when he was high or drunk, he would talk in long, intricate monologues, his bony hands eloquent, flaming with ideas. Marco had told Kristin that Jay was a genius, but also that he was mad. A screw a bit loose, he'd said; not like other people; someone who could tip alarmingly into high excitement, depression, even rage. 'We shouldn't have been surprised by what happened to him, what he did,' he'd told Kristin, and she wondered whether to ask Jay about it directly.

'What do you do, Jay?' she had said instead.

'I work in a residential home for people with dementia,' he replied.

'What a wonderful thing to do,' she said warmly. 'You're a hero.'

Jay hated that word.

'I like it,' he said. 'It suits me.'

'It must be hard though.'

'People say that a lot. I think that everything's hard if you do it right.'

'I so agree. And you live up north?'

'Derbyshire.'

'Beautiful,' said Kristin, who'd never been there and didn't really know where it was, except it was somewhere in the north. 'So why are you here, Jay, in hot, crowded London, on the longest day of the year? I mean.' She gave a laugh so loud he started. 'Marco's here because he wants to have it out with Tyler, tell him what he thinks of him. I don't think he will, mind. He's more bark than bite, our Marco. What do you want from this evening?'

'I'm here because Clara thinks it will be good for me,' he said.

'And do you always do what Clara tells you?'

He considered this seriously.

'Usually I do.'

'You poor man,' said Kristin merrily. 'Still in love with her.'

The colour rushed into Jay's face. He bunched his fists. But he was saved from answering because Beatrice was coming down the steps, arm in arm with a distinguished-looking man wearing expensive clothes.

'Is that her husband?' Kristin whispered loudly.

'No. That's Rudi Scott.'

16

'Everyone,' called Beatrice from the base of the steps. 'Rudi came after all.'

The scattered guests drew together again to greet him, apart from Tyler who didn't move.

'Now there's a lovely-looking couple,' said Marco, who was conscious of being both stoned and drunk, and what's more, was starting to feel mildly sick.

What did he sound like? Stupid, he thought; stupid and brash and lewd and loud. Why didn't he just shut up? He knew what he looked like as well, a balding middle-aged man dressed like a teenager in a grubby tie-dyed shirt and trainers with fraying laces.

Rudi came across to Ellen and smiled at her. They hugged. Beatrice rejoined them, handing a dry martini to Rudi, who sipped it with an expression of approval. He was doing his best not to stare at Tyler, who was standing beside a mossy statue, but his eyes continually flickered that way.

'How's the writing going?' Will asked Rudi after they'd shared a careful hug. 'I heard you're a writer, yes?'

'I am. And it's all right,' said Rudi, and took a long swallow of his dry martini before picking up the chunk of lemon and putting it into his mouth. He didn't want to talk about his writing. 'I'm working on something. Hello, Jay.'

He and Jay used to show each other what they'd written.

Now Jay worked as a care assistant and struggled to pay his fuel bills, while Rudi lived in a six-bedroom house in Oxfordshire.

Jay raised a hand.

'I've thought about you over the years,' he said in his quiet, uninflected tone.

'Have you?' It was hard to be cool and ironic with Jay. 'I've thought of you as well.'

He hadn't really. He'd thought of Tyler, of Leo, of Beatrice. Not so much of any of the others, except as a group, almost as a system to which he had once belonged.

At last, he turned to Tyler as if he'd only just noticed him.

'Tyler,' he said, and was suddenly and unexpectedly moved by the sight of the man who'd once told him that the purest relationship in life was friendship. 'Tyler,' he repeated, searching for the next words.

'Hello,' said Tyler, not moving towards him. 'Ellen is here because she feels the need to forgive me. Why have you come?'

Rudi stood rigid, his smile locked in place. The rest of them waited in hushed silence.

'I don't know,' he managed at last. 'I wasn't going to. Then I thought of everyone gathering, and me not being here as well, and it felt all wrong.'

'And Will's here because he's my friend,' said Tyler.

Will, standing a few feet from him, looked worn out and defeated.

Beatrice felt unsettled by Tyler, his hooded eyes and his scar, the way he spoke slowly and deliberately. She was about to ask him why he had summoned them all, what his motives were, but Kristin spoke first.

'If you want to know why I'm here, it's out of curiosity. Marco's always been a bit vague about all of this.' She gestured

towards Tyler. 'About you. He just says it was the most important thing that had ever happened in his life. I simply want to
know what happened. That's natural, isn't it?'

Both Marco and Ellen started to speak, but the soft tone of
Tyler's voice cut through them.

'You really want to know? All right, I'll tell you.' He paused
and closed his eyes for a moment before starting to speak. 'It
was twenty-nine years ago, almost exactly, on the midsummer weekend of June 1993. We were staying in a house in the
Yorkshire Dales. The house belonged to Leo's aunt. It was very
remote, so we drove there in two cars, one belonging to Leo
and a large people carrier that we rented. Most of the group
had just done their finals. Not me, because I was studying medicine, and not Jay because he had left a few months previously.
It was like a celebration and a way of marking the end of an
era. It was always going to be intense. We took a great deal of
booze with us and also drugs – mostly weed, but other stuff
as well. Jay in particular took a lot of drugs. I didn't, because
I was a medic and could have got struck off. I'd wanted to be
a doctor since I was a little boy.'

He was still looking straight into Kristin's eyes. He spoke
dispassionately, as if talking about someone else. Which in a
way he was, thought Beatrice: the young man training to be a
doctor, his life unfurling before him, must feel like a stranger
to the man he was now.

'We drank a lot, smoked a lot, talked a lot, played board
games, quarrelled, made up, joked, laughed, stumbled around
on the moors, set fire to sausages on the barbecue, had sex
with each other, well, some of us did, promised to be friends
forever. It felt like anything could happen, normal rules didn't
apply. The newspapers made a lot of that when they got their
claws into the story.'

It was as though Tyler had lost any ability to have a reciprocal conversation: he either spoke only in blunt monosyllables, or he talked like he was a kind of preacher.

'On the Saturday evening,' Tyler continued, 'I had a violent argument with Leo, who I'd known since our schooldays. I've had a lot of time to think about my relationship with Leo. At school, from the age of eleven, I would have said he was my best friend, but he was a bewildering kind of friend, sometimes full of affection and generosity; at other times, rivalrous and undermining.'

'So why did you keep on being friends?' Kristin asked.

Tyler nodded at her, acknowledging the aptness of the question.

'When I was in prison, I thought a lot about that. Why stay friends with a person who does you harm? Though of course, a lot of us do that, one way or another.' His eyes flicked round the group then returned to Kristin. 'I don't think I understood then that he was toxic, a bully, needing to be in control. When we found ourselves at the same university, he took it for granted we would still hang out together, and I went along with that. It didn't occur to me that I could cut ties with him.'

He paused for a moment, looking from face to face.

'That weekend, I guess I finally realised that not only was he domineering, but I didn't even like him; in fact, I actively disliked and resented him, and more than that, I had no obligation to be loyal to him.' He nodded at Kristin again. 'Loyalty was always a big deal to me. It was as if I had made a pledge to him, or something. I used to think I had to hold faith, to Leo, to everyone. Will still thinks that way, I think.'

Will flushed an unhealthy red and murmured something inaudible, but Tyler continued with his speech.

'But I saw what I'd probably always known – known without

knowing: that Leo had set out to continually undermine me. That evening, full of booze and the sense of things coming to an end, I badly wanted to punish him for what he'd done to me and to other people as well. Several of you heard me saying that one day he was going to pick on the wrong person, that perhaps he already had. We had a stupid, messy, feeble kind of fight. We must have looked ridiculous. I seem to remember that you . . . ' Tyler pointed at Marco. 'You even urged us on. As if it was a cockfight or something. No one was really hurt; we were too drunk, or I was anyway. In the early hours of the morning, when everyone had gone to bed, Leo was killed. His throat was cut; he must have bled out in seconds. The pathologist said later that whoever did it might well have medical knowledge. The knife was discovered in my room. I was charged with his murder and the jury found me guilty by a unanimous verdict.'

'Thank you,' said Kristin, looking startled.

'I spent twenty-nine years in prison. Even now, I'm only out on licence. I'm not free. My mother died when I was there. My father disowned me. Of my friends, only Will visited me, and he came less and less often. I was forgotten. I felt I knew what it was like to be dead.'

No one made a sound. Tyler took a sip of water. He was formal, precise, like a professor reaching the end of his lecture.

17

'You're free now,' Ellen said. 'You can begin again.'

She looked slightly ashamed of the last sentence.

'Hang on. Are we meant to feel sorry for you?' Marco, fuelled by drink, had decided now was the time to say his piece. He walked up to Tyler, jutting his chest out. 'Really? So prison's awful. It should be awful. Particularly for a man who murdered his friend. Our friend, don't forget that. My friend. Who believed in me.' He felt tears prick his eyelids. He felt his voice thicken. 'I don't know why they let you out at all. If it was down to me, you'd still be there. Do you know what I think?'

'No,' said Tyler politely. 'What do you think?'

'I think,' said Marco, 'that you are, are . . . ' He stopped, rubbed his face furiously. His eyes were bloodshot.

'We don't all need to hear this,' said Beatrice. 'And you probably don't need to say it.'

'I do,' said Marco. 'I need to.'

'I'd like to hear what you have to say,' said Tyler.

The two men walked further down the garden.

Marco took a spliff from his pocket and lit it, hesitated, then offered it to Tyler.

'If I'm caught in possession of a Class B drug,' said Tyler, 'I'm liable to be returned to prison to serve the remainder of my sentence. In fact, it's possible that I'm violating the terms of my licence even by being present in a house knowing that illegal drugs are being consumed.'

'Oh, come on,' said Marco. 'It's basically legal now.'

Suddenly they heard a voice from the other side of the garden wall.

'We know what you're doing. Do you think we can't smell it?'

'All right, all right,' said Marco in a raised voice. He knelt down and extinguished the spliff and replaced it in his pocket. 'Nosy neighbours, eh?'

'Perhaps he's going to call the police,' said Tyler. 'I don't even need to be convicted of a crime. Just being associated with the suggestion of public disorder.'

'You're being paranoid,' said Marco.

'No civil servant ever lost their job for taking a convicted murderer off the streets,' said Tyler. 'And if you don't care about me, you might think about Beatrice. If she's accused of allowing drug-taking on her property, she could be disbarred. Her husband's a minister. That would probably be the end of his career as well. Not bad for an evening's work.'

'It sounds kind of funny, when you put it like that. I guess I was thinking about the old days. Making music together. But to be honest, I don't care much about you.'

'I get that.'

'Do you? Do you? Why should I?' Marco was working himself up into anger again, holding on to his resolve to hold Tyler to account. But he wasn't feeling very well, and really he just wanted this to be over, so he could tell himself and tell Kristin that he had done what he set out to do. 'The thing is, you're a fucking killer, but you seem to think you can come here and treat us with contempt.'

'Interesting word.'

'Contempt,' repeated Marco. He was losing his thread.

'Is that what you wanted to say to me?'

'You ruined my life, do you know that? Everything could have worked out differently. And you could at least have the humility and honesty to apologise. Instead of which, you're acting like a kind of judge. Who are you to judge us?'

'I remember the music,' said Tyler musingly, seeming not to have listened to the last part of what Marco had said. 'There was that summer party you played at. It was you and a couple of people you were in a band with then. You started playing and everybody was talking, and then gradually the talking stopped and everyone was listening. You could feel it. The whole crowd was listening like one person.'

'That was a good evening,' said Marco, and before he could stop himself, he smiled with genuine pleasure. 'Sometimes it all comes together.'

'As I was listening, I was thinking that, a few years in the future, everyone here will be saying: I was there. I was there at this summer party and I saw Marco Burney before he was famous.'

'Before I was famous.' Marco's face puckered slightly.

'So what happened?'

'What do you mean, what happened?'

'Maybe I mean, what didn't happen? Was there a moment where you realised you weren't going to be what we all thought you were going to be, or did it happen gradually? You know, like the air just leaking out of a balloon.'

Marco laughed awkwardly.

'You know that I'm still a musician, right? I earn money from music.'

'What was that song you wrote? "Baby Blue", wasn't it? I couldn't get it out of my head for days after hearing you sing it. I almost felt jealous. You were going to write the songs that people would dance to and fall in love to and get married to. When did that go away?'

'Is this a serious discussion?' Marco said. 'Is that something you actually want to know? Or are you just trying to make me feel rotten because I'm not bloody Paul McCartney or Sting or whatever? I did my best, right? I've nothing to be ashamed of. Not like you. How do you live with the shame?'

'But what was it? You didn't get a record deal? You didn't have a hit?'

'Or maybe I wasn't quite good enough. Is that what you're trying to say? I don't know what your problem is. I'm a musician. I teach people music. I'm a mentor. I'm teaching the next generation. Passing on the baton.'

Kristin had come down the garden to join them, and she giggled at this.

'What?' said Marco crossly.

'You teach middle-aged dads who've bought electric guitars as part of their mid-life crisis. You're not exactly nurturing the next generation of young musicians.'

'One of them's a teenager,' muttered Marco.

'Is he the one who says he was forced to do it by his mum and never practises, but you take the money anyway? That one?'

'Thanks for the moral support. I'm sorry I haven't lived up to your image of artistic integrity. But for fuck's sake.' His voice rose into a shout. 'This isn't the point. Not at all. So I'm a failure, but you're a killer. And if Ellen says she wants to forgive you, that's fine. Because I'll never forgive you.'

'Stop, both of you.' Beatrice spoke sharply, trying to control the high note of panic in her voice as she walked towards them. 'Tyler, you wanted this. Marco, you chose to be here. You can leave if you want, or you can come inside and eat dinner.'

Tyler and Marco looked at each other.

'If you're waiting for an apology,' said Marco, 'you'll be waiting another twenty-nine years.'

'I'm waiting for dinner,' said Tyler.

Beatrice led them down the steps to the patio, through the sliding glass doors and into the lower ground floor. The other guests were standing round the table.

18

'Is there a seating plan?' said Clara.

Beatrice had in fact made a careful plan. Now she couldn't care less. She just wanted this to be over as quickly as possible so she could go to bed, put her hot cheek on her lovely Egyptian cotton pillow case and close her eyes. What time was it? It was still light outside, though the day had deepened into a glowing dusk.

'Sit wherever you want.'

She sat down and Rudi sat next to her.

'It's like being back at school,' said Kristin. She had drunk a second martini and rolled up the sleeves of her lace dress as if she was about to wash dishes, or start a fight. 'Choose who you want to sit with. I choose . . .' She squinted, grinned, pointed at Will. 'You! Marco says you were always the life and the soul of the party. You can tell me all about Marco when he was young.'

Ellen took Jay by the sleeve and led him to the table.

'I'll sit next to you. We need to catch up.'

Jay darted a desperate look at Clara.

'Except for you, Tyler,' said Beatrice. 'You should sit at the head.'

The room went silent, and everyone looked at Tyler to see how he would react.

'Don't worry,' said Will with forced cheeriness. 'You won't be expected to make another speech.'

'Oh, but I am going to,' said Tyler, as he sat in the prominent position at the end of the long wooden table. Beatrice sat at the other end, flanked by Marco on her left, Rudi to her right. Kristin pulled out the chair next to Rudi, and pulled Will to sit beside her. Ellen took a seat between Marco and Jay, which left Clara to sit on Tyler's right and Ali on his left. He didn't look at either of them and they didn't look at him. His muscled forearms were resting on the table; his large hands palm up. His eyes were hooded.

Beatrice gestured at the huge spread of food that ran the entire length of the table: a whole poached salmon, multiple salads and dips, crusty baguettes.

'I don't know what you all eat nowadays, so I hope this is all right,' she said. 'You'll have to pass them round. I hope there's enough to feed everyone.'

There was too much, she thought, repulsed by the spread of food, pomegranate seeds winking on top of the heaped aubergine slices, puddles of yoghurt on charred cauliflower, potato salad with capers. She looked from face to face, colour in their cheeks, skin glistening in the heat: excited, scared, drunk.

'It's enough to feed the whole street,' said Kristin to Rudi cheerfully.

There were open bottles of wine arranged along the table. Kristin took one and filled her large glass nearly to the brim.

'It looks wonderful,' Rudi said to Beatrice, putting a hand on hers and squeezing it.

He had hairy wrists, she noticed; had he always? She couldn't remember. So long ago.

'It's nothing,' she said, and smiled lopsidedly at him.

The conversation around the table was awkward and fragmentary.

'How come you're a dentist?' Ali was saying to Clara at the other end of the table. 'If you studied French and Italian?'

'I changed my mind,' said Clara.

'Don't you hate looking into those mouths all day?' Kristin said. 'Cavities and receding gums.'

There was a clattering as the guests spooned food onto their plates. Tyler only took a small helping of green salad, and filled his tumbler with water from the jug.

Will told Kristin about the vegetables on his allotment.

'I grew this asparagus,' said Will, picking up a charred spear between thumb and forefinger. 'Fruit bushes. Blackcurrants, redcurrants, white currants. I freeze all the fruit and use it in the winter.'

There was a sudden silence and the guests looked at each other, waiting for someone to speak.

'What did you do during all those years?' Beatrice asked Tyler from the other end of the table. As soon as she spoke, she felt like an old person awkwardly asking a teenager about their favourite subject at school.

'I read,' he said. 'I studied.'

'Studied what?'

'I did a literature course. When you're locked up for twenty-three hours a day, you've got a lot of time for reading. And I did electrics and plumbing. They said they were giving me skills for the outside world.'

Marco gestured at Rudi opposite.

'Why didn't you bring your wife along?'

'I wasn't sure that partners were welcome.' His eyes shifted to Kristin and back. 'I got the impression it would just be us.'

'I googled you last week,' said Marco. 'In fact, I googled everyone just to see what people were up to. Jay was the only one I couldn't find anything about.'

'I don't really do online stuff,' Jay muttered.

'So I see,' said Marco. 'You've left no trace. You should be a spy. But Rudi and his wife. That was another story. She seems like an interesting woman.'

'What does that mean?' asked Ellen.

'I learned two things about her. One, her father owns some company that makes something I don't understand, but it moved to Malaysia to make it more cheaply. Your wife must be a very rich woman.'

'I don't know about rich,' said Rudi.

'I thought her name was familiar for some other reason, and then, I found her campaign about family values. It's about women in the home and about sex, isn't that right?'

'What is she saying about sex?' Ellen asked.

'She's against it, basically,' said Marco. 'Except in very specific marital circumstances.'

'That's ridiculous,' said Rudi. 'She's just promoting certain values.'

'Like the Taliban,' said Marco with a grin. 'They're just promoting certain values as well. In fact, they're rather similar values.'

'I don't think she'd approve of us,' said Ellen. She drained her wine glass and then refilled it.

'Do you have children?' Beatrice asked Rudi.

'Three.'

'I just have one,' said Beatrice. 'And he's almost grown up now.'

'I win,' said Ellen.

'What about you?' Kristin said to Will, putting her face very close to his.

'No.'

'Why not? Didn't you want them?'

'It just didn't happen,' said Will after an awkward pause.
'That's sad.'

'Has no one told you?' Ali leaned across Will to speak to
Kristin directly. 'There are some questions you shouldn't feel
free to ask, particularly to people you've never met before.'

'It's okay, Ali,' said Will. 'It's a long time ago.'

'Kristin always says what she's thinking.' Marco's plate was
overflowing with food but he didn't seem to be eating any of it.
'And when she's not thinking, she speaks anyway.'

'I can see that,' said Ali. She was sitting very straight in her
crimson dress, her narrow face white and angry.

Then Tyler spoke, softly as if only to Ali, but the room was
quite silent and the words seemed to ring out.

'I thought of you as someone who wanted children. Did you
mind very much?'

Ali lifted her glass in her shaking hand. She took a long
drink.

'I don't know,' she said, her tone matching his. Beatrice had
the sense that she shouldn't be listening to their exchange, but
like everyone, she held her breath and waited to hear what they
would say to each other. 'I think Will minded more than me.
He wanted us to adopt, but by then it was too late. For me,
anyway.'

She made a gesture with the hand that held the drink. It was
as though there was nobody else there. Will sat slumped, his
head lowered, listening to his wife talking about him to the
man she had once loved more than she could ever love him.

'He wanted a proper big family – three or four children. He
had this vision of us living in some house in the country, with a
garden full of vegetables and lots of kids; rowdy meals; books
at bedtime; holidays on the beach, building sandcastles and
throwing a frisbee; mad games. You know what he's like.' She

seemed to suddenly remember he was there and she cast him a glance; her mouth quirked. 'His enthusiasms. He likes mess and noise and being a bit out of control. Not like me.'

She stopped abruptly.

Ellen nodded.

'I always thought you were a bit like a boy yourself, Will. My kids would love you.'

'Now he's just got his allotment,' said Ali.

'And you've got your dog,' said Tyler.

She nodded, drank.

'And I've got my dog.'

'I always thought I'd have children,' said Tyler.

'It's never too late,' said Kristin, bright and loud into the silence. 'For men, at any rate.'

'Will would have been a good father,' said Tyler.

'We'll never know, will we?' said Ali.

'It's so odd,' said Clara dreamily. 'I'm seeing you all like you are now, middle-aged, marked by life, and I'm seeing you as you were then. The face beneath the face. And everyone seems to be talking about what didn't happen, rather than what did. Ghost lives. It's sad. Is it always this sad, or is it just us?'

'He would have been a good father,' continued Tyler, as if nobody had spoken and he was simply continuing his sentence. 'But tell me, Ali: do you think you would have been a good mother?'

19

A sharp intake of breath went round the group. It was as if Ali had been hit. She jerked back in her chair and put both hands to her stomach.

'What?'

'I asked you if you thought you would have made a good mother?'

'Of course she would,' said Will forcefully. 'She would have been amazing.'

'Why would you say that?' Ali spoke in a whisper.

Clara reached across the table and tried to take her hand, but she jerked away.

'Here we are,' said Tyler calmly. 'Meeting after almost three decades. My life was stopped, frozen in time. But you've all had your lives, for better or for worse. You've made your choices. Lots of things we thought would happen never will now. I can't work out if you really wanted children, and I was simply asking if you thought you could have been a good mother.'

'Tyler,' said Clara warningly.

'If you were capable of that kind of unconditional love.'

'Tyler, stop now.'

'Because you don't seem like that to me. And I'm wondering if you've changed so much, or if you were always this way, and I just didn't see it because I was in love with you.'

Tyler was still speaking in a dispassionate voice, as if he was genuinely trying to understand something that stood far off, a problem to be solved.

'He's just trying to hurt you,' said Clara urgently.

'I would have loved my children.' Ali's voice was barely audible. 'I would have loved and protected them. I wanted to do that.'

'In which case, Ali,' said Tyler with a curious formality, 'I'm sorry that you never got the chance.'

She leaned towards him, looking at him almost wonderingly.

'Do you hate me so much?'

'I don't hate anyone. I've achieved that much in prison, at least. You can go mad with hating. Or with wanting.'

'Do you know what I can't quite work out,' said Kristin in her carrying voice, so that the whole room seemed to ring with it. 'I can't work out if you're heroic, or if you're a monster.'

Tyler smiled at her, a small twist of his lips.

'I'll be interested to know what you decide.'

Ali got up.

'I'm going to have a cigarette,' she said.

'I'll come with you,' said Will, half rising as well.

'No.' She spoke sharply. 'I want to be alone. I just want to smoke a cigarette and be by myself for a few minutes. But I think we won't stay much longer, if that's all right with you.'

'Of course.'

Jay leaned close to Clara, almost putting his head on her shoulder. He spoke in a moan.

'We need to go. If we don't go now, something terrible's going to happen.'

She stroked his hair, like he was a scared child who needed soothing.

'We'll get through it together, my dear,' she said. 'You can't run away from this.'

20

Kristin raised her fork and pointed it towards Tyler, and then she pointed it round the table.

'You're all just skirting round the subject. All of you.'

'Which subject is that?' asked Ellen.

'You're all talking about being a dentist, or about the food, and all the time there's your friend Leo who isn't here.'

'Actually the food is worth talking about,' said Rudi.

Beatrice looked at the plate in front of Tyler.

'You haven't touched it.'

'It's a little rich for me. I'm still adjusting.'

'What would you like to talk about?' Clara asked Kristin.

'It's not what I want,' said Kristin. 'It's what you want. What about your friend. He's barely been mentioned. Except by the man who killed him, that is, and surely he deserves more than that.'

'You're right.'

It was Tyler who spoke the words. Everyone stared at him.

'Yes,' said Kristin, after a long pause. 'I mean, what was he like? What did you feel about him? Do you miss him?'

'Of course we do,' said Will.

'Speak for yourself,' said Marco.

'I am speaking for myself. He was my friend. One of my best friends.'

'And mine,' said Rudi.

'I don't know about best friend,' said Beatrice. 'But he was certainly unforgettable. Handsome and confident and clever. Everything he put his mind to, he succeeded at.'

'Charisma,' said Clara, as if it was a dirty word.

'I guess,' said Beatrice. 'Whatever that is.'

'And he knew it,' added Jay in a quiet voice.

'If he wasn't such fun,' Rudi said, 'then you could almost have felt jealous of him. He seemed to have everything. Including money.'

'But he was generous with that,' Beatrice said. 'He was always treating us.'

'He sounds too good to be true.' Kristin wrinkled her nose.

'He could be a bit difficult,' said Will.

Ali came quietly back into the room and took her seat again, not meeting anyone's eyes.

'We were just talking about Leo,' Will said to her. 'I was saying how he could be difficult.'

'That's a mild way of putting it,' said Ellen. 'He got Jay expelled from the university.'

'That's not exactly true,' mumbled Jay.

'You did that practical joke that went wrong, didn't you?'

'Practical joke?' said Marco. 'You trashed that guy's room. Wasn't it months until someone could live there again? What was his name? Jack something.'

'I don't want to talk about it,' said Jay.

'Jim Marriott,' said Rudi. 'He'd pissed you both off. That's what Leo said.'

'Both of you?' said Ellen. 'Or just Leo? And then Leo used you to get his revenge.'

'And you were the one who was caught,' said Clara. Her face was angry. 'And got punished. The authorities found out about you, but not about Leo. He was rich, he was handsome, he had a famous father, he'd gone to a posh school: he was one of the entitled of the world who always got off scot-free. Whereas someone like you, you could always be the scapegoat, couldn't you?'

'It's all right,' said Jay to her in a tone that was unexpectedly gentle, as if he was comforting her for his misfortune. 'It's a long time ago now.'

'Water under the bridge,' said Ellen.

'It was probably even good for me, though I didn't know it at the time,' Jay said. 'I wasn't happy at university. I'm glad I left; I just wish I'd never joined you that weekend.'

'All the same, it was a shitty thing of Leo to do,' said Marco.

'See,' said Kristin. 'This is more like it. Who else had reason to hate Leo?'

'Stop.' Beatrice's voice was sharp. 'What do you think you're doing?'

Kristin turned to look at her.

'What are you scared of?' she asked. 'The truth?'

21

'I remember Leo called you "Fatty",' said Rudi to Will.

Will laughed ruefully.

'I don't remember that.'

'It was his name for you.'

'Well, I was. Am.' Will looked down at his stomach, then at his full plate.

'I like a man who knows how to enjoy the good things in life,' said Kristin.

Ali leaned closer to Tyler.

'What will you do?' she asked abruptly, as if she had been steeling herself to speak to him.

'Do?'

'Yes.'

'I don't know.'

'I was thinking that—'

'Ali!'

Ali stopped mid-sentence at Beatrice's voice.

'Where's your dog? He's gone awfully quiet.'

'What?'

Ali got up and went up the stairs. She returned looking relieved.

'He found a cushion he was using as a toy.'

Will laughed.

'"Using as a toy" is code for utterly destroying.'

'Stop it, Will,' said Ali wearily.

She sat down again and pushed her plate away from her.

'Are you okay?' Clara asked.

'I feel a bit tired, that's all,' Ali said quietly, not wanting to be overheard. 'A bit frail,' she added.

'All these memories,' said Ellen sympathetically.

Ali nodded but didn't speak. She was running her finger round the rim of the glass, staring in front of her.

'Why don't we just say it? What happened to Leo was horrible, but he was a bully.' Clara looked round the table. 'To all of us.'

'You never hid your dislike,' said Marco. 'Even before Jay got chucked out.'

Clara shrugged.

'More to the point,' continued Marco, 'he didn't like you either, did he?'

'Probably not.'

'Why?'

'Why would he? I wasn't disarmed by him, not like you were. He once tried to seduce me – seduce is the right word, I think, though it sounds ridiculously old-fashioned. I told him to fuck off. He probably didn't appreciate that.'

'Sounds like an arsehole,' said Kristin. 'Yet you tolerated him. You went away on that weekend with him.'

Clara turned towards her, her eyes blazing.

'Things are never simple. I didn't much like Leo, but the others—' She corrected herself. '*You* others. I loved you all once. If tolerating Leo was the price to pay for being part of the group, then I thought it was worth it.'

'I'm thinking of that word, *once*,' said Rudi. 'How sad it sounds.'

'Let's leave this,' said Ali with sudden urgency.

Marco gave an ugly bellow of mirth.

'It's a bit late for that, for fuck's sake. Why did you come if you didn't want to revisit the past? Look at us. And him.' He jerked his head at Tyler. 'Sitting there in judgement. Though how a convicted murderer can sit in judgement, I do not know.'

Ellen leaned forward. She had mayonnaise on her chin. Her eyes glittered.

'I was just looking around the table, and you know what I was thinking?'

'Are you waiting for someone to answer that?' asked Beatrice.

Ellen took a gulp of wine.

'What I was thinking is that I've slept with every man round this table. Except Jay, that is,' she added, as if Jay didn't count. She looked at Kristin. 'Does that shock you?'

Kristin laughed.

'No, that's great.'

'It was great, mostly,' Ellen continued. 'I'm sure some people thought I was just sleeping around. Well, first off, people who thought that can just fuck off. But the reason I'm saying this is that it might have seemed casual to some people, it may have looked casual, but it was never casual to me. It was always special. It was always intimate. When I shared a bed with someone, I learned something. I remember Marco playing music to me. It was the most romantic thing ever.'

'You don't have to work your way round all of us,' said Rudi.

'It's all right,' said Ellen. 'Your wife isn't here. And I have only happy memories. I remember you showed me the novel you were writing. I thought you were so talented. What happened to that novel?'

'I never finished it.'

'And Tyler.' Ellen looked at Tyler. 'Tyler. You made me feel like I was fifteen again. You broke my heart a little, but it was always really Ali that you loved. The point is—' Here her expression changed; her smile faded. Suddenly, she looked like a different person. 'The point is that Leo was different,' she said. 'He came to my room one afternoon. He fucked me and then he left. You know the old expression, a notch on the bedpost? It was like that. I'd never experienced anything like it, and I never experienced it again. It was like an animal marking his territory. It wasn't about pleasure, and there wasn't that sweet time afterwards where you lie together and talk and giggle and share secrets. He left, and it was done.' She looked at Ali once more. 'I know you're not meant to say that about someone who has died, but I'm not going to lie. Leo was a friend. But he wasn't always a nice person. He was horrible to you.'

'Leo?' Ali said. 'Not in particular.'

'Don't you remember?'

'Remember what?'

'The bet?'

22

Ali stared across the table.

'What do you mean, the bet?'

'Ellen,' Will said warningly. 'Leave it.'

'Didn't you know?'

'What are you talking about?'

'God, I assumed you knew. I'm so sorry.'

'I'm warning you: leave it,' said Will again.

'Tell me.'

'I think you better had,' said Kristin. 'Now you've got this far.'

'Maybe it's better you know the truth,' said Ellen. 'He had a bet that he could get you into bed. I don't mean literally into bed.'

When Ali's voice came, it was small and flat; her face had a greenish pallor. The room was heavy with silence.

'No. I never heard.'

'Did he win the bet?' Kristin's voice rang out.

'Oh, for God's sake,' Rudi snapped. 'I don't know why you're even here, but you could at least keep your big mouth shut for once.'

'Yes,' said Ali in a small voice. 'He did, as it happens.' She put a trembling hand up to rub her face. 'Did everyone know?'

'It was so long ago.' Beatrice was leaning across the table. One of her sleeves was in her plate of food.

'Did you know?' Ali asked Will, and he looked away in discomfort. 'I see.'

'Ali, my darling—'

'He wanted power, Ali.' Beatrice pushed her sticky hair back from her face. 'He needed to have a hold over people. Just so you don't feel you're the only one he tried to humiliate, once when I was a bit drunk I came on to him and he turned me down. He said I wasn't his type. It was awful. I felt utterly ashamed. I never told anyone. Until now.'

Ali turned to Tyler.

'What about you? Did you know? Is that what your fight was really about?'

It was as if everyone in the room was holding their breath to hear his answer.

'It doesn't matter now,' he said at last, gently. 'It never did.'

'Everyone then,' said Ali. She looked round the table. 'I feel like I've been stripped naked this evening. Flayed. Publicly humiliated.' She looked at Tyler. 'Is that what this gathering was all about?'

'Satisfied?' Will asked Ellen savagely. 'You've made us face the truth. Shone a light, is that what you say? Better now?'

He took a large gulp from the glass and put it back on the table in front of him. Ellen looked at him with concern.

'You're very angry,' she said.

'Stop talking to me in your therapist's voice.' Will ran a hand through his wild hair. There was sweat on his forehead and darkening of his shirt beneath his armpits. 'You think you can blunder about, prodding and poking at everyone's wounds, talking about your jolly sex life as if it was all just good fun, as if nothing meant anything.'

'That's not what I said.'

'People don't all have the hide of a rhino. You hurt people by being so crass.'

'Will,' said Ali, 'I know that—'

'You know what Leo said to us guys about you, after your encounter, when we were in the pub? He said you were pathetic. He said that you put on an act of having carefree sex and that it was all fun, but that really it was just a desperate way of getting some kind of attention. You thought it was about being sexually attractive and liberated, but really, deep down, you knew that we would fuck anything with a hole in.'

Jay laid his face down on the table.

When Ellen spoke, her voice was calm, but she had gone pale, except for two red patches on her cheeks.

'And what did you say to him?'

'What do you mean?'

'You were all sitting together in a pub, and Leo was being foul about one of your friends. I was just wondering how you responded?'

'Yes,' said Ali. 'How did you respond, Will?'

'Did you defend me,' asked Ellen, 'or did you just nod along, or did you chime in with your own anecdotes about me?'

'Of course not,' said Will. 'But—'

'But?'

'I think when people are having lots of one-night stands it can be a sign of something that's going wrong.'

'Interesting,' said Clara. Her voice was scathing and her face white with anger. 'Did you say that about boys you knew who were sleeping with lots of girls? Or is it just girls? If a girl sleeps around, she's a bit of tramp, a bit of a slag.'

Ellen leaned towards him.

'If you were in therapy with me, Will, do you know what I'd tell you? I'd say that people like Leo are manipulative bullies, but that people like you are worse. The people who go along with them because they're cowardly and weak.' She looked around the table and rubbed one eye, as if she had something caught in it. She looked back at Will. 'I know what Leo was like. I didn't quite realise what you were like.'

Her face wore a malicious expression.

'Do you want know who was the best fuck of all of you lot?'

'Oh, please,' said Beatrice, covering her face with her hands.

'It wasn't you, Will. You seemed a bit desperate, if I'm honest.'

'It's because he was always in love with Ali,' said Clara. 'Anyone with half an eye could see that.'

Ali lifted her head. Rudi put his forefinger and thumb on the tender stem of his glass and twisted it round and round.

'I don't think so,' said Ali. 'I don't think that's true.'

'He was always just waiting for his chance,' continued Clara. 'Being the life and soul of the party. The clown. But always hoping.'

'No,' said Will thickly. 'That's crap.'

'Don't worry, I knew you were smitten,' said Tyler. 'And now you two are together.' He paused and looked between Will and Ali for a long moment. 'How's that going, by the way?'

'Did you think,' said Ali harshly, 'that I would wait for you to be released? Wait with open arms for a murderer? Stand by my man?'

Will gave a groan.

'Oh, God,' said Beatrice. 'Someone make this stop.'

Rudi put an arm round her and she leaned into him.

'Mum?' A lanky teenager stood in the doorway gazing at them all. 'What the actual fuck?'

23

'Finn!' Beatrice jerked away from Rudi, but he kept his arm draped over her shoulder. 'What are you doing here?'

Her son looked around at the scene with disgust.

'What's going on?'

'I told you I was having friends round.' Beatrice made a large gesture to the table. 'Everyone, this is my son, Finn. Finn, this is everyone.'

There was a mumbled chorus of hellos, but Finn just glared at them.

Beatrice made an effort to sit straight. She noticed food smeared over the hem of her white silk blouse and covered it with a napkin. Finn watched her.

'I thought you were out for the evening,' she said.

A young woman appeared behind him, blinking at them all in surprise. She was wearing a long green dress and had flowers pinned into her hair.

'Hello,' she said. 'I didn't know there was a party here.'

'It's not exactly a party,' said Beatrice. 'Hello, Connie.'

'We've had a horrible, horrible time,' said Connie, a high note of panic in her voice. 'We thought you'd know what to do.'

'Yeah, well, that was a mistake,' said Finn. 'Look at her. She's drunk.'

'The disapproval of the young,' murmured Rudi.

'I love your dress,' Kristin said to Connie. 'And the flowers. You look like a wood nymph. Have a drink.'

'What horrible time?' Beatrice said. 'Are you okay?'

'It was his friend Arlo,' said Connie.

'There was a bit of an argument,' said Finn.

'What kind of argument? Was anyone hurt?'

'He had a knife,' said Connie. 'It was awful. He was waving it around. We thought he was going to kill someone. Show them, Finn.'

Finn put a hand into the deep inside pocket of his canvas coat and drew out a long-bladed knife. He laid it on the table, amid the debris.

Beatrice grimaced and looked around at her guests. When she spoke, her voice was harsh.

'You realise that just carrying that in the street is a criminal offence?'

'I didn't know what to do,' said Finn. He suddenly looked young and anxious. 'I thought you'd approve.'

Rudi reached out and touched it with his finger. Will picked it up and tested the blade, making a small exclamation at its sharpness.

Then Tyler spoke.

'You did the right thing,' he said.

Finn looked at him, his young face flushed and unsure.

'Yes,' said Beatrice. 'Yes, darling, you did. I was just a bit thrown.' She gestured at the table. 'Do you want some food? As you can see, there's plenty left.'

'No,' said Finn contemptuously. 'I don't think this is our type of thing. We're on our way out; we only stopped by to get rid of that.' He jerked his head towards the knife. 'We'll leave you to your fun.'

Tyler nodded at him.

'That sounds right,' he said. 'I don't think you should be here.'

Finn looked at him curiously, but he didn't reply.

24

Marco reached out for the long-bladed knife that glittered on the table. 'This is quite some weapon.'

He held it in front of his face, inspecting it.

'Put that down,' said Beatrice.

'Are you scared I'll use it?'

He waved it towards Kristin.

'Give it to me,' said Beatrice, and took it from him.

'Tyler,' said Ali in a dry, tight voice. 'I wanted to say that I'm sorry I never came to see you.'

'I understood,' he said.

'This evening,' said Kristin, 'is not turning out the way I expected. I don't think I'm enjoying it anymore.' She caught Rudi's eye. 'You're pretty quiet. Why haven't you joined in the wrangling?'

'That's not really my style,' he said mildly.

'Is that because you're a writer?' Marco asked, dragging a hand across his mouth. 'Are you gathering material?'

'So what was it?' asked Jay abruptly. His voice was scratchy. Everyone looked at him, surprised that he had spoken up. He was huddled over the table, his face pinched, a muscle twitching in his cheek. 'What's the actual point of this reunion? Why am I here, why are any of us here? What do you want? Or is this what you want?' He gestured round the table. 'This horrible disintegration. Are you getting a kick out of it?'

'Of course he is,' said Clara.

Tyler leaned across the table for the water jug and carefully filled his glass.

'I'll tell you what I want and why I'm here.'

He took a slow drink and then placed it carefully back on the table.

'If I close my eyes,' he said, in his calm and measured voice, as if he was reading from a prepared script, 'I can picture you all as I last saw you. It's like a freeze-frame: everyone standing there, watching me as I was led away. I can remember the expression on each of your faces, the horror I saw. It's like something that has only just happened, and it will always be something that only just happened, a moment on repeat. Me being taken away from the path that had been laid out for me since I was a boy, and knew I wanted to be a doctor. I have spent well over half my life – almost all of my adult life – in prison, and it feels to me that those decades are like a terrible darkness spooling out from that single clear moment.'

He took a small sip of his water, let his eyes move from person to person.

'It's true that I can picture the expressions on all your faces, but their meaning changed over time. In those first moments, I assumed they were ones of disbelief. Of course none of you thought I had killed Leo. I was your friend. It was just a ghastly mistake.

'I don't know when I realised it wasn't like that. Was it when nobody wrote to me, told me they stood by me, told me they knew I couldn't have killed Leo? When I was convicted, and no one came to the trial, except as witnesses of course? Witnesses who didn't insist I was innocent. Or when nobody visited me in prison? Except you,' he added, speaking to Will. 'You must have hated those visits; I know I did.

'I was a fool. It took me a stupidly long time to understand that it wasn't just a mistake.'

He picked up the glass and took another slow drink of water.

'One of you murdered Leo and let me go down for it.'

A sound came from Jay, like a sigh he had been holding in check. Nobody else spoke or moved.

'Two people here know I didn't murder Leo – myself, and the person who did it.'

'You don't get to do this,' shouted Marco, pushing his chair back with a violent scrape. 'You killed Leo. Everyone always says they're innocent. That's what convicted murderers do.'

'That's what they say,' said Tyler. 'And some people really are innocent. For nearly thirty years, I've been locked away for a crime that someone round this table committed. I wonder how that feels: not just to take one life, but to take two. And taking Leo's life – perhaps that was a single moment, a violent instinct. But taking mine: that was a choice, a choice you had to make every day for twenty-nine years, knowing that because you were free, I was not. Yes, I do wonder how that feels.'

'Tyler,' said Ellen. 'Very few people who kill someone ever admit they did it, even to themselves.' She was in the process of coming undone. Her grey plait was barely holding any hair, her skirt had twisted round, her cheeks were blotchy. 'Most of them block out the act. They protect themselves from what is unendurable by forgetting it. The red mist, that kind of thing. Have you seen a therapist, Tyler? I'd be glad to recommend someone.'

Tyler didn't react to her.

'I won't bother describing what it's like to spend three decades in a high-security prison. Nobody who hasn't been in prison can know what it's like. The violence. The drugs. The dirt. Blood and shit and vomit. Cockroaches. The boredom.

The fear, which you wake with and you go to sleep with. The bureaucracy like a boot in the face. The rage and despair. The hope is the worst thing. It takes a long time to cure you of that. The things that are done to you and then the things you find yourself doing. And all the time you're slowly rusting away.'

He paused again. In the thick silence, Beatrice cleared her throat.

'But you survived,' she said.

'Did I?' said Tyler. 'Something survived.' He put up a hand and ran a finger down his scar, remembering. 'Perhaps that was what saved me. I spent two months in the prison hospital, and I made up my mind. I'd come through. I'd walk out of the prison gates and back into a life of some kind.'

He smiled round at them.

'But I'm not telling you why I wanted this reunion, am I? During the first years in prison, after I'd been denied an appeal, I was consumed with my sense of rage and betrayal. I swore I'd find out who had murdered Leo and implicated me, and I would have revenge on them. I went over and over the events of the weekend, working out who had said what, who could have done it. Do you know what I realised? That I don't trust any of you. It could be any one of you.'

Beatrice cleared her throat, then spoke.

'Tyler,' she said. 'I would like to talk about these things to you and hear what you have to say, but not like this. It's harrowing.'

Tyler ignored her and pointed at Ali.

'I was in love with you and I think you were in love with me. How many letters did I write to you in prison in those first months, pouring out all my anguish, imploring you to answer, to come and see me?'

Ali gazed at him, her eyes pools of darkness in her blanched face.

'I couldn't,' she whispered. 'I would have gone mad if I hadn't cut myself off. That was the only thing I knew to do.'

'And you.' Tyler's finger shifted towards Will, who sat beside his wife but didn't look at her. 'You never told me you were with Ali. You never told me anything. You sat there and prattled on about politics, or how you'd taken up gardening.'

'At least I came.'

'That's true. You and my mother. My poor mother. It was almost a relief when she died, so I didn't have to endure those visits, when she tried to smile and all she could do was cry and tell me she knew I was innocent, while I knew she thought I was guilty.

'But cheer up.' Again, Tyler smiled at each of them in turn, taking his time. 'I decided against revenge. One of you here must be scared that I somehow discovered the truth. I didn't. I don't know which of you killed Leo, only that I didn't. I came to understand that if I was to leave prison a free man – or as free as someone is who's on licence for the rest of his life – I needed to stop thinking about you lot, and getting justice, or being revenged. I promised myself that shortly after I came out, I would meet you all.' He nodded towards Beatrice, who sat with her head resting on Rudi's shoulder. 'So thank you for your hospitality; I know it's not been your ideal evening. I would look each of you in the eye, see who you had become. After that, I would never see any of you again.

'But do you know what?' His smile widened; for a moment he looked like his buoyant younger self. 'It turns out that I've had my revenge after all. Because while I've been in my own particular hell since Leo's murder, you don't seem to have lived the lives you longed for when we were young and full of promise. You've not made much of a fist of it, have you? Perhaps you're okay,' he said to Clara. 'It's always been hard to tell. But the rest of you – I don't think so. It probably sounds strange, but I don't envy any of you. So perhaps there is a kind of justice after all. Karma. You're locked into the lives you chose.'

He took a final sip of water.

'I needed to see you in order to forget you. I'm here to say goodbye.'

25

The room, which had been quiet, was full of noise and motion, people talking over each other and gesticulating violently. Marco was on his feet. Beatrice's voice cut through it all.

'Enough,' she said. 'I want to speak to Tyler. I should have done so earlier. The rest of you, get out of here. You can go upstairs or into the garden, or you can go home. I don't care. Just give us some space.'

They left, and Beatrice poured herself a tumbler of water and drank it down before sitting next to Tyler, pushing the plates of half-eaten food into the centre of the table.

'That was quite a speech,' she said.

'It was something I needed to say.'

'Ellen's right, you know. Almost everyone in prison says that they are innocent.'

'Yes.'

'We've all spent the last three decades thinking you killed Leo. Do you expect us to believe you?'

'I don't expect anything. One of you knows I'm telling the truth, of course.'

'If what you say is true, then yes.' Beatrice shivered, suddenly cold in her thin silk blouse.

'And what about you, Beatrice. Do you believe me?'

Beatrice lifted her tumbler and laid the cool glass against her burning forehead.

'I don't know what I believe. I'm going to be candid, Tyler: I've never known what to believe.'

'So you were never certain.'

'No. But Tyler, don't you see, I never will be certain. There's nothing you could say that would make a difference to that. The jury unanimously found you guilty. The judge was certainly convinced of your guilt. You can be eloquent and passionate and persuasive, but I'll never know. Nobody will ever know except you – and if you're telling the truth, the person who did it, of course.'

'I agree.'

'So what's the point?'

'I just told you the point.'

'Isn't it more important that you're free?'

'You're a lawyer,' said Tyler. 'You know I'm not. I'm on licence. I'm still serving my sentence, but I'm doing it outside. Just being here, for instance: if I stay the night, I have to tell my probation officer. If I commit any kind of a crime, I'm back inside. If someone even thinks I'm a risk, I could be back inside.'

'Are you planning an appeal?'

'Claiming you're innocent isn't grounds for an appeal. As you know.'

'But Tyler, if you're innocent, don't you want it officially accepted?'

'I've got more important things to do.'

Beatrice leaned in more closely.

'If you want legal advice, I know the right people. I can put you in touch with them, if you like. I would like to help if I can.'

'Why? To assuage your guilt?'

'Guilt?'

'Yes. You're sitting there, calmly telling me you were never certain that I killed Leo. But you never told me that before. You never wrote. You never visited. You got on with your lucky life, in your beautiful house, with your politician husband and your well-paid job. And you left me to rot, and probably, bit by bit, you let yourself forget about me and about that nagging doubt you had. And now you sit there, looking at me with your concerned, professional face, and say that you'd like to help. It's a bit late, isn't it?'

Beatrice hesitated a long while. She could hear voices from upstairs, and see figures in the garden, but here at the table they felt apart from everything else.

'It is a bit late,' she said. 'I should have come to see you. But I was swept up by my life. Probably I was a coward. I couldn't bring myself to think you were innocent, because that would mean one of the rest of us was guilty: any one of us, as you said just now. It was more bearable to accept the verdict and try and put you out of my mind. I am not proud of myself. And to be clear,' she added with a touch of asperity, 'I still think it is more likely than not that you did it.'

Tyler nodded.

'It's a conundrum,' he said amiably.

'But I would genuinely like to help you. I know good law-yers, the best.' She hesitated. 'I could help fund that.'

'What about you?' said Tyler. 'You're a lawyer.'

'I'm not that kind of a lawyer.'

'What kind of lawyer are you?'

'I do corporate law.'

'I don't know what that means.'

'Mergers, acquisitions. When companies do that, they need lawyers.'

'When companies do what? You're just saying words I don't understand.'

'You do understand,' said Beatrice wearily. 'When companies buy other companies. When companies merge with other companies. It involves complicated legal issues, and I help them with that.'

'I guess that pays well.'

'It's not bad.'

Tyler shook his head slowly.

'That doesn't fit with the Beatrice I knew,' he said. 'The Beatrice I knew wanted to blow companies up. She didn't want to help them get even richer and even more powerful.'

'The Beatrice you knew was twenty-one years old. Yes, I was an anarchist and I took illegal drugs and I wanted to overturn the system. And when I was seven I used to play with pink plastic ponies and—'

Tyler interrupted her.

'And now you're an adult, and you've put aside childish things.'

'Something like that. I know it's different for you. Maybe you got frozen at the age of twenty-two.'

At this, Tyler gave the first hint of a smile.

'Yes, it's difficult to sell out when you're in a prison cell.'

'By selling out, you mean, growing up, getting a job, getting married, having children, that sort of thing.'

'I'm sure you're doing God's work,' said Tyler. 'But I don't need your help, Beatrice. I don't intend to appeal; there would be no point. As I said, I just wanted to look at each of you, see you for what you are, and go and never come back.'

26

Ali had walked along the gravel path, and under a wrought-iron archway to the secluded far end of the garden, where there was a tennis table and a garden shed. She needed a moment to herself, but she also needed a cigarette. She felt in her pockets.

'I'll get it,' said a voice behind her.

She turned round. Marco was holding a lighter.

'I've always found Zippos sexy? It's like cocking a pistol.'

He flicked the top off. She leaned forward and lit her cigarette, then offered him her packet.

'I've got my own, thanks.'

He took a crinkled little spliff from his pocket. He lit it and took a deep drag, holding it in his lungs before releasing it.

'I needed that.'

Behind him, Ali saw Clara and Kristin walking along the garden towards them. As they got closer, she held out her cigarette packet.

'I really shouldn't,' said Clara, taking one of them.

'If it belongs to someone else, then it doesn't count,' said Marco.

Ali offered the pack to Kristin, who just shook her head. Marco offered his spliff to her, and she took a drag and passed it back.

'I feel I'm a survivor of an earthquake or a terrorist attack,' said Marco.

'He only has power if we allow him to,' said Clara. 'He's trying to needle us.'

Kristin let out a violent peal of laughter.

'Needle you? What do you mean? He's just said that one of you lot is a murderer.'

'Fuck that,' said Marco, his voice sounding almost sticky. 'How dare he take the moral high ground and sit there at the end of the table, looking silent and disapproving? Fuck him.' Despite his tone, Marco looked around, and then dropped his voice slightly as if he thought that they might be overheard. 'I mean, obviously I feel sorry for the guy. God knows what happened to him during all those years in prison. But the fact is, he was convicted of murder, and it was an open and shut case. We all heard him threaten to kill Leo, and then Leo was found dead. The knife was right next to him, for God's sake.'

'What if he's innocent?' said Kristin. 'What if he's innocent and spent all those years in prison? The idea of it just does my head in.'

'He's not innocent,' said Clara.

'How do you know?'

'I just know. He can't be.'

'Why? Because that would mean that one of you did it?' Kristin took another long drag from Marco's spliff. 'And you got away with it. It's a creepy thought. That there's a killer loose and—'

'Stop it,' said Clara. 'Just shut up.'

'Oh, hang on,' said Kristin. 'Hang on. I think I might get what's going on here.'

Her eyes were gleaming in the dusk.

'Nothing's going on.'

'Are you so certain it's Tyler, it just has to be Tyler, because actually you've always been scared that—'

'Stop right now. I'm warning you.'

'It makes sense. You'd be willing to sacrifice Tyler for him.'

'What the fuck are you on about?' Marco said. 'Who?'

Kristin patted him, not very gently, on the cheek.

'Don't you worry.'

'Listen.' Marco leaned in close, his eyes bulging. 'You've said enough tonight. Keep your big mouth shut for once in your life.'

Kristin laughed merrily.

'Oh, I get it. I've offended you.'

'You wouldn't understand.'

'I've offended you because I haven't bigged you up in front of your friends. If that's the right word for people you haven't seen for nearly thirty years.'

'Stop, before you regret it.'

'What? Are you going to hit me?'

Marco swung on his heel and walked off, a silent howl in his throat, his eyes burning with futile rage.

27

Rudi came down the stairs. He put a hand on Beatrice's back.

'Am I allowed back in here?'

'It's all right. We're done. I've been defending my choice of profession to Tyler.'

'We've all made our compromises,' said Rudi.

'I've not made compromises,' she replied.

Tyler stood up and pushed his chair neatly into place.

'I'll leave you to it,' he said. 'I'm going to sit in your garden for a few minutes, let my thoughts settle, if that's all right with you. Then I'll be gone, and you never need to see me again.'

He walked out through the garden doors.

'What a fucking awful evening,' Beatrice said on an exhale. 'I was dreading it, but nothing could prepare me for how ghastly it's been.'

'I like you when you swear,' Rudi said softly, and touched the nape of her neck with the tip of his fingers.

'Don't,' said Beatrice, shaking him off. 'Tyler seems to think that he's somehow the pure one, and we've grown old and corrupt. I think Tyler still sees me the way I was when I was twenty-one. Maybe he's right, and if the Beatrice I used to be could see me now, she'd be disappointed.'

'You shouldn't think that.'

'I was so eager to please. I look back, and feel sorry for the person I was.'

'Whereas I,' said Rudi morosely, 'feel sorry for the person I am.'

'Aren't you happy? You seem to have everything. Your writing, your children, your marriage.'

'Is that all there is?'

Beatrice gave a melancholy sigh.

'You know, sometimes I get sick of being seen by everyone as the boring, sensible one.'

Rudi gestured around him.

'You've got a sensible house,' he said. 'A gorgeous, grand, big, sensible house. If that's boring, most of us could do with some of it.'

'That's just what I'm talking about,' said Beatrice. 'People look at me and my job and where I live, they look at my politician husband, and God forbid I should do anything to bring him into disrepute, and they think that's all there is to me. I'm more than that. I'm more than a middle-aged, married woman.'

'Let's not think about our marriages this evening. They don't seem real.'

'A midsummer night's dream,' said Beatrice softly.

They smiled at each other, and then the smiles faded and they looked at each other more seriously. Rudi leaned forward and kissed her softly on the lips. He put his hand up and cupped her cheek, and he kissed her again, properly this time. She felt heat all the way down to her stomach. He moved his hand from her cheek to her neck, and then down her silky blouse and inside, cupping her breast. She gave a gasp and moved back from him. She wiped her mouth with the back of her hand, trying not to smear her lipstick, then spoke with a kind of puzzlement, as if she had been observing the actions of someone else.

'If my husband saw what we just did . . .' she said.

'My wife would be worse,' said Rudi. 'If she saw me kissing someone else like that, I think she'd divorce me. I really do. She's not exactly understanding.'

'Then why did you do it?'

Rudi hesitated for a moment before replying.

'I wanted to remember what it was like, what you were like, what I was like. So long ago, when we were young and everything lay in front of us. I was so in love with you. I was in love with you for years after you left me. And it felt that I was stepping back in to the past – my wife can't blame me for what happened before she met me.'

Beatrice gave a small laugh.

'I don't think your wife would accept that argument.'

'You didn't try to stop me.'

'I should have,' she said. 'I've got a husband. I've got a teenage son.'

Rudi raised his hand and touched her cheek.

'You said it yourself. You're more than that.'

Sounds came from the garden. Beatrice stood up.

'We'd better go and join the others. I think this evening needs to come to an end.'

28

Marco went back to the house. Nobody was sitting at the table anymore, which was strewn with dirty plates, serving dishes still half-full of salads, wine glasses and screwed-up paper napkins. He sat on the chair at the end of the table, where Beatrice had sat, and picked up a glass that still had wine in it, which he drank in two large mouthfuls.

Time was behaving strangely and short-term memories were blurry and unstable. He couldn't remember his journey here, only leaving the flat with Kristin, pulling the door shut behind them. He couldn't remember much of the dinner either, only the sense of being somehow on the edge of things, jangled and uneasy. Overlooked, he thought now, with a flash of resentment; unrecognised. Tyler's words niggled at him; his anger stirred like embers being blown on. He thought of his poky flat, his half-empty days, the evenings spent in pubs playing old songs to a few half-drunk people who weren't even listening, his stupid relationship that he knew was a mistake.

He thought of the old days. That time lay clear and radiant in his memory, like a stage blazing with light. He summoned the figures from the past. There was Beatrice, insecure and eager; troubled Jay; Ellen, with her warm hands and generosity; studious, watchful Clara; acerbic, sexy Ali; clever Rudi; Will, so full of appetite and warmth.

He drank the remains of the wine from another glass.

Then Tyler. Tyler with the kind gaze, the steadiness, the sense of being a safe place. Tyler who had been led away by the police on that beautiful summer day and Marco could still see the look on his face as he turned back towards them, before getting into the car. He would never forget it. The anguish. He had never talked properly to anyone about it. When he had tried to describe it to Kristin, it had felt garish and unreal, and Kristin had reacted with a kind of ghoulish excitement that had grated.

And then Leo of course; Leo, who he rarely let himself remember. There he was among them all. Solid and tall – as tall as Tyler. The two of them had been the leaders of their group, though Leo had claimed that role and Tyler hadn't seemed to know he was at the centre of things. Leo with his tangly dark hair; dark stubble; bright blue eyes. A smile he blazed at people when he wanted to charm them. So good-looking, and how well he knew it.

But cold. A cold, cold man.

He didn't want to think about Leo. Not now, not ever. He drank some more leftover wine and sat back in the chair. Everything was fuzzy around him, the room unsteady; only the past was hard-edged. That weekend.

He blinked, trying to bring himself back into the present. His eyes fell on the knife that lay glinting in the last of the light that glimmered through the window. He picked it up and held it, put a thumb carefully against the sharp blade. Then he stood up, and went with it up the stairs, into the living room, where Beatrice, Rudi, Ellen and Will sat chatting, while Jay sat apart at a chessboard, moving the carved wooden pieces with apparent concentration, though actually his face looked dazed.

Marco laid the knife on the coffee table.

'What the hell are you doing wandering around with that?' Beatrice asked.

Rudi leaned forward and picked it up, turning it between his fingers before laying it down again.

'Nasty,' he said reverently.

Marco subsided into an armchair.

'I'm done in,' he said.

'We're all done in,' said Beatrice.

Rudi murmured something, and she turned to him. For a moment, Will, sitting across from them, caught a glimpse of the Beatrice he used to know, shy and beguiling, just wanting to be loved.

'No,' said Marco. 'You don't understand. I'm done in. Fifty-two and done in. What happened? Where did everything go?'

And he started to cry, shielding his face with one broad hand while the other gripped the arm of his chair, shoulders shaking, guttural sounds coming from him.

'Oh, mate,' said Will.

'Marco, honey,' said Ellen.

They crouched on either side of him, patting him, murmuring to him, as if he was a frantic animal.

'What shall I do?' he said through his sobs. 'Oh, Jesus, what shall I do?'

'I know,' said Will. 'I know, I know. It's okay. It's all been so horrible, but you'll be okay. We'll all be okay. I know, I know, I know.'

A wash of words that went on and on, while Marco cried his heart out. Will kissed the top of Marco's head, his own broad face creased in distress. Ellen had her arms round him; his wet face was pressed against her breast.

Jay stared across at the three of them pressed close together. They looked like some medieval sculpture about grief, he thought.

'What are we all doing here?' he asked the room.

Nobody answered. Rudi was still stroking the nape of Beatrice's neck and she had closed her eyes. Jay moved a bishop slantwise across the board.

29

Jay's eyes stung; they felt as if they were buried deep in their sockets. He tried not to look at Marco and his two comforters. The air was warm and heavy. Darkness was seeping into the sky and the garden was a place of shadows.

He stared down at the chessboard. The pieces suddenly felt menacing rather than distracting. He could feel panic like a thick sludge inside him, and was finding it hard to breathe. It had been years since he had been this bad, but then for many years, he had scrupulously avoided anything that could derail him. He thought of his tiny house on the edge of the moors; his scant possessions all in their proper place; the evenings spent alone, eating thrifty suppers at the small pine table, a book propped up in front of him; his job in the care home, where he made his voice kind and his movements gentle. He had arranged his life to eliminate the unexpected. He travelled the same route to work each day, turned down the rare invitations to dinner or parties, did a weekly shop where he bought what he had bought the previous week to make meals on a rota. He slept for seven hours each night, meditated in the morning before breakfast, and went on long, arduous walks on his days off, always alone. Perhaps the only drama in his life was the weather he endured and even relished. There was a kind of happiness, or of peace at least, in knowing that the scary and chaotic part of his life was in the past, and that he no longer needed to dread anything, or hope for anything.

He still didn't know why he had come to this reunion. He couldn't simply blame Clara. Perhaps, he thought now, he had seen it as a kind of test. If so, he had failed. He wasn't as detached from the world as he had believed. It still had power over him. He could feel the terror clutch at his throat.

'No,' he said, and abruptly stood, dislodging the board so that the pieces scattered onto the floor.

Rudi looked at him across Beatrice's head, but didn't speak. Instead, he slowly and deliberately winked.

Jay recoiled. Then he went quickly out of the room, running down the stairs to the lower ground floor, past the congealing mess on the long dining table and through the doors that led outside. He needed to find Clara. They needed to leave.

The garden was full of night fragrance. Roses, night-scented stocks, something he didn't recognise, like the overbearing odour of lilies, which were flowers for the dead.

He stopped for a moment, looking around, trying to get his bearings. He saw that metal steps led into the garden from a terrace on the first floor, and that there was a little shed at the end of the long lawn. But for a moment he couldn't make out any figures. Something rustled in the undergrowth. A dry stick cracked.

He heard voices. Women's voices.

'Clara,' he called urgently, and two shapes moved towards him.

'Jay?'

Clara had her arm around Ali's shoulders. Ali was very upright and moved stiffly, as if her joints had seized up.

'What's happened?' he asked.

'Ali's upset,' Clara said.

'Why?'

'Maybe he's telling the truth,' said Ali, pulling away from Clara's arm. Her voice was scratchy.

'Of course he's not,' said Clara urgently.

'It's all too much. I need to find Benjy. Has anyone seen Benjy?'

'Not recently,' said Jay.

'I can't even look after a dog properly.'

Ali left them and walked back into the house, jerkily, like a marionette.

'Tyler wanted to hurt her,' said Clara. 'He wants to hurt all of us. That's why he's here.'

This is the real test, Jay thought. This moment, now. I can prove myself to myself. He balled his fists, and spoke with a sudden energy.

'He can't hurt me. Where the fuck is he?'

His voice was loud, almost guttural. Clara looked at him in surprise, then pointed. In the dim light Jay made out a figure at the far end of the garden. He strode towards it. Clara followed, calling him to wait.

'Tyler,' Jay said as he approached. 'You're not fucking God. You're not a saint come among us to show us the way. You're a murderer.'

'Do you think so, Jay? Really?'

'Come away, right now,' said Clara. 'Leave him, Jay.'

'You don't need to protect him,' said Tyler. 'Though that was always your role, protect him no matter what.'

'Shut up,' said Jay. 'Shut the fuck up.'

And punched him.

His fist landed on the side of Tyler's face. Tyler was jolted back, but apart from that he barely reacted.

Jay hit him again, but with less conviction this time, a soft thump that landed on Tyler's shoulder. His face was screwed up. He looked as if he would cry.

'Jay!' Clara cried. 'Stop.'

'You always were an angry man,' said Tyler calmly. 'That room you and Leo wrecked – it might have been Leo's idea, but it freed something in you, didn't it?'

'I'm not angry,' shouted Jay, like a small child. 'I'm not.'

'I imagine that's what your breakdown was about, that and Clara leaving you,' Tyler continued. 'It must have been painful to face up to the truth of yourself. The rage boiling away inside you. Now you work as a carer, live a good life, perhaps a self-punishing life, but you're always scared that the anger might erupt again.'

'Stop it,' said Jay, and he put his hands to his ears.

'Just ignore him,' said Clara.

'You've no right,' said Jay. 'You've no right to come here and upset us all.'

'Funny concept, that,' said Tyler. 'Right.'

'Tyler.' Clara spoke fiercely. 'As far as I'm concerned, you're the man who killed Leo, and however bad Leo might have been, you're worse. You're a—'

'Ssh,' said Tyler softly, and put his finger to his lips.

Clara stopped abruptly, and the three of them stood in a suspended silence. Then she linked her arm through Jay's.

'Come on,' she said. 'It's over.'

30

Kristin clattered up the stairs from the lower ground floor, lurching on her heels. Her lace dress was torn at the hem.

'What's wrong with him?' she asked, when she saw Will and Ellen crouched beside Marco, who had stopped weeping, but whose face was puffy and smeared with snot and tears.

'He's just a bit emotional,' Ellen said comfortingly.

'You wouldn't understand,' Marco said bitterly.

Kristin gazed at him, then her face broke into a smile.

'Oh, I see,' she said. 'You're still feeling hard done by.'

'I'm not feeling hard done by.' Marco's face stretched into a grimace. His eyes were red and swollen. 'I'm feeling wounded.'

'Oh, Christ. The man with the wound. Do have any idea of how much I'm done with wounded men. You think I should have defended you earlier when Tyler said your life hadn't lived up to your high hopes.'

'That wasn't very nice of him.' Ellen stroked Marco's cheek.

'It was true though.' Kristin pointed a finger at Marco, who lay back in his chair and squinted up at her. 'And that's the trouble, isn't it? He said out loud what you're always thinking. He said it in front of other people. In front of your partner.'

'Shut up.'

'What should I have said? That you were my hero? That I had faith in you? That it isn't too late, and you could still be discovered?'

'Guys,' said Will. 'Don't do this. Please.'

'Shut the fuck up, you fat cow,' said Marco.

'I don't like it when you swear at me.'

'And I don't like it when you take other people's sides against me.'

'You take other people's sides against me.'

'When?'

'When I talk about the vaccine. When I talk about mobile phones.'

'That's completely different.'

'It's not.'

'It is. It's just ignorant.'

'There you go. See. You make fun of me. You think I'm stupid. I don't even know why you're with me.'

'That makes two of us.'

'Please,' said Beatrice. 'Leave this till morning. Everything will feel better in the morning.' She stood up. 'I'm going to put this horrible knife somewhere it's safely out of everyone's way. I'll decide what to do with it tomorrow.'

She left the room, holding the knife between thumb and forefinger. They heard the footsteps mounting the stairs, a door opening.

There was a brief silence, then Kristin's expression became spiteful again.

'When we met,' she said with renewed vigour, leaning over Marco as he sat splayed in the chair, 'I thought you were rather sweet. You're not sweet at all. You're pathetic.'

'Stop!' Ellen rose to her feet. 'At once. You're going too far. You'll regret it.'

'And you're ridiculous,' said Marco. 'Laughable.'

'Says the man who can't get it up anymore.'

'What did you say?'

'I said, you can't get it up.'

Marco lurched upwards. His fist was clenched, but Will got hold of his arm.

'I was lying when I said it didn't matter,' Kristin concluded triumphantly. 'It matters!'

'Stop it, or leave my house!'

Beatrice re-entered the room. She was in disarray, shirt hanging loose, hair falling over her make-up-smudged face, but her voice had the ring of authority.

'I wish I'd never come anyway,' said Kristin.

'You were never invited in the first place.'

'Yeah, well, I thought it would be fun. I'd heard so much about you all; I had this glamorous image of everyone. It turns out you're just washed-up middle-aged people wittering on about the past.' She went towards the stairs, then turned for her final words. 'The only one I like is the one who's meant to be the killer.'

31

They listened to her going clumsily down the stairs.

'She doesn't know what she's saying,' Ellen told Marco.

He stared at her, dull-eyed.

'You should all go,' said Beatrice.

There were voices from the lower ground floor; then a high-pitched scream.

'Is that Ali?' Will asked, his bewildered face screwed up in an effort of concentration. 'I think it's Ali.'

'Is that glass breaking?' said Beatrice.

There was another scream, then a dog growled.

'Come on,' said Ellen, as if she was rallying the troops for a last stand. 'Let's go and make sure it's nothing serious. Marco, stand up.'

'Why? I prefer it where I am.'

'For goodness' sake,' Ellen said and took hold of his upper arm, dragging at him till he half slithered from his chair. 'Move yourself.'

The four of them made their way down the steps. A scene of carnage greeted them. Dishes were tipped over on the table, food was spread across the surface, along with flowers from upended vases. Rivers of water mixed with rivers of wine. A cigarette was mashed into the wood.

Ali stood at the far end of the table, clutching Benjy.

'What happened?' asked Beatrice, just as Clara and Jay came in from the garden, hand in hand.

'Benjy got up on the table,' said Ali. 'God knows what he's eaten.'

'What a mess.' Ellen sounded almost admiring.

'Red onions are poisonous!' Ali yelled at her. 'And so are raisins. Don't you know anything?'

She sat heavily on a chair and put her head into the dog's fur, which was greasy and matted with food.

'What's that?' Beatrice pointed, her voice ominous.

'Just an old decanter,' Kristin said, looking at the shards of glass on the floor. 'I needed to get rid of my anger. Don't worry, I'll pay for it.'

'You couldn't begin to afford to pay for it.'

'Sorry,' said Kristin blithely.

'I thought you were leaving.'

Kristin ignored her and took a seat facing the glass doors to the garden.

'Where is he?' asked Ellen. 'Has he gone?'

'He's in the garden,' said Clara.

'But then he's said he is going,' Beatrice said. 'I'll see him out. Nobody needs to meet him again.'

The guests sat in different chairs, drinking wine out of other people's glasses. Suddenly, it was as if a great storm had passed through the house, and now they all sat in its aftermath, dazed but strangely peaceful.

'It's only a bit after eleven,' said Ellen. 'I've got to stay out till at least midnight. I've come all the way from Bristol for this.'

Beatrice shrugged.

'I'm going to go to bed soon. As soon as Tyler leaves, that is. You can all let yourselves out. Just be gone by the time I get up in the morning. There are chocolates.' She waved her hand towards the kitchen area. 'And brandy and cognac and liqueurs if anyone wants anything.'

Will held up a glass, almost full of red wine. When he spoke, his voice was thick.

'I think most of us, meaning mainly me, have already had more than enough. You should probably remove this glass from my hand before I do myself any more harm.'

'I never wanted to come,' Jay said. 'I should have listened to myself.'

'I'm sorry,' said Clara.

'You said it might be healing.' He made a helpless gesture. 'I get it. The guy's been in prison for most of his life. But listening to him. I've never heard anything like it. The icy hatred of it. He hates us.'

They sat in silence again, then Kristin suddenly laughed loudly.

'You know what I've just realised.' She pointed at Ellen. 'You never said who was the best fuck.'

'Jesus Christ,' Marco said. 'Are you insane?'

'Don't you want to know?'

'Please, if you have a shred of common sense, shut the fuck up.'

Rudi moved closer to Beatrice.

'You okay?' he asked.

'I don't know,' she said. 'I don't know what I feel.' She looked around. 'He wanted to drive us apart. Maybe he's brought us closer together.'

Rudi squeezed her arm.

'I didn't really listen to what he said,' said Clara, speaking slowly. 'As soon as he started, I had the most vivid flashback to when we were last together.' She looked around at everyone. 'It was as if I was back there on that awful morning. I just heard the commotion, and I saw people crowded at the doorway, and even before anyone said anything, I knew that something awful had happened. I don't remember who it was who found the body.'

'It was me,' said Ellen.

'I thought I was the first,' said Marco.

'You might be right,' said Ellen. 'It's one of the things I've learned from talking to couples. Everyone remembers things differently. You tell yourself stories, then the stories become real. But I'm pretty sure I found him. I think I realised at once that our lives had changed forever. There would always be a before and after.'

'He was almost smiling,' said Marco. 'It was horrible.'

'I remember his eyes,' said Ali. 'I remember them staring up at me.'

'I don't remember that,' said Clara. 'I remember the way his arm was flung out, palm upward, as if he was reaching for something. Or someone.'

'I remember,' said Will, almost dreamily.

'Remember what?' said Marco.

'The eyes. Open. The way Ali described it. Lifeless, but somehow gazing at me. I'll never forget that.'

Ali moved closer to him and touched his arm. There was a look of almost ferocious intensity on her face. Will just stared forward, his eyes fixed on an invisible point as if he was reliving the scene.

'I'd never seen a dead body before,' said Beatrice. 'And I've never seen one since. I remember feeling that he'd been in the world with us just a few hours before, and now he wasn't in the world anymore.'

'I need some more of that brandy,' said Marco. 'Or whatever you brought in. Any of it. All of it.'

The bottles were opened and glasses were filled. Marco raised his glass. When he spoke, his voice sounded as if his tongue was too large for his mouth.

'I was going to say "cheers", but it doesn't seem quite the right word. And I was going to say "here's to us", but that doesn't feel right either. I think we all need something to numb the pain.' He took a gulp from his glass. 'Back in the day we were this special group.'

'Is this still part of the toast?' asked Clara.

'It was never a toast. It was like a howl of anguish.' He contemplated his half-empty glass. 'As I was saying, back at uni, I think people used to look at us and think we were special. We were like the cool kids. It's as if God looked at us and wanted to punish us for being smug and arrogant.'

'It was a tragic crime,' said Clara. 'That's all.'

'That's all?' said Marco. 'It was all cursed. All of it. Like you and Jay. We all thought you were the sweetest couple. You were going to have a sweet wedding and have sweet children. You didn't just dump Jay. You dumped the entire male sex. You dumped half of the human race.' He looked at Jay. 'Did that make it easier? Was it easier to be left because you were just basically a man?'

'No,' said Jay. 'It didn't make it easier.'

'Marco,' said Clara. 'Stop. You're doing what Tyler wants.'

'What does he want?'

'I don't know exactly, but he probably wants to turn us against each other.'

'I don't think that's what he wants,' said Jay. 'We turned against each other long ago. I think he knows.'

'Knows what?' asked Will.

'He knows who killed Leo. He knows, and he's playing with us.'

'Jay! Are you crazy?' Clara's lips were a thin line. 'He killed Leo. Do you believe all his bullshit about it being one of us? Because then he's won.'

Will turned to Ali, who was looking straight ahead at nothing, and quite still, as if carved from marble.

'I can't take this anymore,' he said. 'I need a moment.'

Rudi had been speaking to Beatrice in a murmur, but he looked round as Will left the room and they heard the sound of his footsteps on the stairs.

'Is he okay?' he said. He took his phone from his pocket. 'I'll look in on him. I need to make a call anyway.' He gave a faint smile. 'It's half past eleven, and I said I'd be home by midnight. My wife gets restive.'

He left the room and they could hear his footsteps going up the stairs. The remaining people looked at each other awkwardly.

'I'm going to start clearing up,' said Beatrice. 'I don't want my son to see the house in this state. I think people should think about going.'

She left as well.

'I need the bathroom,' said Ali. 'Then we'll go.'

32

There were only five of them sitting at the table now. Kristin leaned over to Ellen and clinked her tumbler against the one that Ellen was holding.

'You okay, hun?' she said. Ellen didn't reply. She just took a sip of her drink. 'In your job,' Kristin continued, 'you're probably used to people saying terrible things, aren't you? Isn't that the rule in therapy? You can say anything at all. I sometimes think I'd like to go and see someone. I've got issues that would be good to talk about. For example . . .' She made an exaggerated gesture in the direction of Marco. 'I've always been with older men. Much older men. It's probably to do with my dad. Don't you think?'

'I can hear what you're saying,' said Marco. 'If you're going to whisper about me to one of my old friends, you need to talk in a whisper.'

'I wanted you to hear,' said Kristin. 'So what do you think?' she said to Ellen, nudging her a little harder than she intended, making her flinch.

'I think everyone would benefit from the right therapy.'

'But what about you?' said Kristin.

'What about me?'

'I want to hug you,' Kristin said. 'You've done what you've wanted. Like you said, you explored things. That was your word, right? And you're married and you've got about a million children and you help couples sort out their problems. But how do you deal with humiliation? It's like when I was at school and I heard that people were whispering about me behind my back, and I started doing this.'

She pulled back her sleeve, revealing livid streaks on the underside of her arm. As she did so, she spilled most of her drink. But she didn't seem to notice.

Ellen looked at Kristin's scars, reached out and touched them gently with her forefinger. She looked older; her flesh seemed to sag.

'Sex is complicated,' she said. 'There's so much shame and anger and fear. I've gone through life trying not obsess too much about what other people think.'

'Wow,' said Kristin. She looked at Marco. 'Don't you think it would interesting if we went and had therapy with Ellen? We'd learn something.'

Marco stared at her for a long moment, until she flushed and looked away.

'I'm not drunk or stoned enough,' he said. 'I can still feel things. I want to stop feeling them.'

'Let's play a game,' said Jay.

'What?' Clara looked at him in astonishment. 'Have you gone mad?'

'Let's play spin the bottle.'

'Why the fuck would I want to play spin the bottle?' Marco asked. 'I'd rather just drink from the bottle.'

'Whoever it pointed at could say why it wasn't them who killed Leo.'

'We know who killed Leo. We don't need a bottle to tell us that.'

'Are you scared?'

'Jay, don't. I know what you're doing.'

'What am I doing?'

'You're going weird again.'

'Don't use that word.'

'Sorry. I didn't mean – just don't, okay?'

'Or the knife. We could use that knife the kid brought in.'

'I took it upstairs,' said Marco, standing up with difficulty, swaying, then making for the stairs. 'I'll get it.'

'Don't,' Clara said with an urgency that everyone ignored.

'It's got so dark,' Kristin said. 'We need to turn on more lights.'

'We should go,' said Clara.

'Spin the knife,' said Jay.

'I'm warning you, Jay,' said Clara. 'Stop this.'

'You're not my mother.'

'The knife's not where I left it.' Marco came back into the room. He half fell into a chair and picked up the whisky bottle. 'I have a dim memory that Beatrice took it somewhere. This will have to do.'

'Whoa,' said Kristin, as he lay the bottle in the middle of the table and gave it an energetic spin. 'Watch out. It's still half full.'

Golden liquid was spraying out, trickling over the table.

'Who's that pointing at?'

'It's pointing towards the garden.'

'Tyler's in the garden,' said Jay.

33

Slow footsteps were coming down the stairs.

The group at the table turned to see Ali. She was cradling Benjy to her chest as if he was a newborn child. Her face was bony with tiredness. She slid into a chair and looked from face to face.

'What?' she said. 'Why are you all looking like that?'

'We were talking about Tyler,' Jay said.

'Tyler,' said Ali in a dull voice. 'Yes. Where is he? I have to speak to him. I've waited too long.'

She stood up, stumbling, but still clutching Benjy.

Jay stood up and went to the sliding door, pressing his face to the glass and holding his arms out, crucifix style.

'Can you see him?' Marco asked.

'No. That doesn't mean he's not out there in the dark. Looking in at us.'

'Why do I feel scared all of a sudden?' Kristin asked.

'Scared?' Rudi came down, taking the stairs two at a time, holding his mobile in one hand and a tumbler in the other. 'Scared of what?'

'I don't know.'

'Who were you talking to just now?' Marco asked. 'I heard you talking when I went upstairs, but couldn't make out the words.'

'That was Will,' said Rudi. 'He's upset, and he's also very drunk.'

'Will?' Ali subsided once more, pressing her face into the dog's body.

'He'll be fine,' said Rudi. 'He probably won't remember anything in the morning. He'll have one hell of a hangover, but so will the rest of us.'

'I need a cigarette,' Ali said, patting her pockets frantically. 'Where are my cigarettes?'

'I can see someone.' Jay's face was still pressed against the glass.

'Tyler?'

'It's Beatrice.'

Jay stepped back as Beatrice approached the sliding door, holding glasses in her hands.

'There are bloody glasses everywhere. It's as if an army has been in the house,' she said crossly, and went over to the dishwasher. 'I thought you were all going to leave. The party's over.'

'I'm waiting for Will to appear,' said Ali. 'It seems he's very drunk. I'm going to go down the road to buy some cigarettes, then we'll leave as soon as I'm back, I promise. We've all out-stayed our welcome.' She put Benjy down on the floor and scratched him behind his ears. 'Back soon, my darling.'

'It's nearly midnight,' Clara said.

'There's always a twenty-four-hour shop or a garage.'

'I'll come with you then. You shouldn't go alone at this time of night.'

Ali shrugged. 'I'm fine. But okay, if you want to.'

'Shall I come too?' Jay asked.

'No.' Clara's expression was stern. 'You should go home, Jay, like Beatrice said. Go home and put all of this behind you.'

'I've missed my last train.'

'You can't stay here,' said Beatrice, who was no longer

bothering to be polite to her guests. She stacked more glasses into the dishwasher. 'No one can. You all need to get out. There's been enough wreckage.'

'I want to speak to Tyler first,' Jay said stubbornly. 'I think I can make him out now. He's at the bottom of the garden, near that little statue thing. Just standing there. As if he's waiting for something.'

'I don't care what he's waiting for. He needs to go. He never wants to see us again, and I don't want to see him.'

Clara and Ali went up the stairs together to the front door, while Jay stepped through the glass door onto the patio, where he stood for a moment before striding off towards the motionless shape at the end of the garden.

'Marco,' said Beatrice wearily. 'Can you go and make sure they don't have some stupid fight again?'

'Me? What do you expect me to do?'

'I don't know why you're asking Marco,' said Kristin. 'He's scared of physical violence. I'd be better than him if it came to a fight.'

'I should take the hunting knife with me,' said Marco. 'Where is it? You took it, didn't you, Beatrice?'

'I'm not going to give you a knife.'

'I'll get my coat,' said Ellen. 'And call an Uber.'

'Where are my car keys?' asked Rudi, following her. 'Where did I put them?'

'Don't tell me you're driving. You're way over the limit.'

'I'll be fine,' said Rudi. 'I just need to get away from all of this.'

34

The room had emptied. Beatrice was alone. She stood by the dishwasher and looked back at the table where they'd all been sitting.

Five hours ago, this open space with its glowing terracotta tiles and steel girders had been like a beautiful stage set: the table laid, stainless steel cutlery gleaming, the colourful plates they had bought in Portugal, wine glasses at the ready, the opulent flowers standing sentinel, and through the glass doors, the garden lushly green in the soft evening light.

It had all been trashed. Whisky and red wine puddled the surface of the table, along with crusts of bread, smears of dip and butter, screwed-up paper napkins and even the stub of a cigarette on a plate still half heaped with aubergine salad. Candles had melted down into queasy shapes that spread out from their holders. Shards of glass glinted on the floor. Outside, it was windless and dark; a few stars and the pale rind of a moon pierced the blackness. The warmth had gone from the air and it was beginning to feel cold.

Beatrice shivered in her thin silk shirt, which was missing one of its little buttons. She put her arms around herself and listened to the beating of her heart. She felt slightly sick and entirely comfortless. A few dim shapes drifted in the garden like ghosts. She could hear people moving about upstairs, but no voices. They still hadn't left. She had to make them go.

She stood for several minutes amid the ruin, unsure what came next, and then she too slowly left the room.

PART TWO

35

When Maud O'Connor arrived at Archie and Fran's flat in Leyton, it was nearly midnight. As she entered the room, she collided with a man who was leaving.

'I'm sorry,' the man said in a distracted tone. 'I'm in the middle of an emergency.'

'Is everything all right?'

'No, it's not all right.' He made a helpless gesture. 'It'll probably seem funny to you but my neighbour's just called. My cat's up on the roof again. They've tried everything. Now they're talking about calling the fire brigade. I'm the only one who can lure her in.'

'It doesn't seem funny to me,' said Maud. 'I had a cat once.'

'Did it go up on the roof?'

'No, but he used to run away.'

'He always came back, right?'

'Yes, he did,' Maud said. She omitted to mention that he always came back until the time he didn't and, ever since, she wondered whether he was alive somewhere, happy with someone else.

'Thank you,' said the man. 'That makes me feel more hopeful. My name's Ross, by the way. Goodbye.'

He left and she turned to look at the living room. It was crammed; people stood in tight groups, drinking from cans, smoking, leaning close together to talk over the music, which was loud and insistent. She was deciding what to do next, when she felt a tap on her shoulder. She looked round. It was Ross.

'I've got to go,' he said.

'Yes, you said.'

'If it wasn't for the cat, I'd have stayed and we'd have had a conversation. I'm already completely sure that at the end of it I'd have asked you if you'd like to meet again. Maybe for lunch tomorrow.'

She looked at him more closely. Was this just a line he tried on women? But there was something in his brown eyes, a kindness, which made her think he didn't.

'There is a real cat?' she asked. 'This isn't just something you say?'

'There really is a cat. In imminent danger.'

'I've had a bad week,' Maud said. 'I was planning to sleep for most of Saturday.'

'A late lunch,' he said. He thought for a moment. 'At The Lantern. It's by the canal, near Victoria Park. Two o'clock. Meanwhile.' He looked towards the outside.

'Your cat.'

'So come if you can. Or want.'

And he was gone. Maud wasn't sure what to make of what had just happened. She had been caught unawares.

She looked around for people she knew, searching for Silas, wondering if being here was a mistake. She had come on from a different party in East London, and had been in two minds about coming to this one. Archie and Fran belonged to her past. When she and Silas had split up, their friendship group had separated as well, obeying the gravitational pull of its origins. Archie and Fran had belonged to Silas, and although they kept in touch with each other, they rarely met. Maud hadn't seen them for more than two years.

Time was funny, she thought. Emotions played havoc with it, stretched and shrank and shredded it. Getting over Silas had been a slow business. People always said that relationships took work; so did ending them. Maud had spent the last two years working at her job, working at friendships, having flings and one slightly more serious affair, working at taking joy in small moments, at not minding being alone. Her father had always told her you should put your shoulder to the wheel, and that's what she had done. When it first happened, it had felt like a wound that wouldn't heal. Everything hurt, and she inched her way through the days, a step at a time. Bit by bit, it got better, until it was just a fading bruise; press it and it throbbed, but it was bearable. Now it was more like a scar: a memory of pain. But it took effort and willpower, and every so often, she relaxed and memories caught her off guard.

He had left her, torn up their shared life, and by the time he regretted what he had done, it was too late. Several times he had turned up at her door to ask if they couldn't try again, once with flowers and once in tears, and sometimes Maud allowed herself to imagine what that would be like. But she knew there was no going back. She had once loved him fiercely and joyfully; now he was like an intimate stranger. She both knew him better than she knew almost anyone, and yet she didn't know him at all.

Maud had no idea if he was in a relationship now. Sometimes she met shared friends, but she never asked about him. Most of her friends had partners or were married. Several had children, or were pregnant, or talking about getting pregnant. She and Silas had been trying for a child when he had panicked and ended things. Was that why she still sometimes felt a terrible pang of sadness? It wasn't him she missed, but she had a ghost life, where she was in their beloved flat in East London, and she had a baby.

But he was an arsehole, she told herself. A coward.

She pushed her way through the people in the living room and went into the kitchen, where she found Archie deep in conversation with a man wearing a kaftan. Archie looked up, saw her, did a double take, then threw his arms around her, kissing her exuberantly and telling her that he'd missed her, that she looked terrific.

'You'd better hide that,' Archie said to the man in the kaftan who was rolling a thin spliff, and he was half joking, half serious.

Maud winced. Her job had often got in the way of her relationships, especially with Silas and his friends. The fact that she was with the Metropolitan Police made her into the enemy, or at least into someone to be wary of. She wasn't just Maud, she was Detective Inspector Maud O'Connor.

She picked up a bottle of sparkling water from the table, unscrewed the top and took a swig, wiping her mouth with the back of her hand. She stepped out into the long, narrow garden, which was also full of people. In the distance, fireworks soared up into the clear sky and scattered their fountains of colour.

She caught fragments of conversation – the planet is fucking dying . . . Oh, my God, that's so creepy . . . I just want to try it once . . . The babysitter said midnight . . .

A woman she used to know looked at her, through her, no flicker of recognition on her face. Maud felt like a spectre in her old life, invisible and forgotten. She saw a familiar couple standing at the end of the threadbare strip of grass and made her way towards them. As she drew closer, she noticed the man was wearing a sling; she could see the bunched-up shape of a small baby inside. They looked round, and for a moment their faces wore an identical expression of blankness. Then the woman's face cleared.

'Maud!'

They kissed each other on one cheek, then the other.

'Good to see you, Maud,' said the man. Paul, she thought his name was. 'It's been ages.'

'It has,' said Maud, and looked at the downy crown of the baby's head. 'Who's this little beauty, then?'

'Corin,' they said at the same time, smiling the same proud smile.

'Hello, Corin,' said Maud. 'I had no idea. How old?'

'Three months and a week,' said the woman.

'How very lovely,' said Maud warmly.

For one awful moment, she thought she might cry. She raised her bottle to the couple.

'Congratulations.'

Someone touched her on the shoulder, and she knew who it was even before she turned to see him.

'Hello, Silas.'

Dark hair, blue eyes. He had been there for most of her twenties, her early thirties, her hoped-for future. Now here he was smiling at her – an intimate stranger.

'How are you?'

She smiled back.

'I'm well,' she said.

'You look well. I like your hair.'

'It's the same as it always was.'

'Really? Do you want a drink?'

'I'm just on water this evening,' she said, and saw the fractional narrowing of Silas's eyes as he remembered her job, remembered all the times that her job had been an issue for them.

'Are you on duty?'

'On call.'

'So you might be rushing off. It feels like the old days.'

It felt like the old days to Maud as well, with Silas making snide little comments about her work.

'It's good to see you, Maud. I've been wanting to speak to you.'

Maud's phone rang in her pocket. They both heard it. Maud shrugged.

'I need to get this,' she said. 'Sorry.'

She listened to the voice on the other end, her expression not altering. Then she ended the call and turned back to Silas.

'Whatever you were wanting to speak to me about will have to wait.'

'Wait a moment. It's important. I've missed you. Can I come and see you?'

'I have to go.'

'Tomorrow. Can we meet tomorrow?'

She thought of Ross and her lunch invitation.

'I'm probably busy tomorrow,' she said.

'Maud—'

'Stop,' she said.

She walked quickly back up the garden, her hand raised in a gesture of farewell.

36

The police vehicle was outside the house, blue lights flashing. Some of the party guests were out on the pavement smoking and they stared at it, and stared at Maud as she walked towards it. A young woman asked her if something had happened.

'Not here,' said Maud.

A uniformed driver was standing by the car. He looked young. He had a round face, and as if to make up for the high dome of his forehead, he had a fluffy ginger beard. He was chewing gum in a vigorous, practised manner.

'Constable Paul Hale,' he said. Then his eyes narrowed. 'You know we're going to a crime scene? Do you want to change into something more practical?'

Maud glanced down at her short-sleeved yellow shirt and baggy cropped trousers, then shrugged.

'We'd better go straight there.'

Sometimes detectives sat in the passenger seat. It showed that you were one of the lads. But Maud got into the back. She needed to clear her head. She didn't want to make conversation.

'Where are we going?' she asked, as the car moved off.

'Tufnell Park, ma'am. St Matthew's Avenue. Number 44.'

Forty minutes away, she thought.

'You do this a lot?' asked the officer.

'What do you mean? Investigate crimes?'

'No, I mean, get called in the middle of the night.'

'I'm on call a lot. This is the first time I've been called out. Usually it can wait till morning.'

'Must be something important.'

'I hope not,' said Maud.

'If you're in luck, I can take you back to your party.'

Maud was trying to think of a way of politely ending the conversation when her phone rang. She looked at the caller ID and it was who she was expecting: Weller. Her boss.

'Hello, sir.'

'I just looked at the rota and saw your name.'

He made it sound like it was a bad thing.

'I'm on my way there now.'

'What have you been told?'

'I was just told it was a murder, and that a car was being sent for me. To be honest, I was a bit surprised.'

'And why was that?'

'Can't the guys on duty deal with it?'

'Do you want out, Maud? Have you been drinking this evening?'

Maud looked at the bristly back of Constable Hale's head, aware that he was listening to everything she said.

'I was just surprised. I thought you were only called on if something really big had happened.'

'Have you heard of Sebastian Harris?'

Maud considered.

'The politician?'

'The cabinet minister. He's a cabinet minister, and he's a close friend of the PM, and the murder took place in his house.'

'Did he do it?'

'Is that a joke?'

'It was a question.'

'He wasn't on the premises. He's on an official visit. But

that's not the point. A murder has been committed in his house, and the searchlight is well and truly on us. As you well know, Maud, our relations with the government are not of the best. They seem to think that we don't investigate crimes anymore, and when we do, we don't solve them.'

'I'll do my best to solve it.'

'I'll be frank,' said Weller. 'I'm a bit worried about you doing your best. If you were on *Mastermind*, your special subject would be rubbing people up the wrong way. I've got to admit that when I saw your name coming up, I considered going in myself.'

Maud was tempted to make various replies to this, but she looked once more at the back of the driver's head and resisted all of them.

'If you want to take over, I'll step aside,' she said.

There was a pause. Was he really considering it?

'There's not going to be any stepping aside. I just want you to be aware that everybody's going to be watching this one: the government, the press. This isn't the time for you to make some kind of point.'

'I'm just going to do my job,' she said.

There was what sounded like a snort at the other end of the line.

'Let's see how you do it. I'll send Mark over to join you.'

'No, thank you,' said Maud firmly. Mark Forrester was a bony-faced young man with pale red hair. He was weak and bombastic; eager to please and anxious to be one of the lads. Maud had worked with him several times before, and she had no intention of doing so again.

'What d'you mean, no?'

'Sorry, sir. I've actually already asked someone.'

'Who?'

Maud bit her lip.

'Carrie Kessler, sir.'

'You have, have you? That was quick.' He sounded dissatisfied. 'You think Carrie's up to it?'

'Yes,' said Maud. 'Sir.'

'And she's available? I thought she was on another case.'

'That's finished. And she's good. We work well together. She was invaluable on the Charlotte Salter case.'

'That's not much of a recommendation. I don't know, Maud.' Maud waited. 'All right,' he said eventually. 'Just make sure she stays on side.'

'Can you tell me anything about the case?'

'I was just getting to that. That's the other problem. All I know is that there was some kind of a party, or gathering of friends, going on. And here's the thing: one of the guests was a recently paroled murderer – Tyler Green. He was only let out a few weeks ago. As soon as the press hears about that, all hell's going to break loose. Also, I'm pretty bloody sure that while we're talking, someone is waking up the Home Secretary, and I can tell you he's not going to be happy about it. He's not going to be happy about it at all.'

'So. Someone has been killed at the home of a cabinet minister, who wasn't present. And one of the guests was a convicted murderer, out on licence.'

'That's about it.'

'Who's the victim?'

'I've told you all I know. You think you can handle it?'

'Yes. Sir.'

'You'll tread carefully?'

'I'll be professional.'

'Why does that make me feel worried?' he said. 'I'm trusting you, Maud. There's a lot riding on this.'

37

Avoiding the eyes of the constable in the mirror, Maud called Carrie Kessler's number. The phone rang and rang, and just when Maud was thinking she should hang up, it was answered with a groan.

'Carrie? It's Maud.'

'Huh? Maud? What?'

'Sorry if I woke you.'

'If? *If*? I went to bed at half past nine, and I was just in the middle of a nice dream about frogs. I think it was frogs. What time is it?'

'Nearly one.'

There was another groan.

'In about four hours, Sadie will wake up.'

'Have you drunk anything this evening?'

'What?'

'I said—'

'I know what you said. If you want to know, at about seven o'clock I drank half a glass of red wine with my supper of de-frosted lasagne. What's going on?'

'There's been a murder. I want you to assist. Can you come?'

'Of course I can't come. It's the middle of the night. I've a two-year-old daughter asleep a few feet away.'

'Is there nobody you could ask to look after her?'

'What? At one in the morning?'

'I think you'd be particularly interested by this case,' said Maud. 'If there's any way of making it possible, I'd really like to have you with me on it.'

Constable Hale put two more tabs of chewing gum into his mouth and chomped loudly. Maud met his eyes in the mirror. She turned away.

'Also,' she said, 'I've already told Weller you've agreed to assist.'

'You have, have you?' said Carrie. 'At whatever time this is in the morning. I mean, honestly.'

Maud waited.

'I suppose I could ask my mother. She lives about ten minutes away.'

'That would be fantastic.'

'She'll be even more pissed off than I am, but I'll try her. I'll call you back in a minute.'

Maud looked out of the window at the buildings that flowed past. Her mobile rang.

'She's on her way in an Uber and in a bad mood,' said Carrie. 'I'm not going to spend my whole weekend working, though. I'm taking Sadie to the aquarium tomorrow afternoon. By which I mean this afternoon.'

'Thanks, Carrie. I owe you.'

'You can come and babysit sometime.'

Maud gave her the address and ended the call. In the mirror, Hale raised his eyebrows slightly, but said nothing.

38

She saw the flashing lights as soon as they turned into St Matthew's Avenue. There were two ambulances and at least three police cars. They were parked askew, blocking the whole road. Behind them, people were beginning to gather, including, Maud saw, ones with cameras. Two female paramedics were leaning against one of the ambulances. They looked round as Maud approached them.

'Is there anyone injured?'

'No,' said one of the women. 'Just dead.'

Maud walked up the steps to the front door, which was open. She almost collided with a uniformed officer coming out.

'Who's in charge?' she asked.

'Who wants to know?' he asked.

She held up her warrant card. The officer flushed.

'DS Hawkins is upstairs,' he said. 'It's a bit crowded.'

'Has anyone left?'

'What do you mean?'

'I am told there's been some kind of party or gathering here. Have any of the guests left?'

He gave a helpless shrug.

'I don't know. I think everyone's in there.' He gestured towards a closed door. 'You could ask upstairs.'

Control the crime scene, Maud said to herself. It's lesson number one. But she didn't say anything out loud. She could hear a hubbub on the other side of the door, and she opened it a crack to look into a large room full of people, some of them standing, others sitting, all of them looking like survivors after a bomb has gone off. Their expressions were glazed, bleary with shock. A man in a grubby T-shirt with a mouth that hung crookedly, as if the hinge of his jaw had come loose, gawped at her unseeingly.

She turned away.

'Is DS Hawkins here?'

A man on the stairs lifted a hand. Grey suit, close-cropped dark hair.

'Can I help you?'

She introduced herself.

'Craig Weller sent me,' she said.

'Is there a problem?' Hawkins asked with a frown.

'No problem,' said Maud.

Maud stepped further into the hall. She didn't want the guests to see her before she was ready to talk to them.

'We need to separate them,' she said.

'Are you taking over?' said Hawkins. 'Is that what this is about?'

'I'm in charge of the inquiry, that's all.'

'Why? What's up? Aren't I good enough?'

Maud looked around. Hawkins had spoken loudly and rudely. She replied with icy politeness.

'If you have a problem with this, you can take it up with Weller. But in the meantime, so far as is possible, please can you keep the witnesses apart from each other. They should not be conferring. Now, can you take me to the body?'

'Which do you want me to do first?' said Hawkins.

Maud stared at him for a moment, then gestured to a young female officer by the front door to come over.

'What's your name? I don't think we've met.'

'Constable Sarah Fortune, ma'am.'

'Right, Sarah. I'm DI Maud O'Connor, and I'm in charge of the investigation. I'm making you responsible for keeping all the guests apart. Please take their names and details, check if anyone has left or arrived. Got that?'

'Yes, ma'am.'

'Also, if it hasn't already been done, grab all their mobile phones. I want to have a list of all calls that have been received and made between the hours of six and now, and also co-ordinates – we need to know who, if anyone, left the house, and where they went. Got that?'

The young woman looked anxious.

'You can delegate,' said Maud. She pointed at a young officer, who was staring at his phone. 'Get him to do it. Send me the information when you're done. Also, please ask one of your colleagues to organise blood tests for drug and alcohol consumption asap.'

She turned back to Hawkins.

'Now you only have one thing to do. Shall we do it?'

She saw Hawkins's jaw flexing, but he didn't say anything. She followed him up two flights of stairs to the second floor. On the landing, Maud could see the activity inside the room, the white overalls, the murmur of voices.

'It's a bit of a mess in there,' said Hawkins.

He was taller than her, and bulkier, and he was standing too close, almost pushing against her.

'What kind of a mess?'

'Blood. Knife in the neck. Spoilt the lawyer's lovely house.'

A fold-up table had been set up outside the door, piled with equipment and supplies. The two detectives ripped open cellophane bags. They pulled the plastic booties over their shoes and pulled on the surgical gloves with a snap. Maud stepped forward, but Hawkins put a hand up to stop her.

'You should prepare yourself,' Hawkins said. 'It's the smell that gets you.'

Maud had been at many crime scenes. She had seen people who had fallen from high buildings, a man who had been pushed under a train, a man who had been targeted by a gang wielding machetes. She waved Hawkins aside and stepped into the room.

A body lay spreadeagled on the floor in a pool of sticky blood that was almost black.

'Do you have the name of the victim?'

'The name's Garvey,' said Hawkins. 'William Garvey.'

39

The man in white overalls who was bending over the body moved aside, and Maud crouched down beside it. Beside him. Will Garvey was lying on his front, his right arm reaching above him; the left was curled by his side. He had long, thick fingers, she saw, and a gold band on his wedding finger, a watch on his wrist that told the right time: ten minutes past one. His legs, in old jeans, were stretched out, ending in trainers. His face was turned sideways, one cheek resting in the pool of blood, his hair slick with it. His eyes were open, or the one eye she could see was. His neck was open too, like a gaping second mouth. On the floor a few feet from his body was a long-bladed knife. His artery must have been severed, pumping out gouts of blood. So much blood, she thought, as her eyes travelled up and down Will Garvey's body, noting the stubble on his cheek, the way his hair rested on the collar of his checked cotton shirt.

'He must have died almost immediately,' she said out loud, though really she was talking to herself.

'It's the way they do it in prison,' said Hawkins. 'One stroke of the knife and they bleed out, no noise, it's over almost at once. I don't know why Weller felt the need to send you here. We've already arrested him. He's back in prison, where he belongs. He should never have been let out in the first place.'

'Arrested him on what grounds?'

'For violating the conditions of his licence for a starter. But it's pretty clear we've got our man.' He looked at her, mouth quirking at her inappropriate clothes. 'You should just go back to wherever you came from when Weller called.'

'Is there evidence that points to Tyler Green?'

'We've not been here much longer than you. It's just bleeding obvious.'

Maud frowned, but didn't answer. She was looking round the room, which was small and square, the window looking out onto the garden. It seemed like a second spare room that also served as a storage space. There was a sofa bed pushed against one wall and a rack of dresses against the other. Several had been dislodged from their hangers and were lying in a bright heap near the body, stained with blood. On the shelves were piles of papers, as well as a collection of paperback novels.

The room was thick with the familiar sickly-sweet smell, but also something else that was sour and also familiar. She saw there was a thick splatter of vomit beside the sofa bed; some of it had gone all over the nice oversized cushions in their ticking stripe fabric, and some into a terracotta pot that held a plant with a twisted stem and pale green leaves.

She stood up. There was a framed poster on the wall of a woman in a bath tub.

'Any idea of time of death?' she asked the man in white overalls who was standing at the door.

'It wouldn't have been long ago. The body's still warm; the blood isn't yet fully congealed. He can't have died much more than an hour or so ago.'

'Thank you. Who found the body?'

'One of the women found him.' Hawkins was surly with her, resentful. 'Name of Ellen Sweeney.'

'And she's downstairs?'

'They all are, including the wife. Widow, I should say. There are eight of them. Some kind of reunion, I gather.'

'Had anyone else been in here?'

'Dunno. It was complete chaos when we arrived. Some of them were hysterical.'

And it had still been chaos when Maud had arrived, she reflected.

'Right,' she said to the men and women in the room. 'I'll let you guys get on with it.'

As if on cue, a white light flooded the room. Maud looked back at the spotlit body of William Garvey in its dark lake of blood, at his visible eye staring at her, and at the thin blade of the knife shining as if it was the source of the unforgiving light.

40

Maud peeled off her gloves and removed the over-shoes, then went back down the stairs. As she reached the ground floor, the front door opened and a woman burst in, as if she was crossing the finishing line of a race. In spite of the horror of what she had just seen, Maud couldn't help smiling.

'Carrie,' she said.

Carrie Kessler was small and skinny, with a triangular face and a sharp chin. Her dark hair looked as if an electric shock had crackled through it, making it stand crazily on end, and this gave her a permanent air of astonishment and urgency, but Maud knew she was smart, brave, drily humorous, stubborn, honest and loyal. And she held Maud to account, wasn't afraid to speak her mind.

Two years ago, they had worked together on a case that involved the disappearance of a woman called Charlotte Salter, missing for decades, and a bungled police investigation. It had been an intense and bruising experience, all the more so because in the middle of it, Silas had ended their relationship, running scared at the idea of starting a family. Carrie had been hugely pregnant then, and the day after the investigation ended, she had gone into labour, swearing like a trooper as she rolled into hospital accompanied by Maud and two other women friends. Now she was the single mother of Sadie, who was small and fierce like her mother.

'I got here as soon as I could.'

'Thank you. I've not long arrived myself, so I can't tell you much. A man called William Garvey was murdered about an hour ago. His throat was cut. He's upstairs on the second floor. There was a gathering in this house; Hawkins called it a reunion. One of the men present was a convicted murderer who's recently been released on licence. His name is Tyler Green. He's been arrested for breaking the terms of his licence, though I'm not sure what the grounds are for this, and is now back in prison. Obviously he must be a suspect, but so must everyone else who was here at the time. We're keeping an open mind, right?'

Carrie grinned.

'You mean, other people aren't?'

'Something like that.'

Carrie nodded. She took a notebook out of her backpack. She was wearing jeans and her shirt had a stain on the collar.

'You should know,' continued Maud drily, 'that we're in the home of a KC called Beatrice Macmillan.'

'Nice house.' Carrie looked around. 'I could fit my entire flat into this hallway.'

'It belongs to Sebastian Harris.'

'You mean, *that* Sebastian Harris? The one with the jaw?'

'That's him. The minister in charge of transport. Close to the PM, I'm told. So they want us to clear this up and keep media speculation and controversy to a minimum.'

'Bit late for that,' said Carrie. 'Have you seen the circus gathering outside?'

'I know. It's going to be a frenzy. But there'll be a lot of pressure on us to get a quick result. I was told – how was it put to me? Not to rub people up the wrong way.'

'You know me – the soul of diplomacy.'

Maud smiled at her.

'I need you because I know you won't be pushed around.' They moved aside as an officer came down the stairs holding an evidence box. 'As far as I understand it, all of the guests who were present are in the living room, including the wife of the victim. They'll be in shock, but it's important to talk to each of them as soon as we can. We need to start building a picture of what happened while it's still fresh in their minds. We can get full statements later.'

Heavy footsteps came down the stairs and Hawkins presented himself. He looked from Maud to Carrie, and then back.

'Is your driver still outside?'

'Why?'

'I assume you'll be wanting to interview the killer, of course.'

Carrie raised her eyebrows.

'Which killer?'

Hawkins looked down at her; she was tiny next to him.

'The man we've got banged up in a prison cell. That fucking parole board . . .'

'I'll interview Tyler Green,' said Maud. 'Because I'm going to interview all the people who were present when William Garvey was murdered. But we begin here, in this house, where it happened. We do this properly. A clean, orderly investigation.'

Hawkins's face darkened. He muttered something.

'I don't think I heard that,' said Maud. 'Please make sure that the garden is gone over, especially around the exit to the street. We need to find out if anybody could have got in and out of the house from the back.'

'Yeah, yeah,' he said, as if it was all too obvious. 'But we know who did this, don't we?'

'That's the trouble with people like him,' said Carrie as they walked towards the living room. 'Now I want it not to be Tyler Green, just to wipe that smile off his face.'

41

They all turned towards Maud and Carrie as they entered the living room. The female officer had done her job, and everyone sat separately, while one officer stood by the door, another by the French windows that led out onto the decking.

Maud stopped in the centre of the room, looking from face to face, her eyes taking in the grandeur of the room, the framed photos of a younger Sebastian Harris and his wife and son, the large sofa and the armchairs, the fireplace with logs stacked beside it, the bookshelf lined with hardbacks, the flowers in tall vases, the richly coloured rugs and the walls painted in a muted yellow, the mirror on the wall that reflected the calm space back to itself. She had been in grand houses before. This one felt almost impersonal, as if the owners had brought in an interior designer and given them free range.

'I'm Detective Inspector Maud O'Connor. This is Detective Sergeant Carrie Kessler. I'm leading the investigation into the murder of your friend, William Garvey. I know you'll all be feeling shocked and distressed, but I'd be very grateful for your co-operation. Perhaps you can each tell me who you are, and what your relationship is to the deceased.'

As she turned towards them, they gave her their names. Beatrice Macmillan, the owner of the house, was crouched over in a chair she had pulled up to the window, her arms wrapped round her body. Jay Murphy had curled himself into one end of the long sofa, an angled heap of bones, his head in his hands, and Maud could barely make out his words. Clara Keane, the one person who looked calm, had retreated to the piano room, where she sat on the stool as if about to play for everyone. Marco Burney – the skinny man with a buzz cut in old jeans and a stained T-shirt she had noticed earlier staring out at her – was now huddled on the floor near the hearth, his arms round his knees, rocking to and fro. Rudi Scott, in stained linen trousers and silver hair in peaks, stood by the French windows, hands thrust deep in his pockets. The widow, Ali Marais, a thin woman in a crimson dress, was the only one who was moving. Even as she gave her name, she continued walking up and down the long room with small jerky steps, holding her old raggedy dog pressed tight against her chest. Her lips were bloodless and her face chalky.

Maud turned to Hawkins.

'Where are the others? You said there were eight witnesses, and also that an Ellen Sweeney had found the body.'

'I don't know about that,' Hawkins said, as if it had nothing to do with him.

'Can you tell me where they are?' Maud asked Beatrice.

'They took Tyler away,' Beatrice answered in a dreary voice. 'That's all I know.'

'Kristin's gone,' said Marco, half snorting with laughter. 'Done a runner.'

'To where?'

'Who cares? Good riddance.'

Maud turned to Hawkins.

'Find her and bring her back.'

'I think—'

'We can discuss any concerns once she's back. And where's Ellen Sweeney? She discovered the body, right?'

'I think she's doing a bit of clearing up,' said Clara. 'She wanted to be useful.'

Maud could now hear the sound of someone moving around downstairs, crockery chinking together.

'Oh, for God's sake,' said Carrie.

She brushed past Hawkins on her way to the stairs.

'Everything in this house is evidence until I tell you otherwise,' said Maud.

She stood where all the people in the room could see her. She could hear Carrie speaking briskly to Ellen downstairs.

'I'm going to tell you what happens next. I and my colleague ...' She nodded towards Carrie, who reappeared in the room, Ellen Sweeney – a woman with greying, badly plaited hair in a pleated, sky-blue skirt that looked like it had been fished out of a drawer of clothes belonging to the Fifties – dishevelled and shamefaced behind her. '. . . will collect initial statements for you, so we can start to make sense of the events that took place here. You'll all be interviewed more fully later.'

'I have to go home!' Jay had struggled into a sitting position. His whole body seemed to be trembling. Maud saw Clara rise and take a few steps towards him, but then stop herself. 'I need to get out of here.'

'Everybody in this room is a material witness. We need to take preliminary statements from you, and then we'll interview you properly to establish what happened. I'm asking you to remain until that happens – particularly those of you who live outside London.'

'You don't understand,' he said. 'I can't be here.'

'I'm sorry,' said Maud.

Beside her, Ali laid Benjy down, then pulled out a packet of cigarettes, her fingers fumbling to extract one, then giving a small groan as several fell to the floor. She bent down to retrieve them.

'Not in here,' said Beatrice.

'Oh, my dear,' said Ellen briskly. 'Of course she can smoke, Beatrice. It's no time for silly rules. Her husband has just been murdered.'

'Sebastian hates the smell of smoke.'

Marco started choking with sudden laughter.

Maud looked round the room. The witnesses, all apparently guests at Beatrice Macmillan's gathering, appeared to have stepped from different worlds. A few looked wealthy, like their host, or Rudi Scott; others poor, like the twitching, starved man on the sofa.

'Which of you was the last person to see Will Garvey alive?' she asked.

There was a silence, then Clara spoke.

'That was you, Rudi, wasn't it?'

Rudi looked startled.

'Me? I don't think so.'

'Yes. Don't you remember? You went upstairs. You said you were going to call your wife about being delayed. A bit later, we heard voices from upstairs, and then you came down and said you'd been talking to Will, who was rather drunk and distressed.'

'Didn't anyone see him after that?' asked Rudi, his face grey. 'I'm sure they did.'

'I don't think so,' Ellen said.

'What time was that?' Maud asked.

'Shortly before midnight,' said Clara. 'Maybe twenty or a quarter to. I remember, because Ali said she was going to get cigarettes. I offered to go with her, because it was nearly midnight and I didn't think she should go alone.'

'That's right,' said Ellen. 'I remember.'

'Is that your memory, Mr Scott?'

'What?'

'Can you confirm that you saw Will Garvey at about a quarter to twelve?'

'I don't know the time.'

'But do you agree that you spoke to him and that he was drunk?'

'Yes. Yes, that's right.'

'Where was he?'

'Where?'

'Yes.'

'Upstairs.' Maud waited. 'By the bathroom,' Rudi added.

'Thank you. And nobody saw him after that?'

They looked at each other, shook their heads.

'Good,' said Maud. She looked over at Rudi. 'We'll go over the details of this soon. Bear with me. Mrs Sweeney, I understand you found the body?'

'I did.' Ellen smiled, and then seemed to realise that was inappropriate. 'It was very shocking. I've already given a description to the other officer.'

'I will want to hear it from you myself, but that can wait. Ms Macmillan, can I perhaps start with you.'

'Me?'

'Yes. As the owner of the house. It won't take long.'

Beatrice stood up. She pushed her hair back behind her ears, put her hand to her throat to find the gold necklace there, twisting it so that its clasp was invisible. She pulled her shirt straight, noticing the missing button.

'Of course,' she said. 'Where do you want us to go?'

'Do you have a study?'

'Yes. I'll show you.'

42

When the door clanged shut and the key turned in the lock, it seemed to Tyler that time was on a loop. He had returned to the world he had spent so much of his life in. It was beginning all over again. Escape had been an idle dream. This is where he would always return to: this airless room, this smell of human sweat and piss and shit, this creep of minutes, and this body that would grow old and would die. Except now he knew what he would have to endure, and he couldn't. Not again. Not one week, not even one day.

He heard the prison officer walking away and pressed his face to the door.

'I need my bloods tested,' he called out. 'I can prove I haven't broken the conditions of my licence.'

The footsteps grew more distant.

'Now,' he shouted, and his voice cracked with the futility of it. 'Tell the governor. I know my rights.'

There was a gurgle of laughter. At first Tyler thought it came from the corridor, then he realised it was behind him, in the dark. He wasn't alone.

'Who's there?'

A shape moved in the bottom bunk.

The shape laughed again.

'I wasn't expecting a cellmate.'

Tyler didn't reply. For a moment he thought he would split

apart with the emotions inside him. How was it possible to feel so shockingly defeated and still be able to stand, breathe, speak words that had meaning?

'What's your name?' the man asked in the darkness.

Tyler didn't reply. He shuffled towards the bed. His shoes flapped because they had taken away the laces; his trousers were loose because they had removed his belt. He climbed into the top bunk. Through the thin curtains at the one small window he could make out the shape of the moon. He had stood under that moon, he had felt the soft air of the evening.

'Friendly,' said the man. He tutted.

Tyler lay rigid as a plank, his arms straight. Under their closed lids, his eyes throbbed. His cheek throbbed where the police officer had hit him. His heart pounded like it was trying to get out of his chest.

Underneath him, he heard the man shift about in his bed. The springs creaked. Soon, the man's breaths became ragged. Tyler heard the familiar, rhythmic sound, then a groan of satisfaction.

'That's better,' said the man.

Tyler waited. The breathing beneath him softened and became even. There was a small, stertorous snore.

After a few minutes, he opened his eyes once more. The moon had gone from the window, which was now just a dark grey blank in a darker room. Poor Will, he thought, remembering the heavy body stretched out on the floor in the pool of blood. Will who had come to see him in prison, when everyone else kept away. Will who had married Ali. He needed to concentrate, try to work out why this was happening again, but his mind was slow and he was tired, so tired.

The events of the evening returned to him in all their garish colour and confusion, like a fever dream. Middle-aged faces overlaying young faces; friends who had turned into strangers. The woman he had loved in the way only the young can love, with such innocence and ardour, who had become brittle and angry. The way they had looked at him, with ugly curiosity and excited pity, and fear.

43

The study was on the first floor, next to the master bedroom. It had a long wooden desk, an office chair and a softer chair. There was a tall filing cabinet in the corner. One wall was lined with books, most of which were legal volumes, while framed certificates hung on the others, among formal family photographs. A richly patterned rug lay on the floor. Maud and Beatrice took a seat, while Carrie stood at the door with her pen poised above her notebook.

The window looked out onto the street. Beatrice gave a stifled moan when she saw the scene out there: the ambulances and police cars, blue lights still flashing, the thickening crowds pressing against the cordons, the TV van parked down the street. Cameras were pointing at the house.

Carrie pulled down the blinds.

'My husband,' said Beatrice. 'You know who he is?'

'I do,' said Maud.

'Why is that relevant?' Carrie asked.

Beatrice pressed her fingers to her temples.

'He's a public figure. This nightmare will be very—' She stopped, passed her hand in front of her face, touching her skin softly with the tips of her fingers. 'Very—' She tried again, searching for the appropriate word. 'I'm sure you understand.'

'I understand that your friend has been killed,' said Carrie.

'We know you want to help us,' said Maud.

Beatrice's face flushed. Maud saw her gather herself.

'Obviously.'

'Can we go back a bit, so that I have some context. You and eight friends were in the house this evening when Mr Garvey was killed.'

'I wouldn't exactly call them friends,' said Beatrice.

'If they weren't friends, what were they doing here?'

'It was a – a reunion of sorts.'

'So you used to be friends, is that it?'

'Yes.'

'And was this reunion to mark Mr Green's release from prison?'

'I suppose so.'

'Perhaps you could tell me in your own words?'

Beatrice bit her lower lip, nodded.

'When we were at university, we were friends,' she said. 'Close friends, you might say,' she added with a reluctance that Maud found interesting. 'But we lost touch with each other. Most of us haven't seen each other since—' She stopped.

'Since?'

'Since Tyler killed our friend Leo Bauer. It was very shocking.'

'I'm sure,' Maud said neutrally.

'I saw Ali and Will occasionally, no one else. I know Jay and Clara kept in touch. They used to be a couple, but now ...' She made a tired gesture, batting away irrelevant information. 'That's all, I think.'

'But you kept in touch with Tyler Green?'

'No. Only Will saw him in prison. But not for ages.'

'So why this reunion? What was it for?'

'Oh, God, I don't know. Tyler asked Will to organise it, and Will asked me because, well, there's enough room. And everyone came, for their own particular reasons, which I hadn't expected. It was a horrible evening; it felt wrong from the start, a sense of gathering dread. I should have told them all to leave.'

'Did Mr Green ask for these particular guests?'

'Yes.'

'Why?'

'Why?' Beatrice hesitated, stared down at her smooth hands with their manicured nails. 'Because we were the people present the weekend he killed Leo,' she said. For a moment, she lost her reticence, leaning towards Maud to speak. 'We were staying in a house Leo's aunt owned, in Yorkshire. It was after most of us had done our finals, a kind of celebration and farewell. Quite intense,' she said, and for a moment, Maud saw her eyes go cloudy with memory. 'Then Leo died and it was the end of everything. You need to understand, it was like being hit by lightning. One of our friends was murdered, one of our friends was convicted of murder, and we were all there when it happened. For some of us, even seeing each other was a reminder.'

'Hang on,' said Maud, startled. 'You were all there when it happened?'

'That's right.'

'Were other people there too?'

'Just us.'

'So,' said Maud slowly, 'Tyler Green comes out of prison after twenty-nine years and arranges a meeting between him and all the people who were there when Leo Bauer was killed. Why?'

'I don't exactly know. He said it was to say goodbye.'

There was a long pause, then Beatrice spoke again.

'The others will tell you, so I might as well. He said he hadn't killed Leo. That one of us had.'

44

Maud waited a few beats before she continued her questions.

'Ms Macmillan, Mr Scott apparently saw the deceased at about a quarter to twelve, upstairs by the bathroom. He was heard speaking to him. Does that sound right to you?'

Beatrice rubbed her face.

'Rudi?'

'Yes.'

Beatrice frowned.

'I think that sounds right. I don't really remember.'

'And what time was the body discovered?'

'Time? I don't know. I'm not sure. People were about to leave.'

'Can you pin it down at all?'

'I think it was around midnight,' she said slowly. 'I think it must have been. It was just after Ali and Clara came back from buying cigarettes. Ellen went up to find him. Because I wanted everyone to go. I told them to go.'

'You'd had enough of the party.'

'It was terrible.'

'All right.' Maud could hear Carrie's pen on the notepad. 'So you're saying around midnight?'

'Yes. Though I can't be sure.'

'Thank you. Can you tell me when you last saw Will Garvey alive?'

There was a long pause.

'No,' said Beatrice. 'I don't know. He was there when Tyler told us he never wanted to see any of us again. We all were. But after that – I'm sorry. I don't know. People just . . . it's a big house. I wasn't . . . I don't know.'

'And what time was that?'

'I'm not sure. I don't think I can tell you with any accuracy. I wasn't looking at the time.' Maud waited, but Beatrice didn't add anything, just looked down at her hands. Eventually Carrie spoke.

'So you're saying that you can't remember when you last saw Will Garvey alive, and that Ellen Sweeney found his body sometime around midnight?'

'I think so.' Beatrice's lip quivered.

'Did Mrs Sweeney go up there alone?'

'The first time. She went up. She came running down to say that Will was dead. Then most of the others went back up with her.'

'Who?'

Beatrice took her time in answering.

'I stayed downstairs with Ali, Marco and Rudi. So Clara went,' she said. 'Kristin. Jay, I think, God knows why; he's not exactly resilient. And Tyler. Ellen said he'd know what to do. I don't know why she'd think that.'

'Did she think Will Garvey might still be alive?'

'I don't know. You'll have to ask her. I called the emergency services. That'll give you an exact time.' Suddenly her head jerked up. 'What time is it now?' she asked urgently.

'About ten minutes to two,' said Maud.

'Finn. Dear God. What if Finn comes home?' She stood up with a screech of her chair. 'I need to call him.'

'Finn?'

'My son. If he comes back now ...' She gestured wildly towards the window.

'Are you expecting him?'

'I don't know. I mean, maybe. He could come back any time. And if he arrives and finds this. He mustn't. My phone. I need my phone.'

Maud gestured to the landline phone on the desk.

'You can use this.'

'Yes! Of course. I didn't think.'

She leaned across the desk and picked it up, started pressing the buttons with clumsy fingers.

'I can't remember his number,' she said. 'Why can't I remember? Hang on.'

She pressed her hand to the side of her face, her lips moving silently, then started pressing the buttons again. Maud watched her: Beatrice seemed a mixture of control and panic.

'He's not picking up,' she said. Then: 'Finn, it's me. Call me as soon as you get this. You can't come home. The police are here. There's been a – an accident. I'll tell you. Just don't come at the moment. It'll be all right though. I promise. Just call.'

She put the phone down.

'What now?' she asked.

'Can you tell me about the weapon?'

'What do you mean?'

'I mean the weapon that was used to kill Garvey.'

Beatrice shook her head.

'I know that. I don't know what I'm meant to say.'

'The murder was committed with a knife. I want to know whether it was a knife that belonged to you.'

'I don't know. I didn't see it.'

Maud twisted round.

'Carrie?'

Carrie raised her eyebrows and left the room. Maud turned back to Beatrice, who didn't meet her eye. She seemed to be looking at nothing, expressionless.

45

'While we're waiting,' said Maud, 'is there anything you'd like to say? Anything that might be helpful?'

'I don't know how to answer general questions like that. If you've got a specific question, then I'll answer it.'

'You're sounding a bit like a lawyer.'

'I am a lawyer. Corporate law,' Beatrice added, and gave a strange, mirthless twist of her lips as she said this.

'I meant that you sound like one of those lawyers who stops their client answering questions. Aren't we just two people who want to solve this crime?'

'It's all a bit more complicated than that. You've seen the people out there. Soon it'll be the media. Tomorrow ...' She stopped herself and sighed. 'It's already tomorrow, isn't it? Later today, it'll be in the papers and on the television.'

'The sooner we find the murderer, the sooner it'll all go away.'

'When you say that, you sound young and inexperienced.' Maud smiled at her.

'Let me ask you this. Did you kill Will Garvey?'

'Of course not.'

'Do you know who did?'

'"Know" isn't the right word. But I assume Tyler did. That's what you lot think as well, isn't it? He's the obvious suspect.'

'Oh, yes,' said Maud. 'He's certainly the obvious suspect.'

Carrie came into the room with the evidence bag. She held it up.

'Is this knife your property, Ms Macmillan?' she asked.

'No.'

'Do you know whose property it is?'

Beatrice hesitated noticeably.

'No, I don't,' she said finally.

'Am I missing something?' Maud asked.

'Is that a question I'm supposed to answer?'

'Ms Macmillan, I'm starting to feel a little puzzled. An old friend of yours has just been murdered in your own home, and when I ask you about it, you're treating my questions as if they're some kind of irritating intrusion. It looks as if I'm going to have to repeat the question until I get a proper answer. The knife. Have you ever seen it before?'

Now there was a long pause. Beatrice swallowed before replying. When she finally spoke, it came out in a rush.

'I do recognise it, yes. My son, Finn, brought it to the house this evening. It didn't belong to him. From what I understand, he took it away from someone in order to avoid the possibility of trouble. In my opinion, he was doing the right thing.' She swallowed again. 'But I was aware that carrying a knife in a public place is a criminal offence, even if you're not intending to use it. So I was just acting like any parent would.'

'As you must know,' said Maud, 'you are allowed to carry a knife for a lawful reason. If your son behaved the way you said he did, then he had nothing to worry about. And you do need to answer all of my questions in full.'

'I didn't think it was relevant.'

Maud raised her eyebrows.

'This knife is the murder weapon. How could it possibly not be relevant? Did your son give it to you?'

'Yes.' Beatrice frowned. 'He came downstairs with Connie, his girlfriend, while we were eating. I hadn't been expecting him. He was upset because his friend had been brandishing it, and it seemed like things were going to get out of control. He put it on the table. Or someone did.'

'Who touched it?'

'I don't know. I can't remember.'

'Did you touch it?'

'Maybe. I think so.'

'How did the knife end up in the room where Garvey was killed?' Carrie asked.

'I put it there. It somehow made its way to the living room. I think Marco brought it there. People kept picking it up, and it was making me uneasy. It felt like an accident waiting to happen.' She grimaced. 'Anyway, at some point I took it upstairs, into the little spare room – nobody ever goes in there. Out of harm's way, as I thought. I was going to decide what to do with it in the morning.'

'Thank you. Where exactly did you put it?'

'Where? On a shelf, I think.'

'And there's nothing else you want to tell me?'

'No.'

'Okay, we'll interview you fully at the station. Before I talk to the others, I'd like you to show us round the rooms on this floor.'

'What on earth for?'

'A murder happened here. This is a crime scene. We need to have some sense of the layout. For example, one question. You had a party this evening. When I was here, it seemed to be taking place in the garden and in the sitting room on the ground floor. I suppose for dinner, you went to the room on the lower ground floor, is that right?'

'Yes, that's right.'

'But William Garvey was found in a bedroom right at the top of the house. Why was he up there?'

'I don't know.'

'Did you notice him go up there?'

'No.'

'Did he go upstairs alone?'

There was a long pause.

'I'm sorry,' said Beatrice eventually. 'I'm just trying to think. Yes. I think so. I don't know. People were drifting about. They came and went.'

Maud looked around.

'So this is a study. You work here?'

'Yes. My job involves a lot of preparation.'

Maud, Carrie and Beatrice left the study and turned into a room that overlooked the garden. It felt different from the rooms downstairs, less manicured, less formal. Maud noticed the big-screen TV, a baggy sofa, cushions on the floor.

Carrie walked to the far side where there was a door leading onto spiral metal stairs that led down to the garden. She pulled on her gloves before she turned the handle and pushed it open.

'So you can get to the garden from every floor except for the top floor, is that right?'

'We had these little stairs built,' said Beatrice. 'We don't use them much. Finn used to when he was younger.' She smiled bleakly. 'He sometimes sneaked out at night.'

'And the door was unlocked this evening?' Carrie asked.

'As you can see.'

There were two rooms on the street side of the house. Maud also pulled on gloves before she opened a door into what was clearly the master bedroom. She flicked on the light and looked around. It was hard not to be distracted by the feeling of money everywhere. This was a house that had been built in the nineteenth century for an office clerk and his family and a servant or two. Now it was owned by millionaires, and you could see it in every artisanal door handle and light fitting. The bedspread was perfectly smooth. She walked across the room and opened the door to the ensuite bathroom, with its free-standing tub. She touched the towel hanging from a rail.

'There's a loo downstairs as well,' said Beatrice. 'And another one on the second floor.'

Maud and Carrie crossed the hallway into what was obviously the spare bedroom. It had the plush impersonality of a hotel, with an abstract painting of a red circle and a blue square on the wall. The bedspread was creased.

'We don't really use this room,' said Beatrice, reaching out a hand to smooth the spread, but Maud put out her hand to stop her.

'I just wanted to straighten it out,' Beatrice said. 'Force of habit.'

'Leave it,' said Maud. 'I think there's been a bit too much cleaning up already. Please avoid touching anything.'

She steered Beatrice out of the room and shut the door.

'Do we have to go up there?' Beatrice asked, gesturing towards the bright whiteness of the second floor, where the crime scene officers were still at work, and where Will's body still lay.

'Not now,' said Maud, then called downstairs and waited until a uniformed officer came up to join them.

'I want all of these rooms sealed. Nobody goes in without my permission.'

'Where am I going to sleep tonight?'

'After you've given your statement at the police station, do you have friends or neighbours you can stay with?'

Beatrice frowned.

'If that's a problem we can sort something,' said Carrie.

'I can make my own arrangements.'

46

Beatrice went down the stairs, and Maud beckoned Carrie back into the study, where she closed the door.

'Thoughts?'

Carrie sat down in one of the chairs and stretched her legs out luxuriously. She yawned so widely Maud could see her tonsils.

'Coffee would be good,' she said. 'And something sweet. My blood sugar feels low. So first off, a really basic comment. This is a big house, but it's not that big. How can there be a murder in a house with lots of people in it, and nobody knows who did it? I mean, obviously one person knows. But you know what I mean.'

'I know exactly what you mean. I think it's important. I don't know how it's important, but I think it is.'

'Then there's Tyler Green, who's obviously the clear suspect. But I haven't had the chance to hear much about him.'

'He was convicted of killing his friend, Leo Bauer, at a weekend house party which was attended by all the guests who were assembled here yesterday evening. He spent twenty-nine years in prison.'

Carrie nodded.

'I know,' said Maud. 'I mean, who gets twenty-nine years? Beatrice Macmillan says that he claimed yesterday evening that he was innocent and one of them was the murderer.'

'Everyone says they're innocent.'

'Yes. Of course, some of them are.'

'God, what a can of worms.' Carrie drummed her fingers on Beatrice Macmillan's large desk. 'If he's telling the truth, which he almost certainly isn't, that could be just as bad for him. Maybe he blamed William Garvey for being convicted. Maybe he thought, or even knew, that Garvey did it.'

'You're right,' said Maud. 'And it looks rather like an execution. A single knife blow. But if you were going to revenge yourself on someone, would you do it at a party that you yourself had asked for, in an enclosed space where it would be hard not to be seen, where you'd gathered all the witnesses of the first murder, and where you would be the immediate suspect? That's like a piece of theatre. Why not get Will on his own? And then, what about the knife?'

'What about it?'

'If you were planning to commit a murder, wouldn't you bring your own weapon? The knife that killed Garvey was brought into the house by Beatrice Macmillan's son. It happened to be lying around. This just doesn't seem planned to me.'

Carrie thought about this.

'There aren't rules for how you commit a murder,' she said. 'He could have relied on finding a sharp knife in the house. I bet there are multiple ones here that could have been used to kill Garvey. When Beatrice's son brings one in, he decides to use that. Or maybe you're right, and the murder wasn't even planned. Tyler Green may have just got into a row with Will Garvey, seen the knife, and picked it up to threaten him. And went that bit too far. All those years in prison might do that to you. You're used to fighting for your life.'

Maud nodded. 'Okay. What did you make of Beatrice Macmillan?'

Carrie wrinkled her nose.

'Something not quite right there.'

'I agree. An old friend has been murdered in her house, just a few yards from where she was standing. Don't you want to do anything you can to help? She answered every question like a lawyer, saying as little as she possibly could.'

'Maybe, like lots of lawyers, she doesn't trust the police.'

'She's a business lawyer. She never deals with the police. When I asked her about the knife, she was almost misleading.'

'She was worried about her son.'

'She may not be a criminal lawyer, but she knows enough to know that there was no way in the world that we were going to hassle him about this.'

'Don't forget her husband,' said Carrie. 'A bomb has just gone off in her life. As she said, in a few hours this is going to get into the papers. Murder in politician's home. Once everyone has been interviewed and it all comes out, it could ruin his career. Maybe hers as well.'

'That's possible,' said Maud. 'Or it might be that she was the one who killed Garvey. She's hiding something, I'm sure of it.'

47

Tyler lay rigidly in his bed. He was trying to remember how to breathe, but it felt that there was a thick sludge in his chest. The sounds of his cell mate, the smell of him just a few inches beneath him, filled him with a kind of nausea.

It seemed to him that a tide was rolling towards him, dark waves swelling like a thick, writhing muscle. Soon it would be on him. All the feelings he had, with excruciating willpower, held at bay for twenty-nine years, knowing that otherwise they would destroy him, were gathering. He no longer had the strength to fight them.

The man beneath gave a liquid snore. Tyler shuddered. He would climb out of his bunk and mash the man's smiling baby face into pulp, punch and punch and punch him until the noise stopped and the unendurable feelings had been used up.

He slid from the bed and stood in the centre of the little room, his fists clenched and his heart hammering. He was acutely aware of his body. The way the blood was pumping, the faint ache of his old scar, the roaring in his head, like the roaring of a stormy sea.

The man snored again, and this time Tyler started to scream. He screamed and he howled, and the sound filled him up and ripped him open. He crouched on the floor and he howled into the darkness as if he was an animal in pain. It was like being violently sick: horror pouring out of him. His head banged against the tiles.

The sound became a word, over and over: no no no no no no no.

'Mate,' said a voice.

Tyler became aware of a sharp, tingling point in the soft flesh just under his ear.

'Shut the fuck up,' said the voice. 'Or I will slit you open like a pig.'

Tyler tipped his head and felt the warm blood, then he roared again, even louder. Heavy feet pounded outside. The door burst open. There was a bright light in his face. Something smashing against his skull, a boot in his ribs, and then he was dragged backwards by his arms, out of the cell.

A voice boomed in his ear.

'We knew you'd be back. This time you won't be leaving.'

48

'Ms Marais.' Carrie bent over Ali. 'I am very sorry to have to ask you, but can we have a few words?'

Ali squinted up at her, as if trying to focus.

'Why?'

'Just a few preliminary questions. If you would come with me, so we can have some privacy.'

Ali got to her feet, holding onto the dog. She stared around her at the others in the room. Ellen and Marco had both fallen asleep in their chairs. Jay was rocking to and fro slightly, and whimpering. Nobody said anything.

Ali put Benjy on the floor, and Carrie took her by the elbow and led her out. She felt like she was made of dry twigs and could snap into fragments.

In the study, Maud was waiting for them. Ali sank into the chair where Beatrice had been sitting.

'Oh, dear God,' she said.

Maud leaned towards her, watching her intently.

'Ms Marais, when did you last see your husband?'

'I don't know,' said Ali. 'I don't know. Everything's just – I don't know what's happened.'

Maud waited, a grave expression on her face.

'I don't know,' Ali repeated. 'I feel sick. I need a cigarette.'

'Approximately?'

'Can't someone else tell you?' There was a pause. 'We all sat together at the table, talking.'

'What time?'

'You can ask and ask. It was dark, that's all. Dark outside.'

'And that was the last time?'

'The last time,' Ali repeated dully. She put a hand across her eyes. 'He went upstairs.'

'Where did he go?'

'I don't know.'

'And you?'

Ali took away her hand.

'I went to the toilet. I felt sick; I thought I was going to throw up. It had been the worst evening. I still feel sick.'

'And then?'

'And then nothing. Nothing. Why are you looking like that? I went to get cigarettes. When I came back, he wasn't there. That's it. Someone went to find him.'

'Thank you,' said Maud. 'Do you have any idea who saw him after he left the room?'

Ali frowned.

'You mean apart from Rudi? I don't know. People were drifting about. Is he up there now?' she asked. 'Will, I mean. Is he still there?'

'Yes.'

'Do I have to look at him?'

'At some point, he'll have to be formally identified. You can designate someone else to do that, if you want.' Maud paused before asking the inevitable difficult question. 'Do you know who killed your husband, Ali?'

'Tyler killed him.'

Her mouth twisted on the name.

'Why do you think that?' Carrie asked. 'What makes you so sure?'

'Tyler loved me.'

'Tyler loved you?'

'He loved me once. And once, I loved him. Before he killed Leo. And then he was sent to prison, and Will married me instead. Nobody had told him. I saw his face, and the way he looked at me. He could have killed me instead.'

'You're saying that Tyler Green killed your husband because of you?'

Ali wrapped her arms around her thin body.

'I'm so cold,' she said. 'I'm so tired. Yes. Because of me.'

'It was a very long time ago that he loved you,' said Maud gently. 'Do you really think that—?'

'I don't know,' Ali said. 'I don't know what to think.'

'Okay,' said Maud as the door closed on Ali. 'One theory is that Tyler Green killed Will Garvey because he found out that Will was Leo's murderer. Another theory is that it was because Will Garvey married the woman he loved. Another possibility is that the two murders are not connected at all.'

'So it could be that Green didn't kill Leo Bauer, but he did kill Garvey because he found out Garvey was the murderer who had let him take the rap.' Carrie was counting things out on her fingers. 'Or he killed Bauer three decades ago after a violent argument, and now he's killed Garvey because Garvey took the woman he loved. Or because of something else we don't yet understand. Or he killed Bauer, but didn't kill Garvey. Or he didn't kill either of them.'

'That sounds about right.'

'It's enough to make your head spin.'

'I've just been sent over the information from the collected mobiles, by the way. If I ping it to you, can you go through it, see if anything leaps out?'

'Sure.'

'In fact, I think we need to see the whole dossier from the Leo Bauer case.'

'You're sure it's connected?'

'Sure? No, of course I can't be sure.'

'Okay then, I'll ask one of the guys at the station to send it over. Who do you want to talk to next?'

'Ellen Sweeney.'

Her mobile buzzed in her pocket and she pulled it out to answer.

'Have you charged him yet?' It was almost a bark.

'No, sir,' said Maud coolly.

'Is he saying he didn't do it?'

'I haven't seen Tyler Green yet. I'm still at the house.'

'What the fuck are you doing there, Maud?' Maud held the phone slightly away from her ear. 'I told you I want this wrapped up quickly.'

'I'm conducting an investigation.'

'Well, conduct it by interviewing the man who we all know did it and getting his confession. I'm under the cosh here.'

49

Carrie had to wake Ellen Sweeney up. She opened her eyes and stared around her in bewilderment before she remembered where she was. Then she struggled into a sitting position, her thick grey hair in a tangle, her skirt twisted.

'I must have nodded off,' she said, and laughed heartily. 'Isn't that odd? This terrible thing has happened and I went to sleep. I was dreaming about something. What was it now? No, it's gone.'

'A few questions, please.'

'I need to contact my husband.'

'All in good time.'

'He'll be worrying. Actually, that's probably not true. He'll be fast asleep. Him and the children. I have five children, you know, though only two still at home. I call them my—'

'We can talk in the study. DI O'Connor's waiting for you.'

'How long are we going to have to wait here?'

It was Rudi, speaking in what was almost a drawl.

'You're under no legal obligation, but we're very grateful for your co-operation, and we will require formal statements from all of you in the next few hours. And I imagine you all want this to be over as soon as possible.'

Then Clara spoke.

'Jay isn't well,' she said.

'I'm sorry to hear that. What's the trouble?'

'He's stressed,' said Clara.

'We're all stressed,' snapped Beatrice.

Marco's head lifted up; he gazed about him in befuddlement, then closed his eyes again.

'What time did you discover the body of Will Garvey?' asked Maud.

'Time?'

'Yes.'

'I feel thick-headed. I could do with some coffee.'

'Time, Ms Sweeney.'

'I'm a Mrs actually. I used to be Eleanor Hooper, but I changed my name when I married. I'm old-fashioned that way.'

'Mrs Sweeney, what time did you discover the body?'

Maud was chilly in her thin yellow shirt, and behind the alertness that she always felt at the start of a case, her brain working away, assembling facts, making connections, storing up impressions, she was weary. She too could do with some strong coffee.

'It was around midnight or just before,' Ellen said at last, with a note of triumph in her voice. 'But not much before.'

'How can you be sure?'

'Because I remember Clara saying that it was nearly midnight when Ali said she was going to buy cigarettes.'

'You're sure that it was before midnight.'

'Yes. Ali was steeling herself to speak to Tyler. They'd barely exchanged a word all evening. There was a horrible tension between them. Not surprising really, when you think about it. They were ridiculously in love when they were young, you see. At least, he was with her. She was less demonstrative. But anyway, she said she needed to get cigarettes, and she and Clara both went out because Clara said she shouldn't go alone. When they came back, which couldn't have been more than five or ten minutes later, that's when I went to call Will. Because Ali was impatient to leave, you see, and she was rather angry with him for not being ready. Poor thing. I imagine that will come back to haunt her – that she was being cross with him and all the time he was lying dead upstairs. Poor, poor Ali. She'll need a lot of help to get through this. And she has no children to turn to. They couldn't, you see.'

'That's useful, thank you.'

'So,' said Carrie, scribbling on her notepad. 'Ali Marais and Clara Keane went out shortly before midnight, and on their return five or ten minutes later, you almost immediately went upstairs to look for Will Garvey. Is that correct?'

'Yes.'

Maud scrutinised Ellen Sweeney. She was intrigued by her garrulous cheerfulness.

'How did you know where he was?'

'I didn't. I thought he must be in the bathroom, or asleep in one of the rooms, so I just looked in all of them, turning on the light and calling out his name. "Will, are you there?" I said. "Time to go home, Will." And then—' She came to a halt.

'And then?'

'Then I came to the rooms at the top of the house. I looked inside the son's room, and then the other one.'

'Was the door open or shut?'

'Open. No, shut.' She stopped to consider. 'Usually I'm good at details like this. I have to be, as a therapist. It's the tiny things you have to pay attention to. Maybe it was shut, but not properly. Anyway, I found the light switch and that's when I saw him, lying on the floor. And at first, I just thought he was passed out, and I thought, poor Will, he must have been even drunker than I realised. But of course, then I saw the blood.

Everywhere.' There were blotches of red on her cheeks; her eyes gleamed.

'Did you immediately know he was dead?'

'I did, of course I did, yet I still thought we could help somehow. I mean, isn't that peculiar? One part of me knew he was dead. You've seen the body. But another part of me just wouldn't accept it.'

'Did you touch the body?'

'I reached out and patted his shoulder. To wake him. I knew I couldn't wake him, but I had to try. I don't know. I think that was all. I didn't step in the blood. I don't think I did. I saw his neck. It was horrible. And I could see one of his eyes, staring up at me. I've only seen one other dead body, apart from my dead mother in hospital, and that was Leo's.'

'And then?'

'Then I ran down the stairs shouting that someone should help. That Will had been killed. I think I said he'd been killed. That wasn't a very nice way to break the news to Ali, was it? But I wasn't thinking straight.'

'Of course.'

'And Kristin said she'd come. I don't know why she was the one to offer. And Clara, so Jay came too, like her shadow. That wasn't a good idea – he's a delicate soul. And I told Tyler to come, because he was a doctor. Well, not a doctor, but you know, a medic, all those years ago.'

'So Tyler Green was with the rest of the guests at this point?'

'He must have been. Or maybe he came in from the garden when he heard me shouting. That's where he'd been before. All I know is that the five of us went back up the stairs.'

'And then?'

'Then Tyler knelt down and he just shook his head and said there was nothing anyone could do. Which we knew of course.'

'Did he touch the body?'

'I don't know.'

'Or Clara or Kristin or Jay?'

'I don't know. Well, Kristin didn't, at any rate, because she was busy being sick.'

So she was the one who had vomited, thought Maud.

'Thank you.'

'Then we all went downstairs and everyone was crying or shouting, and I hugged Ali and it was like hugging a marble statue. Poor thing.'

'Thank you. You'll have to go through this in detail at the station.'

'Mrs Sweeney,' said Carrie. 'Why did you start clearing up?'

'Why? Well, it was a mess, and I hate a mess.'

'It was a crime scene.'

'It was still a mess. I thought Beatrice could do with some help.'

'What did you clear away?'

'I couldn't tell you. I stacked plates and started to load the dishwasher. Things like that.'

'Nothing else? Did you wipe surfaces, pick things up from the floor, anything like that?'

'I have no idea. I was just trying to be helpful.'

She gave a merry trill of laughter, which died away when she saw the expression on Carrie's face.

'I'm sorry,' she said, and her face looked suddenly pouchy and old. 'I'm very sorry. I'm a meddling fool.'

50

'Thank you for your patience. I understand this isn't easy, and I know you will be wanting to go home. You are free to go, of course, but with your consent, you will first be taken to the station, where you will give your statements.'

It was the small hours of the morning, and Maud was standing in the middle of the living room.

'And then we can go home?' Clara asked.

'If you live in London, yes. But if you come from outside of London, we might ask you to stay in the vicinity a while longer.'

'That's not right,' Clara said.

'What's not right is that your friend is lying dead upstairs.'

'Of course, but I still think—'

'I hope we won't keep you for long. Wake him up.' Maud pointed at Marco, who was heavily asleep in his chair, drool running from his open mouth. 'And where is Kristin Foster? Has she been found?'

'She was back in the flat she shares with Marco Burney, apparently packing a bag,' said Hawkins, grinning widely.

'Please request her to come to the station at once.'

'Can we have coffee there?' Ellen asked.

'Of course. You will be taken care of.'

Maud turned to Hawkins, who was standing by the door.

'Make sure the whole house is sealed off. And we need cars to take everyone to the station for their statements.'

Before they left themselves, Maud and Carrie went downstairs and stood for a few minutes, looking around. Despite Ellen's efforts to clear up, the table was still strewn with dirty dishes, smears of food and puddles of wine.

Maud slid the door open, and the two women stepped outside, where the moon laid down a path for them. Standing at the far end of the lawn, they took in the house, with its large, lit-up windows and the steps that led into the garden from three of its floors.

'You could leave one way and enter another, and nobody would be the wiser,' said Carrie. 'You could say you were going outside and actually head for the top of the house, or vice versa.'

'Just what I was thinking.'

There was a narrow gravelled path that led up one side of the house. Maud gestured to the gate that opened onto the street, which was heavily bolted and padlocked, and topped with iron spikes.

'Can you make sure to ask Beatrice Macmillan about the keys to this?'

'I will.' Carrie made a note for herself.

Returning to the house, Maud went up three flights of stairs to the top floor while Carrie checked on the arrangements for the witnesses. In the room where the murder had happened, paramedics in green coveralls were carefully lifting Will's large body into a body bag before sliding it onto a stretcher. Maud thought they seemed almost tender. She watched them a while, then left to look into the other rooms. The largest obviously belonged to a teenager. Two guitars were propped up against a wall, and a TV and a gaming console stood at the end of the bed. There was a closed laptop on the pillow, and on the bedside table, next to the lamp, was a tangle of chargers. Clothes were heaped by the door, shoes were scattered around, a couple with studded soles, and the wardrobe stood open. There were three mugs on the desk, and a driving theory handbook. An upturned wooden chair lay next to the desk. Satsuma skins and a green towel were tossed on the floor. The one gesture to childhood was the corduroy octopus on a shelf, along with school text books and other random volumes. Maud saw a vegan cookbook and a book called *How to Live*. There was a poster on the wall of what looked like a flying, armoured castle, with Japanese writing underneath.

Next to it was a small bathroom, and the second study that overlooked the street. The final door opened onto a windowless space crammed with rolls of carpet, tins of paint, tennis racquets, a couple of pairs of skis, some large suitcases, and boxes marked in felt-tip pen as containing things like Christmas decorations, Finn's old toys.

She went slowly down the stairs, stopping for a moment on the landing. Her eyes were bright with thoughts. She could feel ideas gathering, their outlines becoming firmer. She knew she had to hold on to them, but not pursue them.

Carrie was waiting in the hall. Maud pulled her hair more tightly back from her face. 'Okay. Let's go.'

51

Even though it was still night, it felt like they were stepping into daylight. Maud counted three different news crews, lights blazing. Ahead of them, on the pavement, Maud recognised the back of DS Hawkins. A neatly coiffeured female reporter was holding a microphone up to him, on her face an expression of concern and empathy.

Carrie scowled.

'Do you think he might by any chance be giving the impression that he's really the person in charge of the inquiry?'

Maud smiled.

'I think he very well might be.'

'You're not going to tell him to shut up.'

'Life's too short. We've got work to do.'

They walked along the pavement, ignored by the media. Suddenly a shiny black Range Rover pulled up right in front of them with a screech of tyres, so that they stepped back in some alarm. The driver got out and rushed round to open the rear door. Maud found herself face to face with a man she recognised from the newspapers and from television panels.

'Mr Harris,' said Maud.

Harris didn't seem to notice her at first. He was looking round at his driver, who had opened the hatchback door and taken out a suitcase and a shoulder bag. He muttered some instructions to him, then finally looked at Maud. He had a large florid face and curly grey hair. His celebrity seemed to have given his face a glow, as if there was a spotlight on him.

'Are you connected to all of this?'

'I'm Maud O'Connor. Detective Inspector.'

'Can you take me to the person in charge?'

'That would be me,' said Maud.

He looked at her with apparent suspicion.

'How's my wife?'

'She's distressed, of course,' said Maud.

'What about my son?'

'He's not here.'

'What?' His eyes narrowed. 'Come inside. We need to talk.'

He marched along the pavement without waiting for Maud. Cameras were pointed at him and questions shouted, but he didn't look around. As Maud and Carrie followed him, Hawkins stepped into their path.

'Perhaps I should talk to him?' he said.

'No,' said Maud, walking around him.

She followed Harris into the hall, where scene-of-crime officers were crouched in one corner. He turned to Maud.

'Where's my wife?'

'She's on her way to the police station. We're conducting interviews.'

'What? At this time?'

'There's no point waiting.'

Harris looked around, taking deep breaths, and noticed his driver, hovering with the bags.

'Take them upstairs,' he said.

'Hang on,' said Maud. 'We're sealing the house off for the next few hours. I don't want anything brought in or taken out. And you need to leave.'

Harris gestured Maud to move closer. When he spoke it was in a low mutter.

'I've already talked to James,' he said. 'You know who I mean?'

'James is quite a common name,' said Maud.

He sighed.

'James Moore. The Home Secretary. Have you heard of him?'

'What did you talk to him about?'

'I made it clear to him that this is an extremely sensitive case and he assured me that I would be kept fully informed at every stage.'

'Of course,' said Maud. 'I'll arrange for a liaison officer to contact you . . .'

'Don't give me that,' said Harris. This came out more loudly than he intended, and he looked around to see if anyone had noticed. 'You say you're in charge of the investigation, right?'

'That's right.'

'You saw that circus outside. They're like animals sniffing around for the slightest hint of something they can use. I want to make sure they don't get anything. And I don't want any surprises, have you got that? I want to be informed of absolutely everything, do you understand?'

'I hear your concerns,' said Maud politely. Out of the corner of her eye, she could see Carrie rolling her eyes. 'Now if you'll excuse me—'

'Wait,' said Harris, holding up his hand. 'As I said, I talked to the Home Secretary and he assured me that this case would be handled with total efficiency and total discretion.'

'We don't need to be told that,' said Maud.

'I'm not so sure about that,' said Harris. 'I've had dealings with the Met before, and let's just say that I wasn't particularly impressed.'

Maud didn't reply. She had her own issues with the Metropolitan Police, but she wasn't going to express them in front of this man.

'I understand that you've got the main suspect in custody. This Tyler Green.'

'Tyler Green is in custody.'

'Are you going to charge him?'

'I'm on my way to interview him.'

'But do you think that charges are imminent? Off the record.'

'Off the record or on the record, I've no idea.'

He glanced around again.

'Is there anything you know of in this case that might embarrass me?'

'Embarrass you? What do you have in mind? Is there something in particular that you are anxious about, Mr Harris?'

Harris leaned in so close to Maud that he could smell his breath.

'Let me be clear, I'm a good citizen and I want to co-operate with our police in every way possible. But if I suddenly get doorstepped by a reporter or film crew, and they ask me something you haven't told me about in advance, then you will find yourself in a world of trouble. Do you understand?' Maud didn't reply. She didn't even nod her head. 'Do you have anything you need to tell me?'

'Not so much tell,' said Maud. 'More like ask. Did you know about this party in advance?'

'Are you interviewing me?'

'I'm asking you a question.'

'I have nothing whatever to do with this.'

'It took place in your house. Did you know about the party in advance?'

'Vaguely.'

'Did you approve of it?'

'What does it matter whether I approved?'

'Did you approve of it?'

He took a deep breath.

'Obviously I wasn't particularly happy about the idea of a convicted murderer in my house.'

'Did your wife know you weren't happy about it?'

'We talked about it, and I said she should go ahead if it was important to her.'

'So it was important to her?'

'I don't think I used those exact words. I was fine with her hosting the party, if that's what you mean.'

'Did you know any of the people who were present?'

He hesitated.

'My wife hadn't kept in touch with the people from her past. Except for one or two, but even those were, well, distant acquaintances. Beatrice told me about Tyler Green, of course.'

'And what were your thoughts about that?'

'Well . . .' Harris began and then coughed and cleared his throat. 'In my career I have always believed in rehabilitation, while on the other hand I've always thought it was important to consider the feelings of victims and their families. And if,' he continued, his voice deepening, gearing up for the climax, 'if the parole board has let a killer back onto the streets, let me tell you that there will be an inquiry and we will not rest until we know that such a mistake will not happen again.'

Maud suddenly felt like she was not so much interviewing Sebastian Harris as watching him hold forth on television.

'What about William Garvey?'

'Yes, William Garvey. I'm not sure I'd ever actually met him but I think I knew his name. I believe he and my wife had kept intermittently in touch. Needless to say I was very . . .' He coughed again. 'I was distressed and dismayed to hear that he had been murdered. And it was especially terrible that it happened in my . . . in our house.' His expression became sterner. 'But I really don't see the purpose in asking me these questions.'

'The media are going to be asking those questions as well. You'd better get used to them.'

He frowned.

'I'm not sure I like the tone of that.' He paused and took a breath and then made a visible effort to look more affable. 'Look, Detective, er . . .'

'Detective Inspector O'Connor.'

'I don't want to pull rank. I am simply asking you to be co-operative. I want you to be frank with me. Are there any issues that might turn into a problem?'

'You mean, apart from the murder?'

'This will be used as a weapon against me, you'll see. Well, I won't go down quietly, and you should bear that in mind. I can be a useful ally and a dangerous enemy.'

'Thank you for warning me,' said Maud. 'By the way, can you account for your movements over the last few hours?'

'Are you serious?'

'I need to ask everyone,' said Maud. 'It's just a matter of routine.'

'I've spent the last few hours in the car on the M1, being driven from Nottingham, where I was attending a conference. If you feel you need to check this, there are any number of witnesses.'

'Thank you,' said Maud.

52

'You ladies took your time in there,' said Constable Hale, as Maud and Carrie got into the car. 'Where to now? The station?'

'Fordham Prison, please.'

'Got it.'

He pulled away from the kerb. There was a large bag of crisps open beside him, and as he drove, he dipped his hand in and pushed crisps into his mouth. A tang of vinegar caught in the back of Maud's throat.

'It's the best way to stay awake,' he said. 'Want one?'

'No, thanks,' said Maud.

But Carrie leaned forward and extracted several, eating them in quick succession, tiny crumbs scattering over her lap.

'We badly need coffee,' she said to Maud.

'I've got a bit of coffee left in my flask,' said Hale. 'It's got quite a lot of sugar in, though. And it might be tepid by now.'

'That's kind of you,' said Maud. 'But not for me.'

'And I've got some cheese and ham sandwiches.'

'Really?' said Carrie.

'I always come prepared.'

'You'll need them yourself,' said Maud. 'We'll get something at the station.'

'What was it like then?'

'Sorry?'

'In there. What was it like?'

'If it's all right with you,' said Carrie, 'there are a few details we need to discuss.'

'Don't mind me,' said Hale.

Carrie pulled out her mobile and notepad, and spoke in a lower voice.

'While you were upstairs, I had a quick look at the information sent through about the phones that were collected. I can tell you that mobile positioning data shows that the only people who left the house were Ali Marais and Clara Keane, at twelve minutes before midnight. They went as far at the Shell petrol station, about three hundred metres away. They returned nine minutes later.'

'Which is exactly what they said.'

'Yes. I need to go through the list of calls properly, but there's one thing I noticed at once.'

'Yes?'

'Not about a call made, but about one that wasn't made. Rudi Scott never called his wife.'

'And he was the last person we know of who saw Will Garvey alive.'

'Chewing gum?' Hale asked.

'Also, the file on Leo Bauer will be waiting for us at the station.'

'Excellent.'

The car sped through the dark streets, the large houses of Tufnell Park rapidly giving way to poorer streets, smaller houses, blocks of flats, a twenty-four-hour corner shop where a fox was nosing at an overturned bin. There were several homeless people sleeping under the railway bridge, their belongings piled up in supermarket trolleys. Maud saw a scruffy dog lying next to one of the curled-up figures. At least tonight it was warm, she thought.

They rounded a bend and saw a massed shape against the horizon. The high brick walls were studded with small, unlit windows. There was a helicopter hovering above it like a giant insect.

'Here we are,' said Hale. 'Welcome to Fordham Prison.'

53

The warder was in a bad mood as he led Maud and Carrie through gate after gate.

'He's already been trouble,' he said.

'What does that mean?' asked Maud.

'Shouting, banging. He was out of control. It took four of us to restrain him. Fucking psycho.'

He unlocked the door of an interview room. It was windowless, grey, with nothing but four orange plastic chairs, a table that was screwed to the floor with a raised metal bar running across the width of one end, and the recording device in its centre. Maud sat at the table, Carrie to one side. The warder waved the two officers to chairs at the other end.

'We'll bring him along,' he said, and left the room.

After a few minutes they heard footsteps in the corridor outside. The door opened and Tyler Green was led into the room between two warders, one clutching each arm. His wrists were fastened in front of him with rigid handcuffs. They forced him into a chair opposite the detectives. One of the warders took another pair of handcuffs from his pocket and used them to attach him to the metal bar on the table.

Tyler Green's left eye was half closed and badly bruised. One cheek was purple and his lower lip was swollen. His shirt was stained with blood.

'What the hell has happened?' Maud asked.

'He had to be restrained,' said one of the warders.

'Restrained? He's been beaten up.'

'He brought it on himself.'

Maud looked at Green, and he looked blankly back at her.

'I'm Detective Inspector Maud O'Connor. This is my colleague, Detective Sergeant Carrie Kessler. What happened here?'

'What do you think?'

'Are you all right?'

'I don't even know what to say to that.'

Maud looked at the two warders.

'I'm conducting an interview. Could you please uncuff this man?'

'No chance,' said the warder. 'He's a danger to others, and a danger to himself.'

'I'm the detective in charge of this inquiry. I want him treated in a civilised way.'

The warder smiled faintly.

'If you've got any problem with anything here, you can put it in writing and send it to the prison governor. We'll see that she gets it when she comes in.' He looked at his colleague. 'When's she coming in? Monday morning, isn't it?'

'He's not even under arrest,' said Maud.

'He's a murderer out on licence, and his licence has been revoked.'

'Who by? The murder only happened a few hours ago.'

'As I said, if you've got any complaints, put them in writing.'

'All right,' said Maud. 'Since you've shackled him for our protection, you can leave us now.'

The warders looked at each other doubtfully, then one of them nodded.

'Don't take too long about it.'

After they had gone, Maud looked at Tyler Green more carefully. He was a tall man, his silvery grey hair was cut short, his hooded eyes were a flecked walnut brown, and a long scar snaked down one side of his face. There was an air of watchful containment about him, but at the same time he looked spent, utterly exhausted. And something else, she thought: he looked defeated.

'Is there anything I can do for you?' she said.

'I've just seen your power to do something for me. You can put it in writing.'

'Did they assault you?'

'What are you? Twelve years old? What do you think it's like when someone like me gets back in here?'

'Do you want to take it further?'

'You heard,' Green said. 'I started it.'

'Can I get you anything?'

'No, you can't get me anything. It's the middle of the night. Unless you want to ask those guards to make us all a coffee.'

'Mr Green, I'm here to talk to you about the murder of William Garvey. The quicker we can sort the matter out, the quicker we can get you out of here.'

Green started to raise his hands but it was as if he had forgotten they were shackled to the table. He leaned down and rubbed his face. When he raised his head again, his face was wet.

'I'm not getting out of here,' he said. 'Don't you understand? They've got me back. They're going to keep me.'

54

Maud turned on the bulky recording device, waited till its red eye was blinking, then gave her name and Carrie's, and the date and the time: 3.49am, Saturday 22 June. Then she nodded at Tyler Green.

'First of all,' she said, 'have you had your blood and urine tests?'

'No.'

Carrie stood up with a scrape of her chair, before Maud had a chance to speak.

'Leave it to me,' she said. 'I'll get it sorted.'

Maud nodded then turned back to Tyler as Carrie strode from the room. 'I apologise. This should have been done at once.'

'Thank you.'

'What will the tests find?'

'That I haven't drunk any alcohol and I haven't taken any drugs.'

'There was clearly a large amount of alcohol consumed at the party.'

'I haven't drunk anything for twenty-nine years,' said Tyler.

'Not even on your release.'

'It felt safer that way.'

'Safer? Because you didn't know how you might behave.'

Tyler shook his head. It was because he didn't know how

he would feel, what would come unloose in him, the great damned-up flood of emotions.

Maud scrutinised his gaunt, bruised face, his flecked brown eyes that were giving nothing away.

'So you haven't contravened the conditions of your licence?'

'No. But it doesn't matter.'

'What do you mean?'

'I'm going to be charged with Will's murder, aren't I? The fact that I didn't have anything to drink is hardly going to make a difference.'

'I'm in charge of this investigation, and it's my job to find out who killed Will Garvey. I intend to assemble the evidence, talk to everyone who was at the house, discover the truth. You are among the people I am interviewing.'

'Am I meant to believe that?' he asked.

She shrugged.

'Believe what you want. Let me start by asking you: did you kill William Garvey?'

'No.'

'Do you know who killed him?'

'No.'

'Right. I want you to take me through the events of the evening.'

'From the beginning?'

'From the beginning. Starting with how this reunion came about in the first place. It seems a pretty startling idea to me: gathering all the people who had been together when the murder of Leo Bauer happened.'

Tyler looked past her, reflecting. His bruised face looked deathly tired.

'I asked Will, and Will asked Beatrice. And Beatrice said yes. And then so did everyone else.'

'But why?'

'Why did I ask Will?'

He closed his eyes for an instant. How could he tell the detective that it was part of the process of believing that he could be free, or partly free at least. He didn't mean free from prison, but free from the deathly grip of the past – from what had happened to him, what had been done to him, from how his life had been annihilated.

He simply said: 'I spent nearly thirty years in prison, locked away for something I didn't do.' He made a small gesture with his cuffed hands. 'I was found guilty. You don't want to hear me argue my innocence. I know as well as anyone that we all say we're innocent.'

'You're not quite explaining why you wanted the reunion,' said Maud.

She saw him making an immense effort. When he replied, it was slowly and painfully.

'I was a person to whom things had been done. I'd been wrongly convicted, I'd been locked away, punished, beaten up, robbed of all sense of power over my own life.' The words were coming more easily now, as if something had been dislodged inside him. 'In prison, it's easy to feel you're a passive object – something like an old, waterlogged branch being washed along by a river. Or just like a body. It's a very bodily experience. I needed some kind of control, even if it was meaningless and futile. I wanted to reshape what had happened to me, make it belong to me. I wanted to take the power away from them all. I thought if I saw them, talked to them, looked them in the eye, found out what their lives had been like, they would all be reduced to human size again.' His voice cracked. 'And actually, that was true. Because what I saw was that they were all unhappy in their different ways.'

'Did you want them to be unhappy? Did you want to punish them?'

'I'd be lying if I told you that in those first years in prison, I didn't sometimes long for that. It could have consumed me. By the time I was let out, I just wanted to forget about them. I didn't want to dream about them anymore, or wonder who was the killer, who had seen me put away for twenty-nine years and let that happen. My friends. When I was young, I honestly thought I loved them all. I would have trusted them with my life. I was a naive young man who'd led a sheltered life. A dreamer, you could say.'

He gave a smile that wasn't a smile.

'So, you asked Will Garvey to set up this reunion.'

'Yes.'

'What was his attitude?'

'He was a bit reluctant,' said Tyler, then he gave a groan that seemed to come from his guts. 'Poor Will. Poor sod. He wanted to be a good friend to me. Even yesterday evening, he was talking about that. Friendship.'

Maud didn't answer, just sat very still and watched Tyler Green's face, the way the muscles worked, the way his slightly hooded eyes stared at some distant point.

'When he was young, he was a bit of a clown, but very endearing. A nice man. Kind. I saw his body, you know.'

'I know. We'll come to that.'

'They must have done it from behind.'

Maud waited, but he didn't add anything. She remembered thinking it looked like an execution.

'I gather Garvey came to see you in prison.'

'Yes.'

'Anyone else?'

'Of the group? No. My mother used to come.' His hands

moved again, restrained by the cuffs. Maud guessed he wanted to cover his eyes at the memory. 'I dream about her as well. Night after night. She died when I was thirty-nine, and I was almost relieved because her visits were like a special kind of hell – for her, and for me. She and my father separated not long after I was convicted; because of me. He would have nothing to do with me. She always said she believed I was innocent, but I knew she didn't really. For a long time, even after she was dead, I longed to show her that I wasn't a murderer, to comfort her with that at least. Anyway, after she died, I started to dream about her.'

Tyler Green didn't seem to notice that tears were pouring down his bruised face. Questions were crowding in on Maud, but she remained silent and let him follow his thoughts.

'So yes, Will came to see me. Not often, and less and less as the years passed. I can't remember when he last came. We never talked about what had happened. He never said he believed me, or didn't, or anything like that. We didn't talk about Leo, or any of the group. He kind of prattled on and I sat and let the words flow over me and wished him gone.'

'And Ali Marais,' said Maud. 'He didn't mention her.'

Tyler looked at her, a mirthless smile twisting his mouth.

'Ah,' he said. 'Ali Marais.'

'Tell me about her.'

55

At that moment, the door to the room opened once more, and Carrie entered. She was accompanied by a prison officer and a nurse, and neither of them looked happy.

'You know what time it is?' said the nurse. 'Couldn't this have waited?'

'Come on,' said the officer, who was short and broad and strong. 'Let's watch you take a piss.' He peered at Tyler. 'You've been crying?'

'Are you the person who assaulted him?' Maud asked.

'I don't know what you're talking about.'

'I need to warn you that I'll make sure there's an investigation into this.'

'I'll bear that in mind,' said the officer.

He unfastened the cuffs and Tyler stood. Maud saw he had a slight limp as they led him from the room.

'Can you bring the drug kit straight back to me?' she asked.

'Don't trust us?'

She didn't, but made no answer, just switched the recording machine off.

'Has he said anything?' Carrie asked as the door closed behind the three men.

'He hasn't confessed, if that's what you mean.'

'He's not what I was expecting.'

'What was that?'

'I don't know. Just not someone so, well, compelling, I guess.'

'Compelling? Yes, I suppose he is.'

'It isn't looking good for him, though. He's already murdered another man. He's spent twenty-nine years in prison. On his release, he brings together the group who were with him when that happened, which is a pretty damn weird thing to do. I mean, what's that about?'

'It's to do with a kind of freedom,' said Maud slowly.

She felt that she knew something, but she didn't know what that was.

'Either he's a hardened criminal,' Carrie said, 'or he's the unluckiest man I've ever met, and that's saying something.'

56

In the police station five miles away from the prison where Tyler Green now sat opposite the detective with snaking yellow hair, Rudi had been allowed to call his wife. He bent over the phone as if he was imparting secrets.

'It's horrible,' he hissed to Celia, who was sitting up in bed now, blinking in the dazzle of the bedside lamp. 'Horrible.'

'I said you shouldn't go,' she said. 'Come home at once.'

'I told you, I can't. I'm in the police station. We all are.'

'This is ridiculous.' He could hear her getting out of bed, picture the determined set of her jaw. 'They have no right. You haven't done anything.'

'They've taken a blood sample,' he said. 'And a urine sample. They watched me.'

'Do they think you've taken drugs?'

'They have to check,' said Rudi. 'There were . . .' He hesitated. '. . . drugs on the premises.' He sounded like a police officer himself, he thought.

'Drugs? Who was taking drugs?'

'A couple of the others. I didn't have anything.'

'Were you drunk?'

'I had something to drink. That's not against the law.'

'But you were going to drive home. You can't drink and drive.'

'I only had a bit,' said Rudi, feeling the throb of his headache as he spoke.

'Rudi, I'm going to come now.'

'Don't do that. There's nothing you can do here. I'll be home soon, I'm sure.'

'I'm going to call my lawyer, and then I'll drive to London and insist they release you at once.'

'I'm here of my own free will. We all are. But I've agreed to be interviewed first. This is the simplest way. It'll all be done with, and I'll come back straight after.'

'They don't think any of you had anything to do with it?'

'Of course not,' he said, but he heard a shrill note of panic in his voice.

'Why are they holding you all then?'

'Because we were all there,' Rudi said wearily, wishing he had never made the call.

'There's something you're not telling me.'

'Celia, please. I don't need you to interrogate me. It's been ghastly. I'm having a truly awful time. I thought you would be sympathetic.'

'You should never have gone.'

'You've already said that.'

'My phone says it will take me an hour and twenty-seven minutes. I'll be there by half past six.'

'Don't come,' said Rudi.

'You need me. I'm on my way.'

57

Finn Macmillan Harris was walking swiftly up the lamplit street. He was on his way home alone because he'd had an argument with his girlfriend at the club. He was thirsty, clammy from all the dancing, hot and cold and suddenly dog-tired after the adrenaline spikes of the evening. All he wanted to do was climb into bed, pull the covers over his head, sink into oblivion. He would sleep into the afternoon. His father was out of town, smarming up to rich businessmen or whatever he did when he went away, so Finn wouldn't have him on his back.

There was a missed call and a voicemail message on his phone from his mother, but he didn't bother to listen to it. She would be asking him when he would be home, or apologising for the scene he'd come across earlier. He felt slightly queasy at the memory: all those drunk middle-aged people; his mother, usually so carefully elegant, looking rumpled and bleary, with that silver-haired man coming on to her. But they would all be gone, and she would be long asleep.

As he neared his house and was feeling in his pocket for his keys, he saw a blue light flashing ahead, a small group of people standing about. He saw that the road was blocked. Perhaps one of the neighbours had been robbed, he thought. Or one of them had been taken ill, maybe old Nelson Greer, who his mother said always looked like he was about to have a heart attack.

Shit happens, but it happens to someone else, not the Harris and Macmillan family.

58

They led Tyler back in, and the officer shackled him to the iron bar once more. The nurse was holding a small, squat pot, with perforated strips running up the side and a plastic cylinder inside a sealed transparent bag.

'You'll have to wait for the blood results,' he said.

'Yes,' said Maud.

He laid the pot on the table in front of her.

'Be my guest. The main drugs we test for are amphetamine, barbiturates, ketamine, MDMA—'

'I know.'

She pulled the pot towards her and tore off the perforated strips. There was a little panel at the base, and they all watched as one faint blue stripe appeared, gradually becoming clear, but not the second stripe which would confirm drug use.

'Negative,' said Maud at last.

Tyler didn't seem much interested. He stared down at his shackled hands and his expression didn't alter at Maud's words.

'Thanks,' Maud said to the two men in dismissal.

The two women waited in silence until they had gone from the room, before Carrie turned the machine back on.

'So,' Maud said. 'Tell me how you felt when you found out that Ali Marais had married your old friend Will Garvey.'

Tyler met the grey eyes of the detective, and it seemed as if she was looking right into him, into the self he had kept hidden away for so very long. He bore the gaze. Neither of them looked away. A strange space had opened between them, and his chest ached with the unfamiliarity of it: someone who was absolutely intent on him, and who was working to understand him.

He could hear the recording device clicking, and the sound of the other detective shifting in her chair. Even when he looked away from her, he could feel Maud's eyes on him. You'd have to be a fool to lie to DI O'Connor, he thought.

'Do you mean, did I want to kill him because he'd stolen my woman?'

'Well?'

'Ali became my girlfriend when I was only just twenty, barely more than a boy. It's true I was in love with her, or at least I thought I was, and at the time I felt absolutely certain it was going to last forever. We had talked about how we were always going to be together. Or maybe that was just me doing the talking. She was always hard to pin down; there was something unreachable about her – perhaps that was part of her appeal. I think she did love me, though. Once upon a time. But all of that was long, long ago. Another world, and I was a different person. I can't even remember what it feels like to be in love like that. It's just a memory of a memory of a memory.'

But that wasn't quite the truth. Tyler could remember. He remembered like a man dying of thirst remembers the taste of cool water in his mouth. For a moment he could feel Ali's small, firm hand in his, see her smiling at him. He looked up and saw Maud's unnerving eyes fixed on him.

'I was a stupid, soft kid,' he continued, his voice suddenly harsh because that dark wave was gathering in him again. 'Who knows what would have happened between us? Probably we would have drifted apart, though I was convinced we were meant for each other. She never saw me, or wrote to me in prison, and after a bit I gave up on her. Maybe I began to hate her. In those first years, I was full of hatred and despair and hope and terrible, terrible sadness. I couldn't separate the feelings out from each other: to get rid of one, I had to get rid of all of them.'

'When did you find out that she and Will Garvey had married?'

'Yesterday evening.'

'So he never told you, even though he came to see you multiple times.'

'He never told me.' Tyler gave a bleak smile. 'He probably didn't want to upset me.'

'And he didn't mention it when he was helping to organise this reunion?'

'He never told me.'

'What did you feel when you discovered it?'

'This is all stupid. Who cares what I felt about Will, or any of them?'

'Obviously, we do,' said Carrie. 'You had a possible motive. Or maybe,' she continued, 'you didn't kill Leo Bauer and you discovered that Will Garvey did. Which is another motive.'

Tyler turned his face to look at Carrie.

'I don't know who killed Leo. I don't care that Ali married Will. I was surprised, but I wasn't upset, that they'd got together. I was almost amused. I didn't nurse a love for Ali over all the years, if that's what you're thinking. When I saw her yesterday, she was simply a middle-aged, not-very-happy woman with a stupid dog. I didn't feel Will had betrayed me. It's all nonsense. I don't care about any of that. I don't care about love and revenge and justice. That's over. I care about the sky above me, rain and wind in my face, earth underneath my feet. You think I walked out of prison after almost thirty years and wanted to murder someone, practically in public, so that I'd immediately be shut up again? And never be free again. Never again.'

Tears were coursing down Tyler's face once more, and like last time, he didn't seem to notice.

'I can't spend another day in this place,' he said. 'Not another hour.'

Maud leaned forward and switched off the machine.

'We're going to stop for the moment,' she said. 'We'll rustle up some coffee for you. I'll see if you can be moved to a police cell, but at this time of night it might be difficult. In about fifteen minutes, we'll come back and I will take you through the events of last night.'

As she and Carrie walked down the corridor, Maud looked up at the small window and saw that it was growing paler; the moon a fugitive shape. It was half past four. The short night was over; day was beginning to break.

59

Finn sat in the back of the police car. He was shivering and didn't know if that was because of the drugs, or because he was cold, or because he was scared.

What had just happened? There were police cars and ambulances outside his house, neighbours, journalists. All the lights had been on, so the house looked like an ocean liner in the darkness, but he hadn't been allowed inside. Instead, he'd been led to the car and ushered into the back seat. Like a criminal.

He thought of the stash of dope in a sock in his underwear drawer. Would they find that? Would they go through his laptop? Was there anything on there that could get him into trouble? He felt nauseous; tears pricked at his eyes. He just wanted to crawl into bed and wake up when this was over.

Where was his mother? He remembered the missed call and pulled his mobile from his pocket. He looked at the unyielding neck of the police officer in front of him, then pressed the phone against his ear to listen to the voicemail. His mother's voice sounded strange, a sense of high-pitched, precarious control.

'Finn, it's me. Call me as soon as you get this. You can't come home. The police are here. There's been a – an accident. I'll tell you. Just don't come at the moment. It'll be all right though. I promise.'

She didn't sound as if she thought it would be all right. He called her number. It rang several times and then her voice – her ordinary, professional voice – asked him to leave a message.

'Mum,' he said. 'It's me.'

His voice came out thin and wavery. He ended the call. He thought of his father, and that made him feel even sicker. Outside, the sky was lightening, and the plane trees stood like sentinels on either side of the road. He leaned forward in his seat and closed his eyes. The car turned into the high street and started to slow.

'I don't feel very well,' he said as the car drew up outside the station. 'I don't feel very well at all.'

60

Jay could hear something tapping. At first he thought it was the ticking of a clock, but the clock in this room made no sound. Its long hand crept round silently, and now it was nearly five o'clock.

He stood up, his limbs cramping. He'd been given water, but his mouth was still parched and his tongue felt furry. The coffee they had brought to him had tasted metallic; it was like sipping blood.

Where was the sound coming from? Tap, tap, tap, like a fingernail on the door, a little code that he couldn't decipher. Sometimes it felt like it was inside his head, the machinery of his brain coming loose.

Then he saw what it was. A fly was repeatedly hitting its fat body into the window high above him. Click click click. Jay pressed his hands against his head. He couldn't listen to it anymore. Click click click. He couldn't. Click click click.

He went to the door and pulled it open.

'I need the toilet,' he said, hearing the terror in his voice.

He was pointed down the corridor to a little door opening onto the washroom. He leaned against the wall, breathing in and out, in and out, the way he knew to do when these panics came at him, but there wasn't enough air in his lungs, and he started to gasp. He splashed cold water onto his face. Was that him in the mirror, staring out like a man who was trapped in a burning building? Him now, or him thirty years ago, or him as he would be when he was old?

He put his hands on the edge of the sink and leaned forward. The past felt alive, and it was writhing inside him, a long, muscled eel. Breathe in and out, he thought. Don't think. Concentrate on the inhalations, exhalations. Remember what Clara had said to him as they walked into the police station. You'll be all right. I promise you'll be all right. Just give your statement, and then you can go home. He tried to conjure up Clara's face, but instead he saw Will. He saw Leo. He saw Tyler Green, and he felt himself hitting him, the scorching anger he had felt, so long held tamped down, but always there, a glowing ember.

Jay stood up straight again. He couldn't be here. He opened the door, stepped into the corridor. The police officer was talking to a young woman officer a few feet away, his back turned. Jay walked swiftly to the entrance and pulled the door open. No one called out or tried to stop him. He was outside. Down the steps. Into the forecourt, past the cars. Onto the street. It was that simple.

He walked swiftly, looking around him as he went. The sun had risen; the sky was gradually turning from silver-grey to a cloudless, glinting blue. He had no idea where he was, and no idea where to go next. Home, he told himself: get the first train out and head for home. He could lock the doors, close the curtains, unplug the phone, climb into bed and pull the covers over his head. He could hide away in the darkness and wait this out.

He wished it was still dark now. There were already cars on the road and people in the street. Some of them were starting their day and some ending it; night revellers reeling along, holding on to each other; men in T-shirts and women in short dresses. He shielded his face with one hand and tried not to look at them; he didn't want to meet anyone's eyes or feel the pinprick of their curiosity. He wanted to be swallowed up.

For many years, it had been his wish to be unseen and to leave no mark. Sometimes he thought of himself almost like mist on a landscape: there, but not there. Why had Clara made him come? The horrible night, people talking to him, asking questions, probing at him. Too much food, too much drink, too many bodies crowded together, and the past swirling about them.

There was the blare of a horn and screech of rubber on tarmac. Without noticing, he had wandered out into the middle of the road. A motorist was leaning out of the window shouting something at him, jerking his middle finger. Jay stumbled away.

He suddenly realised he had left his jacket over the back of the chair in the interview room – or perhaps he had left it at Beatrice's house; he couldn't remember now. He had no wallet. He had no phone; they'd taken that. He stopped on the pavement. He could walk for hours and still be trapped in this monstrous city.

'What shall I do?' he said out loud.

He lowered himself to a sitting position, put his arms around his shins and his head on his knees to blot out the sun. A dog wandered past, raised its leg against a lamppost a few feet from him.

In the station, just a few hundred metres away from where Jay crouched, DS Hawkins was shouting for that fucking Jay Murphy to be found, or someone would have to answer for it.

61

Conrad Bauer was woken by the phone ringing in the living room downstairs. He turned over, put his arm across his eyes, and tried to ignore it until it fell silent. Then he heard his mobile from his study next door, its jingly tune repeating. It stopped, then started once more. The landline rang again.

He sat up in bed. His wife remained steadfastly asleep, her grey hair spread out on the pillow and a sleep mask across her eyes. It was light outside and there were birds singing, but when he put on his glasses and looked at the radio on the bedside table, it was only a few minutes before five. Yet still the phones continued.

He climbed out of bed, pulled on his dressing gown and went into the study.

'Yes,' he barked. 'What is this?'

'Mr Bauer?'

'Yes.'

'I'm sorry to wake you. This is Nick Shelby from BBC News.'

'Why are you calling me at this ungodly hour?'

'I don't know if you've heard, but there's been a murder at the house of Sebastian Harris, and Tyler Green has been arrested.'

'What?'

Conrad Bauer rubbed his eyes. The reporter was still talking, asking him for a comment.

'Tyler Green,' the man repeated.

'You're saying there's been another murder?'

'Yes. A William Garvey, very late last night.'

'Will Garvey,' said Bauer. 'Dear God. He's killed Will too?'

'Garvey has been murdered, but as yet nobody has been—'

'You want a comment?' Bauer sat down, feeling the stiffness in his body. The phone was ringing again from the living room. 'I'll give you a comment.' He raised the hand that wasn't holding the mobile and brought it down with a thump on the desk. 'Why was he let out? I tried to stop it. I could have told you he would kill again. I did tell you.' He paused, took a calming breath. 'Tyler Green is a very dangerous man. Twenty-nine years ago, he killed my son. There are some people for whom life should mean life. I have always said he was one of them. Tyler Green should never have been released.'

After he had answered several calls, he went back into the bedroom.

'What's going on?' his wife murmured sleepily from the bed.

'I can't believe it,' he said. 'Tyler Green's back.'

'Back?'

She pushed the sleep mask to the top of her head, half opened her eyes.

'Out. And he's done it again.'

'No,' she said, sitting up. 'No.'

She looked old, thought Bauer, but then she was. They were both in their eighties now, but somehow even older than that. Grief wears you out.

'Yes.' He was pulling on his clothes. 'He's killed Will Garvey.'

'Where are you going?'

'They're on their way to interview me.'

'Conrad.' She was dismayed. 'Are you sure you want to get dragged back into all of this?'

But she could see any objection would be useless. Her husband was fired up, almost excited. She thought back to the months and years when he had been consumed by his campaign to keep Tyler Green locked away for life. It had been his way of mourning, or perhaps his way of refusing to believe Leo was dead.

'I'm going to raise such a stink,' Bauer said, buttoning up his shirt, running a comb through the white wisps of his hair. 'Such a stink.'

He already looked younger, she thought, and lay back on the pillow, pulling her eye mask down again, although she knew she wouldn't sleep. She listened to the birds singing outside the window, and thought about the man who had killed her son.

62

Maud put a styrofoam cup of coffee in front of Tyler.

'I don't know how you have it,' she said. 'Add your own milk or sugar.'

Tyler prised off the lid and picked up the cup in both his shackled hands as if he was cold, though the room was stuffy. He took a cautious sip, then another. He had control over himself again.

'I want to take you through the events of last night, as far as you remember them.' Maud nodded at Carrie, who turned on the recorder. 'What time did you arrive at number 44, St Matthew's Avenue?'

'I arrived at two minutes before seven o'clock.'

'That's weirdly precise.'

'I looked at my watch before I rang the bell.' He glanced at his bare, cuffed wrist. 'The only thing I collected from prison was my old watch, and the first thing I did was to replace its battery. I always wear it. They've taken it again, of course.'

'Who else was there?'

'Everyone except Rudi. He arrived about twenty-five minutes later. We started out in the living room, and then went into the garden.' He looked up from his coffee and half smiled. 'It's a very nice garden.'

'What were people drinking?'

'Dry martinis. It was something we used to have on special occasions. We thought they were cool.' His voice was ironic. 'I had water. The young woman Kristin didn't drink at first, though that changed later.'

Maud gathered her thoughts.

'So you're saying for that first part of the evening, the group was in one place?'

'Pretty much. At one point, Beatrice and Will went to the kitchen to do something with asparagus. Rudi and Beatrice went there a bit later to put the food out. People drifted around a bit, and they chatted in groups of course, it wasn't one big conversation, until Kristin asked me about what had happened that weekend.'

He was a good witness, thought Maud; very precise. She distrusted too much precision. At a time like this, most people became vague and confused.

'I told her, and described being in prison. What it was like. The atmosphere changed then; I suppose that was inevitable. That was when Kristin had her first drink, I think. Around ten past eight, I'd say.'

She raised her eyebrows at him.

'I'm very conscious of time,' he said, and for a moment there was a tiny crack in his regained composure. 'Time passing. Even without my watch, I always know what time it is.'

'What time is it now?' Carrie asked. He looked across at her.

'I think it must be about half past five, twenty to six.'

She took out her phone and glanced at it and smiled.

'It's your mundane superpower.'

'So after that, did you all stay together?' Maud said.

He waited, staring into the distance as if he could actually see the room he had been standing in, the comings and goings of the guests.

'Marco got very angry with me. We walked down the garden together, and he told me I'd ruined his life. Then I asked at what point did he realise he would never make it as a musician. He got very upset.'

'I see. Did you intend to upset him?'

'Not really. I was genuinely curious. I wanted to get a clear picture of what had happened to each of them. Kristin joined us, and then Beatrice came down the garden to tell us to behave in a civilised manner; something like that.'

'Then?'

'We all went downstairs and sat at the table. I sat at the head,' he added, before she could ask him, 'which was Beatrice's idea. Between Clara and Ali.'

'What happened next?'

'We ate. And some of them drank a lot. Wine this time.'

'Can you remember what people talked about?'

'At first it was all fragments. Rudi's rich wife, who campaigns for family values – women in the home, no sex before marriage, that kind of thing.' His voice was neutral. 'And then there was a conversation about children. Ellen has five. Ali and Will couldn't have children, which was obviously a painful subject. Ali was upset.'

'Upset with who?'

'With Kristin for asking her about it.' He put his cup down. 'But mainly with me.'

'You upset her as well as Marco?'

'It seems so.'

'Why?'

'I asked if she thought she would have made a good mother. She was distressed.'

'And you're surprised?'

'No. Will was angry,' he continued. 'I guess he wanted to

protect Ali. The whole evening, he seemed hyper-aware of her feelings. Perhaps that's not so strange.'

Maud wondered if perhaps DS Hawkins was right and Tyler Green was a psychopath after all.

'I sound cruel,' Tyler said, as if hearing her thoughts. 'Maybe I've become cruel. That's what all those years in a prison do to you.

'Ali left the table to smoke a cigarette in the garden. She needed time to herself. She returned a few minutes later. It must have been shortly before nine, something like that anyway. Then, at Kristin's bidding, people started talking about Leo.'

He stopped, but neither detective spoke, and after a few moments he continued.

'It started off with everyone saying how wonderful he was. Handsome and charming and clever. That kind of thing. You know, don't speak ill of the dead. But it quickly became something quite different.'

'Okay,' said Maud.

'Someone talked about how Leo had basically got Jay thrown out of uni. They wrecked a boy's room together, really trashed it, but Leo got off scot-free and it was Jay who was expelled. Jay insisted he didn't mind much. I don't know how true that was. After that, it was as if everyone had been given permission to speak freely. I think someone said Leo had always called Will "Fatty", but Will didn't seem bothered; he made a joke of it. Clara said Leo was a bully. She didn't specify. He was, though. I know from experience.'

'He bullied you?'

'At school. Very badly. You've got my motive,' he said. 'Revenge.'

The recorder blinked its red light. A message pinged onto Carrie's phone, then another.

'Then?'

'Then Ellen talked about having sex with Leo. She'd slept with every man round the table except Jay, and seemed gleeful about that. Well, why not? Anyway, she told us about her encounter with Leo. She said it was ugly, something to do with control, like an animal marking his territory.'

Maud was aware of the scratching of Carrie's pen. She nodded at Tyler to continue.

'Things turned nasty. Ellen mentioned a bet that Leo had made with friends that he could get Ali into bed. People tried to shut her up, but it was too late. Ali hadn't known about it until that moment round the table. It was clearly extremely painful, and it seemed indecent.'

It was an odd word. Maud stored it away.

'It almost felt that Leo was still damaging us, all these years later,' Tyler said. 'As if he was in the room.'

'And you? Did you know?'

'Yes,' he said simply.

Maud sat back in her chair.

'You talk about all of this as if it didn't concern you. Weren't you angry?'

'At the time I was.'

'Some dinner party,' said Carrie.

'What next?' Maud asked.

'Will turned on Ellen, accused her of being crass and cruel. One thing led to another. He told her that Leo had told all of us – all of the men, that is – about their encounter, and how she thought she was being liberated, but really was just a bit desperate. Things became heated. Clara in particular was furious with Will. Then Beatrice's son and his girlfriend arrived with the knife.' He gave his unsettling half smile. 'The one that was used to murder Will.'

'And you know that how?'

'I saw it beside the body.'

'How can you be sure it was the same one – lots of knives look similar.'

'It was the knife.'

'Did you touch it?'

There was a tremor of hesitation.

'No.'

'Back to the table. Beatrice's son and his girlfriend arrived at what time?'

'A bit after half past nine,' Tyler replied without hesitation. 'I don't think he cared for us. He left ten minutes later, leaving the knife behind.'

'Can you tell me who handled it?'

Tyler closed his eyes, opened them again. He looked like a bird of prey.

'Rudi did,' he said. 'And Marco waved it around. And Beatrice – she took it from Marco. I don't think the others did – or not then, at least. Anyway, after the boy had left, I gave my speech.'

'Your speech?'

'Yes. I said I was innocent. I said one of them had killed Leo and framed me, but I didn't know who. I said that if I had wanted revenge, I had got it: they were all trapped by the lives they'd led since the murder, and I was the only one who was really free.' He gave his mirthless smile again. 'Something like that anyway. I said I never wanted to see them again, and I was simply there to look them in the face for one last time, and to say goodbye.'

'That must have caused a stir.'

Tyler lifted one shoulder.

'I guess,' he said. 'Beatrice cleared everyone out of the room.

I don't know where they all went. I remember Ali went into the garden to have a cigarette, and Marco followed her. And Clara and Kristin went outside as well.'

'So I make this shortly after ten,' said Maud.

Tyler nodded.

'So you were left with Beatrice?'

'Yes. She was able to have her little talk with me. The one I think she had been waiting to have all evening. She basically said she had always thought I might not have been guilty, and she offered to help me financially if I wanted to appeal.'

'And what was your response to that?'

'I said I had no intention of appealing. And I asked her why she had never expressed her doubt before.'

'And?'

'Oh, you know,' said Tyler wearily. 'It was all so distressing, blah blah. She felt bad about it, blah blah. Anyway, I also left the room, after upsetting her.'

He said it as if he had knocked into a chair.

'How was that?'

'I asked about what the twenty-one-year-old Beatrice would think of Beatrice the corporate lawyer.'

'And she was hurt?'

'She was defensive, a bit angry. I mean, how can a murderer criticise a law-abiding pillar of the establishment? And then Jay came into the garden and he hit me.'

Maud pictured the thin and fragile man taking a swing at Tyler, who was tall and strong and menacing.

'Jay hit you?'

'Yes.'

'So basically,' said Carrie, 'you came to this reunion, found out everyone's weak spot, and exploited it until each person was in a state of anger and pain.'

'That wasn't the point.'

'And what was the point?'

'I needed to see them for who they were.'

'So you could be free of them?'

'Yes.'

Carrie nodded.

'Pretty brutal.'

'I can see you would think that.'

'And deliberate,' said Maud. 'As if you had planned it all out.'

'Can we take a break?' said Carrie. 'Five minutes.'

63

Carrie waved her mobile at Maud as they left the room.

'Apparently Sadie woke half an hour ago. I just need to make a call, sort a few things.'

She turned away from Maud, who caught fragments of Carrie's conversation with her mother. The green beaker that Sadie was having a tantrum about was in the cupboard next to the sink. The T-shirt with kangaroos on it that Sadie was insisting on was in the wash. It didn't matter if she didn't clean her teeth for once, and if Sadie wouldn't eat porridge, her mother could give her anything she wanted.

'She'll want to wear her wellies when you go out,' said Carrie. 'She wears them everywhere. They're in the broom cupboard. Okay, let me talk to her.'

Her voice changed, went up an octave. She used words like 'poppet' and 'pigeon', and made animated gestures, as if her child could see her.

'Mummy'll be home soon,' she said.

The light was streaming in through the small window when they returned to Tyler Green. It was past six o'clock. Soon Maud would go to the station to interview the rest of the group.

'We're getting near the time of William Garvey's death,' she said. 'From what you've told me, the whole group had been drinking heavily, some of them had taken drugs, and they had been stirred up by you. A bit of a toxic brew.'

'It was,' said Tyler.

'What happened after you went into the garden?'

'You'll have to ask them.'

'What did you do there?'

'Do?'

'From what other witnesses have said, you were in the garden for about fifteen minutes. What were you doing?'

'Nothing.' Maud waited. 'I was breathing,' said Tyler. 'Breathing in and out. Long slow breaths. It's like meditating. I was settling myself, letting everything that had happened go from me.'

'That's all?'

'Yes.'

'Fifteen minutes is a long time to just breathe,' said Carrie.

Tyler turned his gaze on her.

'Fifteen minutes is rather a short time, I find.'

'This is important. Who else came into the garden?'

'I'm not sure. I wasn't looking.'

'You've been very sure up till now.'

'I felt it was all over. It was time to go. I was tired.'

'So you have no idea who came into the garden?' Carrie pressed him.

'I know Jay did. He was all over the place, not really making sense. And Marco for a bit. They didn't stay long. Then Ellen shouted that I needed to come. She said Will had been stabbed.'

'You're telling me you didn't leave the garden until Ellen called you.'

'That's right.'

'But you have no witnesses to this?'

'Unfortunate, isn't it?'

'Tell me about the body.'

'What is there to say? He was dead. Blood everywhere. There was nothing I could do.'

'Did you kill him?'

'No.'

'Did you hate him?'

The shortest of pauses.

'No.'

'Do you know who killed him?'

'No.'

'Do you have anything to add?'

'No.'

Maud stood up.

'We're done for the moment,' she said.

64

The warder was waiting outside the interview room.

'Did he confess?' he asked.

'No,' said Maud.

The man shook his head.

'You could talk to him for a year and he wouldn't tell the truth.'

Maud hesitated. She felt uneasy about leaving Tyler Green in this situation, but she had so much else to do.

'I've requested that Tyler Green be moved into a police cell,' she said. 'In the meantime, he should be put on full suicide watch.'

'We'll pass on your concerns.'

'Pass on my concerns?' said Maud. 'What does that mean?'

'It means that we'll notify the relevant authority when possible.'

'When will that be possible? It's six in the morning on a weekend.'

'I don't know.' The warder gestured around him. 'You may have noticed that we've got staffing challenges here.'

'Tyler Green is an imminent threat to himself.'

'This prison is full of people who are threats to themselves and others. We can't watch all of them all of the time. Some people might think that a bastard like Green doesn't deserve special treatment after everything he's done. But we'll look in on him every hour or so. And we've put him with Harvey Skinner for a cell mate, so he'll have someone checking on him twenty-four seven. That's one of the benefits of overcrowding.'

Maud wasn't sure of what she should say to this. She felt that there must be something she could do, someone she could call, but she couldn't think of anyone and she was running out of time. She looked at the warder's tag.

'Mr Boyle,' she said. 'I'm holding you personally responsible for his safety.'

The warder smiled.

'Why don't you just do your job and leave me to do mine.'

65

Ellen Sweeney pressed the phone to her ear. She was smiling, and she gestured with her free hand, holding it out placatingly even though there was no one to see. Her voice was higher than usual.

'I would have called earlier, Michael,' she said. 'But I didn't want to wake you up.'

'Don't be ridiculous. Ollie was up an hour ago, making his usual racket.'

'I'm sorry.' She gripped the phone tighter.

'Too late for that.'

'You must be exhausted.'

'What I want to know, Ellen, is what is going on? And if you would be so good, tell me why I have to find out about it from the radio?'

'Please, Michael. One of my friends was murdered. And I was there.'

'Hardly one of your friends if you haven't seen him for decades.'

'Don't be angry. I'll be home soon.'

'I hope so.'

Her smile stiffened, until her mouth was a sad rectangle. With her unravelled plait and her hectic cheeks, she looked like a small child who was trying not to cry.

'It's been horrible,' she said. There was a catch in her voice.

There was an ominous silence.

'Ellen,' her husband said at last. 'Please don't be histrionic. It was your choice to go to this ridiculous reunion of people you haven't seen since we married. I really don't need my wife to be involved in some sordid drama. Do you know how that's going to look?'

'I'm sorry,' she said once more.

'You know who I am. You know my position. And I've got the job interview coming up.'

'Of course, darling.'

'It's bad enough not knowing when you'll do something embarrassing. God knows it happens a lot. But this is of a different order.'

'It's not my fault that—'

'Stop!'

She stopped.

'When will you be back?'

'As soon as I've given my statement, I'll go and pick up my things from Georgia's house, and then I'll get the first available train. I'll be as quick as I can.'

'That's several hours,' Michael said. 'You do realise I've had a particularly stressful week.'

'I know.'

'And now you expect me to look after the boys while you kick your heels in a police station. I'm not happy.'

'No.'

'Not happy at all.'

66

Conrad Bauer had played a successful businessman for many years in the TV series *Fletcher's Fortune*. But his best performance had been as the father of a murdered young man. At the moment they had heard, on that terrible morning twenty-nine years earlier, two young police officers sitting on the sofa in their living room, Conrad and Susan had started to cry. Their lives had broken apart, and they thought they could never put it back together. But gradually their lives did come back together. Susan Bauer had counselling, she had friends and, above all, she had her two other children.

Conrad Bauer rejected the idea of therapy with contempt. Could it bring Leo back? He rejected everything with contempt. Instead, he turned his grief into a cause. When Tyler Green's trial began, Bauer had assumed that he and his family would be at the centre of it. They were the victims, weren't they? But it turned out they were virtual bystanders. The police and the prosecution lawyers barely contacted them. During the trial, they were just watching the process like anyone else. Nobody asked them to testify. They weren't allowed to tell the jury about the pain they had suffered.

Bauer hated the lawyers. He hated the defence team, with their nitpicking attempts to deny the obvious truth. He hated the prosecution lawyer as well. For all the passion he showed, it might as well have been a shoplifting case. More than once, he saw the defence and prosecution barristers leaving the court together at the end of the day, chatting like old friends, laughing about something, like it was simply a game. He thought of them going home and having dinner and watching the TV, as if it had been a normal day at work.

But he didn't hate the judge. He had stared at him day after day. At first, Judge Kendall had looked almost detached. Giving evidence, one of the police officers referred to suggestions of illegal drug use during the weekend in question. They hadn't actually been found at the scene, but there were suspicions that they had been disposed of before the authorities had arrived. At this point the judge had shown a sudden interest. He had interrupted the prosecution and asked about these drugs. He had asked what they were, about their effects, about how drugs of these kind were obtained. As he heard the officer's answers, the judge's expression was one of obvious disgust. The defence counsel had got his feet and stated that the officer's evidence was based on suspicions about drugs that hadn't even been found. It was scarcely relevant to the issues of the case.

In response, the judge had turned towards the jury.

'I think it is possible that you members of the jury may find this information about the circumstances of the crime very relevant indeed. Of course, it is entirely a matter for you, but you may regard this as an explanation of the sordid circumstances in which this terrible crime was committed.'

Bauer could see that Judge Kendall despised Tyler Green and everything he represented, a world of drugs and privilege and sexual vagrancy. When Green himself was on the stand, the judge occasionally interspersed pointed questions of his own. They were ostensibly to clarify points of information, but Green's answers were always received with a grunt or a little shake of the head. Bauer had felt himself entirely ignored and marginalised, but just once, during Green's examination, the judge had looked round and had caught Bauer's eye. There was the merest flicker of recognition and Bauer saw also – or had he imagined it – an acknowledgement of shared disgust at what had happened.

After Green had been convicted, Bauer feared that there might be some recommendation for mercy: a promising student, unblemished character, a glittering future before him. But the judge went the other way. He dismissed the very idea.

'What we should be thinking of, here in this court, is of a young life cut off in the flower of his youth.'

After the trial was over, people spoke to Bauer of drawing a line under the whole terrible affair. They talked of closure, as if the matter could ever be closed. Bauer had heard of murderers being released early if they had reformed and shown repentance. A columnist wrote an article about the case, condemning the length of the sentence, and saying how unlikely it was that a man like Tyler Green would ever reoffend.

A man like Tyler Green. Bauer knew what that meant. It meant that respectable people, students, didn't belong in jail. He could imagine Green doing the correct things in prison, studying, pretending to repent, saying the right things to the right people and then being quietly released after a few years. From that moment on, Bauer devoted his life to preventing such a thing happening. His life as an actor continued and thrived. But his true passion was keeping Tyler Green in prison.

He founded a victim support group. He gave interviews on radio and television. He spoke at conferences and demonstrations, anywhere that would have him. He had the phone number of every radio producer and editor and journalist, and they had his number. He was always available, always articulate and well-briefed. He made himself an expert on the probation service. He knew how to work the system but, even more important, he knew how to work it from behind the scenes. He made connections with people in the judiciary and the Home Office who couldn't afford to be seen to be soft on crime. He understood that nobody ever paid a political price for keeping a convicted murderer locked up.

He realised that it wasn't enough to feel grief. When you were on television or on the radio, you had to be able to perform it, with the right crack in the voice, just as you shed tears on stage in a play you had performed a hundred times before.

Within an hour of learning the news, Bauer was sitting on his sofa with a TV news crew. He had dressed, as usual, with great care. He wasn't wearing a suit and tie. That would look mad on a breakfast TV show. He had a chosen a sober, dark blue shirt, open-necked. Casual but serious.

The young woman interviewing him was new. Bauer was familiar with almost all the reporters and presenters in current affairs and features, but he hadn't met Freya Davison before. She looked concerned.

'Before we start the interview,' she said, 'we had a call with the lawyer and we've got to be really careful about what we say about this.' Her eyes flashed with distress. 'What happened to your son, it's a terrible tragedy,' she continued. 'I recognise you're still living with it. Of course you are. But we still have to be careful.'

Bauer was tempted to say that he knew as much about contempt law as a lawyer, just as he knew as much about the probation service as a probation officer.

'It's all right,' he said. 'I've been doing these interviews for years.'

'Now there's an active police investigation though.'

'It's only when charges are imminent that the contempt laws really become relevant,' Bauer said. 'But don't worry, I'll be careful. I simply want to convey how I feel. I want to speak from the heart on behalf of victims, as I always do. By the way, am I right that the victim of this terrible crime is William Garvey?'

'Yes, that's right.'

'Was he married?'

'Yes.'

'And is he known as William? Or Will? Or Bill?'

'I'm sorry, I don't know.'

'Better stick with William,' said Bauer. 'One of the awful things about what happened to our son was when the media said things about him that weren't true, and then other people repeated them.'

'We'll try to get things right,' said the woman. She nodded at the camerawoman and then turned back to Bauer. 'I'll do an introduction later. I'll fill in the background, say who you are, et cetera, et cetera. Are you all right if we go straight into the interview?'

Bauer looked round. On the wall behind him was a photograph of Leo Bauer, eighteen years old, grinning as if someone had just made a joke. Whenever he did television interviews at home he sat so that the photograph was visible behind him. He nodded at her.

'Conrad Bauer, when you heard about the terrible events of last night, how did it make you feel?'

Bauer paused, as if he needed to gather himself.

'Before I say anything, I must acknowledge that a man has been murdered. His name is William Garvey and I would like to offer my deepest condolences to his widow and . . .' Bauer paused. He had forgotten to ask whether Garvey had children or not. 'And to his loved ones generally. I know what it's like to lose a family member in these circumstances.'

'And you have a painful personal connection to this event. That must bring back terrible memories.'

'Yes,' said Bauer. He felt his eyes prickle. 'I can't comment on the details of this awful crime. It's currently being investigated. But it's a simple fact that one of the people present at the house where this murder was committed was Tyler Green.' He took a deep breath. 'Many years ago, Tyler Green was convicted of the brutal, unprovoked murder of my dear son, Leo.' Another deep breath, then another.

'I know it must be difficult for you,' said the interviewer softly.

'It never stops being difficult. The murder was committed decades ago, and Tyler Green was sentenced to life imprisonment. I have devoted my life ever since to fighting for the rights of my son, and the rights of other victims of crime. I wanted to make sure that life really meant life. But . . .' A deep breath. 'The authorities thought differently. A few weeks ago, despite all our protests, Tyler Green was released. I'm not going to comment on what happened. We'll see what the police find out. If they find out anything. But the fact is that Tyler Green is back in custody, where he belongs.'

'Have these terrible events opened old wounds?'

Bauer rubbed his eyes.

'The wounds don't need opening. They never go away. Tyler Green was sentenced to life, but my wife and I, we were the ones who received the real life sentence.'

Bauer looked at Freya Davison, who left a few seconds of silence.

'Conrad Bauer, thank you very much.' Another pause. She looked at the camerawoman. 'That was great. That was

exactly what we needed.' She caught herself. 'I mean, you expressed your grief so movingly.'

'Do you need to do cutaways?' said Bauer.

'Just a few. We'll only be a few minutes.'

67

'Where to now?' asked Constable Hale.

'Give her Weetabix then,' said Carrie into her mobile.

'Back to Hitcham Road Station, please.'

'Or anything. There are some pancakes in the freezer compartment.'

'Grim in there, was it? I've never actually been inside. But you hear the stories.'

'Pretty grim,' said Maud.

Her mind was racing. She tried to put thoughts of Tyler Green aside, and concentrate on the tasks ahead of her.

'Give her anything. Or nothing. She won't starve.'

'Bed bugs, they're the worst,' said Hale with relish.

Maud looked out of the window at the city waking up, corner shops opening, people in running gear jogging along the pavement, dog walkers, heading out into the beautiful morning. Her eyes felt gritty with tiredness.

They drove past the front of Hitcham Road Station, where a crowd of journalists was gathered near the entrance, and turned into the car park. The station had an anonymous and bureaucratic appearance. It could have been a benefit office, red-brick and symmetrical, its square windows glinting in the sunlight.

'I'm so sorry,' said Carrie. 'Tell her I'll be back soon. Put her in front of the telly. Whatever she wants. I can't thank you enough for holding the fort.'

'The doctor gave Alison Marais a sedative,' DS Hawkins told Maud. 'You'd better give her a couple of hours before you talk to her.'

'How are the rest bearing up?'

Hawkins grinned.

'Where do I start? The KC has demanded her big-shot lawyer, who's on his way. That Ellen Sweeney is giving some kind of inspirational lecture about fuck knows what to whoever will listen. The guy with the shaved head, Burney, is jabbering away about being the victim of a miscarriage of justice. His drug test was positive, by the way.'

'What's happened to his partner? Have you tracked her down?'

'Yep. She was back in the flat, packing a bag. And she's not the only one who did a runner.'

'What do you mean?'

'That Jay Murphy. He tried to escape.'

'What do you mean, escape? He's not been arrested. He was always free to go.'

'I don't think that's how he sees it. He snuck out, but only got as far as the corner where he curled up in a ball. A kind lady came and told us about him.'

'I see,' said Maud.

'Oh, plus the boy's here. It's quite a party. I gather the wife of Rudi Scott is also—'

'The son's here?'

'Yes. I put him in Interview Room Seven to calm down.'

'Is he upset?'

'He's crying. He wants his mother.'

'Not until he's been asked about the murder weapon. Is an appropriate adult with him?'

'What?'

'An appropriate—'

'I know what you said. He's not a child. He's seventeen.'

'Exactly.'

Maud turned to Carrie.

'I was going to speak to Rudi Scott,' she said. 'He was the last known person to see William Garvey. But we need to talk to Jay Murphy at once, given his mental state.'

'Don't you want to know about the media furore?' Hawkins asked. 'Leo Bauer's father has been on telly, and now his fans are gathering out there with banners.'

'No, thank you. Not just now.'

She walked swiftly down the corridor, but at the door of the interview room suddenly paused. Her pale face wore an alert expression; her eyes were narrowed. Carrie thought she looked like a dog who'd found a scent on the breeze. In fact Maud was remembering something, a tiny moment in the house which she had noticed without even realising she had noticed.

She turned to Carrie.

'Join me in a minute,' she said. 'First, can you collect the file on the Leo Bauer murder. And track down Matt Moran. Ask him to contact me as soon as possible.'

'The forensics guy?'

'Yes. I need him.'

68

The young officer paused before opening the door to the interview room.

'He tried to make a run for it,' he said. 'Sounds like an admission of something, doesn't it?'

'I'd just like to talk to him,' said Maud.

'I just thought you should be informed.'

'I already have been. Maybe you could bring us some coffee.'

'You don't want me to sit in.'

Maud didn't reply.

'All right,' he said. 'Two coffees.'

'Three. One for my colleague.' Maud gestured towards Carrie, who was hurrying in the opposite direction. 'She'll be back before it arrives.'

The officer grunted, then pushed the door open.

Jay was sitting, hunched over, his head moving up and down, as if to a rhythm that nobody else could hear. Maud pulled a chair across and sat opposite him.

'Why did you run off like that?' Maud asked.

Jay slowly raised his head and looked at her. He was blinking quickly and still nodding his head.

Maud repeated the question.

'I can't deal with this. I never wanted to come. I said it would be too much. But she said it would be all right.'

'Who said?'

'Clara. She said it would be good for me. I knew it wouldn't. And now it's happened again.' The nervous motion of his head increased, his hands opened and closed on the table. He was making strange smacking noises with his mouth, as if he was trying to spit out a hair.

'Jay.' Maud leaned across the table towards him, trying to hold his gaze, but his eyes flickered rapidly round the room. 'I've asked them to bring us some coffee. Then I simply want to ask you some questions, as I'm doing with all of you. You are not under arrest. You have not been charged with any offence. You were present when a crime was committed and are a material witness. We need to find out who did it, and you may be able to help us. Do you understand?'

'Home,' said Jay. It was more like a question than a demand.

'Have you taken any substances?' asked Maud, who was wondering if he needed urgent medical attention.

His eyes flicked towards her.

'I have been all right,' he said. 'I have been careful. I have done what I was told.'

The door opened and Carrie came in, the young officer behind her with a wooden tray, which he put on the table before leaving again, shutting the door too loudly.

'Here. Sugar's good for shock.' Carrie ripped open several sachets and tipped their contents into one of the cups of coffee. 'Nothing to stir it with,' she said, and dipped her pencil into the liquid instead, swirling it vigorously. 'Milk?'

He didn't reply, so she splashed in some milk, before pushing the cup across to Jay.

He stared between the two women with a glassy expression, then fixed on Maud.

'Don't look at me like that.' He pointed a finger at her. 'You're looking at me as if you can see inside me, and you can't.' He pressed himself back in his chair, as if he was trying to shrink from sight.

'What are you worried about people seeing?' Maud asked gently.

'You don't understand.'

'Help me understand.'

'This is no good.'

He picked up the coffee in both trembling hands; pale liquid sloshed over the brim.

'Do you have a secret, Jay?'

'Everyone has secrets. Don't you?'

'Is there something you're ashamed of, guilty about?'

'Shame?' He gave a wild laugh.

'Did you kill William Garvey?'

'That's not the point.'

'Please answer the question. Did you kill him?'

'No.'

'Yet you ran away.'

'I keep telling you, I can't be here. Nobody listens.'

'I'm listening. You can tell me anything.'

'That's what they always say.'

'Who's "they"?'

Jay focused on her for a moment.

'I don't know,' he said tiredly, almost sane. 'Just I've been here before.'

'What was your relationship to William Garvey?'

'Nothing,' he said. 'Not really since I left university before they all did.'

'Clara is the only one you've stayed in touch with?'

'She stayed in touch with me. She feels bad.'

'About what?'

Maud could sense Carrie shifting in her chair, slightly

impatient at Maud's line of questioning, but she kept her eyes fixed on Jay Murphy's thin, twitching face.

'She left me,' he said. 'After Leo. I fell apart. The last straw.'

'Twenty-nine years is a long time to feel guilty about a break-up.'

'Break up, break down,' said Jay. He gave a snort of wretched laughter. 'She keeps an eye on me, like my mother. Not that my mother keeps an eye on me. Anyway.' He rocked in his chair. 'Anyway,' he repeated. 'I told her, I live in the ashes.'

'The ashes?' It sounded grandiose, but it made a kind of sense. Jay Murphy was like the grey embers of someone, a bleak and burnt-out man. 'You didn't keep in touch with William Garvey?'

He shook his head.

'Or Tyler Green?'

Again a shake of the head.

'You said you left university before them – why was that?'

Jay moved his head slowly from side to side, like a cornered animal.

'You know already.'

'I don't know. I'd like you to tell me.'

'I was thrown out.'

'Why was that?'

'I don't want to talk about it.'

'Better you tell me than someone else does.'

'I acted violently,' said Jay. 'Is that what you wanted to hear? Is that enough? I was violent. I wrecked a room. I hurt someone. I left. I never went back. I should have never gone on that stupid weekend. I should never have come to this bloody reunion. Everything's gone wrong. Everything. Everything. Everything.'

'Mr Murphy,' said Maud. 'Jay. Have you been violent since then?'

'I don't want to talk anymore. I'm better now. I work in a care home, and I am careful with everybody. They like me. They know they can trust me. It won't happen again.'

'Were you violent last night?'

'No,' said Jay, putting up a hand to shield his face. 'No.'

'Did you attack Tyler Green?'

'No. No. No.'

He was rocking again, and his words weren't denials, more like a chant to himself.

'It's better for you if you tell me.'

'No,' he said.

'Did you attack William Garvey?'

'No. Please. No.'

'What did you do when you went back into the garden after Tyler Green had made his speech?'

'Do?' He stared at her wildly then covered his eyes. 'Do?'

'Did you go back into the house? Did you kill William Garvey?'

'No.'

'Then talk to me, Jay. Tell me what you remember. Tell me what you know.'

'Nothing. I don't remember anything. I don't know anything. Please let me go home now.'

His rocking was more rapid and Maud could sense that he was slipping further into himself, out of her reach.

'Are you on medication?' she asked. 'Is there anything you need?'

He didn't answer, just huddled in on himself and rocked to and fro, murmuring a word she couldn't make out.

'Call the mental health social services,' Maud said to the officer.

'It's Saturday. The interview rooms are full of your witnesses. There's a crowd gathering outside. Now you want me to bring in the social services as well?'

'Call them at once, and don't let Jay Murphy leave here. He isn't safe.'

69

'I can see why someone would want to kill Tyler Green,' said Carrie. 'But why would someone want to kill William Garvey? Except Tyler, maybe. Or Garvey's wife. But why would either of them do it in public, at a reunion? And the others hadn't seen him for decades. Or maybe we're making it too complicated, and it was just a random act of violence committed during a moment of drunken rage.'

'Maybe,' said Maud. Her brows were knitted and her face intent. 'Or maybe something happened that evening to trigger the murder, something we don't know yet, or haven't understood.'

'Mostly it seems like chaos.'

'Which we need to sift through. Can you start putting together a timeline of events. We have to figure out where people were around the time of the murder – I mean, in what room, who they were with, in the very small window in which it could have happened.'

Her mobile buzzed and she fished it out of her pocket, making a grimace when she saw who was calling.

'Maud.'

Even with that one syllable, Maud could tell her boss wasn't happy.

'Sir.'

'Where the fuck are you?'

'In the station.'

'Well, so am I, and so is half the country, as far as I can see. The place is full to the gunnels. There are people waving banners on the pavement outside. What am I supposed to tell the Home Secretary?'

'You can say that the investigation is—'

'And what about the press?'

'What about them?'

'Come on, Maud. You need to get Tyler Green to confess. Before long, you need to make a statement to the press; they're clamouring. You need to give Sebastian Harris some red meat and get the Home Secretary off my back. Also, I've just been accosted by a very cross lady called Mrs Scott.'

'Let's talk face to face.' Maud slid her mobile back into her pocket. 'I'm starving,' she said to Carrie.

'I'll get you a piece of toast or something while you talk to him, shall I?'

'Terrific. And more coffee – with an extra shot. Carrie, there are two people I've got serious concerns about.'

'Who do you mean?'

'I'm worried about Jay Murphy.'

'Me too,' said Carrie. 'But you've left instructions for them to call the mental health social services. They'll take care of him. Who's the other?'

'Tyler Green shouldn't be in prison.'

'Lots of people shouldn't be in prison.'

'I was thinking: the warder mentioned the name of his cell mate. Harvey Skinner. Did it ring a bell?'

'I don't think so, no.'

'I wonder what he's in for.'

70

Craig Weller was tired and grumpy. His tie was knotted too tightly and his hair was brushed flat against his scalp. When he saw Maud, he pointed an accusing finger at her.

'Give me one good reason why you haven't charged Tyler Green.'

'There's no evidence he did it. It doesn't look like he's broken the conditions of his licence either. He shouldn't have been locked up again.'

'You want to let him out?' Weller's face turned a dangerous shade of red. 'That's your solution to this shit show? Let the psychopath out on the streets, and keep the rest of them shut up in a police station. Including the husband of a prominent campaigner, and a KC who's the wife of a cabinet minister.'

'Nobody's been shut up. I asked them to wait until they gave their statements, that's all. Some of them don't live in London.'

'Well, I'm going to tell Hawkins they should all go home and wait for you to contact them.'

'Why would you do that?'

'Because I'm your boss, Maud. Remember?' He glared at her. 'I know what you've been up to.'

'I'm sorry, sir? What have I been up to?'

'I know you've been studying to be a lawyer on the sly. Did you think I wouldn't find out?'

Maud kept her expression bland.

'It wasn't a secret.'

'You're going to jump ship, is that it?'

'It's just a course I'm doing in the evening. It's useful to learn a bit about the law.'

'I don't know about that. It depends what you're learning. I don't want to think you're not committed, Maud.'

'I don't think I've given you any reason to think that.'

'I've put myself on the line for you more than once.'

Maud didn't reply to that. She wasn't convinced that Weller really had put himself on the line for her.

'I don't want you running around being a lawyer. Arguing for that fucker, Tyler Green, as if you're his defence council.'

'I'm not being a lawyer, but I'm not going to break the law for the convenience of the Home Secretary. I'm going to conduct this inquiry in an orderly fashion, follow the rules.' She gave him a cautious smile. 'As I know you'd want, sir.'

Weller narrowed his eyes, as if searching for sarcasm in her tone.

'I know you've got to do your job, but I've got to do mine as well, and you're not making that easy. Help me out here, Maud.'

'I'm not trying to be difficult.'

Weller tapped on his watch.

'It's a quarter past seven now. You obviously aren't ready to charge Green, and this is going to take longer than I had hoped or expected. We reconvene at ten and assemble a proper team. Then you talk to the press. Fair?'

'Fair,' said Maud. She thought for a moment. 'Okay. Hawkins can tell people to go home, and we'll contact them to make their formal statements. Except there is someone I'd like to tell myself.'

Weller looked suspicious.

'Why?'

'A few questions before they leave. Observe their demeanour.'

'There are already lawyers buzzing around,' said Weller. 'Like flies around a turd. Tread carefully.'

'Just a few questions.'

Carrie handed her a mug of coffee and a large, slightly stale Danish pastry.

'You wondered about Harvey Skinner,' she said.

'Yes?'

'I looked him up. Three years ago, when he was working as a kind of handyman in Kent, he beat an old couple to death with a claw hammer. She was eighty-seven and he was ninety. He stole eighty quid that was hidden in their teapot.'

'Oh, fuck.'

'He was caught because he went into the local shop to buy cigarettes covered in their blood. Apparently he showed no remorse. When the judge sentenced him, he started humming. He sounds like a properly scary character. Here, this is what he looks like.'

Carrie slid her mobile across, and Maud looked at a face, eyes magnified by the thick glasses, the oversized, smiling red mouth.

'What the hell are they playing at?'

71

Rudi Scott had clearly been the most elegantly dressed of the guests, with his linen suit and his beautiful shirt. Now he was glassy-eyed with shock or exhaustion. His linen jacket was creased, and there was a smear on one of the sleeves where something had been spilled. Maud and Carrie sat opposite him; Carrie handed him his mobile.

'You can leave in a minute,' Maud said.

'Thank God,' said Rudi. 'I just need to sleep. Except I feel like I'm never going to sleep again.'

'But first I'd like to ask you a couple of questions.'

Rudi frowned.

'What about?'

'I hope you won't object if we record this interview?'

'What?'

Carrie placed the recorder on the table.

'I don't want to be difficult,' said Rudi, 'but I'm just so tired. With the shock of it all, I can't even think straight. Is this an official interview?'

'Well, it's an interview,' said Maud. 'And we're detectives. But you're free to leave at any time.'

'Is this a moment when I should ask for my lawyer? I have one, you know.'

'You're allowed to have legal advice at any time,' said Maud. 'Including now.'

Rudi shook his head.

'I just want to be helpful,' he said.

Carrie switched the machine on. Maud identified themselves, gave the date, time and place.

'You were the last known person to see William Garvey
alive,' said Maud.

'I'm sure that's not true,' said Rudi. 'I'm sure someone saw
him after me.'

'Really?' Maud said with interest. 'Who?'

'Well, I don't know anyone specifically, but there were so
many people milling around. I assume someone else saw him.'

'There weren't so many people milling around upstairs,
where the body was found.'

Rudi didn't reply to that.

'Why did you go upstairs?' Maud asked.

He gave an obviously forced laugh.

'Is something amusing?' Carrie asked.

'It seems weird to ask a question like that about a party
where everyone was just wandering about.'

'It may seem weird,' Maud said. 'But I'm going to ask the
question again. Why did you go upstairs?'

'I think I went to the toilet upstairs. I'd been drinking quite
a lot.'

'There's a toilet downstairs, isn't there?'

'It was probably occupied. I was fairly pissed by that time,
and maybe I wanted to get away from all the noise for a
moment.'

'And then?'

'And then what?'

'I'm trying to follow your movements,' said Maud. 'You
come out of the toilet and – what?'

Again Rudi seemed to be forcing himself to think.

'I saw Will.'

'Where?'

'I saw him on the landing.'

'You mean, outside the bathroom?'

'Yes. I think so. It must have been there.'

'What was he doing?'

'He wasn't doing anything. I assumed he was waiting for me to come out.'

'How long were you there?'

'You mean with Will?'

'How long were you upstairs?'

'I can't remember exactly.'

'Five minutes?'

'Maybe.'

'Ten minutes?'

'Why does it matter?'

'I'm just trying to get an idea. Ten minutes? Fifteen minutes?'

'Not fifteen. I was just in the bathroom.'

'And how long were you with Mr Garvey?'

'Barely any time. A minute? Two?'

'And you talked to him?'

There was another visible hesitation. When Rudi started to reply, he stammered slightly and had to correct himself.

'Yes, yes, I talked to him a bit.'

'What did you talk about?'

He shook his head helplessly.

'You're asking me about a party where I talked to person after person for hours. We were all drinking and arguing and remembering, and sometimes it got out of hand. It's really hard to remember one particular and very brief conversation in those circumstances. And Will had drunk a great deal.'

'Try and remember,' said Maud. 'This was different. It was

in a different place, separate from the rest of the party. It was just the two of you. You must be able to remember something.'

'We just chatted.'

'Chatted about what?'

'About the oddity of getting back together after all these years.'

'There was some conflict during the evening. Did he say anything about that?'

'No.'

'Did he say why he had gone upstairs?'

'I think he said he needed to get away from the party for a moment, away from all of us. He was very drunk. Quite emotional. We had all been remembering Leo's murder, the moment of finding him dead.'

'Yes?'

'It was intense, after so many years of trying to forget about it. Ellen found the body, you know, just as she found Will's, though Marco seemed to think it was him who had found Leo. Ellen said she knew in that instant that our lives would never be the same. Marco said there was a faint smile on Leo's face, though I can't say I saw that. And Ali and Will talked about the way he had stared up at them. Someone else said something.' He frowned. 'I think it was Clara who said he seemed to be reaching out for something or someone. Everyone had different ways of remembering him, as if they had to focus on a single detail to make sense of it, or to make it bearable.'

'And what do you remember?'

'Me? Honestly, I don't know. He was just – well, just so dead. I had never understood before how dead a dead person can be. If you know what I mean.'

Maud nodded. She did know. She waited a few seconds, looking at Rudi.

'You also said you went upstairs because you needed to get away from the party.'

'Oh, yes, that's right.'

'Did you follow him upstairs?'

'No. I told you. I went up to the toilet.'

'Did he follow you?'

'He was already there.'

'Can you be more specific? Where exactly was he?'

Rudi looked suddenly confused.

'I mean, he was there when I came out of the bathroom. We exchanged a few words, then I went downstairs again.'

'So did he go into the bathroom when you left him?'

'What?'

'You said you assumed he was waiting to go into the bathroom, even though there are several other lavatories in the house. Did he go in?'

'I don't know. I didn't notice. I wasn't paying attention.'

'So you left the party to go the bathroom, and to get away from it all?'

'Yes.'

'For no other reason?'

'What other reason could I have had?'

He sounded irritated.

'But apparently when you left the dining area where everyone was gathered, you said you were going to call your wife.'

'Oh. Did I say that? I don't remember.'

'You did say that. Did you call her?'

'What?'

'Did you call your wife, as you told the assembled guests you were going to do?'

'I'm not sure,' Rudi said cautiously.

'Let me help you. You didn't. Your mobile shows that you made no calls that evening.'

'So why ask me? I didn't call her. I was going to, but then didn't want to wake her. What's that got to do with anything?'

Maud didn't reply. She just looked at him.

'I'm so tired,' said Rudi. 'I'm not thinking straight.'

'That's all for the moment.' She stood up. 'Before you go, I'm going to send an officer in. You'll need to remove all your clothes.'

'What the hell for?'

'You were at a murder scene.'

'Does that mean I'm being accused of something?'

Now Maud was the one who suddenly felt weary.

'People are combing through that room with tweezers. They'll find fibres. It will be helpful to know which of them are yours, and which of them aren't.'

'My lawyer might have something to say about that.'

Maud made herself respond calmly.

'I've already told you that you can have a lawyer present at any point. But if you refuse to co-operate with this, you won't be allowed to leave until it's resolved. The officer will bring you some other clothes. They probably aren't very stylish, but they'll get you home. Once your statement is typed up, you'll be asked to return to sign it. The interview is concluded.'

72

As Maud shut the door to the interview room, a woman came down the corridor towards them at a brisk pace. She was neat and streamlined, pale hair framing a long, pale face. Her ears were small and flat against her scalp; her narrow shoulders were encased in a tailored grey jacket. A tired-looking man with iron-grey hair and steel spectacles trailed in her wake, carrying a cardboard tray with three Styrofoam cups inserted into it.

The woman stopped abruptly.

'What were you doing in there?'

'I'm sorry?'

'I said, what were you—?'

'I heard you. I'm Detective Inspector O'Connor. I was interviewing a witness. Can I ask what you are doing here?'

'Why were you with my husband? He must have told you he wanted his lawyer present.' She gestured at the man behind her, who shifted from foot to foot. 'Why were you interviewing him at the very time we had gone to get refreshments?'

'He didn't tell me.'

'You expect me to believe that?'

'You can ask your husband.'

'I'm not happy about the way this case is being conducted. Rudi has been up all night. He hasn't been allowed home. He's been treated like a criminal.'

'He was free to leave. He was asked to stay until he gave his statement.'

'So he can go now?'

'Not immediately. He needs to give us his clothes.'

'What?'

'We'll supply him with others.'

Celia narrowed her eyes. Her nostrils quivered. Maud couldn't tell if she was angry or alarmed.

'Who is in charge of this case? I want to speak to him.'

'Me,' said Maud.

'You?'

'Yes. So address any concerns to me.'

'You know who I am?'

'I know you're the wife of Mr Scott, who was present when a murder was committed.'

'I can make life very difficult for you.'

Maud grinned.

'Join the queue,' she said cheerfully.

'I think she's scared,' Carrie said as they walked away.

'You may be right. Anyway, let's get his clothes looked at.'

'Just his shirt and trousers?'

Maud considered this. Something was nagging at her. She had been irritated by his attitude but that wasn't it.

'No,' she said. 'I want everything. Shoes, socks, underwear.'

'His underwear?' said Carrie, smiling. 'He won't like that.'

'I want Matt to go through it all, every thread, every little stain.' She looked back at the room they had just left. 'So what do you think?'

'He was the last person we know of who saw Garvey alive. He's an obvious suspect, and he didn't do himself any favours with those answers. He sounded like someone desperately trying to think of something to say.'

'I know,' said Maud doubtfully. 'And yet I can't help feeling that if he had killed Garvey, he might have come up with some more convincing answers.' She sighed. 'But then criminals don't always act in their best interests, and I've not had any sleep, and I'm probably overthinking this.'

'I've been looking through the file on Leo Bauer.'

'Anything leap out?'

Carrie shrugged.

'Same execution.'

'Right.' Maud rubbed her face, pushed her hair more firmly back. 'Let me have a quick look, just in case.'

'In case of what? What are you looking for?'

'No idea.'

Maud opened the file and skim-read a few pages. She had been telling the truth when she said that she had no idea what she was looking for. She didn't even know if the two murders were connected. She turned over witness statements, the pathology report; glanced at the toxicology. Then she lifted up the bundle of photos. The house. The room. The body. Leo Bauer lying in a small disordered room, blood puddled around him, his arm thrown up and forward, as if clutching towards something, his white face, the closed eyes, the dark tangle of hair, and the neck torn open. There were close-ups of the wound; the knife; the defenceless body on the slab.

She sighed and put everything back in the folder.

'We need to get to Ali Marais' house.'

Carrie was just starting to answer when Maud's phone rang. It was Weller.

'I want you to get a statement from Beatrice Macmillan,' he said.

'I've already talked to her.'

'This is the official one,' said Weller. 'On the record. I've talked to her husband, and I've said if we do this one statement, get it done and dusted, we can draw a line under their participation.'

'That's not necessarily true,' said Maud, 'and I'm not sure it's the best use of my time at the moment. I want to talk to the widow.'

'If you disagree, you can send me a memo. Meanwhile, just get it done.'

73

Tyler Green was staring at the ceiling, following the cracks in the paintwork. Everything – the paintwork, the frayed sheet that was half covering him, the rusting grille around the light in the ceiling – looked like it was rotting or rusting or cracking. He felt a movement from the bunk below him.

Harvey Skinner was so tall that he had to curl himself in order to fit on the bottom bunk. The cells on this level had been designed for single occupancy, but they had all been adapted for two people. That meant a bunk bed, and a makeshift curtain in front of the stainless steel toilet. Skinner wasn't just tall. He was bulky, as if he had been partially inflated, his bare stomach bulging between his waistband and the bottom of his T-shirt. And he was pale, as if he had been kept underground. He wore thick aviator glasses and his curly hair was divided in the middle. It was shiny with hair oil or just sweat.

His voice, when it came, was surprisingly high.

'Tyler Green,' he said. 'Tyler Green.'

Tyler didn't answer.

'Thirty years they said you did. That's bad. That's very bad.'

Tyler remained silent. The cell felt tiny, as if there wasn't enough air in it for the two of them.

'And now you're back.' Skinner gave a shrill giggle. 'You didn't last long out there, did you?'

He waited for Tyler to speak. In the distance, they could both hear the sound of someone yelling.

'You're not very friendly, are you?' Skinner said. 'Not very talkative.'

'No.'

'Rude, I call it. I don't think I care for that. Not one bit.'

74

Constable Hale drove Maud and Carrie south towards the river. Maud looked out of the window. She saw people walking with their morning coffees. It was the weekend. They were wearing shorts, summer dresses.

She lifted her phone to her ear.

'Hello. Yes, this DI O'Connor. I want to speak to the Duty Governor … Yes. The Duty Governor …'. Now. As a matter of urgency … Yes. I know the time, and no, it can't wait … Thank you, I'll stay on the line.'

She looked at her watch. It was ten past eight. The sky was a pale, milky blue. The leaves on the great plane trees were a fresh lime green. Tiredness pulsed behind her eyes.

'Hello,' said a voice.

'Is this the Duty Governor?'

'Yes. And you are?'

'I am DI O'Connor, and I'm calling about one of your inmates. Tyler Green was admitted in the early hours. I've just learned that he has been put in a cell with Harvey Skinner.'

'Why is this your concern?'

'Harvey Skinner doesn't sound like he should be anyone's cellmate. I want you to move Tyler out of there at once.'

'You do, do you?'

'Harvey Skinner sounds like a psychopath.'

'So we've put him with another psychopath. What's your objection?'

'Mr – what is your name? You haven't told me.'

'Steven Chellick.'

'Well, Mr Chellick, my objection is that someone is going to get hurt.'

'Have you heard that prisons are overcrowded?'

'I am asking you to move Tyler Green at once. I am gravely concerned for his safety. Are you saying that you won't?'

'I'm saying that I've noted your concerns.' She could almost hear his smile. 'For what they are worth.'

75

When the car stopped and they got out, they found themselves in front of an apartment building that was like a hotel. They entered through large glass doors and were greeted by a concierge, who showed them to a lift. On the eleventh floor, they stepped out into an anonymous corridor. Immediately opposite, a door was opened by a young woman dressed in a slim grey suit, with a white shirt.

'I'm not the butler,' she said, smiling. 'My name's Robyn Murdoch. I'm here as Beatrice Macmillan's legal representation. Come through, will you?'

They stepped inside.

'Jesus,' said Carrie. 'Sorry. That's not very professional.'

'I believe it belongs to a friend of Mr Harris.'

The apartment was spectacular enough, bare boards, open plan, minimalist. The floor-to-ceiling plate glass windows looked out on the river, across at the Houses of Parliament. At one end of the room was a long glass dining table. Beatrice Macmillan and Sebastian Harris were sitting side by side with their backs to the window. Maud walked across to them.

'I heard that you want to make your official statement immediately.'

'What we want,' said Harris, 'is to get this over in as quick and efficient a way as possible. The whole thing's turning into a bloody farce.'

'Is your son staying here?'

'Of course. Why?'

'I would like to interview him as well.'

'He's very upset,' said Beatrice. 'Is that really necessary?'

'He brought the murder weapon into the house, so yes, it's necessary.'

Maud nodded at Carrie to join her. They sat down opposite the couple.

'You've changed your clothes,' said Maud to Beatrice.

'Of course I have.'

'We'll need the ones you were wearing,' said Maud.

Beatrice looked at the lawyer.

'Is that really necessary?'

Maud turned to Robyn Murdoch.

'Do you want to tell her or shall I?'

'We just want to co-operate,' said Murdoch.

'Then can we have the clothes?'

Beatrice shook her head impatiently.

'I'll get them after we've finished.'

'How about now?' said Maud.

Beatrice looked furiously at her lawyer, but there was no response. With a theatrical sigh she got up, and Maud followed her along a corridor to a utility room. The clothes were lying in a pile next to a washing machine.

'We got here just in time,' said Maud with a smile. She put on her plastic gloves with a snap, found a roll of bin bags on a shelf, ripped one of them off and stuffed the clothes inside.

'Is that everything?'

'Of course it's everything.'

Maud looked at the half-open door of the washing machine.

'You're sure?'

She knelt down, put her hand inside and felt around. She felt something soft and pulled out a pair of black knickers.

'Oh, for goodness' sake,' said Beatrice. 'This is outrageous. Do you ever look at yourself? Maybe I should have a word with my lawyer about what you're doing.'

'Feel free,' said Maud.

She stood up and put the knickers into the bag with the rest of the clothes. The two of them walked back into the main room.

'Everything all right?' asked Robyn Murdoch.

'No, it isn't,' said Beatrice. 'This is all extremely distasteful.'

They resumed their seats. Robyn Murdoch smiled at Maud. It was as if they were meeting for morning coffee, except that there wasn't any coffee.

'I just want to be clear,' she began, 'that Ms Macmillan is being completely willing and co-operative. But you know the situation.' She gestured at Harris, sitting stiffly beside her. 'It has the potential to be extremely damaging for both of them, however innocent they are. So we just want to be as efficient and professional as we can about this.'

'Good,' said Maud. 'You want your husband to be present, Ms Macmillan?'

'I don't see why you should put yourself through this,' Beatrice said to Sebastian Harris. 'I'll be fine.'

'I'm staying,' he said, and folded his arms.

Maud nodded at Carrie.

Once more they went through the business of starting the recording and identifying everyone present.

'We've just come from talking to Rudi Scott. He seems to have been the last person to see Will Garvey alive. Do you have any thoughts about that?'

Beatrice looked slightly puzzled. She leaned across and whispered to Murdoch, who nodded.

'Do you have specific questions?' Murdoch asked.

'Did you see him go upstairs?'

Again Beatrice whispered to her lawyer, who whispered back. Then she turned to Maud.

'I'm sorry, I don't remember,' she said.

'Did you see him come down?'

'I don't remember.'

'Did you see anyone else go up?'

'I'm sorry, there was so much happening. I probably wouldn't have noticed, but I can't remember anyway.'

'Did you see William Garvey go upstairs?'

'No.'

'The last time you saw Rudi Scott – I mean before the body was discovered – did you notice anything about his demeanour?'

'Not that I can remember.'

Between each of these exchanges, Beatrice exchanged whispers with her lawyer. Finally, Maud gave a laugh.

'Do you ever watch the tennis at Wimbledon?'

'Is this relevant?' asked the lawyer.

'I was just thinking of how in the doubles, the players have a conversation with each other after every single point. It makes the game twice as long as it should be. Have you seen that?'

'No,' said Beatrice.

'Maybe you don't remember it.'

'I'm sorry,' said Murdoch, 'are you disputing Beatrice's right to legal advice?'

'These are the most basic questions. It makes everything take longer.'

'The best way of speeding things up is to proceed with the interview.'

Maud did proceed with the interview, asking most of the same questions as before, almost all of them interrupted by consultations between Beatrice and her lawyer.

76

'I already told the man at the station everything.'

Finn Macmillan Harris looked unwell. His face was pasty beneath its summer tan and he had purple shadows under his eyes. There was a thin string of spots across his forehead. He was wearing tatty joggers and a loose, faded T-shirt and his feet were bare. He looked out of place in the immaculate grandeur of the room.

'Did they give you an appropriate adult at the station?' Maud asked.

He shook his head.

'You should have an adult with you for this interview.'

'I'm not a child.'

'You're seventeen.'

'I'll stay,' Beatrice said, putting her hand on Finn's arm. Her son didn't look at her, but Maud saw the muscles on his forearms tense.

'That's probably not a good idea,' Maud said.

'I'm his mother. I want to stay.'

'We prefer not to have parents present at interviews,' said Maud, keeping it general. She turned to Robyn Murdoch. 'It would be best if it was you.'

The lawyer nodded and sat beside Finn. Beatrice hovered for a moment, then turned and left. Maud could hear her talking to her husband on the other side of the door, then their voices faded.

'Finn,' Maud began. 'We are going to record this interview, and then later we will get it typed up and you'll need to sign it. It's a bit like being under oath – you need to tell us the truth.'

He nodded, chewed the side of his finger.

'Will they have to see it?'

'Your parents? No. Ready?'

Carrie turned on the recorder and Maud gave the place, date, time and who was present.

'What time did you arrive at your house yesterday evening?'

He frowned, shrugged.

'Half past nine?' he hazarded. 'Not late.'

'Was it just you?'

'No. Connie was with me. My friend. Girlfriend, kind of.'

'Why did you come?'

'It's where I live, isn't it?' Maud didn't say anything, just looked steadily into his wretched face. 'You know all this anyway. I came to get rid of the knife. The knife they say killed him.'

'Where did you get it from?'

'I don't – I guess I don't remember.'

'You're not in trouble,' Maud said. 'This is about a murder, not you and your friends. But I need to know.'

Finn rubbed his eyes.

'Just a mate.'

'What was this mate called?'

'If I tell you, will he get into trouble?'

'I can't promise anything, but I'm not investigating your friend or what he got up to. This is simply about establishing where the murder weapon came from.'

Finn plunged his hands into his dirty blond hair.

'Arlo,' he said, so quietly that Maud had to repeat it for the recorder. 'Arlo Wallace.'

'And why did he give it to you?'

'He didn't. I took it from him. He was – he was spoiling for a fight, and Connie and me thought he was going to hurt someone.'

'What did you do?'

'I brought it home because I didn't know what to do with it. I thought Mum would know.'

'So you took it into the house, and then?'

'I heard voices and laughter, so I went downstairs. There was a whole group of people I'd never set eyes on before, sitting round the table. A gross amount of food, like a kind of banquet. I'm a vegan,' he added. 'I handed the knife over to Mum. Then me and Connie left again. That's it.'

'You put it in her hands?'

Finn pondered.

'I think I just put it on the table.' He made a grimace of disgust. 'Some of them seemed really turned on by it. They were touching it, picking it up.'

'Do you remember who?'

'The guy sitting next to Mum, with the silvery hair.'

Rudi, thought Maud.

'And the one who was killed.'

'How do you know it was him?'

'Have you turned on the telly or gone online recently? His face is everywhere. And that other one. The murderer.'

'Tyler Green?'

'Yeah.'

'No one has been charged with the murder yet. Did Tyler Green touch the knife?'

'No. He was the only one who wasn't ooh-ing and aah-ing. And the only one who didn't seem shit-faced.'

'Everyone else seemed drunk to you?'

'For sure. It kind of creeped me out, if you want to know.'

'What about you?' Carrie asked. 'Had you had much to drink?'

'No. A can of beer on the Heath earlier.'

'And drugs?'

Colour spread like a tide up the teenager's face.

'I don't get what that's got to do with anything.'

'Finn,' Maud said gently. 'We're not interested in going after you for taking illegal substances. But it might be relevant in terms of your reliability as a witness.'

'You're not going to go telling my parents?'

'I am not.'

He darted a glance at Robyn Murdoch.

'What about you?'

She smiled at him.

'Of course not.'

'You've no bloody idea what it's like, having a KC and an MP as parents.'

'No.'

'If he knew I was taking drugs.'

'Are you?'

'A bit. Not really, but a bit. Some.'

'And that evening.'

'Not much till after I left. A bit of weed. Then me and Connie went to a club. The Cauldron,' he added, seeing Maud raise her eyebrows enquiringly. 'Near Finchley. I had a bit of ecstasy.'

'Thank you,' she said.

'Is that all?'

'When you left, the knife was still on the table?'

'Yeah. I left almost immediately. I didn't want to be around them. I didn't like it.'

'What didn't you like?'

'Mostly seeing my mum drunk and not like herself. It was kind of scary. Does that sound stupid?'

Back on the pavement outside, Maud frowned.

'What?' Carrie asked.

'I went into this interview thinking that Beatrice was difficult and a little annoying. But it's more than that.'

She took out her phone and dialled Matt Moran.

'Are you there yet? Good. You've got work to do.'

77

'He'd be heading to the allotment now,' said Ali. 'That's what I keep thinking. Every Saturday morning, he'd bring me tea in bed, and then I'd hear him in the kitchen, whistling loudly and banging things. He'd make sandwiches and he'd be out all day. Especially at this time of year. He'd come back glowing, spreading mud everywhere, with all the produce. Broad beans, onions, currants. And his beloved asparagus.'

Her lips quivered. A single hoarse sob escaped her.

Ali Marais was wrapped up in a voluminous white dressing gown. Her short, dark hair was damp, her small, chalky face scrubbed bare of make-up. Maud thought that she looked younger, prettier, more vulnerable. They were sitting in the kitchen of the 1930s house in Clapham. The room was spotlessly clean and tidy, though a jacket that must have belonged to Will was on the back of one of the chairs, and on the doormat by the door to the small garden was a large pair of Wellington boots. On the wall next to the cooker hung a gardener's calendar, with notes scrawled beside dates, presumably reminders of tasks that Will needed to do in the allotment.

Behind Ali, a woman was noisily making a pot of tea for them. Diana Marais was startlingly different from her sister: soft, comfortable, slightly down-at-heel, more like William Garvey than his wife. She had answered the door to them, and at first had tried to refuse them entrance. But Ali had come down the stairs in her oversized robe, and told them to come in.

'There's nothing I can say,' she told them now. Her voice was hoarse. 'What else can I say?'

She reached out and with thin, shaking fingers extracted a cigarette from one of the two packets on the table.

'Will hated me smoking inside,' she said. 'He was quite right. It makes everything stink of stale tobacco. I try not to smoke more than a few a day, but today's an exception. I don't have a lighter. Where's my lighter?'

'Here, darling.'

Diana Marais came over with a large box of matches, struck one and held it out. Ali sucked greedily at the flame, then sat back. Diana kissed her on the top of her head, then retreated to the kettle, which had just come to the boil.

Detective work is full of patient repetition. Statements made and added to and corrected, and the important things in them can often be the small, overlooked slippages, contradictions and absences; timings returned to; facts re-examined; evidence sifted through. Maud was fascinated by it, the sifting, re-examining what was known and seeing it in a new light.

As Ali Marias retold her story, the red light on the recorder blinking and Benjy faintly snoring under the table, Maud listened out for something that would hook her attention, though she didn't yet know what that would be. Ali spoke haltingly, in fragments, saying the same things as she had said before. Sometimes her voice died away, and Maud and Carrie waited without speaking for her to pick up the thread. After Ali described the discovery of her husband's body, there was a silence in the room.

'You didn't go upstairs to see his body?' Maud asked eventually.

Ali shook her head violently.

'Ms Marais.' Maud spoke softly, carefully. 'Can you tell me about your relationship with your husband?'

Ali gazed at her.

'I don't—' she said, and stopped.

'Is this really necessary?' asked her sister.

'Sometimes I got cross with him,' whispered Ali. 'I was cross that evening, when he didn't come downstairs and I wanted to go home.'

Maud remembered Ellen saying how Ali would suffer for her irritation at Will, while all the time he was lying upstairs with his throat slit open.

'He was a kind man,' said Ali softly. 'He rescued me after Tyler. He'd loved me for a long time; I knew that, though when I was with Tyler I pretended not to. I was grateful to him. And there was no one else in our marriage, just us and Benjy. And no children – that absence was always there.'

'Did you love him?' Carrie asked.

'Love,' said Ali dully. 'What does that even mean? Will was a good man. He was faithful. He loved me. I loved him in my own fashion, I guess. Is that enough?'

'Enough for him, or for you?'

'I don't know. I don't know what I'm saying. He's dead. It's over. Everything's over.'

She covered her face with her thin hands and rocked back and forward in her chair.

Diana Marais put three mugs of tea on the table.

'Add your own sugar and milk,' she said to Maud, and pushed one of the mugs towards her sister. 'Here you are.' Her voice was almost a coo, like a mother to her distressed child.

Maud waited. After a few minutes, Ali took her hands away and took a cautious sip of tea.

'Will and Tyler?' Maud asked. 'Tell me about their relationship? They were close when they were young?'

'Very. Will adored Tyler. He looked up to him.'

'So Will loved you both?'

'Yes.'

'Complicated.'

'Not really.'

'And Tyler?'

'He – I always thought he loved Will, too.'

'But you said, when you last talked to us, that you were certain Tyler had killed Will, because of you.'

'Yes.' It was a strangled whisper.

'Which implies that he was still in love with you.'

Ali didn't say anything, but she shook her head.

'Ms Marais is shaking her head,' said Carrie for the recorder.

'So why would he kill him?'

'I think he hates me now,' said Ali. 'Really hates me. And hates Will for marrying me. I felt it yesterday. He hadn't known we were together. Will hadn't told him. I think Tyler wanted to punish us. He was—' She paused. 'Inhuman.'

She pulled another cigarette from its packet, lit it, took a pull at it that hollowed her cheeks. Maud added a splash of milk to her tea and drank some.

'Can you tell me about your husband's relationships with the other guests?' she asked.

'He didn't have a relationship with any of them. We hadn't seen anyone for decades. Except Beatrice, sometimes, when she found a bit of time in her busy diary. Never at the house though. We weren't that important to her.'

'I see. So he hadn't kept in touch with any of them?'

'No.'

'Did anyone have any reason to bear your husband a grudge?'

'Will?' Ali sucked at the cigarette again, a glowing column of ash growing at its tip, followed it with a gulp of tea. 'Everyone liked Will. He's – he was nice. Nice,' she repeated ferociously.

Maud nodded. She was concentrating hard, remembering all the things that had been said to her by all the different people over the course of the long night. She was remembering her initial interview with Ellen.

'I gather that just before going to buy cigarettes, you'd said you wanted to speak to Tyler, who was then in the garden. What were you going to say to him?'

'What?' Ali stubbed out her cigarette. She looked deathly tired. 'Why does that matter? Sorry, or something like that. Sorry for everything that had happened; for never being in contact; maybe even sorry about me and Will. Doesn't that seem grotesque now? To apologise to him. He's a monster. Can't you see that he's a monster?'

'I think she's had enough,' her sister said reprovingly.

'I think so too,' said Maud, rising. 'I hope you can get some rest.'

Ali gave a harsh laugh.

'I feel like I'll never sleep again.'

78

It had been a long, tiring morning for Conrad Bauer, but it had been worth it, he thought. Now that the flurry of interviews was over, he sat with a cup of tea in front of his computer and watched himself on playback. He had been on two breakfast shows and on the morning news, coming straight after the Home Secretary. He approved of the way he looked, in his dark blue shirt, his solemn face. The very slight waver in his voice. He thought he came over pretty well: an old man remembering his own loss, but focusing now on the tragic death of William Garvey, and on the grief of those who had known and loved him.

He listened to himself on the radio as well: brief and eloquent; the careful respect of the presenter.

His inbox was filling up with messages of support from friends and from strangers. There was a gathering crowd outside the police station; the head of the Metropolitan Police was expressing grave concern about the release of Tyler Green. The prime minister had made a statement, as had the parole board. A detective was going to hold a press conference shortly.

He sipped at his tea. He felt alive again, full of rage and purpose. He wanted to do more, speak more, hear the swell of his voice and see the compassion in the eyes of the people he addressed.

Susan Bauer was in the garden. She loved gardening, but she

wasn't gardening now, or reading the newspaper that got delivered every morning, and that she had carried out with her. She was sitting on the wooden bench, her hands folded on her lap, and staring straight ahead of her. She wanted to ask Conrad to stop, just stop. She felt that she couldn't bear his righteous anger, his fervour and determination, for one second more.

Their son had been murdered. His absence was at the centre of her life, its force field, and this is how it would be until she day she died. She hated it when people talked about the good that could come out of the terrible event. No good could come out of it, and there was a kind of peace in her acceptance and her grief. But Conrad couldn't leave it alone. This morning, he had been almost happy, she thought. Happy in his hatred and his thirst for punishment.

She heard the phone ringing indoors. She heard the front doorbell. She closed her eyes and turned her face up to the sun and the sound of the birds singing.

79

For most of the years that Tyler had been in prison, nights had been a torture. During the day, he had had a purpose, a strict plan to the hours that was laid out in a meticulous grid, and he would move through it like a soldier on a military operation. Exercise, eat, shower, study, exercise . . . But nights were formless; time didn't have a shape, but oozed forward with agonising slowness. He would lie in the darkness, hearing another man above him or beneath him, breathing, snoring, whimpering, sometimes crying out, shouting incomprehensible words. Flying into sleep was like a memory, something he no longer knew how to do, and in his dry, hissing wakefulness, his thoughts and feelings felt like a million insects swarming around him. When he did finally sleep, thick, ghastly dreams would close round him so that he woke in a lurch of sweat and terror.

But this morning, Tyler wished it was still dark. The single, small window in the room showed a pale blue; every so often, a soft wisp of cloud would float across it. He could hear, even in this stifling cell, birds singing. Yesterday, he had been under that sky, in that luminous day. Yesterday, he had walked along a canal, gone to a park and sat for hours with his eyes half closed, listening to children playing, the trickle of a fountain, the liquid notes from a blackbird in the tree.

And here he was, and here he would always be. Life means life. Tyler Green will never be free.

Then he let himself think of DI O'Connor, her clever face, and those grey eyes looking at him, into him, trying to see him clear. If anyone could – but he stopped himself.

The key rattled in the lock and the cell door swung open. Harvey Skinner stepped through. He seemed to block out the light, and bring an unpleasant odour into the room, mushroomy and dank. The door clanged shut behind him. Skinner stepped forward until his face was a few inches from Tyler's. He smiled, cracked his knuckles.

'What shall we do today?' he asked in his fluty voice. 'Tyler Green.'

'Step away,' Tyler said. 'Step away now.'

'Did he speak? Did he give an order to me? That's good. That's very good.' Even his laugh felt grubby. 'I have friends in this place, Tyler Green. Do you have any friends?'

Jay was sitting on a chair in a corridor, watching people come and go. He seemed to have been forgotten about. He slept for a bit and then woke up. He saw a police officer looking down at him.

'Can I go now?' he asked.

'Did you give your statement?'

'Yes.'

'I suppose you can go. If they've got your number.'

'Yes, they've got my number.'

He got up and as if he was in a dream he walked down the corridor, through another door and then he was out in the street and the sun was on his face. He was free.

80

Ellen was back at the kitchen table in the home of her friend Georgia Byrne. Behind Ellen, Maud could see the greenery of an Islington square. People were walking their dogs. Georgia was bustling around in the background.

'Would you like some coffee or tea?' she said. 'I've got some pastries.'

'No, thank you,' said Maud. 'We're going to be as quick as we can.'

'Take as long as you like. This is so dreadful.'

'Could you give us a moment?' said Maud. 'We just want to ask a few questions to Mrs Sweeney, then we'll be out of your way.'

'Yes, yes, of course,' said Byrne, looking alarmed. She hastily poured herself a mug of coffee, spilling some on the marble surface. 'Just give me a shout if you need anything.'

She left the room and they heard the murmur of her voice in another room. Ellen leaned forward and spoke in a quiet voice.

'I'm sure she's calling a friend to talk about it. I've rarely seen her so excited.' She sat back and looked reflective. 'I've never been at the centre of something like this before. It doesn't feel quite real.'

'Yes, you have,' said Maud.

'Oh, yes. Sorry, I can't believe I forgot about poor Leo.'

'You probably need some sleep,' said Maud. 'We won't be here long. Some of these questions might seem a little intrusive.'

Ellen looked puzzled, and then gave a small laugh.

'Oh, yes,' she said. 'I talked about sex. Why not? But I think I made some people uncomfortable. Sometimes I do that. Since you're here to investigate a murder, I don't suppose that matters very much.'

'You're probably right,' said Maud, 'but even so, we need to talk about it. You made some people uncomfortable. Which people?'

Ellen gestured with her hands.

'I should preface this by saying that I'm a couples' counsellor. People can say what they like to me. If you're young and single, your sexual conduct is nothing to feel guilty about, so long as you don't hurt people.'

'But,' said Carrie.

'What do you mean?'

'I thought there was a "but" coming. You said that you made people uncomfortable. And my colleague asked, which people.'

Before Ellen could answer, there was the sound of music, the tune of 'Ring-a-ring-of-roses'. She looked down at her phone. 'I'm sorry, I'm going to have to take this. Hello, darling.'

She stood up and walked to the far end of the room, away from the street. She turned away from them and her voice became muffled. Maud could only hear fragments of what she was saying. Fragments of denials and apologies and then a long silence. There was a tinny sound coming from her phone, an unintelligible shouting. Finally she spoke again.

'No, no, I'm sorry, I . . .'

She stopped. She stood with her back to the two detectives, looking at her phone. Slowly, she turned, came back to the table and sat down. She was glassy-eyed, as if she had suffered a blow. She looked at the detectives as if she was struggling to recognise them, then took a tissue from her pocket and blew her nose.

'That was Michael, my, er . . . It's nothing to do with any-thing but he gets very . . .' She waved her hands again. She nodded her head slowly. She was visibly trying not to cry. She breathed deeply.

'Are you all right?' said Maud. 'Can I get you something?'

Ellen rapped the table with her hand.

'No, I'm not all right,' she said, 'in about a million different ways. The idea that I'm sitting in a room giving couples advice, when I . . .'

She stopped and breathed deeply again.

'When you what?' asked Maud.

'Let's not go there.' Ellen spoke in a newly brisk tone. 'You were asking about last night.' She sank her head into her hands and then raised it. 'It doesn't mean anything, but I guess it's better if you hear it from me, rather than from somebody else.' She took a deep breath. 'We were all being emotional and open with each other, and I was talking about my sexual experiences with them, what it had meant to me.'

'Them?' said Maud.

'I talked about how I had slept with all of them except Jay . . .' She gave a faint smile. 'I mean all of the men. I wasn't that liberated. And what it had meant to me. I said that Leo had been the one person who just treated me like an object.' She gave Maud an urgent look. 'I just want to say at this point that I'm not looking for your pity.'

'Pity about what?'

'Will then said that after Leo had fucked me, he met up with the boys and talked in the way that boys always talk about the girls they sleep with. He said I was pathetic, and that I slept with all these men out of a kind of desperate need for attention.'

'How did that make you feel?'

'You mean was I humiliated? No. Just angry.'

'How angry?'

'Oh, right,' said Ellen after a pause. 'You're asking, was I angry enough to stab Will to death?'

'I'm not asking it,' said Maud. 'You're asking it. What's the answer?'

'The answer is that I'm just tired of all these men. They despise you when you want to have sex, and they despise you when you don't want to have sex. But the real villain in that story is Leo, not Will, and Leo's already dead. He can't be killed again.'

'Why did you go to the party?'

Ellen's face clouded over.

'I don't know. I've never been the sort of person who goes to reunions. Maybe it was a way of being the woman I'd been when I was twenty. That'll teach me.' She glanced at Maud. 'You might even call it pathetic.'

Maud left a pause before her next question, giving Ellen some time to collect herself.

'We're interested in a fairly short period of time. At about eleven forty-five, Rudi comes downstairs and says he has had a conversation with William Garvey. He says there was nothing unusual about it, though they were both a bit drunk. About fifteen minutes later, William Garvey is found dead.'

'By me,' said Ellen.

'Yes. Why did you go up?'

'It was time for us to leave. That's putting it mildly. The party had disintegrated. Beatrice needed us out of there. As far as I could make out, most of us just wanted to go and forget it had ever happened.'

'What happened when you found Garvey?'

'I couldn't take it in at first. I thought he'd fallen over or was asleep. And then I was hit by the smell. You don't expect the smell.'

'Were you sure he was dead?'

'I bent down and saw the blood and the way his head was lying. I knew he was dead.'

'Did you touch the weapon?'

'The weapon? I didn't even see a weapon.'

'Let's take a step back. Rudi Scott comes downstairs from talking to Garvey. Where is everyone?'

'I haven't slept for twenty-four hours. I can't think clearly.'

'We'll let you go in a minute. Bear with me. You've already told us that Ali Marais went for cigarettes, and that Clara Keane went with her. Was that before or after Rudi Scott came downstairs?'

'Why does that matter?'

'We just want to establish where everyone was and when.'

Ellen made a helpless gesture.

'After,' she said. 'I remember him saying something, and then Ali saying something, and then saying she was going for cigarettes, and Clara said she would go with her.'

Maud glanced at Carrie.

'I know,' said Ellen. 'Sorry, it's not very clear. I'm exhausted.'

'It's good enough,' said Maud. 'Where was Tyler Green?'

'I remember that,' said Ellen. 'He'd gone into the garden. He wanted to get away. Jay went after him.'

'You say they were both in the garden. You're sure about that?'

'You could see them from the house. Marco was worried that they might get into a fight, so he went out after them. Or maybe Beatrice sent him out. That might have been it. I think other people might have gone as well.'

'Which people?'

'I can't remember. I wanted to leave. I was going to get my coat and call an Uber and . . .' She stopped. 'I think I actually called one, and then I forgot about it. It must have waited outside, and I didn't come. What do they do when that happens? You probably have to pay a penalty.' She rubbed her tired, pouchy face. 'I hate forgetting things.'

Maud switched off the recorder, but she didn't immediately leave.

'Mrs Sweeney,' she said. 'You're a couples' counsellor. Can I ask you a question? What would your advice be if someone was obviously in a coercive relationship?'

Ellen lifted her head, met Maud's eyes, looked away again.

'I don't give advice,' she said. 'That's not my job.'

'What would your response be?'

Maud saw Ellen swallow. Her hands were plaited tightly together in her lap.

'I would ask them why they felt unable to stand up for themselves,' she said slowly. 'I would encourage them to think about their self-value, self-esteem. People who are in abusive relationships have often lost all confidence in their own worth. They think they somehow deserve to be bullied and controlled. Also,' she continued, speaking with obvious difficulty, 'I would say that by continually trying to placate their partner, people in coercive relationships are perpetuating the damaging pattern they have become locked into.'

'Thank you,' said Maud. 'That sounds like a helpful response.'

She stood up and gave Ellen a small smile. Ellen didn't smile back, but she nodded at Maud before turning away.

81

'I'll drive us home,' Celia said to Rudi. 'You're in no fit state.'

'What about my car? It's outside Beatrice's house.'

'Gordon can drive it back. Can't you, Gordon?'

Their lawyer gave a grudging nod.

'After I've had some breakfast,' he said. 'I'm rather tired myself, as a matter of fact.'

'Take your time – there's no hurry at all.'

'I'm not insured.'

Celia took her phone out, tapped away at it.

'Now you are,' she said. 'For twenty-four hours. Give him the key, Rudi.'

Rudi put his hand into the pocket of the navy sweatpants he had been given to wear. He handed the keys across, told the lawyer the address, followed Celia meekly down the road to where her car was. She was right – he was in no fit state to drive. He felt limp and boneless, drained of all vitality. When he examined himself in the car mirror, his face was whey-coloured.

He looked down at himself. The clothes they had given him made him feel like a stranger to himself: cheap drawstring trousers, thin navy shirt, white pull-on shoes that were slightly too large. His hands were sweaty and his scalp itched.

'I feel like death,' he said as the car pulled away from the kerb. 'I'm going to try and get some sleep.'

'Just a minute, Rudi.'

Celia always sat close to the wheel when she drove, and very upright. She looked composed and alert.

'What?' Rudi asked.

'Tell me what went on.'

'What do you mean?'

'What happened last night?'

'You know what happened. Tyler Green murdered Will Garvey. It was a nightmare.'

'I know you, Rudi. I know there's something you're not saying.'

'For God's sake, of course there are things I'm not saying. It was ghastly. Utterly ghastly. A trauma,' he said. 'I have to have time to process it, come to terms with what I've gone through. You can't expect me to tell you the whole story all at once.'

'You shouldn't have secrets from me, Rudi.'

'I don't know what you're talking about.'

'Secrets press down on us,' said Celia, flicking on the indicator to turn left, glancing in her rear-view mirror. 'Secrets trap us. The truth sets us free.'

'I'm your husband, not your target audience. And I've been through a terrible, life-changing experience. You could at least be sympathetic.'

'I'm thinking about what's good for you. I'm always thinking about that. I want to help you, but I can't unless you tell me what it is that's bothering you.'

'A friend's been murdered. I've spent the night in a police station. I haven't slept. My wife is treating me like a suspect. That's what is bothering me.'

'Go to sleep then, Rudi,' she said, like a mother talking to a small, truculent child. 'You can sleep while I drive.'

He took off his glasses, inclined the chair as low as it would go, turned away from Celia and laid his cheek on the cool leather of the seat. The sky was a bright lid of blue; the sun burned at him through the glass, and when he closed his eyes he could still see its hot white ball against his eyelid.

He couldn't sleep. Celia's musky perfume caught in his nostrils. The car purred under him. He lay still, trying to breathe evenly, mimicking sleep. The radio came on and classical music filled the car: something slow and heavy, a funeral march, the sonorous boom of foreboding.

The car was moving slower, and now it came to a halt. He sat up and opened his eyes.

'What's up?'

'There must have been an accident,' Celia said. 'That's all we need.'

Rudi looked ahead. A long line of cars and vans wound up the hill. The sun shone off their metal bodies, making his headache worse.

'It's not moving,' he said.

'I know it's not moving.'

'I'm very hot.'

'Everyone is hot, Rudi.'

'Do we have any water?'

'No.'

'Bloody hell,' he said crossly, and felt his wife stiffen beside him. 'Sorry. I'm not feeling myself.'

82

As Jay walked towards the train station, he felt as if insects were loose inside his skull. Buzzing and buzzing and scratching and itching. He rubbed his head. He had spent his entire adult life, ever since that terrible weekend, constructing a shelter to keep the world out, and also to keep his own thoughts out. It was the most fragile of constructions, held together by tape and fraying string. Sometimes, when he woke in the middle of the night, it seemed that the wind and the rain were finding their way through the gaps of his shelter, so it might collapse and leave him exposed to the elements. But it had just about remained standing. Until now.

He was like an actor, who for almost three decades had played the part of a functioning human being. On days where he hadn't wanted to eat, hadn't even wanted to get out of bed, he had made himself imagine that he was in a film, performing an ordinary person. Never the main person. Just a supporting player, the sort who serves coffee to the leading character or, better still, just passes silently by in the background.

But during this awful evening, the shelter had collapsed and his performance had failed. The real Jay Murphy in all his emptiness and pretence had been exposed. They had seen him for what he was, and he had seen himself for what he was.

He tried to control his spiralling thoughts, but the image of the body and the blood kept intruding. It became so powerful that he tried to block it out by covering his eyes, but that just made it more intense, harder-edged, brighter.

Dimly, he realised that it was a beautiful morning, still quite cool, but with a promise of heat. He walked past people, couples, obviously with plans for the day, things they were excited about. It was a world he was shut out from. He might as well have been looking at it through glass.

He had known he shouldn't have come, that it would only cause harm. Why had he let Clara persuade him?

He had heard about surgical patients who had woken up in the middle of an operation. They could sense the pain, but the anaesthetic stopped them from saying anything. Jay felt like that. He was being operated on while fully conscious and he couldn't do anything about it. He just wanted it to stop.

83

Maud had been staring out of the window as Constable Hale drove them to Marco Burney's flat in Wood Green. It was a lovely morning. People were sitting outside. She could almost smell the coffee. Her mobile buzzed in her pocket.

'Driscoll. Scene of crime. You called.'

Maud had to think. She was tired. Everything took a little more time to process.

'Yes,' she said. 'Are you doing the garden as well as the house?'

'The garden?'

'Let me put it another way. I want you to go through the garden as well as the house. Gather everything up. Litter. Cigarette butts. Everything. Got that?'

'Yes, ma'am.' Driscoll didn't sound especially pleased. 'Anything else?'

'Stuff that's been thrown on the floors or in the bins in the house. Anything at all.'

'We're on that already.'

'Good.'

There was a pause. Maud could feel the man waiting on the other end of the line, waiting to be dismissed. But she was trying to think of something. What was it? Oh, yes. Probably nothing but still.

'There's a spare bedroom,' she began and forced herself to remember. 'On the first floor. Have you checked it out?'

'Should we?'

'No. It's probably not important, but since nobody's been in there, keep it like that. Seal it off. A forensic guy should be arriving soon. Dr Matthew Moran. He'll want to have a look in there. We might as well keep it clean for him. Cheers. See you later.'

'Why are you interested in that spare bedroom?' Carrie said.

Maud gave a faint smile.

'Did you never go to parties when you were a teenager?'

'Of course.'

'Me too,' said Maud. 'It may be nothing but . . .'

She left the sentence unfinished.

84

Jan and Mick were on the platform at Camden Town underground, changing to the Bank line. They were excited. They
lived in London, but they had never been to Borough Market
before. The plan was to take the train down to London Bridge,
walk to the market, get some breakfast and then – who
knows? – they would walk along the river and home.

They didn't know it, but they wouldn't get to Borough
Market today.

Mary Rundell was leaning back against the wall. She was
ninety years old and was standing next to the bench, but
nobody offered her a seat. People stared down at their phones,
or pretended to. She was going to Brixton to visit her son and
daughter-in-law. They were cooking brunch for her: scrambled
eggs, pastries, coffee. She wouldn't eat that brunch. The next
meal she would feel able to eat was early that evening, just a
piece of dry toast.

About a mile away, Narayan Singh, driver of the southbound
Northern Line train, was pulling out of Hitcham Road Station.
He was bored, but cheered himself up thinking of this afternoon's match. When his shift ended, he was going to Highbury
with his son. He didn't know it but he was in the final minutes
of his career.

A gaunt, grey-haired man pushed past Mary Rundell so that
she had to steady herself with her sticks. He stood directly in

front of her and she glared at his back. She had almost fallen, and she had a sudden image of herself hitting the ground, breaking a hip and all that would follow. Stretchers and hospitals. It was her greatest fear. The man was nodding his head slightly, backwards and forwards. Probably not quite right in the head. You saw more of them around nowadays. Awful really.

Mick was saying something but Jan didn't hear him because the man next to her was murmuring something. At first she thought he was talking on the phone but it didn't sound like normal conversation. The man's words were gradually obscured by the growing hum of the approaching train.

As the hum became a roar, Mary Rundell felt that she ought to reach forward, but she couldn't, because she was holding her sticks. And Jan felt an apprehension that she couldn't quite identify, a sick feeling spreading through her chest.

It all happened at once.

The train burst out of the tunnel. The gaunt man stepped forward. Someone yelled. Jan tried to look away, She stared instead at the driver of the train. He was so close that she could see his face, his staring eyes and his mouth opened wide in a silent scream.

85

'I thought we might have woken you up,' said Maud.

Marco took a gulp of coffee, eyeing the recorder nervously.

'Kristin's just gone to bed, but I'm going to try to get through the day. If I go to sleep now, I won't sleep tonight. Then I'll be fucked for the week. I'm playing a gig tomorrow afternoon. I need to get my head straight for that.' He blearily contemplated Maud. 'It's all right for you. What are you, thirty-something? I can't do this anymore. When I was at college, we'd go to a party all night and then go out for breakfast the next morning. We'd have a few hours' sleep, and then we'd start all over again. Some chemical stimulants might have been involved, if I'm allowed to say that in the presence of the law. The statute of limitations probably applies.'

'What about last night?' asked Carrie.

'What do you mean?'

'What stimulants were involved?'

'Is this what it's about?' said Marco angrily. 'If you can't solve a murder, maybe you can make a drugs arrest? It's probably time to ask you to leave.'

'We don't care if people were taking drugs,' said Maud. 'If Tyler Green was, then that might be a problem for him. But we won't report him.'

'You needn't worry about Tyler,' said Marco. 'He gave me a

right telling-off. He made a point about not violating the terms of his parole.'

'It may not be a big deal for you,' said Maud, 'but it is for him. He's already back in a cell.' She raised her eyebrows at him. 'Are you going to say he deserves it?'

Marco looked uneasy.

'That's what I thought,' he said. 'As soon as I heard. But I saw him in the garden.'

'The whole time?'

'Maybe not the whole time. Jay went into the garden to have things out with Tyler, and I went after him to make sure nothing happened.'

'Anyone else?'

'Rudi was with me. And Kristin came along.'

'And you were all together?'

'Yes. At least, I think so.'

'And Tyler was where you could see him?'

'No. But I didn't see him go past us.'

'William Garvey,' said Carrie. 'How did you get on with him?'

Marco looked puzzled.

'You mean, in general?'

'I mean last night.'

'It was all right,' he said. 'We all got a bit drunk. We were a bit boisterous. All of us were.'

'He wasn't as nice as he pretended to be,' said a voice and the three of them looked round.

Kristin was standing in the doorway. She was dressed only in an oversized T-shirt and knickers.

'I thought you were asleep,' said Marco.

'I heard voices,' she said.

Her eyes were swollen, her face smeared with make-up, her hair mussed.

'In what way wasn't he nice?' Maud asked,

'You've heard what he said to Ellen?' Kristin didn't wait for her to reply. 'I mean, someone who says something like that, all these years later, there's something wrong with him. Right?'

'Aside from his remarks to Ellen, were you aware of other tensions between Garvey and any of the guests?'

'Are you joking? Everyone had conflicts with everyone.'

'Not me,' said Marco.

'Oh, you.' Her tone was venomous. 'Don't get me started.'

Maud looked at Marco.

'Was there any problem between you and Garvey last night?'

Kristin answered for him.

'The real problem was between him and Tyler Green. He was the one who really knew how to push Marco's buttons.'

'That's not really true,' Marco muttered.

'Of course it's bloody true,' said Kristin. 'Tyler Green comes out of prison and organises this reunion because he wants to fuck with all of you, get inside your heads. And he knows that the best way to get into Marco's head . . .' Now she was standing next to him, and she gave a small flick to his scalp, making him flinch. '. . . is to ask him about his musical career. Where did it all go wrong? When did you realise that you weren't going to be a star? That sort of thing.'

When Marco spoke, it was in a numbed monotone.

'I think little Kristin is trying to be helpful to me.' Maud could sense his smouldering rage. 'I think she's trying to communicate to you that I couldn't have killed Will Garvey because I was too busy thinking of how much I wanted to kill Tyler Green.' He looked round at her. 'Have I got that right?'

She shrugged.

'If that's the way you want to interpret it.'

'Why did you leave the house, after the murder?' Maud

asked her. 'You must have known you were a material witness, yet you left the house without informing the police.'

'Why?' Kristin gave a nasty laugh. 'I wasn't leaving the house, I was leaving him.' She jabbed at Marco with her forefinger, furious with loathing. 'And once you tell me that you no longer need me, I'm out of here. You won't see me for dust.'

'Good,' said Marco. 'Great.'

He stood up, looked around him wildly, then started plucking items off surfaces and throwing them on the floor: a large hairbrush clogged with hair, a pile of glossy magazines, framed photos. 'Take your crap with you,' he said, upending a rolled orange yoga mat which unrolled across the floor.

'We'll be going,' said Maud. 'Unless there's anything you want to add.'

'Will you be all right here?' Carrie asked Kristin.

'Me? Look at him. He's the one you should be worrying about.'

86

Diana Marais had made scrambled eggs for Ali. That was half an hour ago. The eggs were untouched. The cup of tea was untouched, quite cold now. But Ali had smoked several cigarettes, grinding each out in the saucer that served as an ashtray. The kitchen smelt of them. Will would have hated that, and she felt guilty, as if she was knowingly doing something to distress him. But he was beyond distress, of course. His body would be in the mortuary, or maybe on some table, being cut open. Ali shivered, picturing his soft, white stomach, his defenceless penis under the scrub of dark hair.

Abruptly, she stood up and went to the fridge, pulling open the door. She peered in at the last of the asparagus spears that he had brought home from the allotment yesterday – was it only yesterday? – as well as bowl of the broad beans that he had podded in readiness for this evening, and some green beans. He would have served them with garlicky butter, his lips shiny as he ate them.

She saw his wide, beaming face when he came in through the door yesterday afternoon with the laden bag. She heard her own acid comments about the tyranny of produce, about the mud he tracked across the floor. The flicker of hurt on his face, quickly suppressed; the heavy set of his shoulders.

And now she would never see him again. She would never be able to tell him that she was sorry she had been so waspish;

sorry she had kept so much of herself back; that she hadn't been able to love him as devotedly as he had deserved; that she hadn't had a child with him. Perhaps Tyler was right, and she wouldn't have been a good mother, but Will would have been a good father. He would have poured himself into the role. He had yearned to be unconditional. At the beginning, his love for her had been like that: defenceless, ardent, generous-hearted. But she had resisted him, always holding something of herself back, frightened of his unguarded emotions, policing her borders so that she had rarely let herself out or let him in. Bit by bit he had withdrawn.

Standing now at the open fridge, staring in at the vegetables he had harvested, it seemed like a betrayal to remember how she had been with Tyler thirty years ago. Yet memories came at her, and she couldn't escape them. Walking down the street together, sharing cherries from a brown paper bag. He had been wearing a white T-shirt, dark glasses, smiling. How he looked at her as they made love, serious, intent on her pleasure. What had happened to that person Tyler had seen and adored – where had she gone?

Ali closed the fridge. Benjy was whining at the garden door and she opened it to let him in, seeing the flat blue of the sky. She picked him up, then sat at the table, the cold, grey tea and congealed egg in front of her. She put her face into the dog's rough fur and thought of the detective's alert face, her piercing grey eyes. She needed Maud O'Connor to find the person who had murdered her kind, good, clumsy, sweet husband; the husband she was falling in love with at last, now that he was gone.

She wanted to cry, be softened and healed by tears. But she was dry-eyed, wretched, alone. So lonely.

87

Maud stood at the centre of a green square, pigeons flapping heavily in the tree above her. She had needed to get out of the car for a moment, leaving Hale loudly chewing his gum while Carrie gave instructions to her mother, and in the background Sadie wailed.

Two small children, tutored by a man who was perhaps their grandfather, were trying to kick a squashy ball between them. Another child, a bit older, was sitting on a bench, crying bitterly. Both his knees were badly grazed, and every time his sobs subsided, he would look at the blood and start weeping again. Almost out of sight, a rough sleeper lay curled underneath thick undergrowth, surrounded by empty cans. Nearby, a litter bin was stuffed to overflowing; litter lay all around it, some obviously ripped up and scattered by a fox. A young man walked past, taking loudly to no one, angrily shouting. But there were roses in the flower bed. There was a small tribe of goldfinch in the bushes. A couple sat on the grass and smiled at each other. So much that needed fixing; so much that was just right.

Maud let her thoughts slow. She had accumulated so many of the details; now she needed to stand back and let the big picture come clear in her mind. She must be quick, but not hasty. Like her roofer father, she knew how to be patient. Investigations were like jigsaws; they also contained moments of revelation, when an intricate mosaic suddenly revealed itself.

She took deep breaths of the morning air, filling her lungs. Then her phone buzzed in her pocket. She sighed, knowing even before she saw the name on her screen, who it would be.

'Where the hell are you?' Weller sounded harried. 'It's almost ten thirty. I'm at the station, there's a frenzy out on the streets, the Home Secretary is talking about making a statement, but you're not here.'

'I was about to call. We need to postpone assembling the team, and the press conference . . .'

'No.'

'I can't get back in time for it. Just by half an hour or so. Eleven? Or eleven thirty to be safe.'

'Maud, were you listening when I told you that—'

'I wouldn't ask,' she said, 'if it wasn't necessary.'

She slid the phone back into her pocket and returned to the car.

88

'Coffee?'

'We've just had some, thank you.'

They were in the kitchen of Clara's house, a late-Victorian semi in a leafy road in Kennington. Out in the garden, Clara's partner, Sam, was watering the beds. She was small and sturdy, with long, dark hair tied back into a single thick plait.

'How can I help?' Clara asked. 'I'm very tired. I need to get some sleep.'

She had obviously just showered. Her hair was slightly damp, her cheeks flushed, her feet were bare. She wore a pair of loose-fitting shorts and a sleeveless white tee. She had freckles on her shoulders.

Maud nodded at Carrie to turn on the recorder, then she gave the place, date, time – twenty-five minutes to eleven – and the names of people present. Clara sat across from them, grave and composed, her hands folded in her lap.

'First of all,' Maud began.

'I've got a question first. Did you talk to Jay?'

'Yes.'

'How is he?'

Maud thought of him as she had seen him last: twitchy, shaky, scared, with the air of a hunted animal.

'He's obviously troubled,' she said. 'I've asked my colleagues to call the mental health social services. He'll be kept safe.'

'Safe? Do you know the damage you've done to him?'

'I know this whole process has been distressing and traumatic for him,' Maud replied.

'He's frail,' said Clara. 'Things can trigger him, tip him over the edge again.'

'I understand.'

'Do you promise he won't be harassed anymore?'

'I'm not here to make you promises; I'm here to ask you questions.'

Clara sat back, her shoulders sagging.

'Of course,' she said. 'Though to be honest, it's a bit of a blur.'

'You're not the first to say that.'

'It was like a bad dream. And then, you know, the past gets in the way. It's as if what happened yesterday is lying on top of what happened with Leo all those years ago, like an image on tracing paper on top of another image that is both similar and yet different.' She looked directly at Maud. 'Does that make sense? It's hard to separate the two things out. Even the atmosphere.'

She stopped. Outside, Sam had crouched down to pull out weeds. The sky blazed blue. Maud waited.

'From the beginning, everything felt wrong,' said Clara. 'I should have listened to Jay.'

'What did Jay say?'

'He kept telling me we should leave. Almost pleading. As if he knew something terrible was going to happen. The way you can tell when a storm's coming, electricity in the air.'

'And yet you stayed.'

'It was as if we had no choice,' said Clara. 'Tyler was pulling our strings, jerking us around, watching us behave badly.' She grimaced. 'Actually, I'm making excuses for myself. I made him stay. I thought he should stick it out. I thought it would be good for him.'

'In what way did you—?'

Her mobile vibrated in her pocket, stopped, began again; then Carrie's mobile also rang.

'You'd better take that,' Maud said to her.

Carrie walked from the room as she answered. Maud could hear her low, courteous tones, then a note of something else. Alarm?

'Can you tell me what you were doing between the—?' she began, trying to keep her mind on the task.

The door opened and Carrie put her head round it. Her face was expressionless, but Maud felt a prickle of unease.

'Excuse me,' she said, leaning forward to switch off the machine.

Out in the hall, Carrie spoke in a hushed voice, almost a whisper.

'Maud,' she said. 'Jay Murphy has taken his life.'

There were many words trying to be uttered – *No. How could this happen? When? Oh, God. I promised he would be safe?* – but Maud didn't speak any of them. She just stared at Carrie, and her eyes felt as if they were burning in their sockets.

'He jumped in front of an underground train,' Carrie said.

Maud closed her eyes.

'He was supposed to be kept safe,' she whispered.

'What's happened?'

It was Clara, who had come out noiselessly in her bare feet. Maud turned.

'Ms Keane,' she said. 'I can't really—'

'What has happened? What? It's Jay, isn't it? What's happened to him?' She stepped forward so her face was a few inches from Maud's. 'Tell me,' she hissed. 'Tell me he's okay.'

'He's not okay,' said Maud, very gently.

'You said he'd be okay. Why are you looking like that? Where is he? I've got to go to him.'

'I'm so very sorry,' said Maud. Her voice felt strange to her, as if coming from a long distance. Yet all the time she was thinking, thoughts shifting and new patterns forming. 'Jay Murphy's dead.'

89

'No,' said Clara, stepping back. Then louder: 'No!'

Sam came through the door and stood behind her, sliding her muddy hands around Clara's waist, laying her cheek on Clara's shoulder.

'You're lying,' said Clara.

'I am so sorry,' Maud said again, watching Clara's face, her flared nostrils, her mouth in a snarl.

'You said he was safe.'

'I thought that he was.'

'How? How did he do it?'

There was a silence.

'He jumped in front of a train,' said Carrie.

'You did this.' Clara wrenched herself out of Sam's grip. There were muddy stains on her T-shirt. Her face was blotchy and her eyes glittered. 'It's your fault. I told you to be careful. I warned you. You drove him to this, just because you knew he had a motive. You people don't care who you destroy as long as you find an answer. Everyone abandoned him and let him down and now he's dead, and it's too late, and you're the one who's killed him.'

Carrie stepped forward and put an arm around Clara's shoulders.

'Come and sit down,' she said.

'Don't touch me,' shouted Clara, but she didn't

immediately pull away. Her anger seemed to be leaking out of her, leaving her smaller, older, defeated. 'Jay,' she said. 'Poor darling Jay.'

Sam took her hand and led her back into the kitchen, guided her into a chair.

'Maybe some tea,' said Maud to Carrie, who nodded and crossed over to the sink.

Maud pushed her unruly hair off her forehead and squatted down beside Clara's chair, speaking quietly but clearly.

'Ms Keane—'

'Leave me alone.'

'Ms Keane, what did you mean just now, when you said Jay had a motive to kill Will Garvey?'

'You're just playing fucking mind games.'

'What was the motive?'

'I know Jay told you. I told him not to. I told him you'd jump to conclusions. And I was right.'

'No.'

Clara let out a breath that was like the stifled beginning of a sob.

'I'd like you to tell me now,' said Maud. 'What did you warn him not to say?'

'That Will was the one who shopped him to the authorities at uni, for trashing the room. It was Will who got him thrown out.'

'Thank you,' said Maud. 'Why do you think he did that?'

'I've no idea. Maybe he thought it was the right thing to do. Or that it would help Jay, who was obviously in some kind of trouble. He didn't shop Leo, though. That was what always riled me.'

'How did Jay take it? Was he bitter?'

'He was ashamed. Shame was Jay's enemy. And he was

crushed,' said Clara. 'He took a long time to get over his pal betraying him like that.'

'How did he find out?'

'Leo told him, of course, that weekend when Tyler killed him.'

'Who else knows this?'

'Just me, I guess. Jay confided in me, but he didn't want it to go any further.'

'And you never thought to mention it to anybody else?'

'Like who?'

'Like Garvey. Like the police.'

'No. Jay trusted me.' Her face crumpled. 'And then Leo was murdered, the group disintegrated, I broke up with him, and he was all alone, and he went to pieces big time. He tried to take his own life; I was responsible for that. And now—' She lifted a hand to wipe away the first tears running down her cheek, and Carrie reached over with a handful of tissues she had taken from her bag.

'So just you and Jay knew?'

Clara stared blindly at Maud.

'What a terrible way to die,' she said. 'Jay was scared of everything, and yet he jumped in front of a train. What pain he must have been in, to make him do that.'

'Yes,' said Maud. Her eyes were steady on Clara's face, but her thoughts were racing. 'Great pain.'

'Here,' said Carrie, putting a mug of tea in front of Clara. 'Sugar?'

'No. No, thank you.' She took a sip. 'I always thought I could rescue him. Poor darling Jay.'

She sounded like his mother.

'You say that shame was his enemy. Do you think that—?'

'No. No no no. I know what you're going to say. It's odious.

Tyler killed Will. Jay's – what's that terrible phrase. Yes. He's just collateral damage.'

Maud continued to look at her, into her.

'I think,' she said at last, 'that you're scared Jay killed Leo, and then he killed Garvey.'

'No!'

'I think that's why you've been so adamant that Tyler was guilty – because you believe he might not be.'

Clara put her hands over her ears.

'No,' she repeated.

'Well,' said Maud. 'Your friend is beyond rescue now. And beyond pain.'

'She's right,' Maud said as they went from the house. Her thoughts were like knives. 'I'm responsible for Jay Murphy's death.'

'Of course you aren't.'

'I knew he wasn't safe.'

'You told them to make sure he got help.'

'I didn't check they had.'

'Nobody could blame you for that.'

'I blame myself.'

Carrie laid a hand on her friend's arm. 'You listen to me now, Maud. It's awful, but this is not your fault. Or if it is, it's mine as well. Not forgetting the arseholes at the station who couldn't be bothered to get proper help in place. Oh, and whoever killed Will Garvey, if it wasn't Jay himself. Clara was turning on you because she needs to hit out at someone. Like she said, she was the one who insisted Jay come to the reunion in the first place.'

Maud shook her head impatiently, her wild yellow hair rippling round her face.

'Well, that's for later. We now have two more people with a firm motive for killing Will.'

Carrie nodded.

'Jay and Clara,' she said musingly. 'So do you think—?'

'Let's wait to see what Matt Moran can tell us,' she said.

Carrie suddenly stopped, frowning.

'Where's that sound coming from?'

'Oh, that.' Maud patted her pocket. 'That's my alarm. It's time for me to wake up and greet the day.'

90

'Do you want to know who that was?'

Sebastian Harris sat down heavily in the chair opposite Beatrice.

'Not particularly,' she said. 'But I think you're going to tell me.'

'That,' he said, slowly and emphatically, 'was the PM.'

Beatrice looked across at her husband. He had jowls, slightly protuberant eyes. It struck her that she didn't really like him. She didn't really like herself very much either. Their relationship had become transactional, a smooth and practised affair which had enabled them both to prosper: he rising through the ranks of the party until people spoke of him as a future leader; she a KC earning more money, probably, than the rest of her guests yesterday put together, so they could live in their grand house, go on expensive holidays, wear linen and silk and cashmere, drink excellent wine. Was this what her life would always be, a sleek limo nosing its way through the mess of life? And yet panic rolled through her at the thought of losing it all.

'The PM,' she said coolly. 'Am I supposed to be—?'

'On a Saturday morning.'

'I do realise that it's Saturday.'

'He asked me if there was anything he should know.'

'Know?'

'About the murder.'

Beatrice raised her eyebrows. She was sharply aware of herself, of all her words and gestures; it was as if she was watching herself attentively, making sure she didn't put a foot wrong.

'And I said there was nothing.' He leaned towards her. 'Because there isn't, is there, Bea?'

'Of course there isn't,' she said. 'What could there be?'

'That's what I want you to tell me.'

Beatrice arranged her face into a sympathetic expression.

'It was a horrible, horrible thing to happen in our house. Next to our son's bedroom. And I'm obviously sorry that you're involved in any way. But I'm sure Tyler will be charged very soon, and that will be the end of it. He'll be back in prison—'

'Which he should never have left.'

'No.'

'You should never have invited him to our house. It was a thoroughly irresponsible thing to do.'

'Of course now I wish that I hadn't. But that's the wisdom of hindsight. Everything will go back to normal.'

Normal, she thought. The events of the night lay in fragments behind her, like a blasted landscape after a bomb had torn through it.

'I hope you're right.' Her husband frowned. 'But I can't help feeling there's something you're not telling me.'

'There's nothing.' Beatrice reached out and touched his hand reassuringly. 'I'm obviously very shocked and upset by all of this. And very, very tired. In fact, I think I'll go and lie down.'

She stood up. Her legs trembled. Her throat ached. Her stomach churned and her skin prickled with sweat. She walked slowly, carefully, out of the room, but as soon as the door was shut raced to the bathroom, where she was sick.

91

Tyler wanted to do something violently physical: go for a long run that would leave him sweaty, exhausted and aching; slam his fists into a punch bag over and over again; walk for hours, pain burning his calves.

He stared around him. There was dirt in all the corners, the walls were speckled with mould, the window was smeared, the toilet was stained, the sink grubby. And he was locked into this room with a man who took up all the space and all the air. He could hear Harvey Skinner rummaging through his possessions, small grunts of satisfaction coming from him. Tyler didn't want to know what he was doing. He didn't want to have to look at him: the pimples on the back of his neck, the huge hands, the oily hair and magnified eyes, the smile.

He felt as though he was about to crack open, so his emotions would boil and froth out of him, all his rage and despair, everything he had kept caged up inside himself until he no longer knew who Tyler Green actually was. Was there still a soft and tender self, sheltering beneath the carapace, or had that self withered and died long ago?

He had been let out, and he had thought to begin the next chapter of his life. Instead, he had manufactured a situation, this cursed reunion, so fraught with guilt and regret and danger that of course it had erupted out of control. How could he have been so blind and so foolish, sabotaging his own future for the sake of – what?

It was hard to breathe. He had to labour at it, forcing air in and out of his lungs. He mustn't lose himself to panic. But why not? What did it matter, what did anything matter, now that he was back inside?

As a child, a teenager, a young man, he had known himself to be one of the lucky ones: born to a comfortably-off, supportive family; healthy, popular, academically successful, the career he had always dreamed of within his grasp. His future unfurled before him like a shining path. But he had not had that life; he hadn't had any life at all.

His breath came in shallow gasps. His lungs burned and his throat hurt and his heart hammered. He sat up, swung himself out of the bunk onto the floor. He stood at the door and hammered at it until the little window slid open and he was looking at a section of a face, boiled blue eyes, a pocked nose.

'I have to see the governor,' he said in a rasping voice that sounded unfamiliar. 'I have to see somebody at once. I shouldn't be here. I haven't done anything wrong. This is a miscarriage of justice.'

There was that gurgling laugh behind him, and then his cellmate said: 'We've been through all this before, mate. It's getting boring. My patience is wearing thin.'

The man on the other side of the door laughed as well, the hacking laugh of a smoker.

'It's Saturday,' he said. 'We're on skeleton staff. Do you think we have time for this crap?'

'I demand to see the governor, or a lawyer.'

'In your dreams. Now shut it before we do it for you.'

'The detective—'

'Shut it, I said.'

Then Harvey Skinner rose from his bunk.

'Why not leave him to me?' he said. 'Keep it in the family.'

92

As the car pulled up, Maud saw a familiar figure leaning against a garden wall. She got out of the car and walked towards him. Matt Moran looked as if he had just got out of bed, but he always looked as if he had just got out of bed. He was dressed in jeans and a hoodie and trainers with no socks. His hair had got longer since the last time she had seen him. At his feet was a large, battered canvas backpack. He seemed lost in thought. Then he noticed her and Carrie. He gave a faint smile.

'In trouble again?' he said.

'Sorry,' Maud said. 'I've probably ruined your weekend.'

'Do you want to hear about my private life?'

'I would love to have a proper heart to heart. But I'm a bit pressed for time.'

'Good. I don't want to talk about it either. So what's up? Apart from what I saw online.'

The house had a weary morning-after feeling. The glasses and bottles in the living room were still where they had been abandoned. The scene-of-crime investigation had lost its urgency. Some of the team had gone, others were standing around making desultory conversation. Maud looked out of the ground-floor window and was horrified to see two of the team in the garden, one of them vaping, the other smoking a cigarette. She turned to two officers who were having a muttered conversation.

'The garden is part of the crime scene,' she said. 'They need to stop smoking and pick up anything they've dropped.'

'Is that so?' said one of the officers.

'I wasn't starting a conversation about it. I want one or both of you to go down to the garden and sort it out. Now.'

There was a pause. Maud wondered if they were actually going to argue about this but after some theatrical sighing and shared glances, they left the room. Maud gestured after them and then looked at Matt.

'Sometimes I wish I was doing any other job than this.'

'What else would you be doing on a sunny Saturday morning?' Matt said. 'Anyway, you were going to give me the tour.'

Maud gathered her thoughts. She didn't feel exactly tired, but she could see that her brain was working more slowly than usual. It was like a dream where she was walking through sand. Carrie went into the garden to oversee the work there, and Maud led Matt through the house: the lower ground floor where they had eaten supper, the living room, then up past the bedrooms.

'Nice house,' said Matt. 'Way out of our league, though.'

They had reached the top floor. Maud approached the door of the room where the murder had taken place.

'I can smell it already,' said Matt, putting his bag down in the corridor.

The two of them pulled on the white plastic booties and the surgical gloves.

She pushed the door open. The body had been removed, but nothing else had changed.

'One wound to the neck,' she said. 'It was really ripped open.'

'I can see that.'

'The officer on the scene said that it's the way people are killed in prison.'

Matt looked round.

'You're referring to Tyler Green?'

'You've heard about him?'

'Maud, everyone in the country has heard about him. Have you been following the news?'

'I haven't really had the time. What do you know?'

'That he was one of the guests here last night, and he had just been released after almost thirty years inside. That he's back in a cell. That Sebastian Harris owns this house. That the Home Secretary is calling for an urgent review of the parole board. That's the gist of it. There's a whole lot more I could tell you, some of it quite lurid.'

'So, what do you think?'

Matt looked around and then looked up at the ceiling, deep in thought. Finally he turned to Maud.

'He was lying on his front, right?'

'That's right.'

'Any wounds on the hands?'

'No.'

'So he was probably stabbed from behind. The neck is the one exposed bit of flesh, apart from the hands and the face. If you want to really hurt someone, it's the obvious place to go for. Did anyone in the house hear anything?'

'Apparently not.'

'I'm not surprised. With the wound that caused all of this . . .' He gestured at the floor. 'You wouldn't be able to make a sound. You'd just sink to the ground.'

'Would it take much strength?'

'Was it a single cut?'

'Yes.'

'With a knife that could do that, you wouldn't need much strength. And if you stab someone in the neck, you're doing something . . .' He paused. 'Final.' He narrowed his eyes. 'But you didn't need to get me out of bed on a Saturday morning to tell you this. Why am I here?'

'I've hit a brick wall,' she said. 'There were nine people at the party. Apart from the victim, that is. Five women and four men. One of the women is a lawyer who's married to Sebastian Harris. You know, the government minister. Nobody else could have got into the house without anyone seeing. In the period when William Garvey was killed, they were all together, down-stairs or in the garden.'

Matt considered this.

'So what do you want from me?'

'What I'd really like is for you to work your usual magic, and tell me who killed Garvey.'

It was meant as a grimly ironic joke, but Matt didn't smile. He just looked more closely at the dark, congealed pool of blood. There were obvious footprints and patches of blood across the floor.

'Who's been in here?' he said. 'I guess there were paramedics.'

'Yes, but they didn't touch the body. There was no doubt that he was dead.'

'And the police,' said Matt, 'and the scene-of-crime guys. Someone from the house must have found the body, right?'

'A guest called Ellen Sweeney came upstairs looking for Garvey. She found the body and ran down to tell the others. Then several of them also came upstairs.'

'Did they come inside the room?'

'Yes. One of them vomited over there.'

Matt took a deep breath. For the next few minutes, Maud just watched him as he moved around the room, light on his feet for such a big man. From time to time, he knelt down and peered at something Maud couldn't make out. Once, he got down on his hands and knees and put his face within a couple of centimetres of the floor. She heard him muttering to himself, nodding his head.

Finally he stood up and surveyed the room, as if he was looking for something. He took a deep breath, then looked at Maud.

'No,' he said.

'What do you mean?'

'I don't think I can help you.'

'I can give you anything you need,' Maud said. 'People, time.'

Matt shook his head ruefully.

'This room is like Piccadilly Circus on a Saturday night. There are fibres everywhere. I've counted ten different footprints, and that's just with my naked eye. There are bloodstains all over the place, and I'm sure they go out the door and down the stairs. Maud, I could spend weeks here, I could produce a thousand-page report, and I don't think it would help you in any way. There's just too much noise. This isn't looking for a needle in a haystack. Sometimes it's just hay all the way down.'

Maud nodded. The two of them left the room.

'I had a feeling you'd say that,' she said, as she snapped off the surgical gloves. 'I thought maybe you'd see something I hadn't, but I didn't expect it.'

Slowly, Matt peeled off his gloves and his booties. He glanced at Maud.

'You okay?'

'Why shouldn't I be?'

'It doesn't look good, does it? A murder. No suspect. A totally messed-up crime scene. A politician breathing down your neck. Where do you go from here?' He picked up his backpack and then changed his mind and put it down again. There was something strange about his expression.

'What?' said Maud.

'I know you, Maud O'Connor. You've got something in mind, haven't you? You didn't bring me all this way for a totally messed-up crime scene.'

'Why not?' said Maud. 'I've done it before, and you've delivered. There may be something on the body. It might be worth you taking a look.'

'I'll take a look if you want me to take a look. But you brought me to the house, not to the mortuary. What have you got in mind?'

93

Maud reached into the bag on the floor and took out two new pairs of booties and two pairs of surgical gloves. She walked down one flight of stairs and Matt followed her. Facing them was the closed door of the spare bedroom. As she had instructed, it was sealed with brown and yellow tape. She ripped it off and opened the door. She handed Matt a pair of booties and a pair of gloves. He looked through the doorway. The room was immaculate.

'What am I looking at?' he said.

'The one room that wasn't used for the party.'

'It looks like it's been cleaned.'

'Not since last night. I ordered it to be sealed.'

'Why? If it's a room that nobody went into, then that isn't much use, is it?'

'We'll see about that.' Matt looked puzzled. 'I think you're being a bit ungrateful. You complained about the murder scene being contaminated. Now I've given you a room that hasn't been contaminated at all.'

The two of them pulled on their booties and their gloves and stepped into the room. Matt looked round. Maud was familiar with his particular gaze. He saw things differently from other people.

'Help me out,' he said. 'What am I looking for? Do you think there are bloodstains here?'

'No. And I don't think they'd be much help if you found any.'

'Where should I look?' Before she could answer he quickly continued. 'And don't say everywhere. There's the wall. There's the curtains. In particular . . .' He pointed downwards. 'That rug. It'll be full of fibres, however much they've cleaned in here. But that will take time. I can do it, but it will take time.'

'Try the bed,' said Maud.

'Oh, I see.' He looked at the bed and then back at Maud. 'Are you thinking what I'm thinking?'

'If you're thinking that you ought to start checking the bed out as soon as possible, then the answer is yes.'

He unzipped his backpack and started to rummage inside. He extracted what looked like a pocket torch.

'You've got half an hour,' Maud said. 'I'm meant to be holding a press conference. I just need a preliminary finding, an indication that I'm not wasting my time.'

'I won't need half an hour,' he said.

He walked across to the window and wound the blind down. The room gradually became dark.

'Are you ready?' he said.

'Ready for what?'

There was a click and Maud saw the thin beam of the torch moving over the duvet cover. After a moment she heard the ruffle as Matt swept the duvet back. She saw the narrow cone of light moving this way and that in the semi-darkness. She heard a sudden intake of breath.

'Well, fuck you, Maud, I don't believe it.'

The light disappeared. She saw his shadowy form move across her field of vision and with another click, the ceiling light was switched on. Moran had a curious smile on his face.

'I don't know why you want it, but it's there.'

94

Harvey Skinner tossed his small knife from hand to hand. He looked at Tyler through his aviator glasses, and smiled.

Tyler was very, very weary – not just from lack of sleep, that was the least of it; a surface weariness stung his eyes and made his movement slower. He was weary from striving not to be utterly defeated, to stay alive. It would be so easy to give up, give in. And why not? What was there now to stay alive for? He was back in prison, and like the subject of a grimly meticulous experiment, everything was on repeat: the cell that stank of excrement and sweat, the little window in the door where eyes could peer in on him, and the man who wanted to do harm to him. Cut him. Maybe kill him.

It would almost be a relief to have done with this.

'Let it go, man,' he said.

Harvey Skinner smiled some more. He took up all the air in the little room.

'You know why I'm in here?' he asked.

'It's none of my business.'

'I killed a couple of old people.'

The knife softly thumped on his palms.

'Sorry to hear that,' said Tyler.

'They were so old, it was almost like putting them out of their misery.' Tyler didn't say anything; he kept his expression blank, and watched the toss of the knife without seeming to. 'Though the judge didn't see it like that.'

'Guess not.'

'But you – you killed someone when they were young. Cut them off in their prime.' Harvey uttered the cliché slowly and with relish. 'That's bad. And you've just done it again. Two friends of yours. You know what I'm thinking?'

'No.'

'That it makes you a dangerous kind of cellmate. I'm shut in here with someone who kills his mates.'

'You're in no danger from me,' said Tyler.

He knew what was coming. He kept his eyes on the knife, and tensed himself.

95

Kristin had had a shower and put on a lime green shirt and white jeans. Now she stood in the middle of the living room, brushing her hair until it crackled with static electricity.

'You look rank,' she said to Marco, who was still slumped in the same chair he'd been in when he'd been interviewed by the detective. 'You should wash, at least. I can smell you from here.'

'Why do you care? You're leaving, aren't you?'

'Yes,' she said. 'Yes, I am.'

She dragged the brush through her hair with extra energy.

'When?'

'When am I leaving? Today. As soon as I can. I need to finish packing.'

He looked at her dully; his eyes were bloodshot.

'Where will you go?'

'That's no concern of yours, is it?'

'I guess not.'

'I have friends, you know.'

'Yes.'

'You don't care at all, do you?'

'Jesus, Kristin. What do you want from me? You're leaving; isn't that enough? Do you want me to cry and beg you to stay?'

'You're glad I'm going. You never loved me. You always had contempt for me.'

'Hang on a minute. You spent last night telling everyone what a pathetic loser I was. I seem to remember you even said I was hopeless in bed.'

Her face crumpled.

'I shouldn't have had anything to drink. I got carried away.'

Marco rubbed his eyes and stared towards the window. It needed cleaning, he thought. He should do that. But he knew he wouldn't. He would let the flat gather dirt, let the panes of glass smear up, let his depleted life dribble on.

'Why don't you go and pack?' he said.

Kristin stopped brushing her hair.

'Are you in such a hurry to get rid of me?'

'You're the one who's decided to go.'

'Shall I make us some coffee first?'

'Okay then.'

He lay back in the chair, hearing her a few feet from him, the running water, chink of cups, comforting domestic sounds, another person in the room doing the mundane tasks that make up an ordinary day.

For a few moments, he felt oddly peaceful, the ugliness of the evening sliding away from him, the words he and Kristin had spoken to each other, the humiliation that had been like a harsh spotlight illuminating his entire life, so that he had been a pitiable, hollowed-out creature creeping along in its glare.

'Here.'

Kristin put down the cup too forcefully; hot liquid slopped over its brim.

'Thanks.'

She stared down at him.

'I don't know what happened,' he said into the silence.

He didn't know if he meant what had happened at Beatrice's

house, or what had happened to their relationship, or to him over the years. All of them, perhaps.

'Me neither,' she said tiredly.

The lime green shirt made her face look pasty. He saw the lines on her face. He was older than her, but she was no longer young.

'I'm sorry about everything,' he said, so quietly she could barely make out the words.

'Yeah,' she said. 'It's okay.'

He felt a flare of anger; she was meant to apologise in return. That was the rule. He wanted to snatch back the words.

'Everything got out of hand,' she said after a pause. 'I was to blame as well.'

He took a cautious sip of coffee.

'I guess I smoked too much weed, drank too much.'

'Nothing new there.'

But her face looked softer.

'I'm so afraid,' he said. 'I don't know how to bear it.'

Hearing his words, he understood that for the first time in the years they had known each other, he was being honest about himself.

'What are you afraid of, Marco?'

'My shitty life,' he said. 'What I've become. What will become of me. Everything really. I mean, it's all so fucking useless. I'm useless.' He gave a tremulous laugh. 'Of course you want to leave me. I want to leave me, as well.'

'You're feeling sorry for yourself again. Go and have a shower.'

'Will you still be here?'

'Maybe. Probably, yeah.'

With an immense effort, he stood up, spilling more of the coffee as he did so.

'It's like a dream now,' he said. 'A bad, bad dream.'
'I know.'
'That scary detective. Does she think I did it?'
'I don't know.'
'I think she does.'

96

Ellen Sweeney was hurrying to catch the bus, half running and half walking, her little wheelie bag bumping on the cracked paving. She had left Georgia's house later than she had intended, and it was due in three minutes. If she missed it, she would almost certainly miss the train to Bristol that she had promised Michael she would be on.

She was boiling in the heat, sweat pouring down her face, down her back, gathering between her breasts. She swerved to avoid a small child with star stickers all over its face, bumped into a large man carrying a cat in a box, called out an apology. Her bag caught in a rut and twisted round so its wheels wouldn't turn. Her heart jolted in her chest.

There was the bus stop ahead, shimmering in the heat. She almost cried with relief, but then an ominous red shape was alongside her: the bus, imperviously sliding past, its indicator flicking.

If she made an extra effort, she might just get there. But her ankle turned as she ran; she felt it give beneath her, and she had to slow to a painful hobble. She waved her arm wildly, hoping the driver would see her in his mirror and wait. Now the right-hand indicator was flashing, and the bus pulled away from her.

Ellen came to a halt. It doesn't matter, she told herself, almost speaking the words out loud because she often talked to herself, reprovingly, or giving instructions, words of encouragement and comfort. It doesn't matter; she would just have to get a later train.

But it did matter. It mattered a great deal. She felt dread like a sludge in her chest. She thought she might collapse with the weight of it.

She started walking again, slowly this time, towards the bus stop. Her ankle was throbbing. Once there, she took out her phone to check when the next bus would be. Eleven minutes: she would certainly miss the train. She should call him. Her finger hovered over his name on the screen. Sweat was trickling into her eyes, so that it was hard to see. She wiped the back of a hand across her forehead. Her eyes stung and her mouth quivered and dragged down. Perhaps it wasn't sweat. Perhaps she was about to cry: plump, cheerful, no-nonsense Ellen Sweeney, tears rolling down her hot cheeks, salty in her mouth. She was so tired of having to pretend.

She thought of the young detective asking her how she would deal with a client whose partner was coercive, and of her own sensible response. It occurred to her that both DI O'Connor and Tyler had looked at her in the same way, not unkindly, but as if they could see through the feeble, over-acted, shiny charade into the jumble of weakness and fear.

How had she come to such a pass? Last night – oh, God, was it only last night? – Will had publicly demolished the image she had tried to present of herself as a confident, self-reliant, sexually confident woman, with her useful job and her long marriage and her happy gang of children. He had sensed her secret fear, and he had bullied her. Just as Michael bullied her – because let's call a spade a spade, she said to herself. You are married to a bully. You are the victim of abuse. He should not be allowed to get away with it.

But her children. Her heart swelled when she thought of

them. Did they know? Of course they knew, even if they didn't know they knew.

Another bus was coming up the road. It stopped with a groan of brakes, and the doors slid open. A woman got out and another one got in. The driver looked at her, and she looked back at him. The doors slid shut once more and the bus slowly moved away. Ellen watched as it rounded the corner and disappeared.

What now, she thought. What on earth should I do now?

97

After Matt Moran had loped off, Maud found the officer in charge of the crime scene.

'Do you want me to walk you through everything?' he asked.

'A whistle-stop tour,' she said, glancing at the time: seven minutes past eleven.

'We're pretty much done here. We've got the exhibits bagged up in the basement, ready to be taken to the station.'

They went down the stairs together. In spite of Ellen Sweeney's attempts to clean up, the room was wildly disordered. There were plates of half-eaten food on the table, many smeared glasses and two broken ones; empty and half-empty bottles, the smell of brandy in the air. On the floor near the door, in a plastic crate, was the murder weapon, and beside it multiple sealed and labelled plastic bags and tubes.

Carrie came in from the garden, and the two women squatted down, lifting each bag in turn to examine it. Various fibres and hairs, including some that looked like dog hair; a small white button; some coins; a hairband; some corks; bits of unidentifiable food. Most things looked like rubbish that had been carelessly dropped, but Maud didn't believe that many things were carelessly dropped in Beatrice Macmillan and Sebastian Harris's house.

Carrie pointed to the bags that contained cigarette butts.

'Let's take a look.'

There were six cigarettes in their separate labelled bag, and two hand-rolled spliffs.

'Talk me through them,' said Maud. 'You're the timeline maestro.'

Carrie screwed her small face up in intense concentration.

'These two were found near the bench in the garden,' she said, delicately lifting a plastic bag in her gloved hand; one of the butts had red lipstick marks on it. 'They must be the cigarettes that Marco said he and Ali smoked together early in the evening, before Ali's lipstick had rubbed away. I think Marco said it was about half past seven.'

'Yes,' said Maud.

Carrie lifted the next plastic bag.

'There are two more stubs from near the end of the garden, plus a spliff, presumably from Marco. We know that Clara, Marco and Ali smoked these around ten that evening.'

'Okay.'

'Then this fifth butt, from a plant pot near the steps that led to the first floor, and a second spliff from the patio outside the lower ground floor entrance. At least one was smoked by Ali; we don't know about the other one.'

'And then,' said Maud, 'there's a cigarette that was stubbed out on the table and left on the plate.'

'That presumably was smoked towards the chaotic end of the evening,' said Carrie. 'When Kristin and Ali were downstairs, and the dog got up on the table.'

Maud nodded. From where she squatted, she could see the scorch mark it had left where it had been stubbed out on the grainy wood.

Carrie gently replaced the plastic bags.

'Could there be any more in the garden? Thrown in the bushes, maybe?'

'Does it really matter?' asked Carrie.

'Let's pretend it matters.' Maud turned to the officer. 'Is it possible?'

'I supervised it myself. No, it's not possible.'

'What about the bins?'

'Bins?'

'Yes.'

'I don't think they've been looked at, as such.'

Maud stood up.

'Spread out a tarpaulin,' she said.

'Now? Here?'

'Now and here.'

The officer left the room, tramping heavily up the stairs, and a few moments later a different man came down, carrying a roll of plastic that he unfolded on the floor. He went to the large stainless steel bin by the sink in the kitchen area and upended it onto the tarpaulin. Maud bent down, spreading out the rubbish with her gloved fingers. Most of it was food, and there were also several squares of waxed paper that cheese had been in and some empty tins that should have been in the recycling. No cigarette butts. She picked up a piece of cellophane and looked at it, put it down, spent a few seconds in deep concentration. She pictured the house with its entrances and exits. Screwing up her face, she remembered the times that Carrie had scrupulously drawn up for her.

She felt that tiny fragments of evidence were glinting in front of her, moving into a pattern that had gaps and fissures, but was starting to make a picture. She was no longer tired, but preternaturally alert and alive. This is why I do the job, she thought. This moment, now.

'I see,' she said at last.

'What do you see?'

'It's coming together.'

'Don't go all mysterious on me, Maud.'

'I'll tell you in the car.'

98

'There's something I'm missing.' She pushed both hands into her wild hair. 'Something I know, but can't grasp.'

'Maud—'

'Wait. Wait. Don't say anything.'

Carrie waited. Maud's face was tight with ferocious concentration. Then all of a sudden it cleared. Her eyes glowed in triumph.

'I've got it,' she said.

'What?'

'Hang on.'

Maud pulled her mobile out of her pocket and jabbed at it.

'Hawkins,' she said. 'It's me, Maud.'

'What do you want?'

He wasn't bothering to be polite.

'I need to you to photograph something for me from the Leo Bauer file and send it across. It's urgent.'

'What is it?'

Maud told him, conscious of Carrie's gaze on her face.

'Okay,' he said. 'I'll do it now.'

99

Tyler wanted it to be over, but Harvey Skinner was taking his time. Waiting was part of the pleasure. The little knife glinted in his hand as he smiled.

'There are rules in prison,' he said. As if Tyler didn't know that. 'Like rules in a family. Did you have a family once, Tyler Green? Did you have a mammy? Mine always told me I'd come to a bad end. That's not very nice, is it? Her own son. She smoked sixty a day. Her fingers were dark yellow. Disgusting. I don't smoke. I respect my body, work out in the gym. I could lift you with one hand. One hand. It helps to be strong in prison. People don't mess with you.'

He gave a laugh that was high and gurgling.

Tyler was finding it hard to concentrate. Light came in through the high window and fractured into a hundred pieces around the man's big body, broke the room into interlocking shapes. Things swam in and out of focus, and past and present seemed to mesh together, so that in some mysterious way, Tyler was living in two time zones simultaneously. Was this now or was it years ago? He was so tired. In front of him, Harvey Skinner bounced on the balls of his feet, surprisingly light for a man of his bulk.

'What do you want from me?'

'Want from you? What have you got to give? That's the question.'

'Nothing,' said Tyler. 'I have nothing to give.'

The first strike of the knife was a slow-motion glide through the air, and he had time to think that it would hurt, before it sliced cleanly through the flesh of his forearm. But it didn't hurt, not at once anyway. Even the blood took time to bubble up through the flaps of skin. Only the dizziness told Tyler that something had happened to him, was happening to him. There was a dull booming in his skull, and the little room seemed darker and colder. Had the sun gone behind the clouds?

Was this how it ended? Was this all there was?

Everything was such a waste. His whole life had gone by. The knife glinted again.

100

Rudi and Celia Scott were at a standstill on the Westway, just a few miles from where they had set off; a double line of stationary traffic stretched into the shimmering heat. Every so often, drivers futilely sounded their horns. People got out of their cars and walked along the queue, trying to get a sense of what was happening.

The sun beat through the glass. Celia wound down her window, but the air was thick with exhaust fumes and there was no cooling wind, so she wound it up again. A waltz was playing on the radio, spritely and rhythmic. She turned it off. Three ratty pigeons were pecking at something long dead that lay on the narrow strip of pavement. Strips of plastic hung in shreds from the fence. She breathed evenly, the way she did during her relaxation exercises each morning; she was good at keeping calm and unflustered, holding the world at bay. She glanced at her husband, who looked limp and soiled, and she frowned. Then she turned her eyes on the road again, allowing the cars to become an unfocused blur.

Rudi lay back in his seat and pretended to sleep. Beads of sweat gathered on his forehead. He felt trapped in this car, this body, the heat pressing down on him. He wanted to stand under a cold shower for hours; he wanted winter, ice, wind, purification.

His phone rang. He ignored it.

'Aren't you going to answer?'

He grunted.

'I know you're awake, Rudi.'

So he picked it up: no caller ID.

'Hello?'

The word came out dry and scratchy.

'Mr Scott?'

Just two syllables, but he knew at once who was talking: the low, clear voice with the slight East London accent. His hands were slippery on the phone. He twisted in the seat so his back was to his wife, but he could feel her eyes on him.

'Speaking.'

'In the light of new information, I would like to talk to you as soon as possible.'

He made a sound, like the last bit of air coming out of a shrivelled balloon.

'Are you still in London?'

'We're leaving,' he managed. 'Trying to leave, that is.'

He pressed the phone tightly to his ear, hoping Celia couldn't hear Maud's side of the conversation.

'You need to turn around at once and go back to the station.'

'That might be hard.'

There was a brief pause. He could picture her smart face; her unnerving grey gaze. His stomach roiled.

'An officer can come to your home, Mr Scott, if that's what you'd prefer.'

'No,' he said. 'That won't be necessary.'

Maud ended the call. Rudi stared down at the phone for a few seconds.

'So?' Celia asked. 'That was the detective, wasn't it?'

'Something's come up.'

'What does that mean?'

'Don't worry,' he said, and sliding his phone into his pocket, he opened the car door.

'Rudi? Where are you going? Don't be ridiculous.'

'See you soon.'

He stepped out into the clogged heat of the day. The light screwed into his sore eyes. He started to walk.

101

Sebastian Harris was at the door when Maud arrived. He didn't even say hello.

'I've already made an informal complaint to your superior,' he said. He gestured at the room behind him. The lawyer, Robyn Murdoch, was sitting at the table with Beatrice Macmillan. 'But I can assure you that we're preparing an official complaint as well. You're going to have to answer to the police commissioner about this. I'll also be informing the Home Secretary. I can see what you're doing.'

'Really?' said Maud. 'What am I doing?'

'Kicking up dust, getting a few cheap headlines as a way of distracting people from your complete lack of progress in this case.'

Maud looked at the three people in the room. They were all dressed the way people should be dressed on a Saturday morning, in jeans and sweatshirts, but the kind that looked expensive and beautifully manicured. It made her feel creased and shabby.

She walked across to the table, where there were coffee and croissants and glasses of orange juice. She looked back at Harris.

'Could you give us a moment?' she said.

'Absolutely not,' he said angrily. 'Anything you can say to her, you can say to me.'

'Two minutes,' said Maud. 'Give me two minutes. If after that, your wife wants you to join us, I'll have no problem with that.'

Harris stared at Maud. His complexion reddened. He lifted a finger and slowly wagged it at her.

'Maud O'Connor,' he said slowly. 'Is that your name?'

'Detective Inspector Maud O'Connor.'

'I just wanted to make sure I'd got it right. I warn you once again that you do not want me for an enemy.'

'Two minutes.'

He clenched his teeth and his jaw tightened. Maud had seen it before, at moments where violence was about to break out.

'Two minutes,' he said in a hiss, and left the room.

Maud sat at the table. She waited for the footsteps to recede. First she looked at Robyn Murdoch.

'Sorry to drag you out again on a weekend.'

Once again, the lawyer gave her a warm smile in return.

'Just ask your question,' she said amiably.

Maud turned so that she was facing Beatrice.

'Ms Macmillan, do you know the sentencing guidelines for a Category A offence of perverting the course of justice?'

Beatrice turned to Murdoch. When Murdoch spoke, it was with a note of puzzlement.

'Ms Macmillan has answered all your questions.'

'You'll notice that I'm here on my own, my colleague is waiting outside in the car; this isn't an official interview. I'm going to ask a couple of questions, and I expect you answer them frankly and in full.' Murdoch started to interrupt, but Maud continued speaking as if she hadn't heard. 'If I feel you haven't answered them frankly and fully, then I'm going to come back with my colleague, and it'll be on the record.'

Maud heard a door open behind her.

'Your two minutes is up, Detective. I think it's time for you to leave.'

Maud didn't even look round. She looked straight at Beatrice Macmillan. She felt like they were two chess players facing each other across a board. Beatrice nodded slowly, then looked at her husband.

'It's all right, Seb,' she said. 'We're just sorting something out. I'll call you if I need you.'

Still Maud didn't look round. She just heard Harris stammer something, and then his receding footsteps. The door closed. Beatrice looked at Maud, but didn't speak.

'I find myself in a difficult situation,' said Maud. 'Rudi Scott says that he was upstairs talking to Will Garvey, who was drunk and upset. Some people confirm they heard voices, though they couldn't make out what was said. About twenty minutes later, Ellen Sweeney goes up to look for Garvey. She finds him dead. The problem is, during that twenty-minute period, everyone was either together, or within view of each other, or had left the house to buy cigarettes.' Maud looked at Beatrice's mask-like face. 'So something's wrong. I've been playing around with different possibilities in my mind. What about Ellen Sweeney? She said she found the body. What if she didn't? She could have found Garvey passed out on the floor, stabbed him, and pretended to find him dead. What do you think?'

'I can't comment on that,' said Beatrice blankly.

'It doesn't matter. I don't think it's possible. It was only a couple of minutes before the rest of you joined her. So I turned my attention to Rudi Scott. He seemed like the only suspect.'

She looked at Beatrice, who shook her head slowly.

'Rudi didn't do it.'

'How do you know?'

'I just know. He couldn't have.'

Maud waited a long time before speaking again.

'I want you to be very careful what you say.'

Beatrice's lawyer interrupted. For the first time, she seemed anxious.

'You realise this is all unofficial. Nothing that Beatrice has said is admissible.'

'Ms Macmillan, when you showed me around the house, we went into the spare bedroom. Something very trivial happened. You walked across the room and straightened the duvet where it was creased.'

Beatrice gave a forced little laugh.

'I'm like that. I like things to be straight and neat.'

'I was just in your house with a friend of mine: Dr Matt Moran. He's the best scene-of-crime man I know. He went through that room. He's also got your clothes. So, Ms Macmillan, I would like you to tell me what happened there. Before you answer, I need to tell you: if I believe that you haven't told me the full truth, I will do everything I can to make sure you serve prison time.'

Beatrice's face had gone white. She turned to her lawyer and leaned close in to speak in her ear. As the lawyer heard what her client was saying, her eyes widened in obvious shock. Then the two of them had a whispered conversation. When they were finished, Murdoch put a hand to her mouth, giving a dry cough before speaking.

'Ms Macmillan was, quite understandably, anxious to protect her family. But of course she wants to co-operate fully with the investigation.'

'Then co-operate,' said Maud.

Beatrice took several deep breaths and then looked around as if she thought her husband might still be in the room.

'It feels impossible to say the words out loud. I'm not proud of any of this . . .' she began, but Maud interrupted.

'Let's not waste time. Simply tell me what happened.'

Another deep breath.

'Back when we were students, Rudi and I had a . . .' Beatrice made a vague gesture with her hands. 'It was a secret thing.'

'You were sexually involved with each other.'

'Yes,' Beatrice said in a near whisper. 'It was very intense, but I ended it after Leo died. This evening, when I met Rudi again, matters became a little flirtatious. We had too much to drink and we were remembering old times and . . .' She looked around desperately and then spoke in a hissing voice, leaning towards Maud. 'Sometimes I look at myself, this woman entering her fifties with a teenage son and a gilded life, and I think: that's not me. Now is that such a terrible thing to say?'

'Please tell me what happened.'

'It was a moment of madness. We went up to the bedroom, and I don't need to spell it out.'

'I think you need to spell it out a little.'

'What do you want?' said Beatrice fiercely.' Some pornographic story?'

'I'm going to interview Rudi Scott, and I need to decide whether he's still a suspect. One way of deciding that is whether what he says agrees with what you say.'

'All right,' said Beatrice and then she spoke in a rush. 'We kissed and Rudi pulled my trousers and knickers down and we had sex on that bed, very briefly, fully clothed. There. Are you satisfied?'

'And afterwards?'

'Afterwards, Rudi went down to rejoin everyone, and I used the external stairs to re-enter the house from the garden, so that people wouldn't realise we'd been up there together.'

'So the traces that Matt found on the bed are likely to be Rudi Scott's semen?'

Traces of red appeared suddenly on Beatrice's cheeks.

'Yes,' she said.

'And on your clothes.'

'Very possibly.'

'The clothes that you had put out to wash.'

'I wasn't thinking about it in that way. I felt dirty.' She looked at Maud, her eyes glittering. 'You probably think I'm pathetic; this old woman having sex at a party as if I was a teenager.'

Maud leaned forward.

'You're a KC. What I think is that you derailed a murder inquiry by lying to me. And the fact that it was a murder of a friend of yours makes it even worse.'

'I'm not going to take lectures from you,' said Beatrice. 'Anyone would have done what I did.'

Maud stood up.

'I hope you won't need to use that defence in court,' she said.

She looked at Beatrice. She had been feeling angry, but it ebbed away when she saw the desperation on her face.

'What do I do now? Finn mustn't know. Oh, God, just thinking about that . . . And then what about him?' Beatrice gestured helplessly to the door that Sebastian Harris had gone through. He was probably standing on the other side of it. Maybe he had heard everything that had been said. Then she spoke in a voice so quiet that Maud had to lean in close to make it out. 'You don't know my husband. You don't know what this will do to him.'

'I'm sorry,' said Maud. 'Maybe if you talk to him.'

Beatrice gave a mirthless smile at that.

'Talk to him? And say what?'

'Maybe something of what you said to me.'

As Maud walked towards the door, Robyn Murdoch walked alongside her.

'What happens now?'

'You mean . . . ?' Maud gestured towards Beatrice.

'No. The inquiry.'

'Oh,' said Maud. 'This has changed everything.'

102

Through the small hours of the night, Maud had been cold in her baggy black trousers and her thin yellow shirt; now she was warm again. There had been stretches of weariness, but not anymore. She felt fresh, clear, hard-edged, light on her feet. Energy coursed through her. The sun poured down on her.

She climbed into the car.

'Well?' Carrie asked. 'Was your instinct right?'

Maud fastened her seat belt and tied her hair more firmly.

'It's not really instinct. It's knowing something, but not knowing how you know it.'

'So now we do know,' said Carrie.

'I think we do,' said Maud.

'What I know,' said Hale, 'is that this is turning into a very long day. I've been driving around for twelve hours. I need my beauty sleep.'

'You'll be able to go home soon.'

Beside her, Carrie's mobile rang.

'My mother,' she said, glancing at the screen.

'Answer it.'

'Sorry.' She held the phone to her ear. 'Hello. Is everything okay?'

Maud could hear tinny shrieks coming from the mobile.

'I can't hear you? ... Unwell? ... What's up? ... Does she

have a fever? . . . There's a thermometer in the bathroom cabinet, and some Calpol as well . . . I'll ring again soon.'

She ended the call.

'She's running a temperature,' she said distractedly. 'Talk about bad timing.'

'You need to go home,' said Maud.

'I'll be fine.'

'We've almost come to the end. You've been fantastic. Go home, Carrie.'

'I don't want to leave you in the lurch. And children often have fevers.'

'I tell you what,' said Maud. 'Why don't you go to Hitcham Road Station and take Rudi Scott's revised statement. That shouldn't take long. Then go home. We can drop you off at the underground.'

'It's a few minutes away. It'd be quicker to walk. If you're sure.'

'I'm sure.'

Carrie climbed out of the car. She raised a hand.

'Good luck,' she said.

Maud watched her walk away, then called her boss.

'What the fuck is going on, Maud?'

'I'm very sorry.'

'Where are you? There's a great crowd of journalists here. But you aren't. Even though I gave you an extension. Next time I'll know better than to trust you.'

'I really am sorry. I should have kept you in the loop. But there's new evidence, and I was talking to a material witness.'

'I don't care if you were talking to the Pope. Get here.'

'I will.'

'Now.'

'I think I know what happened.'

'You know?' Weller's tone changed.

'I think I do, yes.'

'Are you going to tell me?'

'Can you give me a bit more time?'

Weller groaned.

'I'll go out there,' he said, 'and tell them we are making significant progress, and will have a further announcement to make soon. But you'd better be right on this.'

'Thank you, sir.'

'Who was this material witness you were talking to?'

'Beatrice Macmillan.'

'Holy fuck, Maud, you're not suggesting—?'

'I'm not suggesting anything.'

'Tell me it's Tyler Green.'

'I'd rather tell you nothing right now.'

'Why doesn't that surprise me?'

'Sir?'

'Yes.'

'I appreciate this.'

'I don't need your appreciation; I need to you end this fucking nightmare.'

'I'm doing my best.'

103

Ali Marais' sister was no longer there.

'I couldn't bear it,' Ali said. 'She was hovering. She wanted me to drink lots of sweet tea and weep, so that she could comfort me.'

'I can see that must have been difficult,' Maud said.

Ali was still wearing the oversized white dressing gown she had been in over three hours ago. Maud wondered if she had simply sat at the kitchen table, staring into the garden, since they had left her. Her old dog lay in his basket near the door.

'Why are you here again?'

'We have new information,' Maud replied. 'There are some things we need to clarify.'

'Yes. Yes, of course.'

They both sat. Ali's face was drawn and there were dark circles under her eyes.

'What new information?' she asked.

'First of all, I want to show you something.'

'What?' Ali shrank back. 'What is it?'

'Bear with me.' Maud opened her phone and pulled up the photo that Hawkins had sent. 'I want you to look at this,' she said.

Ali gave the photo a desperate glance then put her hand over her eyes.

'Why do I need to see that?' she said hoarsely.

Maud closed her phone.

'Leo Bauer's eyes were closed,' she said.

'I don't—' Ali licked her bloodless lips. 'I don't understand,' she managed to say.

'I think you do. Witnesses say that you and your husband remembered them as open, whereas this photo shows that they were closed.'

'I don't know anything,' whispered Ali. 'So long ago.'

'We'll return to that.' Maud rested her forearms on the table and leaned towards Ali. 'So as you know, we have been working on the assumption that your husband was killed between eleven forty-five and midnight. A fifteen-minute window.'

Ali nodded, rubbed her face violently.

'None of it makes sense to me,' she said. 'The times.'

'It appears that we might have been misled.'

'Misled?'

She shivered, though the room was warm, and drew the dressing gown more tightly around her.

'Can I ask you a question, Ms Marais? As you told us earlier today, and as witnesses confirm, you came downstairs at about a quarter to twelve, and you said you needed to speak to Tyler.'

'Yes.'

'You said that you should have spoken to him earlier.'

'Yes.'

'What did you mean by earlier?'

'What did I mean?'

'Yes.'

'I don't understand.'

'Did you mean earlier that evening, or something else perhaps?'

Ali shook her head.

'I don't understand,' she repeated.

'You said you needed to go outside and speak to him. Why didn't you?'

'Why? I don't know. Just—' She shrugged. 'I don't know,' she repeated. 'I don't know anything.'

'Instead, you went to buy cigarettes.'

'Yes.'

'Because you'd run out of them?'

'Obviously. Clara came with me,' she added.

'But you hadn't run out, had you?'

'What?'

'You hadn't run out of cigarettes.'

Ali stared at her.

'Of course I had. Or why would I have gone out at midnight to buy more?'

'That's my question.'

'I don't understand the question.'

Maud drew a sheet of lined paper out of her pocket, with scribbled notes on it. 'Carrie and I have been over it together. Please correct us if you think we're wrong. You opened a packet of cigarettes at about seven thirty yesterday evening, sitting on the bench in the garden. We found the cellophane wrapper to that pack. Let's say it was only a packet of ten. You smoked one and gave one to Marco Burney. Yes?'

'I don't know,' Ali whispered. 'How do I know something like that?'

'At around ten, you smoked another cigarette in the garden, this time with Clara. Marco was with you, but he smoked a spliff.'

'What is this?'

'Shortly before eleven, you had another cigarette, this time alone. And at about ten minutes past eleven, you smoked one more, this time in the dining area of the lower ground floor.

You stubbed it out on the table. I gather things were becoming rather dramatic by this time of the evening. And your dog got up on the table.'

As if he knew he was being talked about, Benjy feebly wagged his tail.

'Why does any of this matter? What's it got to do with Will dying?'

'Six cigarettes, Ms Marais – we've retrieved all of the stubs, along with the cellophane wrapper.'

'So?'

'So you hadn't run out.'

'But I thought I had,' Ali whispered. 'Or I wouldn't have gone out.'

'You came down the stairs at a quarter to twelve, and you said you needed to speak to Tyler. But before you could do so, Rudi Scott also came down the stairs and announced he had just been talking to Will.'

'I can't make any sense of this. Please stop. Please.'

'It's quite simple. You were about to go out to Tyler and say you were sorry for what you had done to him, but Rudi gave you an unexpected lifeline.'

'No,' whispered Ali.

'You were quick-thinking. You knew your husband was al-ready dead, but you saw that if you immediately left the house, you could give yourself an alibi.'

'What are you saying?'

There was a silence. Maud looked at her across the table, and when she spoke, her voice was gentle.

'It's over. You know that. You'll feel better once you tell us what happened.'

Ali lifted her head and met Maud's eyes. Her face was crum-pling; her body was losing its rigidity and folding in on itself.

'I wanted you to find the killer,' she said. 'I've been in hell.'

'There's a way out,' said Maud. 'Just tell me from the beginning.'

'You mean the beginning of the party?'

'No. Way before that. Tell me from the real beginning. When you first met Tyler, all those years ago.'

104

Ali Marais had met Tyler Green in her second year at university. He'd come, a friend of a friend, to the party that she and her three housemates had thrown. She'd only noticed him in the aftermath, when almost everyone had left and the remaining guests drifted around amiably, or sat on the floor, and no one had to make an effort to perform or impress anymore. Ali had been nervous about the evening: perhaps people wouldn't turn up; perhaps they would leave early with a better event to go to. But it had been a noisy, crowded success.

Now, at three in the morning, she sank onto the sofa and yawned, smiled at the emptying room. And Tyler came over and sat beside her. He told her his name, and that he was studying medicine. He said he had seen her before, at a music gig a few weeks ago, and that was why he had come this evening: to see her again. He was always so candid; he never played games or acted cool. There was something almost unworldly about him. Ali had always been slightly tense and obsessive, needing control, but with Tyler she began to soften. He was utterly smitten by her, and he thought she was beautiful, so she began to feel beautiful and desirable. She had always thought she wasn't capable of falling in love, that it was something that happened to other people. She knew that Tyler loved her with a generosity and trust she would never be able to match, but she began to believe that they could make each other happy.

Life opened up for her, and as it did so she became terrified something would ruin it. He would see through her, realise that she wasn't the person he'd taken her for.

Tyler was always certain they would stay together, which also frightened her. After all, she was only twenty when they met, he twenty-one. How can you know at such a young age that you've met the right person? But after a few heady weeks, Tyler was already making plans for their shared future.

She entered his friendship group, bringing Clara with her. She met Jay, Marco, Ellen, Beatrice, Rudi, Will. And Leo. Tyler had told her that Leo used to bully him when they were at school together and Ali asked why they remained friends. Tyler had shrugged. Friendships are weird things, he had said. Sometimes, he said, you choose your friends, but sometimes they choose you. You might not even like them that much, but it's as if you don't have a choice.

Ali was wary of Leo, who was almost absurdly handsome, but who used his charm in a way that she found repellent. She was not going to be charmed by someone who so obviously thought he was irresistible.

In their third year, on an unseasonably warm day in early April, Leo found her, out where she sat by the river reading one of her course books. Sitting beside her, he turned his brilliant blue eyes on her, asked her about her studies, her family, her childhood, her hopes for the future. Touched her on the shoulder, the hand. Told her Tyler was lucky; he envied him. So cheesy. He kissed her on her neck, her jawbone. Murmured her name.

She knew what he was doing, and she knew it would be a terrible mistake, but she allowed him to lead her up the river, into a meadow. He kissed her, laid her down in the long grass, used his fingers until she was panting and moaning with desire in a way that had never happened to her before, then entered her. He watched her as she came, again and again, and she called out for more. As helpless as she had ever been. Sex with Leo turned her into an animal.

After he buttoned himself up again and left, she was appalled and ashamed. She didn't tell Tyler, or anyone; she pushed the event down into the basement of herself. She tried not to be alone with Leo, but whenever she saw him, she hated him, and yet she felt her body turn molten with terrible, burning lust.

Then she overheard a couple of Leo's friends talking about how Leo had made a bet that he could get controlled, demure Ali Marais to sleep with him. One of them had even watched from a distance to make sure Leo didn't cheat.

'He reduced me to nothing,' she said to Maud. 'And I – I wanted it so badly. I kept picturing myself there on the ground. The way he watched me. I wanted him to do it again and again and again, to hurt me and grind me into dust. And I wanted to kill myself, so I didn't have this feeling.'

She had told the story in a monotone, not meeting her eyes.

'Or to kill him,' Maud said.

'It wasn't like that. It wasn't planned. I did my finals. I kept going out with Tyler, having sex with Tyler, making plans for the future with Tyler, who was always sweet to me. I thought he had no idea – I only discovered last night he did. I kept wondering if other people knew. Were they looking at me differently? Were they laughing about me behind my back, or going silent when I entered a room? Leo behaved as if nothing had happened. It was like I was invisible to him again. Until that weekend.'

She paused. Benjy grunted in his sleep, wagged his tail and twitched.

105

Ali had dreaded the weekend, but she told herself it would be the last hurrah for the friendship group. After that, everyone would go their separate ways, and bit by bit they would drift apart. She and Tyler would still see Clara, Will, maybe Beatrice, probably not the others so much. Not Leo. And she could forget about him; forget it had ever happened and let her dark, consuming lust gradually dwindle.

She ate almost nothing; drank too much; smoked some weed. Then, late at night in the garden, she was briefly alone with Leo. He had put his hand on her breast, feeling her nipple harden, and said they should fuck again. She obviously wanted it. And she had felt a throb of that pure, loathsome desire.

'Come to my room,' he'd said. 'When Tyler is asleep.'

She had waited until the house was at last silent, and she had gone to where he lay with a lazy, confident smile on his face, and she had cut his throat cleanly with the knife she had taken from the kitchen. She had watched the blood gush out, watched Leo until his eyes, still wide open, could not see her anymore.

'I was glad,' she said. 'I had to get rid of him. If I hadn't got rid of him, he would have wrecked my life, destroyed me. I couldn't be that person.'

Maud gazed at her, but didn't say anything. Ali's last words seemed to hang in the air. It was very quiet in the kitchen. In the distance, they could hear the sound of the lawnmower.

'There wasn't a plan,' said Ali eventually. 'I just knew I had to kill him. It didn't occur to me that I would get away with it. I think I wiped the handle of the knife, but that was like an instinct. I left the knife by the body. I went downstairs, into the kitchen, washed my hands and face to get rid of the blood.'

'But someone moved the knife,' Maud said.

Ali nodded.

'When I was in the kitchen, I heard someone blundering around upstairs, going into the bathroom to use the loo, coming out again. The bathroom was right next to the room where Leo slept, and I was sure I heard whoever it was go into that room. I thought there would be a shout of horror, running footsteps, the alarm sounded. But there was nothing. I stood for a while, almost wanting to be discovered. Then after a bit, I went into the garden to wait for it to be morning.'

Morning had come. Leo's body had been discovered. There was uproar and chaos: screams in the house, ashen faces, everyone staring at each other with horror and suspicion. The police had arrived. The knife was in Tyler's room. Everyone remembered the nasty row they had had the previous evening. The cut was seen as the work of a professional – something a medical student would know how to do.

'It was as simple as that,' said Ali. 'They took him away in the car. He turned and looked at us. At me. That was the last time I saw him until yesterday.'

'So you let him spend twenty-nine years in prison for a murder you had committed.'

'Yes.'

'The man who loved you, and who you say you loved, after your fashion.'

'It didn't happen as simply as that. At first, I thought he wouldn't be charged. There wasn't enough evidence against him. Then I thought they would give him a short sentence. I don't know. Aggravated manslaughter or something. When he was found guilty, I shut myself down. I made myself not think about it – though of course that meant avoiding thinking about almost anything, feeling almost anything. It was as if I was on a tightrope, and I could keep going only along that fragile slender line, one step at a time, not looking back, not looking down. That's how I survived, if you call it survival. I married Will, because why not? And I tried to have children, because I thought maybe I could find meaning in life again, do something right. I got a dog. I worked hard. I exercised. I kept myself under strict control. I didn't think about Tyler. I didn't think about Leo. I so rigorously, urgently, didn't think about them that of course I thought about them all the time. Every day, every hour, every minute.'

She stood up and went to stand at the window, looking out onto the fresh limy greenness of the garden.

'Do you know what's strange?' she said. 'As the years, decades, went by, I half persuaded myself that Tyler had done it after all. I almost felt like a victim of what had happened. When I saw him last night, I hated him for how he had ruined my life, how he had made me feel about myself. Isn't that strange?'

'Yes,' agreed Maud, though she had had enough experience of people's behaviour to find few things strange. 'So you murdered Leo Bauer because he sexually excited and humiliated you, and you allowed your boyfriend take the rap because that's how it just turned out, by chance, and you let it. Now I want you to tell me about last night.'

106

Ali looked at Maud, almost with surprise, as if she had forgotten she was there.

'Poor Jay,' she said softly.

'Yes,' said Maud. 'Another victim.'

Ali shut her eyes for several seconds. When she opened them again, she stared directly into Maud's face.

'Last night, people said such terrible things, about sex and betrayal and bullying. Childlessness. The bet. I felt as if my clothes had been stripped off my body, and then I'd been flayed. Tyler was talking about the day of the murder, how he was arrested and taken away and then, afterwards, how we had all let him down. After he said all that, he walked out. We were in shock. It felt as if we weren't only remembering that day. We were reliving it. But I made a mistake. I thought no one except Will had noticed. It was such a tiny thing, and so many things were being said, a flood of words and memories.'

'The eyes,' said Maud.

Ali nodded.

'I said that I remembered Leo's dead eyes looking up at me. Will said he remembered it too.' She paused, seeming to turn this over in her mind. 'At that moment, I knew it was the end of everything. I was almost relieved. Will left the room, and I followed him. I met him upstairs. He wouldn't look at me. He was standing at the window, looking out at the garden, out at

Tyler. The whole time he was talking, he was looking at Tyler. He said he knew what I'd done. He knew that I was the one who had killed Leo. And I knew what he had done.'

She stopped for a beat. Maud waited.

'Will closed Leo's eyes himself,' said Ali. 'He couldn't bear them looking at him.'

'Why would he do that?'

'He said that he was drunk, staggered into a random room and passed out. He didn't know that this random room contained the dead Leo Bauer, with the murder weapon next to him. Early morning, Will wakes up, sees the body lying next to him, sees the murder weapon, and panics. He closes Leo's eyes, throws the knife into another random room. Tyler's room, as it happens. But he didn't know who had killed Leo. Not until last night, when he realised it was me, because I had also seen the eyes open, so I must have been in that room before him. He said he was going to tell Tyler.'

'In the same way that you said that you were going to tell Tyler. Why didn't you just let him go ahead and do it? You said a few minutes ago that you were almost relieved that your husband knew.'

'I wish I had. You won't believe that, but it's the truth. I thought I was going to, that it was over at last, the slow-motion nightmare of the last three decades. But it didn't feel real. Everything went red. I felt I was burning up. I knew that I'd done this terrible thing. I'd killed Leo; that wasn't such a wicked thing. The world was a better place without Leo Bauer in it. But I knew Tyler was innocent, and I let him go to prison for his whole life because I was too much of a coward. I didn't do anything to make it happen, but I let it happen. Suddenly I realised that Will, my husband, the man I shared a bed with, also knew that Tyler was innocent, or at least, he knew that the knife had been put there by him, and for years and decades he'd also done nothing about it. And he said to me that without admitting it to himself, perhaps he had done nothing not only because he would have been guilty of perverting the course of justice, but also because if Tyler was in prison, then he had a chance of being with me. He laughed at that, and I knew what the laugh meant – that being with me had been a wretched failure; our marriage had been a mockery of what marriage should be. I felt that a terrible, horrible fate had brought us together, and then last night it made us face up to what we'd done and who we were.'

'Yet you didn't face up to it, did you?' said Maud. 'You haven't answered my question. Why didn't you let Will go down and tell Tyler?'

'I saw the knife. I don't know how it had got there. It was like magic, or it was like destiny. It was as if it had been put there for me to use. I suddenly thought of our marriage like a black hole. For years, I had tried to have a child. I thought if . . .' She hesitated for a moment as if it was now difficult to speak of her and Will as a couple. 'If we had a child, then something good would come into the world. After a few years, it became clear that it wasn't going to happen. I took it as a judgement. At that moment last night, I was so grateful we didn't have a child, because I knew that we were a couple who should be wiped off the face of the earth. Nothing should remain of us.'

'What did you do?'

'I picked up the knife. It happened so quickly. Will still had his back turned to me, looking out at Tyler in the garden. I reached up and jabbed it through his neck. I don't know what I'd expected. Screams. A struggle. Blood spraying everywhere. But there was none of that. He just fell, like when a building collapses in on itself. He sank to the ground. He didn't make a sound, and he didn't look at me. I stared down at him. He was gone.'

'And then?'

'You know the rest. I intended going to see Tyler, to tell him everything. But when I came down, Rudi said he had just been talking to Will. I realised that I had been given this unexpected chance.'

'The perfect alibi,' said Maud.

'That makes it sound calculated,' said Ali.

'Yes, it does.'

'I just needed time to think, to get it all straight. I would have told Tyler later. I would have confessed to everything. You have to believe me.'

Maud looked at Ali with a new fascination. She had to make an effort not to let it show on her face.

You have to believe me. She thought about that, and decided that, no, she didn't believe her. Ali Marais had killed a man who had degraded her sense of self. She could understand that murder, but not how she had stood by for so many years, while her lover was wrongly imprisoned. When she said that she was in hell, Maud believed that. But she had managed to live in that hell. She said she was going to confess it all to Tyler. Maybe. But she had never done so before, when it had really mattered, and when the chance to get away with the crime had presented itself, she had taken it. Again.

She thought all of that, but she didn't say it. If she had, then Ali might have got angry or hysterical, and stopped co-operating. Maud would have been able to assemble the evidence to charge her, but it would have taken longer, and all that time Tyler would have been in jail. Maud didn't want to know the secrets of Ali's soul. She didn't want to be her therapist, or her judge. She wanted to get her back to the station, so that she could make her confession on the record and be charged.

'You should put some clothes on. I think it's time to go,' said Maud.

'Yes, of course,' said Ali.

She looked eerily calm, but then her expression changed to one of alarm.

'What about Benjy? Who'll look after Benjy?'

She broke down, helplessly sobbing.

Hale got out of the car and opened the back door for Ali. There was a new air of seriousness about him. Ali climbed into the car. She looked tiny, as if she had shrunk to the size of a child. Before joining her, Maud called Weller from her mobile.

'You should know that Will Garvey's wife has confessed.'

'You what!'

'To both murders.'

'I thought Jay Murphy killed himself.'

'I don't mean Jay Murphy. I mean Leo Bauer. She killed Bauer and she killed her husband last night. We're bringing her to the station now to be formally charged.'

There was a stunned silence, then Weller spoke.

'The wife? That's good news,' he said in a tone of disbelief. 'Finally some good news. She's confessed, you say?'

'She says she's going to give a full statement.'

'Fantastic. I'm going to call the Home Secretary at once, before the press conference. And Harris, of course. Tell him that he and his wife can stop worrying.'

'Well, actually,' Maud began, 'I don't think that's quite—'

'Business as usual, eh?'

'Sir, before anything else, can Tyler Green be told?'

But the line had gone dead.

108

'Harvey.' The guard rattled at the door. 'Harvey. Time's up. I'm coming in now, okay?'

There was no reply. The guard frowned and slid open the little aperture, peering in. At first he couldn't make out what he was seeing. He fumbled his keys in the lock, dropping them to the floor, retrieving them, cursing under his breath.

'Fuck fuck fuck.'

The door swung open. The guard took a step inside, then stepped back into the corridor again, slipping on the tiles. There was blood all over his shoes. He hit the alarm and the air seemed to shake with its harsh shriek. He shouted. He shouted so loudly that his throat hurt.

'Code red. Fucking code red.'

Then the sound of footsteps running. In their cells, prisoners waited for the news.

Beatrice waited for Finn to go out. She sat at the large table in the grand room, abstract paintings of splashes of colour on the grey walls, and stared through the huge windows. London was shimmering in the heat haze, but she wasn't really seeing the city.

She heard Sebastian's voice from the next room.

'Yes,' he was saying. 'Good. Very good. I'm glad that's sorted.'

The door opened and he came into the room, but she didn't look round. He sat opposite her.

'So,' he said. 'That was the head of the police inquiry.'

'O'Connor?'

'No, not that girl. The man in charge.'

'You sound pleased.'

'I am pleased. Very pleased. They've got the killer.'

The light flooding into the room was giving her a headache. She squinted across the table at her husband, a dark, blocky shape and an unpleasant smile.

'Aren't you going to ask me who?'

'Who?'

She held her breath, waiting for the answer.

'The wife. That's who.'

'Ali? You're saying Ali killed Will?'

'Both of them, apparently.'

'I don't understand,' Beatrice said.

She put her hand to her head, pressed her fingers against the temple to ease the pain flowering in her skull.

'Both her husband and Leo Bauer. At least this will shut that bastard Conrad Bauer up for a bit.'

'Ali,' Beatrice repeated. 'Ali killed them. And so Tyler – oh, God.'

Poor Tyler, she thought. Poor Jay. Her old friends. People she had loved, and who had loved her, back when she was still available for that. Still a proper human being.

'So it's over.' Sebastian put both fists on the table and leaned forward. 'Did you hear me?'

'What?'

'I said, did you hear me? It's over.'

Beatrice looked at him at last.

'I know you heard my conversation with the detective, Sebastian.'

His face darkened.

'You mean, the one about you having a quick, drunken shag with your old boyfriend. That conversation?'

'Yes, that one.'

He sat back.

'What do you want me to say? That you disgust me?'

'Do I?'

'A fifty-year-old woman pulling down her knickers after too many martinis. What do you think?'

'I think we should talk about it. All of it. Everything. All the things we've never talked about.'

'I have no intention of talking about it, Beatrice. I don't want to hear about your squalid behaviour, or your pathetic self-justifications.'

Beatrice considered her husband for a few seconds. Really,

had she ever even liked him, let alone desired him? It seemed impossible now, this barrel-chested, red-faced, pompous man with the jarring voice. Like mist blowing away from a hilltop, her headache began to clear.

'You don't really care, do you?'

'Don't be naive. We both know what was at stake. Now I'm assured that the woman has made a full confession, so none of it will have to come out.'

'You mean, my infidelity.'

He snorted.

'I wouldn't call it that. Sounds a bit too dignified.'

'Or do you mean the fact that I gave a false statement to the police, and deliberately obstructed the investigation, even though it was a friend who had been murdered?'

'I don't want to know about any of that.'

'Of course you don't.'

'Beatrice, I am willing to turn a blind eye to what went on in our house. We have our separate lives, and those can continue.'

'As if nothing had happened.'

'Yes.'

'But it did happen, Sebastian. I'm your wife, and I was unfaithful to you. It wasn't particularly enjoyable, and so I wish it hadn't happened, but I don't feel I betrayed our relationship. Because we don't have one, do we? What we have is a contract of mutual convenience.'

'For God's sake, Beatrice, you know as well as I do—'

'I'm also a KC, and I knowingly interfered in a police investigation into a murder.'

'I told you, that doesn't need to come out.'

'Fine. But I'm going to resign.'

'Don't be a fool.'

'From my job, and from my marriage. Sorry if that interferes with your career prospects.'

His eyes bulged.

'What about Finn? Don't you care about him?'

'Finn? Of course I care about him. I haven't been giving him enough attention recently. I think he's going through a rough patch. But Sebastian, do you honestly think Finn will be upset if we separate? I tend to think he'll be relieved.'

She stood up and left the room. Only when she was out of his hearing did she falter, putting a hand against the wall for support. Will, she thought. Jay. Tyler. All of us.

110

When Rudi stumbled out of the station, blinking in the bright light, he was momentarily bewildered to see his wife sitting in the car, waiting for him. He had left her on the A40, to trudge up the exhaust-choked road towards the police station. Now here she was again, just as she had been a few hours previously.

He made his way towards her cautiously, trying to look normal. He arranged his expression into one of wry affection, lifted a hand in acknowledgement, looked to one side so that he didn't have to meet her eyes as she wound down the window.

'You came back,' he said.

She wasn't returning his smile; her long, narrow face was stern.

'Let's try again, shall we?'

'Try again? Oh, you mean, to go home.'

'Obviously.'

He climbed into the car. He felt her gaze on him as he fumbled with the seat belt: soiled goods, he thought.

'Oof, I'm tired,' he said. 'You must be exhausted as well.'

The car nosed out into the traffic. Celia turned up the air conditioner.

'Anyway, that was a waste of time.' Rudi gestured, palms up, expensive watch glinting. 'I don't know why they needed me really.'

But he felt a blush spreading over his face, down his grimy neck.

'It'll be lovely to be home,' he said.

Stop talking, he told himself.

A message pinged onto his phone, then another, another. He turned to look, shielding the screen from Celia. Beatrice. Why would Beatrice contact him?

'Let me see if this is important,' he babbled to Celia.

It will be public news very soon, so you might as well know. Ali killed Will.

Ali. His first emotion was one of relief. It swept through him like a tidal wave, leaving him weak.

Will and also Leo.

The car swept on, unimpeded now.

She has confessed.

Did that mean it wouldn't come out? He thought it did. He tried to breathe normally.

Sebastian knows everything. I am resigning. We misled the police.

What did that mean? Did she think he should do something similar? He had nothing to stand down from; no noble gesture to make even if he wanted to. He was just a man who wrote novels that nobody wanted to publish. He glanced at Celia, and she stared straight ahead at the road. Then he deleted the messages one by one, though he knew she would never look at them. She was honourable; she set rules for herself and scrupulously followed them.

'It was Ali,' he said. 'Ali murdered Will.'

'The wife?'

'Yes.'

'Who told you?'

Rudi swallowed painfully. His mouth was parched and his

throat sore; he wanted to drink tumbler after tumbler of cool water.

'Beatrice.'

The name felt like a confession; surely Celia would know just from the way he said it. She always saw through him, or saw into him. Why had she married him, when she could see who he was? His eyes burned. If she ever found out ... He touched her on the shoulder and she briefly turned her head.

'What?'

'Thank you for coming.'

'Of course I came. I'm your wife.'

Rudi closed his eyes. The car purred under him; his thoughts churned. He told himself that one day, this would just be a story he had lived through. Or perhaps, he thought, and a half smile crossed his face, it could be his story: one he could write, and by writing put a shape round the shame and dread. A story of the past crashing into the present; of betrayal and death; of survival and recovery. Yes. He let the idea gather inside him as he drifted off to sleep.

III

Sam sat beside Clara on the sofa, their bodies close but not touching, and laid a hand on her heaving shoulder. She felt that she was waiting out a fierce storm. Clara was leaning forward, her head bowed, and her whole body convulsed with weeping. Every so often she lifted her face, which was blotchy and wet, and gazed around her as if something might have happened that would make a difference.

Sam was almost awed at the violence of her partner's grief. They had been together for almost thirteen years, and in all that time she had never seen Clara anything like this.

Bit by bit, the sobbing grew quieter. Eventually it was just an occasional hiccup of distress. Sam pulled a tissue out of her pocket and handed it to Clara, who dabbed at her streaming face.

'Sorry,' she said. 'I'm sorry.'

'Don't say sorry.'

'I just—' Another sob. She pressed the damp ball of tissue to her eyes. 'God.'

'I'm here, my darling,' Sam said.

'It hurts.'

'Yes.'

'It's my fault.'

'No.'

'I made him go. He didn't want to.'

'He chose to go.'

'I let him down.'

'No. No, you didn't. You were his kind friend.'

'Life's so sad.'

Sam lifted Clara's hand and kissed the knuckles.

'It can be,' she said.

'Is there any more news?'

'About the case?'

Clara nodded. Sam collected her mobile from the charger in the kitchen and scrolled through the news. She came back into the living room, her face solemn.

'They've charged someone,' she said. Clara put a hand to her chest. 'The wife. It says she has confessed to Leo Bauer's murder as well.'

Clara stared at her. She opened her mouth to speak, but no words came.

Then the doorbell rang.

'Don't answer,' said Clara. 'I can't see anyone.'

It rang again.

'Tell them to go away, whoever it is.'

Sam nodded and left the room. Clara heard the door opening, a murmur of voices, then Sam returned.

'Sorry.' She made a helpless gesture.

Behind her was another woman, thick grey hair in a matted tangle, skirt twisted, face puffy.

'Ellen?' Clara said.

Ellen blundered towards her, flopped down on the sofa.

'I didn't know where else to go,' she said.

'What's happened?'

'I don't know what to do.'

Sam saw Clara's face change, become calm again, the grief sliding under the surface.

'You can't go home?'

'I have to soon – the children. But not now. He can have them one more night; it's not them he wants to destroy.'

'Your husband?'

'What shall I do, Clara?'

'I don't know.'

'Look at me,' said Ellen. 'Look. Does it make you laugh? The couples' therapist. The good wife. The mother of five. Smily, cheerful Ellen. Look. Look!'

'I'm looking,' said Clara.

'And what do you see?'

'I see my friend.'

112

Conrad Bauer put down the phone and turned towards his wife, who was peeling potatoes at the kitchen sink.

'Who was that?' she asked. Then she saw that his face was grey and slack and his mouth drawn up into a square of pain. 'Conrad? What is it?'

'It's very odd—' he began, then stopped and lifted a hand to his chest.

Susan Bauer put down the peeler and hurried across to him. 'Are you ill? Here, sit down.'

She guided him to a chair at the kitchen table, helped him sink his heavy body into it.

'Is it your heart? Tell me!'

'That was the police.' He looked at her blindly.

'Well?'

'They've got a confession.'

'But that's good news, isn't it?' She drew out a second chair and sat beside him. 'What's wrong?'

'It wasn't Tyler who confessed. It was Alison Marais. Will's wife.'

'I see.'

He looked round at his wife. She was barely reacting.

'No, you don't see.'

'What is it?'

'She confessed to both murders.'

'You mean—' Susan Bauer's thoughts were sluggish. 'You mean, to Leo's as well?'

Conrad Bauer nodded.

'Yes,' he whispered.

'But—' she began, then stopped.

'I was so sure,' he said.

He looked old and defeated.

'Oh, Conrad,' she said, and gathered both his hands in hers. 'Oh, my dear.'

'It wasn't my fault,' he said, but his heart wasn't in it. His expression was one of bewilderment. 'All those years.'

'I know. I know.'

Years of bitter campaigning, she thought. Of self-righteous purpose and zealous certainty. Of hating. Of punishing. Of holding at bay the one unbearable fact: that his beloved son was dead and beyond all rescue.

'What's going to happen now?' Conrad Bauer said.

'What do you mean?'

'What am I going to do?'

She didn't know if he was thinking of Tyler, or of himself. She couldn't think of what to say. She lifted one of his hands and kissed the swollen knuckles.

113

They arrived at Hitcham Road Station, sweeping past the crowd of press into the car park at the back.

'Thank you,' Maud said to Constable Hale.

'Any time,' he said, grinning. 'It's been a rollercoaster.'

They entered the building by the back entrance, avoiding the crowds. Ali was taken to an interview room, where she would make her formal statement. Maud went first to the cloakroom, where she splashed water over her face. Hawkins sat beside her in the interview room. Ali was composed; in a bleak way, she almost seemed at peace. Hawkins switched on the recording device, they gave their names, the place and date and time. The light blinked.

'Let's begin,' said Maud, 'at the beginning.'

After it was over, Maud went to Weller's office.

'We've got a result,' he said, jovial now.

'Yes, sir.'

Weller looked at his watch.

'I make it a bit less than thirteen hours.'

'Sir?'

'It took us a bit less than thirteen hours to solve two murders.'

Maud noted the 'us', and suppressed a smile.

'Something like that.'

'Good job,' he said.

'Thank you. It was Carrie Kessler as much as me. She was invaluable.'

'Ready to face the press? I'll speak first.'

'I don't mind if I don't—'

The door opened, and a young woman put her head round the door.

'What is it?' Weller asked.

'Hawkins thought you should be informed at once, sir.'

'Informed of what?'

'Tyler Green has been attacked and badly injured.'

Maud sprang to her feet. She felt as if someone had punched her in the stomach.

'How badly?'

'That's all I know.'

'But I explicitly told—'

She stopped. What was the use of any of that now? She thought of the warder, Boyle, who was a criminally irresponsible piece of shit. She thought of the officers who had failed to keep Jay Murphy safe. The anger, the blame, much of it directed against herself – all of that would have to wait. She pushed a hand through her tangled hair.

'Where is he?'

'In St Lawrence's Hospital.'

Maud turned to Weller impulsively.

'I must go and see him at once. It doesn't matter if I'm not there for the announcement. It'll come better from you anyway. You know how to do these things.'

Before Weller could reply, Maud ran from the room.

114

She ran past the smokers in the car park, the line of ambulances queued up at A&E, through the revolving doors, past the reception area where people milled around, down the long corridor where the lights flickered and where she dodged wheelchair users and patients walking with painful slowness, up a flight of stairs two at a time, to the double doors of the Intensive Care Unit. She was about to lean on the green button to call for admittance, but at that moment a man was pushed out on his bed, his face a strange grey colour. Maud dashed through, into the unit, where machines beeped, trolleys of equipment rumbled across the lino, and men and women in blue scrubs had a purposeful air.

'Tyler Green,' said Maud to the nurse at the work station, trying to catch her breath.

'Are you family?'

Maud held up her ID.

'I'm Detective Inspector O'Connor. I have to see him.'

The woman looked at her: yellow shirt, weary face, wild hair, glittering eyes.

'Cubicle seventeen,' she said. 'To the end, and then left.'

Maud walked swiftly past the curtained beds. She turned to the left. She saw Tyler at the far end. She couldn't stop herself giving a small cry of distress. He was a mass of tubes and cables, an intubation tube in his mouth. His eyes were closed and his skin had the pallor almost of a corpse, but she could make out the faint rise and fall of his chest.

'And you are?'

Maud looked around. A man was standing next to her. He was middle-aged, his head shaved. Maud identified herself.

'I'm Dr Roth,' he said.

'It looks terrible,' she said.

'He's a lucky man, your Mr Green,' said Dr Roth.

'He doesn't seem so lucky to me.'

'He was stabbed in the chest and in the thigh. If either wound had touched an artery or a major vein, then he wouldn't be alive. Apparently it was some time before they found him.'

'Some time?' said Maud. 'He was officially at risk.'

Dr Roth gestured at the bed.

'I can see that.'

'How is he?' She hesitated. 'He's not going to die, is he?'

The doctor smiled at her.

'As I said, he's a lucky man.'

Maud felt a pain in her chest, curiously close to grief, and hot tears welled in her eyes. She blinked them away.

'Until now, I'd say he's been exceptionally unlucky.'

Roth nodded.

'I've heard about that.'

'Of course you have. Is Harvey Skinner here too?'

'He is. But in a different unit.'

'Was he stabbed as well?'

Dr Roth shook his head.

'As far as I know, Green didn't have a weapon. But he managed quite a bit of damage with his bare hands. Apparently it'll be a long operation. Or series of operations. There's some question about whether his eye can be saved. I imagine there'll be a court case.'

'If I have anything to do with it, Tyler Green will only be involved as a witness.' Maud looked down at the bed. 'Can I talk to him?'

'You can talk to him. I can't guarantee that he'll hear what you say.'

Maud pulled a chair next to the bed and sat in it. She took his left hand in both of hers. The knuckles were badly bruised.

'Tyler,' she said. 'I don't know if you can hear me. I hope you can. This is Maud O'Connor. The detective. I'm sorry I wasn't able to protect you. I did what I could, but it wasn't enough.'

She paused and looked at his face. She thought she saw a slight flicker at the corner of his eyes. She gave his hand a slight squeeze, hoping she wasn't causing him any pain.

'It's over, Tyler,' she said. 'We know that Ali Marais killed her husband. And she killed Leo Bauer. She's confessed and been charged.'

She felt the tiniest movement in the hand she was holding, a ripple. She looked at his face. Again that flicker around the eyes, and then she saw the lids open. She looked into the flecked walnut eyes. She could see the understanding there, but no surprise.

She twisted round to Dr Roth.

'Can you take the tube out?'

'Not yet.'

She looked back at Tyler, directly into his eyes.

'You're in a hospital. You'll be looked after, and you'll be safe. And although nothing can ever compensate you for the great wrong that has been done to you, and the great suffering you have endured, you will be exonerated and you will be free. A free man at last. Do you understand?'

There was no movement, just those eyes looking back at

hers, but Maud knew he was hearing her, and she knew that he understood.

She bent slightly closer.

'Well done,' she said. 'Well done, Tyler.'

Maud strode swiftly out of the hospital, into a summer day which belonged to her at last. Her emotion was not elation: Tyler Green had spent nearly three decades in prison for a crime he had not committed; Will Garvey had been killed by his wife; Jay Murphy had taken his own life on her watch. What she felt was more like a pure, blazing energy that burned away the exhaustion.

She looked at the time on her phone screen, then stopped for a moment, calculating. She smiled her asymmetrical smile, pushed her hair behind her ears. She would only be a few minutes late.

115

Ross was sitting at a table overlooking the canal. She saw him before he saw her. He was watching a swan and her cygnets making their way in a stately procession towards Victoria Park. She saw a faint smile on his face and the wind catching his hair, and she felt a catch in her chest. It was going to start all over again, she knew it, and it gave her a sense of vertigo.

She sat down opposite him; he turned, and he looked relieved and glad to see her. She wanted to cry. She smiled at him, and he smiled back.

'I thought you might have forgotten,' he said. 'Or just have thought I was crazy.'

'Sorry I'm late.'

'We're going to have a competition,' he said. 'Who's had the worst day. I was late too because I locked my bike outside last night and when I came out to get it, it had been stolen. I phoned the police about it, and they told me that they don't investigate stolen bikes. What do you to say to that?'

'You win,' said Maud. 'You've had a worse day.'

'You mustn't let me win that easily. How has your day been?'

Maud stopped to consider this. It suddenly seemed a large and difficult question, a whole world of pain and betrayal that she was still carrying around inside her, and would do for months.

'I've been working,' she said. 'I think my day is only just beginning.'

Ross looked at his watch.

'Work? What do you do?'

She took a breath, kept her gaze steadily on him.

'I'm a police detective. That is what I do.'

Ross put his head in his hands, and then raised his head and looked at her.

'I said the worst thing I could possibly have said, didn't I?'

'That's all right,' said Maud. 'I'm not in the bike investigation department.'

There was a pause. Maud looked at the swans, almost out of sight now. The sun on the nape of her neck was like a blessing.

'Hang on. Am I imagining it, or are you wearing exactly what you were wearing when I met you last night?'

Maud looked down at her yellow shirt and baggy black trousers and smiled, letting happiness grab hold of her.

'I suppose I am.'

'So you haven't slept? It must have been quite some midsummer night.'

'Oh yes,' Maud said. 'It was.'

ACKNOWLEDGEMENTS

A book is made by so many more people than its author – or, in our case, authors. At every stage of *What Happened That Night*, we have been inspired, supported, encouraged, guided, rescued and enabled. We are hugely grateful.

This is a book about a man released from prison after nearly three decades, and of course we could not have begun to plan and write it without trying to understand what life inside a prison is actually like. During our writing career, we have visited many prisons – for men and for women, high security and open – to discuss our thrillers. Thinking and talking about books can be a gateway to thinking and talking about life; reading books is a way of breaking down walls. We salute all the prison librarians who make sure that prisoners have access to whatever book they want, and all the people who run prison reading groups with such commitment and kindness, and also those many prisoners for whom books are a place of refuge and reflection.

We are enduringly grateful to our terrific agents. Sarah Ballard of Curtis Brown is always our first reader, our champion, our clear-headed advocate, our critical friend, and someone we trust absolutely and feel lucky to have. Her assistant Liv Bignold has been a calm, patient, smart and very nice problem-solver. Sam Edenborough of Greyhound Literary has guided us over many years, and we don't know where we would be without him. And Joy Harris of the Joy Harris Literary

Agency in the US, who has also accompanied us over all the years of our writing, has been unswervingly encouraging and helpful. We never forget how lucky we are to have them at our side and on our side, and thank them all

The wonderful team at Simon & Schuster has looked after us beautifully, through the many stages of editing and publishing this book. We are particularly grateful to Suzanne Baboneau and Ian Chapman, to our terrific editor Katherine Armstrong, to Joe Christie, Hayley McMullan, Mathew Watterson, Louise Davies. And our thanks as well to the fabulous team in Australia, above all Anna O'Grady and Dan Ruffino, and to everyone at HarperCollins in the US who has watched over us and encouraged us, especially Emily Krump, Christopher Connolly, Paige Meintzer.

And then there are all the people who work on the front line with such passion, flair and dedication: the booksellers, the librarians, the organisers of literary events and book groups. Their love for books and their hard work is what keeps the whole joyful show on the road.

We want to thank our fellow crime writers, who explore areas of darkness but bring generosity and light and laughter to the job.

And of course, thank you to readers everywhere – not just our loyal, lovely readers, but readers everywhere. Without readers, there would be no writers, and every writer is a reader too.

Finally, our heartfelt love and gratitude to the great, chaotic, ramshackle, porous family we are so proud to be a part of – the one remaining parent, the children and their partners, the grandchildren, siblings and siblings-in-law, the nephews and nieces and cousins, the friends who are like family, all the people who keep us grounded and keep us going through the rollercoaster ride of life.

If you enjoyed *What Happened That Night*, discover more
unputdownable thrillers from Nicci French . . .

HAS ANYONE SEEN CHARLOTTE SALTER?

She's loved by all who meet her. But someone wants her gone . . .

1990

Beautiful and vivacious Charlotte Salter fails to turn up to her husband Alec's fiftieth birthday party. As the days pass and there's still no word from Charlie, her daughter, Etty, and her sons, Niall, Paul and Ollie, all struggle to come to terms with her disappearance. How can anyone just vanish without a trace?

Now

Etty returns home to help move her father into a care home. She is a changed woman from the trouble-free girl she was when Charlie was still around. But when their childhood friends, Greg and Morgen Ackerley, decide to do a podcast about Charlotte's disappearance, it seems like the town's buried secrets – and the Salters' – might finally come to light.

After all this time, will they finally find out what really happened to Charlotte Salter?

'The French magic is at work again' *Daily Mail*

Available now in paperback, ebook and audio

SIMON & SCHUSTER

THE LAST DAYS OF KIRA MULLAN

**She *thinks* it was murder.
But if she can't trust herself, can anyone else?**

Nancy North and her boyfriend Felix are making the move across London to a new flat, a new area, a new start. Because while Nancy is fine *now*, she wasn't fine before. But settling into the new flat and meeting the new neighbours isn't helped by Felix's hovering concern. She *is* all right. She is sticking to her breathing exercises and doctor-prescribed help.

So, when their new neighbour Kira Mullan is found dead by suicide, Felix is understandably worried about Nancy's state of mind. But Nancy saw Kira the day before she died and she didn't strike her as someone who was suicidal – she was upset and angry, yes, but enough to take her own life?

Nancy is the only one convinced that there's more to Kira's death than has been discovered. But all the police and the neighbours see is a vulnerable woman who isn't sure of what she saw, and might even be imagining things . . .

But what if Nancy is right? Are there more questions that should be asked about the last days of Kira Mullan?

'A heroine you'll be rooting for on every page and a forensic study of gaslighting. Pure literary adrenaline' **Erin Kelly**

Available in paperback, ebook and audio

**SIMON &
SCHUSTER**